TOR BOOKS BY MORGAN LLYWELYN

1916
1921
Bard
Brian Boru
The Elementals
Finn Mac Cool
The Horse Goddess
Lion of Ireland
Pride of Lions
The Wind from Hastings
The Essential Library for Irish Americans
Etruscans (with Michael Scott)

THE LAST PRINCE
OF IRELAND

MORGAN LLYWELYN

TOR®

A TOM DOHERTY ASSOCIATES BOOK
NEW YORK

THE LAST PRINCE OF IRELAND

A Tor Book
Published by Tom Doherty Associates, LLC
175 Fifth Avenue
New York, NY 10010

www.tor.com

Tor® is a registered trademark of Tom Doherty Associates, LLC.

ISBN: 0-812-57913-5

First Tor edition: March 2001

Printed in the United States of America

0 9 8 7 6 5 4 3 2 1

For Holly and Sean
and
as always
For Charles

Preface

Since the twelfth century, England had been attempting the conquest of Ireland with varying degrees of energy and commitment. Successive waves of Norman adventurers had been sent across the Irish Sea only to be seduced by the land they came to conquer, and to become in time more Irish than the Irish themselves.

The rise of Protestantism under Henry VIII had small effect on either the native Gaelic Catholic population of Ireland or on the Norman Catholics who had become entrenched among them.

For much of her reign, Elizabeth the First of England paid little attention to the island to the west. She had more pressing matters to consider, and completing the long-delayed conquest of a neighbor could always wait until tomorrow. Then she began hearing warnings that Spain, together with agents of the papacy, was planning to use Ireland as a back door for the invasion of England and the restoration of a Catholic monarchy there.

Elizabeth responded as she always responded to any threat to her sovereignty. Her deputies were ordered to enforce English control, English law, and the new English religion in Ireland by whatever means necessary. They interpreted this to mean bribery, force of arms, and exter-mination.

Clan was turned against clan and brother against brother, weakening the entire fabric of Irish society. The queen's deputies succeeded in coercing some of the Irish chieftains into surrendering their Gaelic titles and lands in exchange for English titles and a fraction of their for-mer holdings—plus their lives. Old enmities were rekin-dled, new ones created.

In order to clear the best land of its native population so it could then be parceled out among English colonists, vast areas of Ireland were laid waste and given over to famine.

Rebellion was inevitable.

Led by Hugh O'Neill of Ulster, the Nine Years' War was Ireland's final attempt to preserve her Gaelic culture and way of life. That struggle for freedom ended disas-trously with the battle of Kinsale.

This is the story of the survivors.

Night

December 30, 1602. *Doire na Fola*, the Oakwood of Blood

The people had been waiting for almost a week while skirmishes were fought all around them. Some had traveled more than twenty miles at their chieftain's summons, bringing their families and what remained of their possessions. They had left the doors of their abandoned homes ajar. Locks and bolts were useless now.

They were gathered in darkness in the dense oak forest that covered a steep hillside beyond *Gleann Garbh*, the Rugged Glen. Their journey to this destination had been hazardous. The enemy was everywhere, and there were few roads. They had had to make their way across a wild and broken terrain, clawing through woodland and furze, wading boggy ooze.

Now there was nothing to do but wait for the morrow. Their bellies cramped with hunger. Provisions were running low. They could not resupply themselves until they found allies, and who could say when that might be.

It was beginning to seem as if every hand was raised

against them in the land that had been theirs for two thousand years.

They were of the Gaelic race of the fretted peninsulas and mountainous coastline of west Cork, in southwestern Ireland. A beautiful place. A place they might never see again.

Niall sat at one end of a fallen tree, with the fingers of his right hand thrust into his mouth for warmth. His left hand was burrowed into his right armpit. He felt, rather than saw, someone sit heavily on the other end of the log.

A surly voice said, "This place is as dark as the inside of a rock."

Niall took his fingers from his mouth. "It is that, Ronan. And cold beside."

"Is that you, Niall?"

"It is myself."

"We are going to be a lot colder in the north, if we get there."

"We will get there, please God. The O'Sullivan has promised."

"We were promised victory at Kinsale," the other man snarled.

There was no answer to be given. Niall put his fingers back into his mouth. They were his harping fingers and he was careful with them.

Someone coughed nearby. A fretful child whimpered.

A face came swimming out of the gloom, becoming a pale gray oval hanging in space in front of Niall. "Have you any food to spare?" a woman's voice asked. "Not for myself, but I have a sick child who is crying for more to eat."

"We are all crying for more to eat," Ronan said. His tone made it plain that he did not intend to share whatever he might have.

"There is a bit of cheese in my pack," Niall offered.

"Bless you!" The woman reached out with trembling hands.

Ronan said, "Apply to The O'Sullivan if you need more food. I suspect he has quantities of it packed away for his personal use."

"I would not dream of asking the prince!" The woman sounded shocked. Niall could not tell if it was because of the suggestion itself, or the inference that The O'Sullivan was hoarding selfishly.

"Where is the commander?" Niall asked Ronan.

"Down below on the glen road, conferring with some guides who just arrived from the Muskerry mountains."

"Guides?"

"Of course, guides. We need local people to lead us through the worst of the mountain passes."

The woman said in a small voice, "My child is not able for mountains, he is too weak."

"Then leave him behind," said Ronan.

"You are a monster!" the woman accused.

"Ssshhh," hissed someone nearby in the darkness. "We are trying to sleep, here."

"I have to get back," said the woman coldly. "The prince's own aunt is caring for my boy. A woman with a heart." They heard her move away, pushing through the undergrowth.

"It is a long way to be carrying a sick child," Niall remarked.

"Ssshhh!" came the disembodied hiss again. "Have you no consideration for your fellow man at all? Be quiet, now."

"And how in the sweet name of Jesus," Ronan challenged, "do you propose to keep a thousand people quiet? Are we not even allowed to belch and fart?"

Niall smiled to himself. "How can we belch and fart with so little to eat?"

The man on the other end of the log said, "Donal Cam has plenty for himself to eat, rest assured of it."

"You should not speak so of the commander."

"Am I not entitled? Have I not followed him this weary time, me and mine . . . and paid for his mistakes?"

"What happened at Kinsale was not The O'Sullivan's fault and you know it, Ronan."

"Do I? Do I indeed?" Ronan's voice rose angrily.

"Ssshhh!" came from several sides at once.

Niall huddled into his shaggy mantle and tried not to think about food. Slabs of bacon. Smoked herring. Pots of soft cheese. Mutton. Buttermilk. Wheaten bread with anise seeds. Salmon. Oatcakes baked in front of a fire until the crust was black and crunchy. His mouth flooded with saliva and he longed for the bit of hard cheese he had given the woman.

Meanwhile, she was making her way back through the trees. She knew her child was near when she could hear his phlegmy breathing. "I am here," she called softly.

Several female voices responded. One was sharper than the others, older, more authoritative; the voice of a woman sure of herself and her place. "You took your time," called Joan. "Did anyone give you any food for the lad?"

"I was given some cheese by one of the *kernes*."

"Did you happen to see Donal Cam?" Joan wanted to know.

"The O'Sullivan is down below somewhere, I was told."

"And my husband with him, doubtless." Sighing, for her legs were cramping, Joan moved over on her bed of dead leaves to make room for the child's mother to sit down beside her. The child was passed between them. He whimpered once, a thin sound like a mouse's squeak.

A woman nearby said, in a voice of exceptional sweetness, "If I still sang I would lullaby the wee mite for you. But my songs are gone from me. They went with Richard."

Her words hung in the air. The other women knew that Maire Ni Driscoll had been the betrothed of Richard Mac Geoghegan, who had died a hero's death during the summer if ever a man did.

At least my old Dermod is still alive, Joan thought to herself. Perhaps it was wrong to congratulate herself on her blessings in the face of Maire's pain, but she could not help it. There was little other comfort to be found in life at the moment, and she and Dermod had been together for thirty years. She could not imagine an existence without him. Now he was with his nephew, Donal Cam, somewhere nearby, the two of them trying to find ways to get everyone out alive.

I wish this day were over, Joan thought. I wish we already were wherever we are going to be tonight.

There was no light but a pallid moon, but it was enough to allow Donal Cam's night-accustomed eyes to see details of the landscape through which he rode. His horse was picking its way up the steep hillside with the dainty, mincing steps that had earned the brown stallion an amusing nickname: *An Cearc.* The Hen.

"An' Cearc never puts a foot wrong, and takes very good care of me," Donal Cam had often said, fondly.

Now the horse was threading its way upward between massive black boulders folded in upon themselves, layer after layer, like clenched fists. Frozen fists, thrusting out of sere and withered grass. Patches of brittle furze stood out starkly against the pale grass. Mindful of their prickles,

An Cearc avoided the furze bushes with the skill of long practice.

Gazing at the boulders Donal Cam fancied he could sense an inheld emotion in them. Mute rage.

Or perhaps that is in me, he thought. Mute rage.

They continued up the hill until the grassland gave way abruptly to a dense stand of oak trees half strangled by an enveloping mantle of ivy. Great swags of moss clung to every tree, leaving only the ends of the bare branches free to claw at the sky, as if seeking to escape.

The Oakwood of Blood. The name itself was enough to frighten people away with its recalling of some ancient massacre.

I hope it is not an omen, Donal Cam said to himself. But what better place for us than this, where at least the trees hide us from the eyes of our enemies? Wilmot's men are only a couple of miles away, but these rugged hills provide us with a fortress—until we can make our escape.

The brown stallion tensed, ears swiveling forward. Donal Cam gave a low whistle. A similar signal answered him, then several men emerged from among the trees. One called cautiously, "Is it yourself, Commander?"

"It is myself. I have come to see if you are ready here, and give you your orders."

"We are as ready as we shall ever be." The man who spoke was one of the elite *buannachta*, warriors recruited from Donal Cam's own clan and allied families. The recruits were further divided into two categories, gallowglasses who were masters of the battle-ax, and kernes like Niall, whose preferred weapons were the sword, pike, or handgun. The rest of a Gaelic prince's army consisted of horsemen like Ronan, and hired mercenaries from other clans.

But it was the buannachta who were the backbone of

the force. A number of these recruits now gathered around their leader.

Donal Cam Ua Suileabhain Beare, O'Sullivan of the Ships, lord of Beare and Bantry, prince of the Gael, descendant of the noble Milesians who had brought the Iron Age to Ireland five centuries before the birth of Christ. The man on the horse was tall and athletic of build, with dark hair and eyes. His narrow face was haggard, looking older than his forty years, but there was no weakness in the high forehead, the sharp nose, the firm mouth. Even in these desperate circumstances his cheeks were freshly shaved, his narrow mustache and small beard neatly combed.

He had discarded the velvets and damasks and lace ruffs he had once worn after the Elizabethan fashion. Since the battle of Kinsale—*Ceann Saile*, the Head of the Brine—he wore traditional Gaelic dress, a shirt of fine linen with wide, pleated sleeves, close-fitting breeches, and a heavy cloak of Kerry wool, striped in bright colors and bordered with thick fringe.

Beneath great shaggy mantles—as much of a uniform as Gaelic warriors ever possessed—his buannachta were variously garbed. The gallowglasses had been chosen for size and power. Some of them possessed mail shirts or quilted iron-reinforced tunics. The lighter kernes wore a haphazard assortment of leather jerkins, woolen breeches, and near rags, evidence of hard campaigning. They all had sunken cheeks and hollow eyes.

They were in a land that had been stripped as clean of edibles as the gnawed skeleton of a dead deer.

An Cearc pawed restlessly. "Did Ronan Hurley come up here?" his rider asked. A recruit trotted off to find him. Meanwhile, Donal Cam spoke in low tones to the others, outlining his plans. There were some things he put off saying, however.

Ronan emerged from the woods and approached the horseman. A burly man, Ronan's features were worn and blunted like those on a coin that had passed through many hands. He greeted Donal Cam with a curt nod. *"Ceann Sluaig."* Head of the host; Commander.

"Ronan. I am glad to find you, I have need of you. Go back down below to the cavalry."

"Cavalry!" A snort of derision. "What have we left, fourteen or fifteen?"

"Twelve," Donal Cam corrected dryly. "With horse. Thirteen counting you as captain."

"Twelve men hardly even need a captain."

"They do, and you will be theirs." Donal Cam's voice took on a cutting edge. "That is my order. Our numbers are only temporarily reduced. You are to find new men for us along the way and see to their training, acquire horses for them, build up our cavalry against the day we begin to win again."

Ronan stared up at the man on the brown stallion. After all that had happened, could it be possible The O'Sullivan still expected victory? The man was as proud as a whitewashed pig! Ronan opened his mouth to say something, but the voice of authority stirred embers of obedience in him and he shrugged, turned, and set off down the slope, contenting himself with cursing under his breath once he was out of earshot.

Donal Cam slid off his horse and led the animal into the forest, holding the reins himself. He felt An Cearc's warm breath ruffling the hair on the back of his head. "Is my uncle's wife here?" he asked over his shoulder.

"She is here," a pikeman affirmed behind him. "She should be off somewhere to your left, I think. At least she was a while ago."

The woods were so dense it was all but impossible to

lead a horse through them. Donal Cam could hear stirrings in the undergrowth and whispered snatches of disparate, desperate conversation. A rivulet of water gurgled almost underfoot, coursing its way downslope. The brown stallion stretched its neck, yearning toward the water. Donal Cam gave the reins a sharp tug. "No time for a drink now."

He could feel, like a tangible weight pressing down on him, the responsibility for the thousand people in the forest around him.

"You, come with me," he ordered the man who might know where his aunt was. "The rest of you, spread out and pass the word. Everyone is to be away now, if they are able."

"Away where? In what direction?"

"Down," he replied curtly. "Down the slope in the direction of the Rugged Glen. At the bottom is a ravine with a small river, and everyone is to gather there. Tell people to slip away in twos and threes, small groups only, as quietly as they can. No torches, they must find their way down in the dark. I do not want a single moving light to alert Wilmot's lookouts."

There were plenty of places from which lookouts would be watching. Doire na Fola was surrounded by hills, and huge erratic boulders stood free and clear like stones thrown from a giant's hand, providing excellent platforms. If he had had enough men to spare, Donal Cam would have posted lookouts over a wide area himself.

Men to spare, he thought grimly.

Aloud he said, "When everyone is collected down below I shall send a signal."

"A signal to whom?" someone asked.

Donal Cam hesitated before answering. Then he barked

out the words in harsh, abrupt syllables; it was the only way. "A signal to the people we leave behind us here," he said.

For a moment no one said anything. His listeners were trying to comprehend. Then, "Leave behind?" a man spoke up. "How can we leave anyone behind? Wilmot's men are only . . ."

"We have no choice," Donal Cam interrupted. "We have people who are badly wounded, or enfeebled with sickness and starvation, or simply too old to travel. Our food supplies are very low, and who can say when we will get more? Our way will lie over mountain and bog, hard traveling. The weak would have no chance.

"So they must stay here. Do not call them by name, they know who they are. Every person is aware of his own condition.

"Explain that those who know themselves unfit to travel are to stay here when the rest of us leave. When they hear the cry of a graylag goose, they are to light as many fires as they can. The enemy lookouts will see the fires and report that we are still encamped here and preparing to cook food for the morning."

Donal Cam's words slowed. He realized he was speaking into an appalled vacuum. The assembled men stared at him, slack-jawed, as he told them, "I do not know how much time this will buy us. Perhaps only hours, but perhaps days. By the time Wilmot realizes something is amiss we shall at least be well away from Doire na Fola."

One of the men found his voice. "But you are condemning those we leave behind to their deaths! You know what Wilmot will do when he realizes he has been tricked!"

"Just do as I say," Donal Cam said in a somber voice. Muttering to themselves, but obedient, his men moved off among the trees. Donal Cam did not envy them their task.

He turned to the remaining man. "You. Niall, is it?"

"It is, Commander. Niall of clan O'Mahony."

"Ah, I remember. You are the one who plays the harp by the campfire at night, the one my men call the bard."

Niall could feel his ears burning. "They are teasing me. I am no bard, my father was just a fisherman, not of the bardic class at all. I have only a small gift for music."

"Music is a large gift," Donal Cam contradicted. "I had a fine harper at Dunboy, Niall, but . . . he is no more. You are at hand. You shall be my harper now."

"I cannot play for a prince!"

"You fight for me when I give the order. If I order you to play music for me, can you not do that also?"

Such an honor was beyond Niall's imagining. He mumbled an embarrassed assent and Donal Cam clapped him on the shoulder. "Good man yourself, Niall. Now, take me to my aunt."

Throughout the forest, people everywhere were having the same response to Donal Cam's directive. As he and Niall advanced, they heard sobs; caught glimpses of anguish among the groups huddled beneath the oaks. Some people had collapsed in each other's arms, weeping. Some caught hold of their loved ones in the gloom and pulled them close, trying to memorize their faces. Some sat quietly, making their soul's arrangements in private.

But no one refused to do as The O'Sullivan commanded.

Day One

December 31, 1602. *Gleann Garbh*, the Rugged Glen

Above the trees, night was fading into the false dawn of a new and terrible day. Throughout the darkest hours Donal Cam's men had searched the forest, seeking out pockets of fugitives and giving them their leader's directive.

Whirlpools of shock eddied in their wake. Then people rose, gathered their belongings, slowly began to move down the mountainside.

Those who were to remain sat on the earth like stones, waiting.

Sometime after midnight Niall had led Donal Cam, more through chance than certainty, to the small group of women that included O'Sullivan's aunt. A child was coughing in a thicket. Donal Cam heard a cracked, familiar voice speak to its mother, and signaled Niall to halt.

He called softly, *"Siobhan Ni Suibhne?"* Joan, daughter of Sweney.

Summoning a cheerfulness not deeply felt, the woman answered, "I am here, Donal. Is my husband with you?"

"Dermod is with The O'Connor Kerry and my officers," Donal Cam told her, pushing through the underbrush to her side. "He asked me to find you and tell you that he will be waiting for you down below. You are to meet him down below," he repeated deliberately.

Dermod O'Sullivan had insisted his nephew deliver the message in just that way. "I know my wife," he had said. "We quarreled, and she just might take it into her head to stay here to spite me. She could say she is too old to travel. But let me remind you that she has borne me seventeen children and is strong enough for anything, so do not allow her to refuse. Insist. Make it sound like an order."

"Meet my uncle down below," Donal Cam said yet again.

"I heard you." Joan sniffed. "That old fool Dermot. A man of sixty years has no business traveling with the army."

"We shall all be traveling with the army," said Donal Cam, "except for those who stay here. The weak, the ill . . ."

Eileen, the mother of the coughing child, cried out, "I cannot leave my boy here! He can travel, I can carry him."

"We can take turns carrying him," Joan assured her. Then she bit her lip. Old fool yourself, she thought. A woman of fifty has no business carrying a child.

She started to ask her nephew if the child could be put on his horse, but he was gone.

There was nothing for it, then. Joan helped the young woman named Maire lift the boy onto Eileen's back, fashioning a sort of sling to support him with strips torn from their underskirts. When they were ready, the party of women set off down the hillside, slipping and slithering, losing their balance, lashed by bare branches, grasping at saplings to slow their descent as the slope grew more treacherous.

In the dark, it was a nightmarish journey. They could hear other people all around them, crashing down the hillside, cursing and frightened.

When they neared the bottom the trees began to thin and they could see the sparkle of water.

The water was a little river, narrow and cold, with no bridge and no ford. Wading across, they had to hold on to one another to keep from being swept away.

On the far side of the river, Donal Cam sat on An Cearc, watching as the streams of people emerging from the forest became a flood. The flood was composed of both soldiers and civilians, a shoving, grunting, shivering mob with no sense of order, groping their way toward him by instinct. He sat impassively as they scrambled up the muddy bank and milled around himself and his officers on their horses.

When the flood dwindled to a trickle, it was time to go before daylight betrayed them.

Throwing back his head, Donal Cam gave a startlingly accurate imitation of the noisy cry of the graylag goose. Natives to the region would know that no graylags wintered here, but Wilmot's army would not recognize the alien cry as a signal.

"I never knew your nephew could do birdcalls," remarked The O'Connor Kerry from atop his horse.

"He was a great mimic in his youth," Dermod O'Sullivan replied with pride. Dermod and The O'Connor were riding knee to knee. They belonged to the same generation and enjoyed reminiscing together about events and people they thought they remembered.

The goose's gabbling echoed through the oak forest. Donal Cam repeated it twice, then kicked his horse in the ribs and set off at a trot for the Rugged Glen.

His followers streamed after him.

Almost at once, the first tiny red dots of fire winked to life in the Oakwood of Blood. They gleamed through the trees like eyes, watching the thousand depart.

The morning had begun in bitter cold. Once the column was out of the forest and under way, however, the temperature began to rise. Perhaps the day would be mild. West Cork had a reputation for moderate climate.

But many people continued to shiver. They were soaked from the river, and chilled with leave-taking and grief. Some, remembering, cried. Others, trying not to remember, stared stonily ahead.

Once they reached the Rugged Glen they began to talk to one another in voices rather than whispers. Some people seemed almost compelled to relate the events that had led to this time and place.

Niall found himself walking beside a stubby priest in his middle years, a man who had recently become confessor to The O'Connor Kerry in much the way that Niall had become harper to The O'Sullivan Beare. They were trudging up the Rugged Glen, a valley filled with winter-naked birch and arbutus, and oaks as thickly swagged with gray moss as those at Doire na Fola. Something about the scene impelled the priest to remark on the ancient trees that once stood near Dunboy Castle.

"I was a guest there, in better days," Father John Collins confided to the sandy-haired pikeman beside him. "I recall the way those trees framed a perfect view of the water, for Dunboy is on a promontory. Do you know it?"

"I never saw the castle," Niall replied. "I was encamped for a time with a company of buannachta a mile or so away, that was as near as I got."

"A pity. The stronghold of The O'Sullivan was worth seeing. A square stone fortress with thick walls and those trees shading the ladies' lawn in summer. Gone now, I should think. The final explosions must have devastated the entire area."

"Were they that bad?"

"Do you not know the details of the siege of Dunboy?"

"Only the rumors soldiers pass among themselves," Niall replied. "When The O'Sullivan left Dunboy for Ardea, before Carew attacked, he took my company with him. We went to meet a Spanish ship that he expected to find loaded to the gunwales with Spanish reinforcements for our buannachta. Instead it carried various important personages and some priests and some casks of wine and huge chests of Spanish gold that the commander shared with his allies. But no Spanish soldiers.

"We were sorely disappointed. We waited in camp while one day became another, but the reinforcements never came. We could have marched back to Dunboy at any time, but we did not, and while we tarried at Ardea, Dunboy fell."

Father Collins sighed. "A tragic loss, that. Carew and his men had already seized most of the Irish strongholds around the southwest coast. Conquering Dunboy was his crowning achievement, I should say, since The O'Sullivan was the last Gaelic chieftain remaining in Munster to defy the English.

"For that reason, I cannot understand why The O'Sullivan was not at Dunboy to lead its defenders in person. I am baffled by his continued absence. He had already taken part in a number of skirmishes as the enemy advanced, he surely knew what their target was. Yet in the end, he slipped away from Dunboy in its final days and let Carew destroy it." The priest shook his head.

"The English queen chose well," he went on, "in naming Sir George Carew as lord president of Munster. He is a clever and cruel man. Perhaps his reputation for cruelty was enough to make The O'Sullivan reluctant to face him personally, after all he had already suffered. Ever since the English victory at Kinsale, Carew had been destroying resistance in Munster with sword and famine, with acts of outrage and horror, and it was obvious there was no mercy to be expected from the man. One could not blame The O'Sullivan for . . ."

"The commander was never afraid of Carew," Niall said confidently. "Never."

"Of course not," the priest said hastily. "I merely meant that perhaps he was acting, ah, prudently, in the face of such overwhelming opposition.

"Carew took a force of four thousand to attack Dunboy, you know, including the earl of Thomond and Donal Cam's own cousin Owen. He brought the major assault force by sea instead of trying to transport them across rough country, but he did succeed in dragging his heaviest cannon overland without being detected, to set up in a concealed emplacement overlooking the walls of Dunboy. He is a shrewd military strategist, one must give him that much credit.

"The first stage of the assault began on June 16, 1602, according to the new calendar of Pope Gregory which the heretics refuse to recognize. There was sporadic fighting, skirmishes as each side took the other's measure. Then Donal Cam learned of the Spanish ships expected at Ardea and made haste to go there. In his absence the fighting intensified. At one point Richard Mac Geoghegan, constable of the castle, rowed out to talk with the earl of Thomond. He warned Thomond as one Irishman to another that it would cost too much blood to try to take Dunboy. But Thomond would not listen."

Niall was shaking his head. "Thomond. Imagine a descendant of Brian Boru siding with the foreigners against his own race."

"The land is full of that now," Father Collins said sadly. "The queen's Os and Macs are in every parish, bribed and bought. Who can say but what there were not traitors within the walls of Dunboy itself? And certainly in Beare there were some whose self-interest lay with Carew and his kind."

"How do you know so much about this?" Niall wondered.

The priest paused to mop his forehead. Donal Cam was setting a furious pace. "Did I not have it from the lips of The O'Connor Kerry himself?" he asked. "He had it from actual witnesses to the siege and fall of Dunboy, local people who hid themselves as best they could during the fighting.

"They said that on the morning of June 23, Carew's forces had overrun Dursey Island while its owner, Dermod O'Sullivan, was with his nephew at Ardea. They butchered the people they found there and destroyed the castle. The O'Sullivan had meant Dursey to be his fallback position if anything ever happened to Dunboy, you see; now it was lost to him. And to poor Dermod as well, who rides with us this day as the landless lord of Dursey.

"Apparently it was not long after this when Richard Tyrell decided to take himself out of harm's way and fled Dunboy. He was the former captain of The O'Sullivan's mercenaries—did you know him?"

"I am a buannacht," Niall retorted coolly. "We do not socialize with mercenaries. But I did happen to see him when he finally arrived at Ardea some days later. Everyone was astonished that he had been able to get through the enemy lines and report to Donal Cam."

Father John Collins cleared his throat and wiped his

brow again. "In the light of his subsequent actions, I have my own theory as to how he got through the lines. And given that Ardea is but a day's march from Dunboy, why did it take him so long to get there? By the time he arrived with news of the assault the castle had already fallen."

"Tyrell did claim to be wounded," Niall said doubtfully. He had heard the question asked before. "Tyrell was with us at Kinsale and fought bravely; I suppose the commander was inclined to give him the benefit of the doubt."

"Perhaps so. But there were others whose attempts at escape were not as, er, fortunate as that of Richard Tyrell. One group of panicked defenders fled the castle and made for the water that surrounds the promontory on three sides. Carew had anticipated this; he had boats waiting for them. Musketeers picked them off one by one, or pressed oars against their heads and held them under until they drowned.

"The local people could hear their piteous cries. They also heard the enemy laughing and shouting, pointing out targets to each other as if they were enjoying a day's sport."

The priest mopped his forehead with his sleeve. But he needed no more urging to continue. He was as lost in his narrative as if he were watching it happen. "As the cannonading intensified, my cousin, Dominic Collins of the Society of Jesus, left Dunboy Castle under a flag of truce to try to arrange an honorable surrender and prevent any further loss of life.

"But Carew's men laughed at him. They seized him and tortured him. When he refused to renounce the true faith and swear loyalty to the English queen they sent him to Youghal, where he had been born, and there he was hanged by the neck. While he still lived they tore his beating heart from his breast!" The priest's voice broke with a sob.

When he recovered himself, he said in a changed voice, "We fought each other the first day we met, as little lads. I loved him ever after."

Unable to speak, Niall walked along watching his own feet.

Father John took up the story again. "Early on the morning of June 27, the final bombardment began. There were still one hundred and forty-three souls defending the castle when the landward cannon opened up. Almost at once a turret collapsed and many men were crushed beneath falling masonry. Demi-cannons and other guns played on the west front of Dunboy until early afternoon, when the walls were finally breached. The enemy poured in.

"The defenders barricaded themselves with the rubble and fought back with shot and stones and sword and pike. A bloody battle was joined in the great hall, lasting until no one was left unwounded. Constable Mac Geoghegan received a wound that would prove mortal in time, though he did not die then.

"When darkness made fighting impossible, the surviving defenders retreated to the cellars while the enemy withdrew and regrouped. By dawn light it was obvious the castle could not be held any longer. But Mac Geoghegan did not mean to let Carew have Dunboy. Dying, he dragged himself to the gunpowder stores and tried to set them alight, meaning to blow up the castle and everyone in it rather than surrender. But the enemy rushed in and stopped him. They killed him on the spot.

"His remaining comrades were captured. There were only fifty-eight of them left alive, and they were hanged in the marketplace at Beare Haven, God have mercy on them."

Niall and the priest signed the Cross in unison. Then Father Collins said, in tones of awe, "Think on it! One hundred and forty-three men holding out against four thousand. Just think on it!"

Niall asked, "What happened afterward? The explosions?"

"Ah. Four days later, Carew's men used the powder stores in the cellars to blow up what was left of Dunboy Castle themselves.

"But before they did," the priest's voice dropped, "before they did, some of the local people came out of hiding and crept back to peer into the ruins by moonlight. They told of seeing congealed blood ankle-deep on the floor of the great hall, and severed limbs everywhere."

He shuddered and fell silent. The two men walked on side by side, each seeing his own horrific vision.

As the morning progressed, O'Sullivan's followers found themselves skirting the head of Bantry Bay, named for *Beann Traighe*, the White Strand, though the beach they were passing was dark and stony. The land had been rising since they left the Rugged Glen, and the incline was beginning to make itself felt in aching leg muscles.

Aware it might be his last chance for a long look at the sea, Donal Cam reined in his horse. The bay waters were a brilliant blue-green, set like a jewel in a circlet of distant peaks. The beauty of the land he was leaving struck Donal Cam like a blow.

He had loved poetry and sport, fine craftsmanship and French brandy, good books and soft beds and sweet music. He had forgotten such pleasures until on impulse he named the kerne to be his new harper, as if he still had a hall to fill with music and great shaggy hounds to rest their heads on his knees as he listened.

The vanished life of a prince of the Gael.

For five centuries, since his distant forebears had fled the arrival of the Normans in Ireland and made their way from its grassy heartland to the remote southwest coast, the sea had supported his clan. The O'Sullivan chieftain claimed a fortune in revenue from shipping and the tariffs charged for using his seaways. Even his income from the pilchards that were pressed for oil in the village of Beare Haven would have been sufficient to support several families for life.

O'Sullivan of the Ships, of the broad galleys.

Now the only vessels plying those seaways were English warships, or tiny boats containing refugees fleeing the destruction Carew was wreaking on Munster.

Honora! Donal Cam thought as suddenly as if he heard her calling to him. He turned in the saddle and gazed back toward the rugged crags only the eagle knew.

Stay safe, Honora. Take care of our littlest son.

The moving river of people caught up with him. A burly gallowglass paused to stare curiously at The O'Sullivan immobile on his horse, seemingly lost in thought.

Feeling the eyes on him, Donal Cam turned his face to the north once more, gave An Cearc a brisk kick in the ribs and trotted forward to the head of the march.

The sick child was crying again. Eileen tried in vain to ignore the pain in her back and shoulders. They seemed to be climbing continually, though they still had not reached the barrier of purple mountains they could see waiting for them like a threat, their peaks as jagged as dragons' teeth. Somewhere up ahead was *Keimaneigh*, the Pass of the Deer. Once through that pass they would be deep in Muskerry territory, in a land of uncertain allegiances.

"Are you weary?" Maire's sweet voice asked. "I can carry him for a while."

Eileen turned gratefully toward her. "God bless."

She managed a smile for Maire, admiring as she always had the young woman who had been betrothed to Richard Mac Geoghegan. Maire's dark hair fell naturally into heavy ringlets; she had clear blue eyes and a dainty mouth, and all her teeth. Once her bosom and arms had been praised for their white roundness. She was thin now, but her limbs retained their grace, as did her remarkable voice.

"Maire Ni Driscoll is the blackbird of Beare," people had said of her in the days when she had reason to sing for joy.

She held out her arms to receive Eileen's child. Joan and the boy's mother refastened the improvised sling around his body while he whimpered and thrashed weakly.

"Be still now," Eileen said, but he did not seem to hear her. His face was without color except for the blue veins in his temples, standing out starkly against translucent skin.

The child smelled sour. Maire wriggled under her burden, trying to find the most comfortable way to carry him. His bony knees dug into her.

The weather was changing. The sky looked white and a cold wind had sprung up, smelling of ice, promising sleet.

They were crossing boggy meadowland. The grasses growing in its deep black soil had, until recently, nourished countless cattle. The cattle were gone now. Where they had been was a nothingness the shape of famine.

"We are coming to the Pass of the Deer soon," Dermod O'Sullivan remarked to his companion.

They were climbing now, through wild and rugged

country, gloomy in the lowering weather. The landscape had an air of menace, but the true menace, was behind them.

Man was behind them. The enemy. Back there somewhere.

The O'Connor Kerry rose slightly in his stirrups and looked back along the route they had come, but he could not tell if they were being pursued. The path had too many bends. He sank back into the saddle, thankful that he still used English stirrups instead of having reverted, as had Donal Cam, to the ancient Gaelic style of riding stirrupless.

The O'Connor appreciated symbols as much as any Irish man, but he liked having a surface to rest his feet upon when he rode. When an old man's legs hung unsupported for any length of time, they went to sleep.

A sheer slope began rising to the left of himself and Dermod, who were following close behind Donal Cam. The land fell away to the right to form the last of the rounded hills, scored by occasional low stone walls. The mountains ahead were badly eroded, appearing to be neither rock nor soil but some striated mixture of the two. Withered grass gave way to the russet hues of dead bracken and heather, and the startling sight of a few dark green furze bushes in bloom despite the season, their vivid yellow blossoms defiantly alive.

The walls of the mountain pass rose on either side. Following Donal Cam, a thousand people began making their way through.

"A good place for an ambush," Dermod O'Sullivan said apprehensively.

The O'Connor surveyed the sheer rock above them. He was shabbily dressed by the standards of Gaelic nobility. A heavy fringed cloak, a stained tunic, woolen leggings haphazardly bound with thongs, soft boots that were badly worn. He was a battered, grizzled chieftain who had worn finer clothes and seen better days, but his eyes were still bright. "Let them come down on me and they will eat my sword," he vowed.

"What happened to that fine handgun of yours, the one with the barrel of Damascus iron?"

"The matchlock arquebus I took off that dead Englishman? Mud got in it and the mechanism jammed. I threw it at someone in some skirmish afterward and lost it."

Dermod grinned, showing stumps of yellowed teeth. "I hope you hit him."

"I broke his nose," the other replied with satisfaction.

Dermod's grin widened. "A fierce pair of old men we are. Let the *Sasanach*, the foreigners, beware!" He shook one age-spotted fist at the sky.

There was no forest to hide them now. They were in the open and vulnerable. With so many people clogging the pass they would be helpless if an enemy fired down on them from the cliffs above. The English might not know the area well enough to take advantage of such an opportunity, but there were those with them who did.

"When you looked back, did you happen to see my wife?" Dermod inquired.

"I was looking for enemies, not friends. Is she still with us?"

"I am afraid she is, though I wanted it otherwise. I tried to arrange a safe place for her, but you know Joan."

The O'Connor chuckled. "She is a strong-willed woman, your wife. But not a young one; she would have been better left in some sanctuary."

"She is ten years younger than me, and she insisted she was able for the journey. She reminded me that women her age drive cattle twenty miles to market."

"We are going a lot farther than twenty miles, I fear. And we have no cattle. They were stolen from us," The O'Connor added bitterly.

Guarding the rear of the column as he had been ordered—though horsemen usually led a march—Ronan Hurley captained the remnant of cavalry. Donal Cam's army now consisted of no more than four hundred in all, including horsemen, buannachta, and mercenaries. Mingled with these were six hundred civilians, comprising the surviving nobility of Beare, freemen, tenants, fishermen, farmers, servants, the usual company of camp followers and attendants, and a group of horse boys of the lowest class, leading rough-coated pack animals.

Little enough food remained in the baggage they carried. For the most part it contained personal goods, weapons, and what remained of Donal Cam's gold, Spanish ducats in a number of small leather bags. The gold would pay his recruits and the mercenaries, but it would not buy food in a land where no food remained to be bought.

Ronan Hurley was very aware of that gold, and convinced that the commander had a private supply of food hidden in the baggage for himself. When the opportunity presented itself, Ronan intended to have the packs searched by an ally he could trust.

Miraculously, the throng got through the Pass of the Deer without incident.

"The ruse worked," one of Ronan's horsemen gloated. "Wilmot must think he still has us penned at Doire na Fola."

His captain scowled at him. "He will discover otherwise soon enough, so move these people on, we can expect pursuit any time. And not only from him—we are still within range of *Carraig an Easaigh*, the Rock of the

Waterfall. The commander destroyed his cousin Owen's castle there only a few months ago; would you care to be found in the neighborhood by some of Owen's men now? Move on, I say!"

At the mention of Owen O'Sullivan, now known as the queen's O'Sullivan, a wave of distaste swept through those who heard.

Beyond Keimaneigh their route curved, doubled back, twisted and doubled again, but there was no other way to traverse the mountains. And more mountains were always discouragingly visible in the distance, waiting for them.

Donal Cam reined in his horse for a brief consultation with his current guides, three local men. Thomas Burke, who had inherited the captainship of the mercenaries by default, caught up with them. "Where are we?" he asked his commander.

"Not far from Gougane Barra, St. Finbarr's holy place."

"Will we seek sanctuary there tonight?"

Donal Cam looked down at the square-shouldered Connacht man, whom he knew as a fearsome warrior, but whose eyes were as blue and innocent as the skies over Clew Bay. "We were just discussing the possibility, Thomas, but I think not. The more distance we put between ourselves and Wilmot, the better. There is another sacral site some miles on, an old church at a remote place called *Eachros.*"

"The Wood of the Horse? Will we be safe there?"

"Safe enough for a few hours. My guides tell me the chapel has fallen into disuse and the surrounding region is considered haunted, so even the English do not venture near. But God knows the place," he added, "so we shall put ourselves into His keeping."

They moved on. The brief winter day was dying. In gathering dusk a thousand people trudged wearily toward an unknown destination.

Since early morning, the three women had passed the sick child back and forth between them. His cries of protest had gradually grown weaker. Most of the time he seemed to be asleep. Dermod O'Sullivan's wife had insisted on carrying the boy for a third of the time, over the protests of the younger women, Eileen and Maire. "But he weighs nothing," she told them lightheartedly.

In truth, he seemed heavier with every step. Foolish woman, Joan scolded herself. Why did you commit to this? You are too old for this, you and your pride . . .

A ragged boy leading a shambling packhorse was walking a few paces ahead of them. With an effort, Joan lengthened her stride and caught up with him. "Could that animal carry some extra weight? A sick child?"

The boy gave her a startled look. "I cannot!" His orders had been precise: No more weight on that horse, take care of the horse. Alarmed lest she try to take it from him, he jerked the horse's lead rope and forced it to trot away.

Joan glared after him. "Wretched little beast," she said under her breath. "I wonder if he is one of ours? Perhaps, considering his bad manners, he belongs to one of the buannachta."

She sniffed indignantly and turned back to her companions.

They walked on. On and on and on. Up and up and up. The climb, if anything, was growing steeper—or perhaps they were merely tireder.

The old woman massaged the small of her back with her hands. A cold wind was blowing steadily in their faces now; her eyes were constantly tearing. She felt as if the skin on her face was cracking open. If she stopped walking, she knew her legs would be trembling.

Joan stretched her neck to try to relieve the stiffness in her shoulders. An icy rain was falling; she could not remember when it began.

Darkness. The return of numbing cold. They found themselves scrambling up the side of what must be the steepest hill in Ireland. Water poured down from the top, making the slope as slippery as fish guts. People fell, got to their feet somehow, fell again. Rocks tripped them, brambles tore them.

"Dismount and lead your horses!" Ronan bawled at his cavalry. The horses were having a harder time than the people. They plunged upward, clawing for purchase with their hooves, panicked by the unstable surface. Civilians scrambled out of their way to avoid being knocked down.

The thousand had come almost twenty-five miles, with hardly enough food in their bellies to sustain them, and with the threat of pursuit like a constant dark cloud over them. This latest barrier seemed the cruelest of all. Strong men were weary; weaker people were in trouble. A few fell down and stayed down, convinced they could go no farther.

Father Collins paused to try to help a woman get to her feet. She slapped his hands away. He caught her under the shoulders and managed to drag her to her knees, but then the tide of people flowed over them, jostling and crowding until he lost his grip on her.

He could not find her again.

The crowd pushed him on without her, up the interminable hill.

In the lead, Donal Cam walked beside his horse with

his guides on either side. The footing was treacherous. Holding the reins at arm's length, Donal Cam allowed the stallion to pick his own way.

He thought longingly of torches, but dared not risk it. Wilmot's men on high ground miles distant might see moving lights and know what they meant.

At last they reached the top of the slope and began following a cart track across boggy land studded with rocks. They almost stumbled into a wall. Putting out his hand, Donal Cam felt boulders so huge they would have taken two men to lift, instead of the smaller stones used in field walls elsewhere. "You raise hardy men in the Muskerry mountains if you can build walls like this," he said to the nearest guide.

"There should not be a wall just here," the man replied doubtfully.

"Are we lost?"

"Not a bit of it! Still, it might not go amiss . . . if we saw someone . . . to ask the exact way to Eachros from here."

"Not likely to find anyone abroad now," said another guide.

They went on. Suddenly An Cearc snorted and threw up his head. Following the horse's gaze, Donal Cam could make out a tiny glow in a grove of stunted trees to one side of the track. They hurried toward it and found a stone hut with firelight leaking through the chinks in its flimsy mortar. Donal Cam rapped on the door.

It opened a hand's width. A man peered out suspiciously.

The guides quickly identified themselves as Muskerry men, explaining they sought the path to Eachros.

Reassured to hear familiar accents, the man opened his door wider. "You are almost there," he told them. "Follow this track until you come to a cairn on the side of the hill, then bear off to your right and . . ."

Donal Cam's weary attention wandered. Through the half-open doorway he glimpsed a woman bathed in firelight, with her children around her. A scene flashed into his memory, as brilliant as a salmon leaping. He saw again the great hall at Dunboy and his own family gathered at the hearth. His own family warm and safe and together within the walls that had sheltered his people for generations.

A small boy detached himself from the other children and came forward to stand close to his father, peeping around at the strangers.

He is the age of my older son, Donal Cam thought. He crouched down and smiled at the boy. "You are a fine lad."

The child made no response, merely stared, wide-eyed.

Donal Cam tried again. "Can you tell me the name of this place?" he inquired conversationally.

The boy was astonished that anyone would ask such a question. "Home," he said, as if it were obvious.

Home.

Fighting back tears, Donal Cam stood up and turned away.

Day Two

January 1, 1603. Eachros, Wood of the Horse

Maire did not want to be awake. She struggled to find her way back into muffled oblivion, but it was no use. She was cold and wet and every muscle in her body ached.

She opened her eyes to a grainy darkness.

With an effort, she remembered. They had stumbled upon this place in the night, and someone said they would be safe here because it was a church. People had collapsed where they stood. She vaguely recalled wrapping herself in her cloak and pillowing her head on some mossy tussock—that was all she knew.

Someone groaned nearby.

Maire sat up. Her body shrieked with pain. Until the last terrible year she had enjoyed being the daughter of a prosperous freeman who had bondservants to do the heavy work. The most strenuous thing Maire had done was carrying bundles on her head, but every Gaelic woman did that. It gave them the queenly walk that lasted all their lives.

Maire thought ruefully that she would not walk like a queen this morning. It seemed impossible that she would stand up at all.

Someone was crying. The strangled, despairing cry of total hopelessness.

On hands and knees, Maire crawled toward the sound. "Eileen?"

The sobbing continued. Finding the other woman, Maire put one hand on her shoulder. "What troubles you, Eileen?"

"My lad is dead" was the muffled reply. "He was dead by the time we got here last night. I knew it then. The last of my children, dead!" Sobbing, Eileen threw herself into the other woman's arms. Only then did Maire realize the poor mother was still holding her dead child, who was now being crushed between them. With a shudder she could not control, Maire drew back and signed the Cross.

Hearing them, Joan crept out of the bed she had made with her cloak and dead bracken. The pain of awakening had not surprised her; she clenched her teeth and ignored it. In fifty years of living one got used to pain. "Is the child gone from us, then?" she asked gently.

Eileen's weeping was her answer.

People were stirring to life around them, hawking, spitting, relieving themselves, scratching. "We must bury the child before we go," said Joan. "Fortunately there is a burial ground here."

Suddenly Maire recognized the shape of the mossy mound on which she had pillowed her head. She thrust her fist into her mouth, eyes wide with horror.

A man said, "I heard the guides talking. There is a burial ground, but it is a *cillín*, unconsecrated earth for unbaptized infants."

Of course, thought Joan. What better place than this

remote site with its abandoned church going to ruins and the trees crowding close to conceal the shame?

The shame of infant souls condemned to limbo, according to the priests, because they were still stained with original sin.

Maire thought with mingled pity and revulsion of the small bodies moldering beneath the hillocky sod. She knew such things happened. Herself and Richard . . . but they had been betrothed. If she had conceived, their child would have been born into holy wedlock and properly baptized by a priest.

"I cannot bury my little lad here!" Eileen was protesting. "He was a Christian!"

"What would you do, carry his corpse all the way to Leitrim?" Joan inquired. "Leave him here, woman. This is a holy place even if the earth is not consecrated, and I shall get you a priest to say the words over him and commend his soul to God."

Joan made her way through the predawn gloom, skirting the few forlorn, uncarved stones that had been jammed into the earth to mark some of the graves. She found Donal Cam at the gable wall of the little church, where Orla had set up his leather command tent the night before. He was talking with Thomas Burke and Rory O'Sullivan, the captain of the buannachta.

Using the prerogative of age, Joan interrupted them to explain the situation.

Donal Cam seemed deeply moved. "A child . . . the first of us to die." He swallowed hard. "Find Father Archer and have him administer the Last Rites."

"Your own confessor? He will not be pleased; the mother is only a farm woman."

"Tell him I insist," Donal Cam replied in a tone of iron determination. "I insist. Make certain he understands that. And hurry. Dawn is almost upon us."

Joan was indignant. "How am I supposed to hurry a woman who has just lost her last child?"

The tall, scarred leader of the buannachta spoke up. "Any way you can," said Rory O'Sullivan, who had seen too much of death.

A small grave was hastily scooped out in the grove, at an acceptable distance from the cillin. The mother had flatly refused to leave her child among the unbaptized. In the murky gloom the hurried burial seemed furtive, almost indecent, marred by Father Archer's obvious resentment at being forced to preside over the interment.

Then they were away, setting off once more across soggy fields. Eileen kept turning and looking back. Joan caught her arm and pulled her forward. "Leave him be," she advised. "He is out of the wind now."

The earth was a morass of coarse grass and hidden bog, making it dangerous to ride the horses. Donal Cam led An Cearc himself, walking along with the reins trailing from his fingers as he continued his conversation with his captains. Thick brown mud threatened to suck the boots from his feet at every step.

Near a waterfall, he felt a sharp jerk on the reins just as An Cearc threw himself violently to one side. In the mud, the stallion's foreleg had slipped between two buried stones. Panicking, the horse gave a wild leap to free himself.

The sound of bone snapping was like a gunshot.

An Cearc screamed like a woman. He lunged forward, trying to escape the pain. Donal Cam fought to steady him, but it was hopeless. The horse's eyes rolled back in his head, showing the whites. He gave one final lunge, lost his balance, fell on his side with a tremendous splash of liquid mud. At once he began to sink. He had fallen into a boghole.

Donal Cam shouted, "A rope, a piece of timber, anything!" but they were just words he had to say. There was nothing to be done. He watched heartsick as An Cearc floundered, inhaling mud. The efforts of the horseboys to pull him out were futile.

"No use," said Thomas Burke. "Not with a broken leg."

Donal Cam took his knife from its sheath on his hip and crouched at the edge of the boghole. He closed his eyes for a heartbeat, then opened them and cut the stallion's throat with one sure stroke. He did not dare shoot him; the sound would have carried.

As they moved away he tried not to look back at the great dark shape sinking deeper into the mud.

"The Wood of the Horse," he said as if to himself. "A prophetic name." He could feel the stallion's blood drying on his hands. He wondered what was happening in the Oakwood of Blood.

The morning had begun without rain, lifting Niall's spirits. The previous day's march had tired but not exhausted him; buannachta were accustomed to worse. He felt sorry for some of the civilians, though. There was one pretty girl with dark curls who looked as if she was crying.

People throughout the column were moaning and groaning, struggling with cramps and stiff muscles. Many who had walked well enough the day before were limping now. Some were using broken branches for walking sticks.

Niall felt a mild contempt for such weakness. He threw back his shoulders and took swinging strides from the hip in case the girl with black curls was watching.

They had already come a long way from the field where The O'Sullivan's horse had died. Niall could see the commander up ahead, riding once more; this time on the best saddle horse they had left, a chestnut who had been the mount of Ronan Hurley.

Ronan must resent that, Niall thought.

Resent was too mild a term for what Ronan felt. He was in a black humor, seated on an inferior animal with a rough trot, a mouth like iron, and an infuriating tendency to snatch at every weed they rode past.

At least the wretched beast could steal an occasional bite of food. Ronan's own morning meal, eaten in the saddle, had been a hunk of stale bread insufficient to quiet the growling of his stomach.

Their route twisted and climbed through the mounds of russet heather that dappled the flanks of the mountains. As they neared the pass of *Gort na Binn*, the Field of the Peak, Ronan fought his horse to a standstill and looked back.

The man riding nearest reined in beside him. "What is it?"

"Just a feeling. As if we are being watched."

Warriors who survive have learned to listen to such feelings. The other man followed the direction of Ronan's suspicious gaze across a long sweep of countryside. Overhead, clouds parted briefly and a ray of sunlight set the heather ablaze.

"Who might it be?" Ronan's companion asked.

The captain shrugged, squinting. "Almost anyone. The O'Sullivan has enemies everywhere now. See there, where I am pointing? Some ten miles in that direction are at least two castles where he was welcome as a friend and ally not many months ago. Now those strongholds are in enemy hands, and the Gaelic chieftains who welcomed Donal Cam are avowing the English cause to save their own skins. Not that anyone could blame them," he added under his breath.

"What did you say?"

"Nothing. Ride on."

Between one step and the next the sunshine deserted them. The smell of rain was on the wind. Soon it was blowing over them in sheets, making the horses pin their ears flat against their heads to keep the water out. People walked bent forward, with their shoulders hunched.

One of the guides told Donal Cam, "We can go no farther with you. Our clan and the clans of this region . . ."

"I know. You are old enemies. It is the common story of a warrior race. I shall not ask you to come with us into unfriendly territory, I need no wars other than the one I have. Just tell me—will this trackway lead us to Ballyvourney? I want to mark the first day of the new month by doing homage at the shrine of Saint Gobnait."

The guides assured Donal Cam that the road he was on would eventually take the group down into the valley of the Sullane river and to Ballyvourney, *Baile Mhuirne*, the Town of the Beloved, a populous village built near the site of an ancient smelter. "Be careful," warned the guides, "for you will be approaching the territory of Thady Mac Carthy."

Donal Cam gave a curt nod. "I know it."

About midday the group drew near the village. They found the shrine of the seventh-century saint on a wooded hillside, where ruins of the convent and school she had founded were still visible. A round stone hut was intact, and a primitive cooking pit was recognizable.

With Father Archer at his side, Donal Cam led a pilgrimage to the shrine. The O'Sullivan had discussed the visit with his confessor before they ever left Doire na Fola.

"Eighteen months ago Pope Clement granted an indulgence to any who visit Saint Gobnait's holy place," Father Archer had said. "There is a great reverence for her throughout the region; we can hardly pass by without acknowledging her. God's saints are precious and time must be taken for them."

The corners of Donal Cam's lips had lifted very slightly. "As I recall the legend, Gobnait once averted a terrible plague through the strength of her prayer. We have a plague of enemies now, and I would certainly welcome her intercession."

Overhearing the conversation, Dermod O'Sullivan spoke up. "It is told of Saint Gobnait that she once routed some raiders who meant to steal her *creaght*, the livestock she kept for feeding her nuns and students. She loosed the bees from her hives on the raiders, who ran away shrieking."

Donal Cam had uttered one sharp syllable of laughter, but there was no mirth in his voice as he said, "A pity we did not apply to Gobnait sooner, then. We could have used her when Wilmot seized my army's reserves of sheep and cattle. If we had that creaght now, we could feed these people enough to give them strength."

When he had ridden away to organize the departure from Doire na Fola, Father Archer had told Dermod, "He blames himself most harshly for the loss of the creaght, you know."

"Why should he?"

"Because he had continued to place trust in Richard Tyrell after the man abandoned the other defenders of Dunboy."

"My nephew had to trust Tyrell. We were running short of officers. We have even fewer now, of course."

"Indeed. Donal Cam's mistake was in giving Tyrell gold to supply a force to march into Kerry and attack the enemy there. Instead, Tyrell and a number of like-minded traitors deserted and took the gold with them. It was news of those desertions that encouraged Wilmot to seize the creaght, realizing it was lightly defended. That in turn precipitated the quarrel between Donal Cam and William Burke. Burke blamed Donal Cam for everything that had gone wrong since before Kinsale. Then he also deserted, leaving a string of curses behind him and taking two hundred of our biggest gallowglasses with him.

"Thus we find ourselves in our present difficulties, without enough men to continue the battle in Munster or enough food to feed the refugees we have accumulated.

"You cannot know as I do, Dermod, how Donal Cam agonizes over every choice he has made. Only his confessor shares his pain," the Jesuit added piously.

Dermod snapped, "Of course I know what he is feeling! Have I not been with him for most of the worst? I was with him the very morning he learned of O'Donnell's death; he wept then. That was when he decided we were beaten, that we must take our people to the north if we were to save any of them. I know better than anyone how hard it was for him to make that decision. I am an O'Sullivan myself, and defeat does not come easily for us. A mere priest could not be expected to understand *that*," he added.

The two men had glared at each other.

Antagonism still simmered between them on this second day of the march. Dermod did not approve of taking time to visit the saint's shrine, when pursuit might be so close behind them, and said so to Thomas Burke, who was a cousin of the departed William.

The new captain of mercenaries agreed. "This is hostile territory now. I would be happier if we kept moving until we are out of Munster altogether. But as long as the Jesuit has our commander's ear, there is nothing to do but accept. Let us hope these devotions do not take too long." He glanced around suspiciously, his eyes examining every copse and hollow.

Meanwhile, Father Archer was telling the devout, "This is the very place where nine white deer appeared to the saint as the angel had promised, showing her where to build her chapel. And there lie the ruins of the pagan fort she demolished with her own hand to show the locals the power of the Christian God."

Those who could, knelt in prayer. Many could not. Their recent exertions made kneeling impossible. They stood in stiff little groups, hands folded as they pleaded with the long-dead saint to protect them from their enemies.

A sizable number had long since gone off into a field to eat instead of praying, sharing out their supplies of hard bread and smoked fish among themselves.

When the devotions were completed, Donal Cam left a purse of gold on the altar of the small church built on the site of Saint Gobnait's original chapel. Then he ordered his captains to gather the party together again and move them out.

As they straggled through the village its inhabitants watched silently from half-open doorways. No hand was raised against them, but no voice called out a greeting, either.

At the edge of the village were two men mending a broken cart. Rory O'Sullivan paused to ask, "Which of these trackways will lead us to the Blackwater?"

The men glanced at each other. A silent message passed between them. With one accord they resumed their task.

Donal Cam called, "Come away, Rory. We can find our own way northward through the mountains, I have ridden this land before."

One of the men working on the cart looked up sharply, staring at Donal Cam with something cold in his eyes.

As they left Ballyvourney a mountain mist, opaque and moisture laden, settled over them.

Eileen crowded close to Joan, taking comfort from the older woman's presence. "What did the prince mean when he said he had ridden this land before?"

"This is Thady Mac Carthy's country," Joan explained to her.

"Mac Carthy? Mac Carthy Mor, overlord of the west country?"

"His family," Joan agreed. "There is bad blood between them and my nephew, dating from the time Donal Cam laid claim to the lordship of Beare and Bantry over the claim of one of his uncles, Owen O'Sullivan. Owen had the Mac Carthys' support, but Donal Cam argued his case before the English government and was awarded the title. I think he won because he knew both Latin and English, whereas poor Owen could only speak Gaelic," she added with a malicious twinkle. She had never cared for her husband's second brother.

"Because Mac Carthy Mor had supported Owen, once Donal Cam held the lordship he often neglected to send a share of his revenue to the overlord as Gaelic custom demanded. At the time, he felt he had more reason to be grateful to the English than to Mac Carthy Mor.

"Then this terrible business of the rebellion broke out, and my nephew sided with Hugh O'Neill against the English. Owen O'Sullivan's son and namesake took the other side out of spite and became the queen's O'Sullivan. The Mac Carthys stood with us, for a while—until Dunboy fell, in fact. Three of the clan were among those who came to Donal Cam at Ardea and took shares of the Spanish gold to help in fighting the English.

"Then they deserted and took the gold with them. Donal Cam attacked Thady Mac Carthy in his stronghold at *Carraig a Phooca*, the Rock of the Phooca, and recaptured some of the gold, but he made an implacable enemy."

The mist around them had become a muffling white fog, heavy as a weight on their shoulders.

"Gaelic, English, this side, that. I could never make sense of it," Eileen said. "It made no difference to our way of life so far as I could see. We held our plowland from the prince and were good tenants to him, paying in corn and butter. We had the grass of seven cows, and such a nice house . . ." She bit her lip. Tears pooled in her eyes.

Unable to say any more, Eileen walked in silence and thought of her dead family and her abandoned house. So snugly built it had been, that house, of good stone, with a flagged floor and a well of sweet water beyond the door. When her husband chose the site he had taken the precaution of testing it, as people were careful to do. There was always the chance it might lie across one of the pathways used by the Good People, in which case it would fall down no matter how sturdily it was built. Fairy folk left no barriers standing on their roads.

Before he began to build, Eileen's husband had set four piles of stones at the four corners of the proposed building. He left them unwatched through the night. In the morning, to his relief, they were undisturbed. Had they been scattered he would have had to chose another building site.

Satisfied that he would not be offending the Good People, he had then erected a house meant to shelter generations of his descendants. The hearth was the heart, large enough to hold a whole pig for roasting. The house grew around this center. It consisted of one large rectangular room where all life was lived, with a loft above for sleeping. The roof on its oak beams was covered with thin shingles of wood cut so that each fitted on the next as snugly as the flakes of human skin fit together to keep wind and rain from human bones.

My house, thought Eileen. My husband, my children. Abruptly, she halted in her tracks and a great keening wail burst from her, an outpouring of anguish she had not willed and could not contain.

"Hush, love, hush! You must not, it does no good. Come away now." Joan put an arm around Eileen's shoulders and turned her head to look for Maire Ni Driscoll. It took the efforts of both women to calm Eileen and get her walking again.

They were making their way along the bare shoulder of *Mullach an Ois*, the Summit of the Fawn, when the feeling that had been haunting Ronan Hurley all day proved justified.

Out of the fog galloped the sons of Thady Mac Carthy, screaming for blood.

They came up behind the column from the direction of Ballyvourney. They avoided closing with Ronan's cavalry, riding instead in huge circles around the column, attempting to shoot or slash the walkers. Wherever they saw an opening they would dart in to attack those who could not strike back.

Some could strike back. As soon as she realized what was happening, Dermod O'Sullivan's wife stripped off one of her woolen stockings and dropped a fist-sized rock into its toe. When one of the Mac Carthys came riding out of the fog toward her, Joan waited until the man was almost upon her, then swung her improvised weapon around her head and smashed it into his knee with all her might.

The man added a new scream to the cacaphony as his kneecap shattered.

At the first sounds of attack, Donal Cam had whirled his chestnut horse on its haunches and galloped back the way they had come, scattering civilians. In the fog and confusion it was impossible to get a clear assessment of the situation. Only the familiar war cry of the Mac Carthys identified the enemy, but that was enough.

"Get people moving!" Donal Cam shouted at his captains. "Protect the column; cover our retreat!"

The leaders of the buannachta, mercenaries, and cavalry did their best. The surprise attack was turned into a running battle, with Donal Cam's people fleeing along the spine of the mountains while their army fought desperately to keep the enemy away from them.

Some people panicked. Their unchallenged passage so far had lulled them; they had let themselves believe they would be allowed to make their journey unhindered. The shocking suddenness of the attack, the eerie quality of the fog, the unfamiliarity of the region, all fueled a mounting hysteria.

If he could not control it now and hold them together, Donal Cam knew his gamble was lost. He would never be able to get any of them safely to the north if they scattered like chickens at the shadow of the hawk.

While his warriors mounted what defense they could, he devoted himself to herding the column from the back of his horse, alternately cajoling and cursing. Once or twice he used the flat of his sword to strike people across the shoulders and force them back into the main body. People out of their minds with a combination of fear and the cumulative weariness of the march were stumbling off through the heather and bracken in aimless flight and would soon be swallowed up in the mist and lost.

There would be no time to search for them.

The buannachta, The O'Sullivan's elite, were well trained. At the first sign of attack they had gathered themselves for battle. With the ease of long familiarity, they could hear their captain's shouted orders even above the yelling and gunfire.

At first Niall had thought they would fight where they stood. He had already shrugged off his pack to free his arms when he heard the order to keep the column moving. He barely had time to snatch it up again. An enemy horseman came toward him, yelling. He clamped his pack under one arm, for there was not a moment to spare for settling it on his back. His pikestaff was ready in his other hand, angled upward toward the man on the horse.

The horseman saw it and tried to swerve, but his animal's reflexes were not fast enough. Niall managed to hit the rider with a telling blow across the chest, and had the satisfaction of seeing the man lose his balance and fall. The horse trotted away, reins dragging. "Someone catch that horse!" Niall shouted.

One more for Ronan, he thought.

He threw himself onto the fallen man. They fought in silence, pummeling one another, until Niall's fist connected hard enough with his enemy's jaw to make the man's eyes glaze. Niall was reaching for his knife to finish the job when the other gasped, "O'Mahony, is that yourself?"

Niall squatted back on his haunches and inspected his fallen foe. "Michael Mac Carthy?"

"It is myself. In the name of God man, let me up. Did we not fight together once?"

"We did. But you are trying to kill my people now."

"I am just trying to do what we all want to do, capture Donal Cam and collect the price the English have put on his head."

Niall did not relinquish his hold. "What price?"

"Three hundred pounds sterling! Lord President Carew has promised to pay that for the live body of the wicked and unnatural traitor, as they are calling him. Help me get my hands on him, Niall, and we shall share it, I give you my word."

Niall held still, as if considering. Then he heard the scream of a woman from somewhere in the column.

Looking into the eyes of Michael Mac Carthy with great regret, he bent forward and cut the other man's throat.

The attackers were inflicting their own share of casualties. As the battle progressed, however, they became more careful about staying well out of reach themselves. Their shouts could be heard quite clearly as they called out to one another, asking if anyone had found O'Sullivan Beare yet.

Not *The* O'Sullivan. The chieftainship of the clan was to be denied Donal Cam, devolving instead upon his cousin Owen, partisan of the English. In the shifting politics of the day Donal Cam was no longer leading his clan north to safety, but fleeing with a band of rebel refugees. The clan O'Sullivan were now considered the queen's people under the leadership of Owen.

That simple change in titles told Donal Cam this much, even in the height and turmoil of battle. He had only time to register the knowledge, but no time to let it sink in and start to hurt. He was too busy for anything but action.

He reined his horse in next to that of one of his cavalry, a thick-necked man with coarse dark hair. "Quickly, change clothes with me," Donal Cam ordered. "Take my cloak; anyone would know it for the cloak of a chieftain. And here"—he paused to reach into the pack behind his saddle and pull out a small leather pouch—"take this gold, too. Ride as hard and as fast as you can to the west, and let the Mac Carthys catch a glimpse of you, but not get too close. Your horse is fast enough to keep you free of them, I think. Go to ground wherever you can find safety and stay there, my friend. This march is not for you."

The other man understood. Like his prince, he was an O'Sullivan. He nodded one swift salute before he galloped off. Donal Cam whispered a prayer after his departing back.

"There he goes, there's the traitor!" they heard someone shout. A band of Thady's men set off after him, reducing the number who were pursuing the column.

The rest continued the fight, harrying the column for four long hours across the spine of the mountains. Although it made the going harder, Donal Cam kept to the peaks. He dared not give the enemy the advantage of getting above him. He ordered those who were equipped with guns to stop and return fire whenever they could, and the air rattled with the sounds of musket and caliver. The caliver, a light form of arquebus, was meant for close range and did little damage under the circumstances, but an occasional cry told when a musket ball had found its mark.

Meanwhile his kernes wielded sword and dagger or the fine ashwood pikes that were deadly in expert hands. The sturdy gallowglasses relied on their axes, heavy weapons almost five feet long in total and capable of pulling a man's arm out of the shoulder socket if mishandled.

The enemy had guns and spears, and one or two had snatched up pitchforks which they hurled at the beginning of the fighting. None of these weapons was suitable for a prolonged running battle across mountains, however, so casualties were not heavy. But fear took its own toll. More than one person scuttled away to hide in some fold in the hills, divorcing himself from the further destiny of O'Sullivan Beare.

When the light began to fade Donal Cam determined to make a stand. He ordered his entire force to the rear in one broad line to turn and face their attackers in traditional Gaelic style. He had timed his move well. Thady's men had begun to weary of riding over rough ground, and knew the dangers the terrain would offer their horses' legs in the dark. When their quarry brought the attack to them they fought one final skirmish, then galloped away, shouting the vilest abuses, to return to their stronghold and await news of the capture of Donal Cam.

When their hoofbeats had faded away, the man they sought took stock of his band. He rode among them speaking reassuringly, praising their courage. Some faces lit up at his words. Others stared blankly, all emotion spent.

"How many casualties?" he asked Rory O'Sullivan.

The captain of the buannachta had a hideous scar across his face, the result of an ax wielded by an enemy gallowglass. The scar was puckered and purple, but thanks to the ministrations of the women it had healed.

Rory said, with a nod, "Ask my wife, she is just beyond the brow of the hill there."

Donal Cam rode in the direction indicated. He found a company of women tending the injured and improvising litters for carrying them. "Orla Ni Donoghue!" he called.

A tall woman with sweat-matted red hair glanced up, beckoned to him, then bent to her task again, binding a wound with plantain leaves.

Among those who followed Donal Cam northward, women outnumbered men. The women could be divided into two groups. One consisted of members of the Gaelic nobility and landholding classes, and their attendants.

The second group, including Orla Ni Donoghue, were generally but not pejoratively described as camp followers. For the most part they were the wives, sisters, and sweethearts of the warriors, women who accompanied their men to battle in the ancient Gaelic tradition.

The passage of Adamnan's Law at the Assembly of Tara in 697 had forbidden women to take part in the fighting as they had formerly done. For the nine hundred years since, they continued to make themselves useful, however, by serving as foragers and cooks and camp makers, by organizing the baggage and tending the wounded, thus freeing their men to fight.

Orla's skillful hands had ministered to Rory's ax wound.

Donal Cam knew those hands, too.

He slid from his horse to stand at her shoulder, looking down at a musketeer who had had his shoulder dislocated by his own weapon. "Can he go on, Orla?"

"He can walk, he just cannot fire his gun now."

"It will go to someone else, then. Are there any dead?"

Orla straightened up and wiped her forehead with her wrist. "A few. We were fortunate there were not more. Will you have someone start burying them?"

"At once; we have to move on."

The man with the dislocated shoulder groaned.

"We cannot make camp for the night out here in the open on the heights," Donal Cam told him. "The mountains, in winter? More of you would freeze to death than the Mac Carthys killed. We must go on as far as O'Keefe country and try to find shelter there."

Orla put a hand on Donal Cam's arm. "There is a price on your head," she said in a low voice. "I heard."

"Did you also hear what they are calling me now? O'Sullivan Beare. Not The O'Sullivan, not chief of the clan. They think to strip me and shame me." His voice was carefully modulated, yet it vibrated with anger.

Orla met his eyes squarely. Her own were hazel, wide

set, with stubby gold lashes. "You will always be chieftain," she told him.

A woman nearby sniggered, then hastily covered her mouth with her hand. Orla glared at her, but Donal Cam ignored her. "What about the baggage, Orla? Have you had a chance to see to it?"

She hated having to tell him, and dropped her eyes before saying, "Mac Carthy's men seized most of it. Many people had overburdened themselves with things they thought they could not bear to leave behind, though when we began to run they dropped them soon enough. The Mac Carthys got all of that . . . and most of the packhorses. Your horse boys were able to save three, the rest are gone."

Donal Cam was dismayed. "Gone? What was lost? The gold, the ammunition . . . *the food*?"

"The horses we still have carry some of the gold and the gunpowder, but what little remained of our food supplies went with Thady Mac Carthy's men," Orla said, confirming his worst fears.

Nothing remained to feed a thousand people for an indefinite time but what crumbs his soldiers might be carrying in their backpacks. And Gaelic warriors traveled light; at most they might have a day's worth of butter and meal.

Donal Cam could more easily have spared gold and gunpowder than food.

"There is nothing to eat at all?" He could hardly accept it.

Orla shook her head. "Nothing."

A quick survey revealed that the soldiers had eaten their daily ration, which was small enough, on the march. The sum total remaining was three lumps of bread and half a handful of meal.

All that careful parceling out of our supplies was

wasted, Donal Cam thought bitterly. We agonized over each bit of food we doled out—it would have been better to let them fill their stomachs at Doire na Fola, at least they would have had the strength of it then.

Now it was imperative the column not only find shelter for the night, but someone to give them food.

First, there were casualties to bury.

The tools had gone with the packhorses. Thomas Burke set his mercenaries to work digging and scraping in the thin mountain soil, using their daggers and sharp stones. The priests said their prayers, the mourners wept, and a few pathetic mounds of raw earth were piled up amid the heather.

While the dead were being buried, the woman who had laughed sidled up to Orla. Indicating Donal Cam with her eyes, she said, "As far as you are concerned he will always have the chieftain's privilege." She laughed again, a suggestive giggle.

Orla snorted. "You are jealous because he did not exercise the right of a prince to take your maidenhead."

"Jealous? Of you? I would not have Donal Cam or your crane-legged excuse for a husband either."

"That is just as well," Orla replied smugly, "since neither one of them would touch you, Grella."

As soon as the burying was done, Donal Cam and his captains devoted themselves to the task of getting people moving again, over loud protests. Racing the night, they set off across the high ground toward the wooded glens sloping down to the valley of the Blackwater.

In the twilight they heard a wolf howl, one of the giant wolves that the giant wolfhounds of the Gael had been bred to hunt.

No beloved wolfhounds loped beside Donal Cam's horse now with their red tongues lolling and their bright eyes merry. He felt their absence.

They began to pass inhabited farmsteads at the edge of O'Keefe territory. "My men know this region," Thomas Burke told his commander. "They are O'Malleys of Connacht who came to the south along this very route, almost. If you need guides through here, call on them."

"Have two or three walk beside my horse. I would be glad of guides; we cannot afford to have torches."

"Even here? Are the O'Keefes not allies of yours?"

Donal Cam took his time about answering. "I cannot say . . . now. The world is torn apart."

As they passed various landholdings, they were aware of men coming out to watch them go by. More than one shouted an angry warning to stay away. Once or twice farm dogs were set upon stragglers from the column.

Tight-lipped, Donal Cam pressed on.

The terrain became a little easier, the wind a little less bitter. At last, in a dip of land sheltered by hills, Donal Cam ordered a halt. A camp of sorts was made, though the lighting of fires was forbidden. There was no food to cook anyway.

The leather tent of The O'Connor Kerry had been lost with the baggage. The old chieftain shrugged philosphically and accepted an offer of sleeping space in Donal Cam's tent. Sentries were posted. The exhausted refugees tried to sleep, only to be pursued through their dreams by a howling mob of Mac Carthys.

Weary though he was, Dermod O'Sullivan left the cluster of officers camped around the command tent and went in search of his wife. Each had long since ascertained that the other had survived the attack, but they had not spoken since, as Dermod rode with his nephew. On previous nights he had slept with the officers. Now, however . . .

He found Joan bedded down near the woman whose child had died.

With a groan and a creaking of joints, Dermod eased himself onto the earth beside his wife. Joan blinked at him; they fumbled together to spread their cloaks jointly.

"I thought I would find you here," he told her. "That boy who died put you in mind of our Philip, did he not?"

"He did, though Philip is older. May God grant he lives to see his eleventh birthday!"

"He will of course. After all, Donal Cam sent him to Spain."

"With his own firstborn son, Donal, to put them under the king's protection," Joan finished. "Salvaging what we could of both families. And not that much left to salvage, with thirteen of ours dead in battle. Now young Philip is a guest of His Most Catholic Majesty, the king of Spain, a token of O'Sullivan loyalty. Much good has our loyalty to Catholic Spain done for us!" Joan added bitterly.

"At least it should keep our boys safe. You should have gone with them."

"How could I seek safety abroad when Donal Cam's wife was staying in Ireland? Am I not at least as brave as Honora? I would have disgraced you if I fled while she stood fast."

Dermod shifted uncomfortably, seeking a soft place that did not exist on the stony ground. "The two of you were a great comfort to us after the loss of Dursey and Dunboy," he admitted. "But that was summer and this is winter. Everything has gone against us. Our armies are depleted through battle and desertion, our creaght is lost, our land is despoiled. With Hugh O'Neill gone back north and Red Hugh O'Donnell dead in Spain, we have suffered blows from which we may never recover."

"So? Now is when you need me most."

"Listen to me, woman! You say you did not want to disgrace me, but I tell you, you have shamed me most cruelly."

"I? Never!"

"But you have; you stained my honor. When Donal Cam decided this march out of Munster was the only way to save what followers remained to us, we discussed it at length, and he told me then his wife and infant son were not strong enough for such a journey. On that day I gave him my promise that Joan Ni Sweney would stay behind with Honora and be her companion in hiding until an escape by ship could be arranged for them. I gave my solemn word!"

"Your word has been kept," his wife assured him. "Is not one Joan Ni Sweney with Donal Cam's wife this very night? I saw them off myself, to the safest, most inaccessible hiding place in the west country. They are where Wilmot could never find them, among the wild crags of *Nead na Fhiolair*." The Eagle's Nest.

"But the Joan I meant was you, not your cousin! When you left your namesake in your place, you disgraced me by breaking the promise I had given my nephew."

"Nonsense. Your words was kept as stated. Besides, my brother will guard both women even more devotedly since one is not only his cousin, but his sweetheart. He will find food for Honora and his beloved Joan even when there is no food to be found. He will keep them safe at the cost of his own blood if necessary. Donal Cam accepted it, when I explained to him. Why can you not do the same?"

"Because I wanted you to be safe, you exasperating woman!"

They lay in silence for a time. Then he felt her chuckling. "You should have seen your face, Dermod, when I appeared at Doire na Fola."

"I can well imagine; I was furious."

"Furious? We had a spectacular row, as I recall. And later you sent Donal Cam to order me to join you, as if you were afraid I would stay behind out of sheer perversity."

"How could I know what you might do? I have not been able to forecast your actions in thirty years of marriage."

She chuckled again, a contented and self-satisfied sound. "My being unpredictable has kept your eyes on me and off other women."

"You are a terrible, wanton creature," said Dermod O'Sullivan with feeling. The old man pulled his wife against him, clutching her fiercely to his heart.

They were almost asleep when the night was torn by shouts and yells.

Day Three

January 2, 1603. *Pobal Ui Chaoimh*, O'Keefe Country

Dawn found the refugees wearier than ever. Sleep had
been denied them. Throughout the night, groups of
local people had taken turns jeering, threatening, taunting
them, beating pots and stones together, setting up a
hideous din but never coming close enough to the encampment to put themselves in danger.

In a way, it was the greatest cruelty they had yet encountered.

Sunrise found a red-eyed Donal Cam preparing to get
the column under way again. Orla and her women had
taken down his tent. It was now packed onto one of the
three remaining baggage animals, and Donal Cam's own
horse was being held by a horse boy, waiting for the commander to mount.

He stood gazing at the bleak winter landscape. Their
tormentors had faded away at first light, but he could still
hear their echoes in his head.

As if reading his thoughts, The O'Connor Kerry said,

"So many enemies! How did we come to have so many enemies among our own people?"

Donal Cam turned toward him. "We lost, Sean," he said simply.

"One battle, Kinsale, after so many victories. And we shall win again, you have said so yourself."

Donal Cam continued to regard him with a grave, dark gaze.

"The loss of a battle—crushing though that one was—is nothing. There will always be more battles, it is the way of the world. I am speaking of that which we lost and may never get back. That which we—and I helped, may God forgive me—that which we gave away. Our way of life, Sean. The whole Gaelic order that had nourished and sustained our race for two thousand years." There was anguish in his voice.

The O'Connor looked questioningly at him, but nothing more was said until the two men were mounted and riding off across winter-barren pastures, the stiff, sore, hungry column straggling with some vociferous protests behind them.

Then The O'Connor turned his face toward Donal Cam and asked, "What were you talking about back there? The Gaelic order?"

"Since your ancestors and mine first conquered and settled this island, Sean, we have been a warrior aristocracy guided by our own complex code of law. Everything was set out for us in patterns suited to our own natures. A man, no matter what his station, had dignity from the moment of his birth, and an honor price that spoke for his value and must be paid to his family by anyone who did him harm.

"We had our high king and our provincial kings, our overlords and our lords, our freemen and the unfree, each level of society dependent on the one above it for protection, and obligated to pay for that protection by supplying produce and goods, or men to fight if need be.

"Freemen held plowland and grassland from lords like yourself and myself, and expected justice from us. By and large, we gave it. We took pride in our honor, we of the Gael.

"Not a perfect system, some might say, but how can imperfect man devise perfection? It worked well enough for us, Sean.

"Not only for the nobility but also for the common classes. No chieftain let any of his followers suffer privation, even if it meant providing for them from his personal stock. It was a matter of honor, and our honor was sacred to us.

"Nor did we war on women and children. That too was a matter of honor," Donal Cam added darkly, turning in his saddle to glance back along the bedraggled column following him.

He resumed, "The Vikings came to plunder the island, but under Brian Boru their power was destroyed and they were absorbed by the Gael. Life went on as before. Clan warfare continued to be practiced to keep our battle skills sharp. Church law and the pre-Christian Brehon law existed together in a complex compromise typical of people who enjoy complexity. Poetry was recited in every hall and hut and we had music for every sort of labor. We lived in the way that suited us, Sean. And we were free.

"Then came the Sasanach from England. The first invaders were of Norman blood, and though their habits were strange to us we had the true faith in common. When they discovered the pleasures of our way of life they set themselves to learn our language and adopt our customs and we absorbed them as we had the Vikings. Ireland remained Gaelic. True, we were now paying tributes—taxes, they were called—to a king in England rather than a high king at Tara, but that seemed the only real difference.

"Then the New English arrived, a new sort of Sasanach, willing to war on their Norman predecessors and eager to convert everyone to the Tudor heresy. The New English were contemptuous of everything Gaelic. They called us barbarians. They, who spitted infants on their spears when they overran Dursey Island, dared to call us savages!" Donal Cam doubled one fist and beat it against the shoulder of his horse in impotent rage. The chestnut stallion responded by shaking his heavy crest and rattling the bit against his teeth.

The O'Connor said, "We beat them at every major battle of the Nine Years' War, until Kinsale. And we shall beat them again. This is just a temporary setback."

Donal Cam gave him a cynical look. "Is that what you call it? I tell you, we have lost, no matter how many battles we may win in future. Look at me," he added bitterly, "I am the prime example of England's triumph."

"Because of one strategic retreat? You do yourself discredit. You are a hero, the last of the great princes of the south to defy the Sasanach."

"Partly because of a bad conscience," Donal Cam told him. "I accepted the English way as cheerfully as any, when I was young. I dressed in velvet doublets and slashed sleeves and strutted about like a cock pheasant, thinking myself a very fine fellow indeed. I spoke the foreign tongue as well as one born in England; I traveled widely and was welcomed in Sasanach halls. When they patronized me—and they did, I see that now—in my blind ignorance I thought they were jesting with me as an equal. All they offered me I accepted, and thought it my due.

"When the time came to argue for my patrimony, did I take up sword and spear and fight for it? Of course not. I was *civilized*." He sneered the word. "I went before the English administrators and paraded my knowledge of English law. It took me two years to prove that the lordship of Beare and Bantry had descended from father to son for generations, and that my uncle's claim on it had been illegally inspired by Mac Carthy Mor, whose creature my uncle was. Owen had promised the overlord more tribute than I would ever be willing to pay; wealth that should have gone to the inhabitants of the region, the fishermen and clan dependents.

"You should have seen me, Sean," said Donal Cam in a tone of voice which indicated he was thankful The O'Connor had not been present to see him. "I appeared before the English administrators with a lace ruff around my neck, like a good Elizabethan. I boasted of the English and Latin scholarship of both my father and myself, insinuating that my uncle Owen, who only spoke Gaelic, was some inferior sort of being, not fit to hold a great title.

"And in the end, I won. Or thought I did. My claim was upheld under English law. I held Beare and the wealth of its seas . . . from the Sasanach." He spoke the last word as if it were acid on his tongue.

"But you held it," The O'Connor pointed out. "Is that not what matters? Would I not gladly receive my kingdom of Kerry back this day, even from English hands?"

Donal Cam shook his head. Suddenly he felt overwhelmed by a corrosive weariness. "If I cannot make you understand, Sean . . . what hope is there?"

"I am trying to understand. I just think that . . . by the deer! Is this horse lame?" The old man leaned out of the saddle, peering down at his mount's legs.

Donal Cam squinted. "Off foreleg. A bad limp, that; you cannot ride him."

But The O'Connor had already drawn rein and was sliding off.

"Have a horse boy lead him for you," Donal Cam said. "God knows we have plenty of unemployed horse boys now, with the pack animals stolen. As for another horse for you, we shall have to take one from the cavalry, but at least we can do that much. Chieftains ride. There is little enough left to us, but . . ."

The O'Connor waved one hand in the air in a negligent gesture. "All those people following us are walking; I can walk."

At that moment Dermod O'Sullivan on his own horse caught up with them. Realizing the situation at a glance, he slid off his animal and fell into step beside The O'Connor. "I am as good a walker as you are, and better," he told his friend amiably.

Donal Cam gave his uncle an exasperated look. "The two of you contest like boys! What am I to do with your horse then, Dermod?"

"Put the weakest of the women on it, or several of the children."

"I would have done that at the beginning if we had enough horses left to us, but there were not. Had I mounted a few and left others walking, there would have been jealousy and quarrels. There would be now, if I put someone on your horse."

Dermod's eyes flashed. "It is my horse, and I can find a rider myself. My wife shall have it."

But when he offered the animal to Joan she refused with a show of indignation. "Do you think I am so old and weak I must ride when others walk? If you can put one foot after another so can I, Dermod O'Sullivan!"

At last four little girls were lined up on the horse's back, with a horse boy assigned to lead them. Once they would have been squealing and giggling at the treat. Now they clung to each other in silence, pale with fatigue and hollow-eyed with hunger.

Ronan Hurley had observed the change in riding arrangements without comment. When the opportunity presented itself, however, he guided his horse toward Orla's women, who were walking in a group, carrying the injured on litters.

He caught his sister's eye and she left the others to walk beside his horse.

Grella Ni Hurley was the woman who had commented on Orla's attachment to Donal Cam. Her features were crowded together in the middle of a round face, but the curve of her hip had been admired in the days before hunger whittled it down. She had followed the warriors for years, enjoying the roistering life of the camps and looking after four brothers.

Of the four, only Ronan was still alive. One had died at Kinsale and two more at Dunboy.

"Did you see that, Grella?" Ronan said indignantly. "A good horse goes to four squirming children, and I am left on this beast who is only fit for the plow."

"A deliberate insult," his sister assured him. "Why do you take it?"

"I would not, if I had a choice. Ever since we left Doire na Fola I have been watching the baggage, waiting for a chance. All that gold. I thought sooner or later I would be able to claim my share as Richard Tyrell did his, then you and I would have been away from this."

"We are owed that much. And more! when you consider our suffering and loss. But you missed your chance, Ronan. The baggage is gone now."

"Not all of it, the commander still has three horses

laden with his personal goods. From the way the horse boys fought for them, I should say they are the ones carrying the gold.

"You and I shall watch those three packhorses as closely as we can. When we stop for the night, try to find an opportunity to search the commander's baggage. No one will question you, you will merely be helping to set up camp. If you find the gold is in there, let me know. Then we will wait for our chance to take it and escape."

"How will we escape?"

"On this horse," Ronan told her. "The wretched animal will carry double; he is good for that much, at least."

The mountainous terrain of Muskerry had given way to the fertile, rolling valley of the Blackwater. Donal Cam still sought the high ground wherever possible, however, and chose routes over hills rather than around them. The high ground was safer; one could see an approaching enemy.

The temperature was dropping steadily. Angry storm clouds huddled like a violent mob in the northwest. Donal Cam had hoped they might find shelter in the distant Glen of Aherlow that night, but there were still many miles to go. He hurried his followers relentlessly.

"These are ferocious hills for starving people to climb," Father Archer protested to him.

"They climbed the mountains; they can manage the hills."

"Not with empty bellies!"

Donal Cam summoned Thomas Burke. "Take a party of your men and do some foraging. Wherever you find a farmstead or a cabin, ask for food. Here." He fumbled in one of the packs on a remaining packhorse and produced a leather purse. "Take this gold and offer to pay."

Burke and his mercenaries broke off from the column

and went in search of food. They were back soon enough. The captain returned the purse to Donal Cam. "There is no food to buy, nor would they sell it to us if they had any. These people are almost as hungry as we are, thanks to the Lord President's policies. We were lucky to escape with our lives in one or two places, they were so angry that we even dared approach them."

Donal Cam circled west of *Ceann Toirc*, the Head of the Boar, then swung northeast toward Liscarroll. *Lios Cearuill*, the Ring-fort of Carroll. He knew there was an English garrison at Liscarroll but meant to bypass it by fording the Allow river at a safe distance beyond. From there he would proceed toward the foothills of the Ballyhouras in search of a secure campsite. If they made it that far, they would have traveled more than thirty miles that day.

Niall O'Mahony did not concern himself with distance traveled or miles yet to go. He concentrated on keeping Donal Cam in sight.

"You shall be my harper now," the commander had promised him at Doire na Fola. Those words still rang in Niall's brain. Even in the worst fighting of the previous day, the pikeman had always known where Donal Cam was; had been aware of him and felt somehow connected to him.

When he was asked to play for his prince, he meant to be ready.

No such honor had come to Niall's immediate family within living memory, but five generations back, on his mother's side, there had been a bard. A true bard, the equal of kings, welcome in every hall. He had been dead many years, but his gift had been passed through the blood of his daughters instead of his sons, to find itself a home in the soul of the humblest of Donal Cam's recruits.

Not so humble, Niall thought, a faint smile on his lips. At least I have one relic from my ancestor, his harp and harp bag. Any man living would be proud, carrying those. He reached over his shoulder and felt his pack reassuringly. No Mac Carthy had snatched it; he would have fought to the death in its defense.

Donal Cam rode past, trotting along the column, urging people to keep moving, encouraging, cajoling, swearing when all else failed. Some swore back at him. Some shook their fists and cursed him. But they stumbled on.

Feeling that he had a special responsibility due to his new position, Niall shepherded those nearest him. Out of the corner of his eye he saw the girl with black curls. If she should stumble, he was ready to help her, but she did not stumble. She walked beside Dermod O'Sullivan's wife with her chin up and her face very white, very closed, and sad.

Niall wondered what she would feel like in his arms.

The sky was too dark for the time of day, and the cold wind cut to the bone. Ice crunched beneath their feet. Niall saw the black-haired girl shiver in spite of her fringed woolen cloak. He was at her side in two strides, unfastening the bronze pin that held his great shaggy mantle in place. The girl started to protest as he wrapped the heavy garment around her, but he pushed her hands aside. "I insist you take this," he said. "I am too hot in it."

She gave him a look of disbelief. Joan said loudly, "Of course she will take it, and we thank you." She pinned the shaggy mantle around Maire's shoulders herself.

Maire managed a faint smile. "It weighs more than I do," she said in the sweetest voice Niall had ever heard. "And it . . . ah . . . it . . ."

"Smells," Joan finished for her.

Niall nodded. "It does smell, but that comes from wetting the fleece. On cold nights, if you wet the mantle and then wrap yourself up in it, fleece to the inside, your body heat warms it and you are snug no matter how bitter the weather. I would not trade it for the commander's tent."

"I shall return this to you before nightfall, then," the girl said.

"Perhaps it would be better to share it," suggested Joan.

Niall felt his ears redden and saw the red stain creep up the girl's cheeks, but Joan went on unabashedly, "Listen to me, Maire, I am giving you good advice."

"But Richard . . ."

"Richard is dead and you are alive," the older woman said briskly. "You—young man. I shall expect you to come looking for your cloak tonight. Two will keep it warmer than one."

To his surprise, in spite of weariness and hunger and the accumulated tension of many days, Niall felt a rising erection pressing against his tunic. He turned his body so the girl would not see.

But Dermod O'Sullivan's wife saw. She gave the pikeman a very deliberate wink.

They had reached the ford of the Allow and were beginning to make their way down the muddy bank and across the black, swift-flowing water when they heard the sound of musket fire. A band of armed men came galloping toward them, yelling for them to surrender and shooting into the air to frighten them.

"English voices!" cried Donal Cam. "From the garrison at Lios Cearuill, surely."

"They are that," confirmed Rory O'Sullivan, preparing to form his buannachta into a defensive line. "Cuffe's men, he is commander there now. And unless I am mistaken that is Viscount Barry's brother with them. We know him of old."

"How did they know we are here?" someone asked as the mass of civilians scurried to seek cover in the shrubbery along the river bank.

"Half of Ireland must know where we are by this time," someone growled. "And himself there with a price on his head."

The company that had ridden out from the garrison to intercept the refugees was small, but well armed. A furious skirmish took place. Donal Cam shouted to his officers to try to lead the fighting upriver, away from the civilians.

Ronan led his cavalry away at an oblique angle and drew the enemy fire. Eight horsemen and forty English infantry took off after him in hot pursuit. The buannachta fell in behind, hoping to pin the English between themselves and the cavalry. The mercenaries supported this maneuver with a flanking action of their own.

Cuffe's men, finding themselves in a dangerous situation, turned and fought, only to have O'Sullivan's force scatter and leave them with no targets. When they tried to go back down the river and attack the civilians, however, the Gaelic army rose up out of the underbrush and the fighting resumed with a will.

At the end of an hour, four of O'Sullivan's men lay dead, but much more English blood had been spilled. Deciding that it was better to be absent than outnumbered, the English captain rallied his men and set off in the direction of Lios Cearuill, shouting threats over his shoulder as he rode away.

Donal Cam surveyed the battle scene. "We won this one, at least," he remarked to his captain of mercenaries. "Are you all right, Thomas? That is a nasty wound on your head."

"Some bastard dragged me off into the undergrowth

and sat on me for a while, but I got away," Burke replied, "after I bashed in his head with a rock the way he had done mine."

"Take it to the women before we get under way again and have them give you some ointment or something," Donal Cam ordered.

"Get under way. You mean, we are not going to camp here?"

"This close to the English? We dare not. This little victory means nothing, the ford is ours to hold for as long as it takes them to catch their breath and get reinforcements, and not one moment longer. We have time to bury our dead, but no more."

The women gathered the dead, wrapped them in their mantles, wiped the blood and the grimace of pain from their faces. Father Archer and Father Collins gave them the final sacraments of their faith and accompanied their bodies to the corner of a high field overlooking distant, beautifully rounded hills.

Amid swirls of blowing snow and chanted prayers, the dead were buried. The ground was frozen hard, almost impossible to dig, and was piled back on top of them in clods instead of in drifts of soft soil.

One of the dead had been a member of the Gaelic cavalry. While his comrades were mourning him, Ronan Hurley appropriated his horse, which was of better quality than Ronan's mount.

Donal Cam noticed. Out of the side of his mouth he said to Rory O'Sullivan, "Go get the extra saddle horse and give it to the weak and wounded."

He would have liked to give all the cavalry horses to those who were unable to walk, but he dared not. They could be attacked again at any time, anywhere, and the mobility of his cavalry was a vital element of defense.

Yet he heard people grumbling about the men who rode while the injured had to walk.

Ronan heard it too, and his eyes glittered with satisfaction. While the great mass of people was struggling to resume the march, he sought out his sister. "People are turning against Donal Cam," he told her. "We will have more and more desertions as we go along, mark it well. Our chance will come soon enough."

In the aftermath of battle, the men who had taken part were silent. They had fought two battles in three days on rations insufficient for one day, and traveled more than eighty miles in bitter weather.

They knew worse might lie ahead of them. Ronan and his sister were not the only ones thinking of desertion.

As they left the high field with its four lonely graves, not a few of them looked back. Some even felt a pang of envy for the men who could, at last, rest.

They had no way of knowing that these were the last four men they would have a chance to bury.

East of Lios Cearuill, the rolling hills gave way to sodden meadows. The Ballyhoura Mountains rose ahead, guarding the Golden Vale.

"Will we have to climb those mountains?" someone gasped.

"Not at all," The O'Connor said reassuringly. "We will seek shelter at their feet, then head straight north in the morning."

Morning. It was hard to imagine morning. It was hard to imagine anything but walking through a bitterly cold winter twilight, with the air so sharp it tore the lungs, and the legs aching, and the feet numb with cold. Walking, walking . . .

Orla walked beside a litter borne by attendants who had formerly cared for Donal Cam in the great hall at

Dunboy. They were too tired to be gentle. The wounded pikeman they carried groaned when they jolted him.

Orla said sharply, "Mind yourselves! You hurt him unduly!"

One of the litter carriers glared at her but she glared back with equal fervor until the man dropped his eyes. For a while, an effort was made to be more careful with the litter.

The injured man looked up at Orla. "Bless you," he said weakly.

"I would do more if I could. I shall, when we stop for the night."

"Will you take the musket ball out of my shoulder?"

"You would lose too much blood, I dare not try. If you could lie still for several days after, it might be possible, but as we are now . . ."

"Take the ball out and leave me, then," said the man. "I will be left sooner or later anyway, with a wound like this. I know it. I cannot possibly get all the way to Leitrim and O'Rourke's stronghold. Leave me as you left those at Doire na Fola. I understand such choices in wartime."

"You are a brave man," Orla told him, "but we shall not leave you if we can avoid it."

The litter bearer who had glared at her before met her eyes again. A silent message passed between them, and this time it was Orla who looked down first.

They both knew the wounded would be left along the way. If the journey continued as it had begun, there would be no choice.

All I can do to save them will be wasted, Orla thought bitterly. She would have cried, if she had not been too tired for tears.

She became aware of a new presence at her shoulder and looked around to see Father Collins beside her. "Is this man going to be all right?" the priest asked.

The man on the litter said, "I shall not need the sacraments yet, but look you; stay within calling distance." His eyes closed. He set his jaw against the pain.

If ever there had been a semblance of order to the march, it was long since lost. Recruit and mercenary strode together, noble and servant stumbled side by side. In their weariness, people bumped into one another repeatedly, and the litters carrying the wounded were jounced and jostled. Orla fell back a pace to use her back as a wall to protect the litter carrying the pikeman, and Father Collins followed her example.

"You are an O'Sullivan woman?" he inquired, making conversation. They were all too weary for talking, but it would help to distract them, the priest felt.

"I am now," Orla said. "My husband is the captain of Donal Cam's buannachta."

Father Collins noticed that she used the commander's Christian name. "You know The O'Sullivan well, do you? Are you from Beare?"

Her reply was clipped. "I know him. He arranged for me to marry the best of his recruits."

"Ah." Be careful here, Father Collins warned himself. Remember that Donal Cam is a Gaelic prince in the old style, which does not always please the Church but has long been accepted in Ireland if not encouraged. When the faith itself is under attack, it would be a mistake to condemn a man for his personal life if he is fighting in the name of the Church.

"Have you, ah, followed the warriors for long?"

"Since my marriage." Her tone was even more brusque.

Father Collins pulled thoughtfully on his lower lip, trying to select a more tactful question. "You were at Kinsale, then?"

At the mention of Kinsale, the man on the litter

groaned. At once Orla's reddened, capable hand was stroking his forehead. "We were both at Kinsale," she said, looking down at him. "I know most of these men. I knew the four buried back there. We had been comrades for a long time. It is hard."

"Of course." The priest tugged at his lip again. "I was not at Kinsale, I was still in Kerry when it happened. Could you tell me something about the battle? Your experience of it must have been unique."

"Unique?" She lifted one eyebrow sardonically and a strange, tortured expression flickered in her eyes. Just then a gust of wind hit them so hard she staggered. The priest caught Orla by the arm, steadying her. She squared her shoulders, swallowed hard, and said, "If we live to see the morning, Father, perhaps I shall tell you about Kinsale. If you really want to hear it. But for now I need my strength for walking."

The priest understood, walking was becoming difficult for him as well. He lowered his head and concentrated on swinging his arms.

Still, curiosity continued to chew at him. History was blooming around him like a flower of fire, and he was a scholar of history. He would continue questioning others and passing information along as if under a compulsion to do so. It was the only way Father Collins's trained and orderly Jesuit mind could cope with the explosive changes taking place in the fabric of Gaelic society. Examine, contemplate, discuss.

Then the rising storm drove out every thought but those needed to keep the body moving.

It seemed to attack them from every direction at once, raging down from the north, blowing in from the Atlantic Ocean to the west, beating upon them from the Bally-houra hills and the snowcapped Galtee mountains to the east. The storm shrieked along the rivers and rioted over the fields. It even sprang out of the earth, with great clouds of snow swirling at ground level, choking and blinding the struggling column.

Joan Ni Sweney tried to help Eileen as best she could, but at some point the dead child's mother pulled away from her and at once disappeared in the blizzard. Two of Ronan's cavalry glimpsed her briefly as she stumbled in front of their horses, and shouted at her, but she waved them away as if afraid they meant to ride her down. She took a few faltering steps out of their path and was lost to sight in moments.

One of the three remaining packhorses decided it could go no farther. It planted itself like a tree taking root. Its horse boy tugged on the lead rope with all his strength, half crying and cursing his charge, but the horse set itself against the pull of the rope and stayed where it was.

"Help!" the boy cried in desperation. "Somebody, help me!"

Ronan Hurley heard him. He was only a horse's stride away when one of Burke's Connacht mercenaries came up behind the stalled animal and gave it a vicious blow on the rump with the flat of his sword. The horse leapt forward, dragging the horse boy. Both disappeared in the snow-clogged gloom.

Ronan stared at the mercenary with undisguised hatred. "Who told you to do that?"

"But the lad needed help. . . ."

"If it ever happens again, just leave it be, do you hear?" Ronan whirled his horse and rode off, leaving the mercenary staring after him in bewilderment.

At the head of the column, Donal Cam asked one of his companions, "Do you know where we are now?"

"There is a place ahead called *Ard Sceach*, the Height of the Whitethorn," the man replied. "The area all around is uninhabited, and the foothills give the place some protection."

"Ah, I know the place you mention. It should be a good campsite for us if we can get that far," Donal Cam said. He turned in the saddle and shouted for Ronan, who trotted toward him wearing his usual surly expression.

"Ronan, bring the cavalry up from the rear of the column and post them along the sides. Have them try to keep everyone together, and urge people to keep going. I know they are tired, we are all tired, but we must find some sort of shelter before the worst of the storm and the night overtake us. Tell the people we are almost at a stopping place, it will put heart into them."

Nothing will put heart into them, Ronan thought sourly. But he rode away to obey the commander's order. The time had not yet come to make a break.

Not yet but soon, he told himself. Soon. That obstinate packhorse I almost seized was a good omen.

At last they dragged themselves up one long, final hill, crowned with whitethorn trees that spilled down into a sheltered glen beyond. For the first time in miles they felt the wind less savagely. Stumbling down the slope from the height, the people threw themselves onto the frozen, icy earth as if into their beds at home.

"We camp here," Donal Cam called out, but there was no need. The column had already stopped.

Orla and her women set about making camp as best they could, but there was little they could do. In normal circumstances they would have cut thin sods from the earth and built walls with them, stretching cowhide covers over the top to form sturdy tents. Now most of the leathers were lost, and in their exhaustion, the camp makers were unable to dig up sods even if the frozen earth had been willing to yield them. They contented themselves with forming a lean-to of branches and draping Donal Cam's leather cover over this, creating a shelter barely large enough for the commander and the prince of Kerry.

"We can build fires for warmth, even if there is no food to cook," Orla said. But the deadwood they gathered was too wet to burn, and in spite of their protected location, random eddies of wind persisted in whirling away the sparks they struck from their flints.

The fugitives huddled in misery, foodless and fireless, to endure the night. Their only comfort was the knowledge that no sane person would venture out in such a storm to harass them.

Above their bowed heads, the wind screamed.

Donal Cam called into the darkness inside his tent, "Sean, are you in there?"

"I am," replied The O'Connor grumpily. "Asleep."

"Not for long. Come out and help me gather some children. They will sleep in my tent tonight and you and I will take our chances outside with the others."

For a while there was silence inside the tent. Then Donal Cam heard the other man stirring, fighting free of the cloaks and blankets in which he had wrapped himself. "You should have thought of this before I got comfortable."

As he emerged from the tent, Donal Cam asked him, "And were you comfortable?"

"Of course not," growled The O'Connor. "How could anyone rest easy on ground as hard as iron? The air in there is deadly still and cold enough to freeze the hair in your nose. You do the children no favor by putting them in there."

"Perhaps not, but I could not sleep sheltered knowing little ones were outside in a blizzard. And neither could you."

"Perhaps not," the older man agreed. He sighed, then stood erect and began stamping his feet in the snow to restore circulation. "Feet!" he commanded. "Prepare yourselves! We have a bit more walking to do."

Day Four

January 3, 1603. *Ard Sceach*, the Height of the Whitethorn

Donal Cam awoke to an eerie silence. He had not realized he had fallen asleep, yet he found himself lying curled in a ball, half buried in snow, with his cloak frozen around him so it crackled as he sat up.

The first sight his eyes saw was a crown of leafless whitethorn trees rising above him, silvered with ice like a Spanish mantilla. Below them were countless white hillocks, snow-covered mounds that did not move.

Donal Cam scrambled to his feet, shaking off snow. "Dermod? Sean? Rory!" he shouted, feeling fear close around his heart like a cold hand. He ran to the nearest silent mound and began frantically uncovering it.

The answers began to come, muffled, reluctant, followed by vague stirrings. Like animals emerging from hiberation, men and women shook off sleep and sought the light. Some faces were pallid, blue-lipped with cold; others bore the first dangerous blush of frostbite. Standing with difficulty, they began beating themselves and each other to get the reluctant blood moving through their bodies.

The sentries staggered in from their posts, drunk with fatigue. From their expressions it was obvious that some had fallen asleep and awakened with great difficulty.

How many people would not awake at all?

Donal Cam bellowed, "Rory!" The voice of his captain answered him, to his intense relief. He ordered, "Gather the buannachta immediately and take them to search the entire area. Dig into every mound you find. Be merciless, but get people on their feet and moving around. Shake them, beat them, kick them if you must. And hurry!"

Putting action to word, he resumed his own attack on the snow-covered mounds.

In some cases it was useless.

Children not crammed into the shelter of the tent had been especially vulnerable to the weather. Some had frozen to death lying beside their mothers. Some mothers had given their lives to keep their young ones warm, using their bodies to cover a nest where children curled together.

Wounded men had also died in the night, surrendering to painless oblivion. Kerne and gallowglass lay stiff and dead.

The storm had harvested the weak.

Orla Ni Donoghue reported, "There are several dozen either dead or missing. Some probably wandered away; they could be anywhere. It will take all morning to bury the dead, because the ground is frozen solid."

Donal Cam received this information with his arms folded and his head bowed. Then he looked up, his gaze sweeping the campsite. A rising sun soon to disappear behind banks of cloud was illuminating the ice-coated trees with crystalline beauty. Leafless whitethorn bloomed with snow.

A sentry trotted up, announcing, "There is a column of smoke rising some two miles distant along the way we came."

Donal Cam nodded. "We must leave immediately, then. Our dead will stay as they are, we have no choice."

Father Archer, with ice in his eyebrows, protested, "We cannot leave them until they have been given the last rites."

A strong hand clamped on the Jesuit's arm. He turned to find himself looking into the innocent blue eyes of the fierce captain of mercenaries. "If we stay here while you mumble," Thomas Burke said, "you will soon be needed to give the last rites to everyone, yourself included. But since you will be among the dead, slain by those pursuing us, the rest of us will at least be spared your dubious attentions."

Father Archer went white with anger. "Take your filthy paws off me, mercenary!"

Donal Cam thrust himself between them. "What are you doing, Thomas? Remember you are speaking to a holy man."

"Not a bit of it. I am speaking to the man responsible for the loss of Dunboy."

Those near enough to hear the exchange gasped at Burke's words—except for Dermod O'Sullivan. At last someone has said it for all to hear, he thought to himself.

Father Archer's eyes were blazing, but before anything more could be said, Donal Cam demanded, "Stop this, both of you! Do we not have enough enemies already without fighting among ourselves? Thomas, we need to move out immediately, so gather your gallowglasses and kernes and prepare to march. As for you, Father Archer, take Father Collins with you and offer a general absolution and blessing over . . . over all those who died in the night. But do it quickly."

For a moment Donal Cam was uncertain whether they would obey. Then, with a grunt, Thomas Burke stalked off to collect his men. Father Archer stared after him. "That man is mad," he said.

Dermod O'Sullivan returned to his wife. They had spent the night in a shelter they contrived together from fallen branches and their combined outer clothing. Insulated by the subsequent snowfall, they had survived the night.

Tragically, many others had not possessed the foresight or the energy to imitate them. Weariness had robbed people of even the ability to think.

Near the now-dismantled shelter, a bright yellow stain in the snow marked the place where Dermod had paused to urinate before going to answer his nephew's worried shout. He glanced at the stain now, thinking ruefully of the heat that had left his body, rising in steam to waste its warmth.

Joan emerged from the underbrush, arranging her own clothing. "Are we moving out, then?"

"We are," he told her. "The sentries have seen smoke in the distance. And Father Archer and Thomas Burke have quarreled," he was unable to resist adding.

"Why?"

"The mercenary accused the Jesuit of being to blame for the loss of Dunboy."

Joan raised her eyebrows. "I hope you did not speak your own thoughts!"

"I am a wise old man," he assured her. "I say those things only to you."

"Did Donal Cam hear this?"

"He did."

"And what did he say?"

"He changed the subject."

"A prudent man, your nephew," Joan commented drily. She leaned forward as far as her aching back would allow, rested her hands on her thighs, and rocked back and forth on her legs, trying to stretch the tightness out of her muscles. "Dermod, did you happen to see the woman Eileen? The one whose child died the first day?"

"I have not." Without thinking he glanced toward the silent white mounds and the priests moving among them.

Joan followed his gaze. "Better if she is there," she said. "She did not really want to live."

"Is there anything to eat, anything at all?"

"Orla Ni Donoghue came by here a little while ago to say that there were cresses in the stream down below."

"Cresses." Dermod made a face.

"They are something to chew and swallow, at least, and full of healthy salts. I ate some," Joan added, "and they will do you no harm either."

While the column prepared to get under way various people followed Orla's direction to the stream and ate the cresses, staining their mouths green with the stuff. It was hard to clamber back up the bank. The extreme cold of the night had exerted a paralytic effect on muscles and joints. Even the strongest was moving with difficulty, and when the march began they moved for a time like a collection of centenarians.

In spite of his youth and strength, Niall the pikeman discovered he could not swing his legs with his accustomed easy stride. Thigh and calf screamed with pain. He propped his back against a tree and massaged them, but it was all he could do to hobble until his limbs loosened.

The night before he had, shyly but hopefully, sought Maire Ni Driscoll and his shaggy mantle. In the storm-swept confusion he had been unable to find her. A fellow recruit had offered a share of his mantle and the two had slept clamped together like lovers, their combined body heat keeping them alive.

First light had given Niall a reassuring glimpse of Maire, getting to her feet not far away from him, still wrapped in his mantle. When he called out to her she came toward him all apologies. "Take this back, I did not mean to deprive you of it last night, I am so sorry."

"Ah no, keep it," he urged. "I will be warm enough once we start walking."

"So shall I, and it is yours."

"It is big enough for two," Niall said, suddenly inspired. "Share it with me, we can wrap it around both of us."

She dropped her eyes. "I could not possibly," she said, but she stood and let him drape the heavy mantle across her shoulders and then his. To make it go around both of them they had to keep their bodies very close together. When they began to walk, each clutched an edge of the mantle, and they soon learned to walk in stride to keep it from sliding off.

A bit of color returned to Maire's pale cheeks.

Joan Ni Sweney saw them and smiled to herself. Her own Dermod had gone up front to walk with The O'Conor beside the horse of Donal Cam, a position of rank she did not begrudge him. Yet she could not resist an occasional wistful glance at the two young people—together.

From Ard Sceach they proceeded toward Ard Patrick through dense woodlands that had sheltered many fugitives before them. At the Height of Patrick they turned northward to leave behind them the aptly named Golden Vale. Lusting for its fertile soil, the Sasanach had slain Gael beyond counting there.

Donal Cam found himself experiencing a sense of unreality. Light-headed with hunger, he fancied the people and the scenery around him were fading to reveal an underlying universe whose structure he had never suspected and whose purpose he could not divine.

He seemed to be leading a starving mob through an ephemeral landscape. Why? Could he not turn aside at the next stronghold and ask hospitality of the local chieftain according to ancient tradition? Could he not warm his hands by a roaring fire and drink whiskey—*uisce beatha*, water of life—flavored with raisins and fennel and perhaps licorice? Would he not be made welcome by the women of the house with their warm bodies naked beneath loose gowns, encouraging him to pass the winter's day in sport and gambling, to spend the evening listening to the tales of the bard and the music of the harper? All these things he had done before as a prince of the Gael. Why not now? How had things come to this?

The answer was beyond believing. The Ireland of his youth was gone. In its place was a stark and bitter land starved to its bare bones and parceled out among opportunists who came like locusts to steal the corn.

Donal Cam felt his soul shrivel to crouch in the darkest corner of his being.

"I said, 'What route do you propose northward?'" The sharpness of The O'Connor's repeated query dragged Donal Cam back to the here and now.

"Ah . . . as direct as possible. I want to avoid main roads, large towns, any place we might meet Carew's people. We shall cross the Slieve Felim range at a narrow part, then on to the Shannon."

"Who do you think is following us now?"

"Probably a patrol from the garrison at Killmallock." *Cill Mocheallog*, the Church of St. Mocheallog.

"How did they know we are here?"

"They may have come across our track by accident," Donal Cam replied. He turned in the saddle and called to the column, "Move along, there. Waste no time!"

"He means to run the legs off us," grumbled a man who had once made a good living fishing the coastal waters of west Cork. "The next time we pass near a village," he said to his wife, "you and I are going to slip away. We can say we escaped and swear allegiance to the English queen or the Lord President of Munster or whoever will accept us and let us live in peace. I have had enough of running."

The sun had disappeared. A spatter of sleet struck the faces of the fugitives.

Niall pulled his shaggy mantle up, covering his head and Maire's. "Now we have a roof," he said.

The mantle deadened the sound of ice pellets striking, but its weight was wearisome. Maire Ni Driscoll did not complain, however. Richard was dead. Nothing else was worth complaining about.

Niall was confiding shyly, "The commander has asked me to be his personal harper. It is a great honor."

His companion said nothing.

"I have a little bardic harp and harp bag that belonged to an ancestor of mine who actually carried them into battle for his prince," Niall went on, seeking to capture her interest. "I am only a recruit, but there is fine blood in me. I am descended from a true bard. And I have no wife," he added, then bit his lip, afraid he had gone too far.

Maire turned her head to look at him. In the dim cavern created by the shaggy mantle, her eyes were huge and lustrous. "I have no husband," she said. "Nor ever will have."

Women say such things as a challenge to men, Niall told himself. I am meant to prove her wrong. And I shall!

The smell of her body reached his nose in spite of the overriding odor of the shaggy mantle and he felt heat in his groin again.

On impulse, Donal Cam reined the chestnut horse to one side and let the flood of people flow past him. He studied the faces going by, not watching for any one in particular, but instead looking to see who was missing.

Of all the diverse and colorful community that had been dependent upon his strength and patronage and followed his standard, how many had failed to get this far?

He was aware of absence more acutely than presence. Missing from the faces were country people and villagers who had once been as familiar to him as members of his own family. He noted the absence of the bald, big-bellied man who could always be found mending nets at the end of the pier, even in savage weather. Only the most howling gale had ever discouraged him.

Gone now.

Missing also were the twin girls who had sold ribbons in the marketplace at Beare Haven. Honora had bought their ribbons. Shining silk and satin, gold and crimson and green.

Missing was the gallowglass who, one drunken night, had recklessly challenged The O'Sullivan to a wrestling match, and beaten him . . . Donal Cam smiled faintly at the memory. The fellow had been so embarrassed the next morning, with his aching head and his red eyes begging forgiveness. And his chieftain laughing and forgiving him and offering him more ale . . .

Gone now. Perhaps a hundred faces missing from the crowd that had set off from Doire na Fola. With every mile they were losing more people. Killed, deserted, lost, simply collapsed and unable to go farther.

I have to make some provision for those who cannot go on, Donal Cam reminded himself.

He gave the reins a shake and trotted back to the head of the march. His face was set and cold, and people glanced nervously at it as he rode by.

Father John Collins was looking for a woman. Several times earlier that morning he had seen her, but she always seemed too busy for conversation. He had never given much thought to the camp followers before. On some lower level of his layered personal judgment he had considered them disreputable, Magdalenes who eschewed the accepted social restrictions of their sex to live without walls and spend their time roistering with soldiers.

As a priest he had known little of the military life. Father Collins's calling had consisted of ministering to the Gaelic nobility of Kerry. *Ciarraidhe*, land of the race of Ciar.

Then The O'Connor got involved in the rebellion, and the old chieftain's confessor was slain by an English musketeer who yelled gleefully, "One less papist!" Months after the debacle at Kinsale, The O'Connor had sent for Father Collins to join him as, with Donal Cam, he fought his way through southwest Munster, trying to resist the closing fist of Carew.

The priest had observed camp followers every day since, and learned a lesson about the error of making judgments in ignorance.

Since the Nine Years' War began many camp followers had been slain by an enemy that did not subscribe to the Gaelic prohibition against warring on women. Yet still their kind stayed with their men, supporting them with as much devotion as any high born wife had ever shown in accompanying her prince into exile.

This last thought brought Father Collins's mind circling around to Honora, wife of Donal Cam, said to be secreted among the wild crags beyond Gleann Garbh. If O'Sullivan could find a safe hiding place for his wife and plan to smuggle her out of the country later, why could he not have done the same for the people he had left to their fate at Doire na Fola?

There were many questions one might ask about the character and motivations of Donal Cam.

Ever since Father Collins had joined The O'Connor, he had been aware of the rumors and accusations being whispered by disaffected followers of The O'Sullivan. Curiosity had prompted the priest to listen, but discretion had prevented his asking the questions he longed to ask.

Was it possible, as some were saying, that Donal Cam had cold-bloodedly sacrificed the weak and wounded at Doire na Fola to buy time for his own escape, when he might have saved them if he really wanted?

Who would know?

Father Collins caught sight of a head of carrot-red hair in the crowd and called, "Orla! Orla Ni Donoghue!"

She waved back and angled toward him until she walked at his side. He eyed her covertly. If rumor could be believed, she was but one of many women whom the prince of Beare had enjoyed, but she had remained his special favorite. Yet she was far from beautiful. Her hair was bushy rather than curly, her frame was broad, she had chapped hands and broken nails and wide feet. No woman could have been less like the elegant, willowy wife of Donal Cam.

Aware of the priest's scrutiny, Orla's eyes twinkled with mischief. "Do you like what you see, Father?" she asked boldly.

"I . . . ah . . . I was worrying that you do not have enough warm clothing," he stammered.

"You were of course." She gave him a sarcastic look, then said more seriously, "None of us has enough warm clothing. But at least the sleet has stopped; that is a blessing. I have learned to appreciate the small blessings."

"As have we all," the priest agreed, grateful to her for having the quickness of wit to recognize his discomfort, and the grace to change the subject. A surprising woman, this. Intelligent. Could he talk around her and persuade her to give answers she did not know she was giving? "Do you remember promising to tell me of your experience of Kinsale?" he asked.

"I do remember, though it seems a thousand years ago we had that conversation."

The priest nodded agreement. Their sense of time was becoming distorted, measured as it was in weather and warfare rather than hours. "If you feel like talking, it will help to pass the time," he said.

"It will be better than walking along thinking about how my feet feel," Orla replied. "Another small blessing, eh?" She smiled at him with comradely ease.

Father Collins smiled back. He was beginning to understand why Donal Cam was fond of the woman. If he was.

They were walking near the bank of a stream that gurgled through a rocky bed. Orla paused to drink from her cupped hands. The unceasing cold of winter would soon mean that all but the fastest-flowing rivers would be covered with ice.

Refreshed, she began speaking. "Kinsale. I can tell you about Kinsale, or what I know of it. When the Nine Years' War began, I was in Beare, very far removed from the quarrels between Spain and England."

"Spain and England? The Nine Years' War was a revolt on the part of the Gaelic chieftains against the Royalists loyal to Elizabeth of England."

"Ah, but underneath it was a power struggle between Elizabeth and Philip of Spain! That Mary who was queen of England before Elizabeth had been wed to Philip's father, and was a professor of the true faith. Elizabeth hated her and her religion, and when Mary died and Elizabeth was on the throne the enmity between England and Spain boiled over.

"As Catholics, the Gaelic race sided with Spain. So did the Old Foreigners who shared our faith. It seemed that the Nine Years' War was about religion, Catholic against heretic, but Donal Cam explained to me that it was really about land and power."

Father Collins lifted his eyebrows. "Is that the sort of conversation you have with him?"

"One sort," she said complacently. "We have talked about everything over the years." She gave the priest a slanting, enigmatic smile. "It was himself who explained to me that Elizabeth saw Ireland as a rear gateway to England, one the Spanish could use to mount an invasion on her kingdom. That was her primary interest in Ireland. That and the timber she could take, because the English have used up so much of their own timber. Then too, she could give Irish land as rewards to her followers. Ireland had become valuable.

"Though the Normans had settled here, we had never totally submitted to English authority. We kept our old ways as we kept our faith. Elizabeth set out to conquer Ireland for good and all, to make us conform to her way. The plantations began, English colonists being given land to hold for the English queen, and the natives were driven out or massacred to make way for the strangers. In fifteen years Munster had been reduced from prosperity to poverty.

"Fearing the same would happen in Ulster, the princes of the north rebelled, beginning The Nine Years' War.

Aod Rua, Red Hugh, the young O'Donnell of Donegal, won spectacular victories against the Royalists. He inspired Hugh O'Neill, whom Elizabeth had made earl of Tyrone, to revert to his Gaelic title of The O'Neill and rise against the queen."

Father Collins was amazed by the woman's lucid recital. Education was no novelty in Ireland; some Gaelic noblewomen could read Greek and quote the classical philosphers, and even a ragged horse boy running barefoot beside his lord's stirrup might have picked up the odd bit of Latin. But how came this camp follower by her education? Had Donal Cam deliberately polished her mind? The priest was intrigued.

"Among the chieftains in Munster," Orla was saying, "the rebellion was the chief topic of conversation. Men were calling Red Hugh the Eagle of the North. Even common folk followed his progress, eager for every bit of news. I was newly married then, to the captain of The O'Sullivan's guard. We in Beare had not suffered as had those farther inland. The O'Sullivan was in favor with the English. But we knew full well what was taking place elsewhere in Munster, and Ulster's defiance of the tyrant inflamed us. When Hugh O'Neill repeatedly outwitted the queen's man, Essex, until at last he was recalled to England and beheaded, we cheered. We did not know Essex but we cheered his death.

"In honor of the two northern leaders we named our second son Hugh," she added.

"Where are your children now?"

He sensed, rather than saw, the stiffness in her. Her tone changed; shields were raised. "Out of Ireland," she said through tight lips.

Diplomatically, Father Collins left the subject. "You were going to tell me about Kinsale?"

"I am coming to it." She relaxed noticeably. "The

O'Neill had been corresponding with the king of Spain and they had exchanged emissaries. The O'Neill urged Philip to send an invasion fleet to Ireland with at least five thousand soldiers to help the Catholics here drive out the heretics . . . so our people could get their lands back, you see," she added.

"O'Neill wanted the Spanish to land somewhere on the northwest coast, convenient to himself and O'Donnell. But when a fleet was sent, under the command of Don Juan Aguila, it met the storms we so often have along the west coast, and memories of the Armada's fate made Aguila turn back. Instead he led the larger portion of his fleet to landfall on the southern coast, arriving in September at the fishing port of Kinsale. Half a dozen of his ships, which had been separated from the main body, made it back to Spain.

"Aguila established a garrison at Kinsale and began fortifying the town. He was soon besieged by the English lord deputy, Mountjoy, together with Carew. Aguila sent urgent messages to O'Neill and O'Donnell, pleading with them to come to his rescue.

"Hugh O'Neill was angry because the invasion had not followed his plan. But he and O'Donnell set out, separately, to gather allies and march into Munster, to Kinsale. O'Donnell traveled at speed like the eagle he was, but O'Neill took time to ravage beyond the Pale and plunder the Royalists settled in Meath.

"Meanwhile, the six ships from Aguila's fleet that had returned to Spain came back again to Ireland with reinforcements. English warships prevented their putting in at Kinsale. They finally made landfall at Castle Haven, in O'Driscoll territory. So then Donal Cam . . ."

Father Collins interrupted, "I can appreciate that The O'Sullivan was seen as something of a Royalist, given that he owed his inheritance to English authority. So what decided him to join with O'Neill and O'Donnell? Was this when it happened?"

Something flared in Orla's eyes; the shields went up again. "Indeed. When we learned that the princes of the north were actually coming to Munster to fight Mountjoy and Carew, it was impossible not to join them. We were heady with the idea of rebellion."

She is witholding something, Father Collins thought. Something potent. What would drive a thoughtful man like Donal Cam to sacrifice his security? If I am any judge of character at all, it would take more than the excitement of the moment.

Orla said, "The day he declared for rebellion, The O'Sullivan built a great fire in the courtyard and burned his English clothing. Then he sent his uncle Dermod to conduct the Spanish captain from Castle Haven to Dunboy. He gave the Spaniards access to the harborages of Beare, and fresh provisions. He summoned the buannachta and put my husband in charge, hired additional mercenaries, and then, leaving the Spaniards garrisoned at Dunboy to defend it, we set out to join The O'Neill.

"Though actually," she added, "Red Hugh O'Donnell reached Munster first."

"Indeed, I recall now. Hugh O'Neill held off for a time. It was said he waited to see how the English would respond to O'Donnell's approach."

"Were you in Kerry then, Father?"

"I was. I did not join The O'Connor until after Kinsale, but I remember seeing him the day he and his followers set out to meet Red Hugh. A brave day that was, with the standards flying."

"We all had standards flying," Orla said with a sigh. "Marching from Beare, we sang and beat the *bodhran*, the war drum, and every beat was like the beat of a heart.

"Then when our men joined forces with The O'Neill,

we learned that not as many Gaelic chieftains were rallying to the cause as we had expected. Some had come from the north, but in Munster Carew and Mountjoy and their agents had been bribing, promising, threatening, even showing forged documents to various chieftains to convince them that others had already deserted to the English side.

"Hugh O'Neill was very concerned about this. He was also beginning to worry that Spain would not give as much help as we had been led to believe. He told Donal Cam that there were wheels within wheels, papal emissaries and crown agents and men of uncertain loyalties all struggling for political gain, too involved with their own interests to care what happened to us.

"He was heartened, however, when Donal Cam told him about the Spanish ships that had put in at Castle Haven. He wanted to believe they were the advance guard of others to come."

"What of the soldiers in the field? What did they believe?"

"Ah, there was great excitement around the campfires," Orla told him. "Every company seemed to have its storyteller, and the old tales of heroes and champions were polished and told anew. We heard endlessly of Cuchulain and Fionn and Brian Boru, and we talked endlessly of the great victory we would win over the Sasanach.

"A man called Niall O'Mahony had a small war harp and knew all the battle songs, and we sang them with him. The men were eager for battle and so were we, because the courage of men is a treasure to their women and an inheritance for their sons."

Orla walked with her head high, as if in the front line of battle. Her chin was lifted, her chest thrust forward. The priest had a sense of being in the presence of an atavism, a survivor from the pagan past of Ireland when the females of the warrior aristocracy were more ferocious than the males.

"Red Hugh O'Donnell's march from Donegal was a hero tale to stand with the best," Orla was saying. "He had left a week before Hugh O'Neill, bringing with him O'Rourkes and Mac Dermotts and a number of men from north Connacht. They covered as much as forty miles a day in winter weather. Once they reached Munster they camped near the headwaters of the Suir river and waited for The O'Neill to join them.

"He never arrived, but the lord president did. When he learned of O'Donnell's arrival Carew set out with twenty-five hundred men to stop him from going any farther south. But O'Donnell was too clever. He left fires burning to make Carew think he was in camp, then led his men away in the darkness across ice-covered mountains where no one could possibly have gone. Yet he did. And he made it while Carew watched his campfires and thought him trapped."

Father Collins snapped his fingers. "Of course! Doire na Fola!"

"Indeed. Donal Cam got the idea from Red Hugh. We escaped Wilmot just as The O'Donnell escaped Carew."

"But . . . was it necessary to leave the weak and wounded behind? Surely Donal Cam could have sent them into hiding with his wife."

Orla turned on him; there was a sudden rasp in her voice. "You do not know what you are talking about! With no people in the oakwood to tend our fires, they would have gone out within hours. Then Wilmot's lookouts would have reported us gone. The O'Donnell only needed a night's grace to escape Carew, for he could march his army at great speed. We have civilians, we needed more time. If we are fortunate, fires may still be burning at Doire na Fola and our enemies may still be watching for birds who have long since flown.

"Besides, Father, none of those we left behind would have been able to make the journey to the Eagle's Nest. That is a savage climb. Gorrane Mac Sweeney probably had to carry Donal Cam's white-handed wife," Orla said with a contempt she could not hide. "The people we left at Doire na Fola could do little more than drag themselves a few paces to gather firewood. Donal Cam made the right decision!" she finished sharply, glaring at the priest as if challenging him to argue.

Prudently, he said, "About Kinsale . . . you and Donal Cam joined O'Neill, did you not, and then met O'Donnell?"

His choice of words mollified her. "We did. And Richard Tyrell joined us shortly after. There was trouble in the combined camp almost at once. Red Hugh let it be known he resented the fact that O'Neill had not joined him earlier. He had no sympathy with the concept of holding off to see which way the wind blew, before acting. His nature was too bold, too audacious . . . and exactly suited the emotions of many others in the camp, who were eager to attack at once."

"Like you," said the priest with a smile.

"Not like me. Not after I saw that grave, thoughtful look on Donal Cam's face that he gets sometimes, and realized he agreed with The O'Neill. I even went among my women then and urged them not to inflame their men. Some listened; some did not." She shrugged.

"Our patrols came back with reports of dysentery in Mountjoy's camp, and said their provisions were running low. A council of chieftains was held and The O'Neill told them our best plan would be to besiege the enemy as they had besieged Aguila. Attack any foraging parties they sent out and wait for hunger and disease to win the battle for us.

"But Red Hugh—and I can see him now in my mind,

that young man who was called the most beautiful and brave in Ireland, as he surely was—Red Hugh was contemptuous of The O'Neill's plan. He pointed out that the enemy was effectively trapped between us and Aguila. To win, we had only to seize the moment. Attack, he cried, attack boldly!

"The O'Neill and his followers, The Maguire, O'Reilly, the Mac Mahons, disagreed. Those who sided with Red Hugh claimed The O'Neill was jealous of the younger man. Soon every chieftain was arguing for his own status and prerogatives."

"How do you know all this? Did you have access to the command tents?"

Orla gave the priest a glance of pity for his ignorance. "Of course not. But we prepared the food. When I took Donal Cam his portion, he told me what was happening.

"Food was part of the problem, though only a woman used to cooking for an army might appreciate that fully. O'Donnell and his followers had traveled very fast and very light, relying on what forage they could snatch on the run. O'Neill had come more slowly, as I said, taking time to plunder. His army was liberally supplied with meat and meal and butter and extra shoes. We had our creaght with us, so we were also well provisioned. But O'Donnell's men were feeling lean and hungry, which makes men quarrelsome.

"The bickering among the chieftains grew worse. It began to look as if the combined forces would disband unless action was taken soon, so O'Neill broke up the camp near Inishannon where we had gathered and led us down the valley of the Bandon river to a place called Coolcarron, north of Kinsale. We arrived there shortly before Christmas and began setting up a new camp.

"During the days that followed O'Neill's men harassed the enemy and made foraging impossible for them, and

O'Neill tried to persuade the others that it was the best method to follow. But Red Hugh made an impassioned speech, saying honor demanded they go to the aid of Aguila. Most of the chieftains agreed with him, and finally Hugh O'Neill gave in.

"We were to attack during the night of January second. Donal Cam told me to have medicaments ready; he feared many casualties.

"Our forces were divided into three columns. Richard Tyrell commanded one, The O'Neill led the main column, and The O'Donnell, because of the speed and mobility of his following, was to bring up the rear and swing wide, to serve as a defensive wing. After telling me where to wait to care for the wounded, Donal Cam rode with The O'Neill. The prince of Tyrone considered him indispensable," she said proudly.

"As the armies were preparing to march, the weather grew worse. There had been storms all month, but as our soldiers gathered in the darkness the father and mother of all storms broke over them. Some thought it an evil omen. Even some of the chieftains were made nervous by the weather, and their nervousness passed into their men. Donal Cam remained resolute, of course, and The O'Neill doubtless drew strength from him.

"In anticipation of our attack, messages had been exchanged with Aguila, who apparently had made some suggestions. Once we got under way he was to come out from Kinsale and attack the enemy from the rear while we engaged the front. But some of the messages must have been intercepted. Aguila and his Spaniards never came out until the battle was over. It was also rumored, later, that our plans had been betrayed to Carew by one of our own chieftains, but I do not know if that is true. If it is, Donal Cam never spoke of it to me."

"Once the battle began, did you see much of it?" Father Collins asked, trying to conceal a growing impatience. The woman was telling him too many details he already knew from other sources. But her Celtic love of intricacy was forcing her to follow every thread, weaving them together until she reached the final four hours.

The four hours at Kinsale that had changed their world.

Orla's throat burned from talking. The priest was milking her of information like a woman milking a cow. She thought with longing of sweet, hot milk foaming into a pail; of wine heated with a poker; of scalding broth taken in great gulps.

"Rain bucketed down on us that night as we were preparing to attack," she told the priest. "We set out in the dark, following the men, waiting for the first sounds of battle. Once the fighting began we would take up safe positions as Donal Cam had ordered and wait to care for the wounded."

"What did you see?" Father Collins persisted.

"Nothing. I told you, we began to move forward in the dark. And it was raining hard, a ferocious storm entirely. We stayed in the rear, behind the soldiers. They were our only guides. But we could hear well enough. We heard the first shouts, a volley, another, the sound of many men moving . . . then more gunfire. And screams.

"It all happened so fast. One moment our men were marching forward in a great formation, thinking to surprise the enemy in the dark. The next moment the English came rising out of trenches right in front of us, and at the same time there was the sound of some sort of battle taking place off to one side—we thought it might be Aguila, come out of Kinsale—and then Mountjoy's cavalry came galloping down on our men over terrain they knew well, but that was unfamiliar to us.

"There was great confusion then, with no one certain

what was happening or where, but The O'Neill and Donal Cam stood firm. The English wheeled off to the side and our men cheered, but then another company of enemy cavalry came up, a great number, and our own were forced to fall back. As always, our horsemen were in the lead, and when they turned to retreat in the darkness and confusion they trampled their own buannachta, who were massed behind them. That was when the screaming began.

"As the night gave way to a stormy dawn, it became obvious our armies were out of their leaders' control. A great cauldron of cloud was boiling overhead and lightning was crackling all around. You could not tell it from the crack of the guns. The air was black with noise, driving men wild.

"A band of English horsemen rode right by us on their way around to attack the main column from the rear. We women screamed for Hugh O'Donnell, but he was nowhere to be seen. We learned later that he had swung wide indeed, got lost in the dark, and was too far out to be of any use by the time he realized his position.

"Richard Tyrell did move his column up, but they could not hold. The main body of men was pouring back over them, you see. When our front line had broken, many of our leaders were carried along with it, and their followers scattered senselessly, mingling with Tyrell's men, breaking their formation and adding to the confusion. We could hear him yelling orders no one obeyed.

"I abandoned my place and ran forward, searching for Donal Cam to tell us what to do. Men came streaming toward me, dazed. Crying, cursing, bleeding. The earth was churned mud so deep it pulled the shoes off me. I stumbled over a dead body, caught myself, and ran on.

"I was shouting for Donal Cam but he could not have heard me. Everyone was yelling and the thunder was roaring and the guns . . . the glory of battle was gone. At last I slipped on the intestines of some poor gut-shot horse and fell on my face."

Orla drew a long breath. "Something broke in me then, Father," she confessed, her voice dropping. "I did not seek Donal Cam any longer. I crouched on the earth with my arms wrapped around my head and howled like a kicked dog. I was past frightened, I was out of my mind with the terror and the confusion. And I was not alone; it happened all around me.

"When an army's spirit breaks it is an awful thing. We had not thought ours could break; we had fully expected victory. Seeing Red Hugh O'Donnell standing tall and brave, with confidence in every line of him, we had felt as if God Himself had promised us triumph."

Father Collins remarked, "No doubt the other side had also prayed to God before the battle began, invoking him on their behalf."

"No prayers were answered," Orla said with certainty, "because God was not at Kinsale that day. There was nothing but chaos there. I know what the word means. Donal Cam used it, after, to describe what had happened.

"Chaos."

"So you found him again?"

"He found me, but not until much later. The battle did not last until midday, you see. It was soon over and done, with a thousand of our people dead and the survivors fleeing in every direction. And Aguila still safe behind the walls of the town," she added. "He no doubt heard the final volley the English fired to celebrate their victory.

"I heard it. It brought me to my senses, and I found myself wandering quite alone across some boggy patch of land, with my feet bare and bleeding and my clothing so sodden with rain I had to wring out my skirts in order to be able to walk. Somehow I made my way northward until I came across a group of our own people, and I joined them. We stumbled on, too shocked to speak. We kept coming across fragments of the various armies—The O'Neill's men, The O'Donnell's, The O'Sullivan's . . .

"Fragments of various armies, but not of one army. We had not fought as one army, that was what Donal Cam said, after. In the first minutes of the conflict, when the English surprised us with their resistance, every one of our chieftains forgot Hugh O'Neill's battle plan and set out to fight as an individual. And of course his men followed him. The enemy fought as a unit, and broke us.

"If we had followed The O'Neill's original plan and let starvation and disease wage the war for us, we would have broken them. That is what Donal Cam says."

Father Collins nodded. His own assessment was the same. No musket, no arquebus was as fearful a weapon as famine. The victims of starvation walked on either side of him, and his own belly was shrinking back to meet his spine.

"Were you able to care for the wounded at all, after it was over?" he wanted to know.

"Ah, we made a camp of sorts on the riverbank that night. People had mostly recovered their wits by then, and the blaming had begun. There was more bitterness than you would find in a vat of vinegar.

"After what I had done I could not find it in me to blame anyone else for anything, though. I just wanted to go off somewhere and sit in a corner and hate myself. Perhaps that was how many people felt, inside.

"My husband Rory had been horribly injured by one of the gallowglasses fighting on the English side. I tended his wound, but we did not speak to each other. Rory was lost in his pain, and I was just . . . lost.

"When Donal Cam rode into the camp beside Hugh

O'Neill, at first I hid from him. I was thankful that he was still alive, but I could not bear to have him look at me, I was filled with such loathing for myself.

"How can a person get over that, Father? How do you ever forgive yourself for being so much less than you thought you were?" There was naked anguish in her voice; all the shields were stripped away.

John Collins was taken aback. He had been trained in platitudes. Facile answers to unanswerable questions were part of his priestly wares, to be dispensed to the needy on request. But upon examining his mental stock he could find nothing to offer Orla. Nothing that would not sound specious in the face of her raw reality.

Intuition told him it would be a waste of breath to tell her, "God forgives you." He knew, as surely as if she had said it to him in the privacy of confession, that Orla Ni Donoghue had ceased believing in God sometime in the morning of January 3, 1602.

The party proceeded northward, crossing now the fertile plain that lay between them and the Slieve Felim mountains. *Sliabh Eibhlinne*, Evlin's mountains, named for the banshee of clan O'Brien. They could see the purple peaks in the distance, for the land lay open. Forests that once stood there had long since vanished, converted into ship timbers or burned for English charcoal—or simply cut down, to prevent their providing any protection for the natives.

A cold wind whistled across the plain, but at least the walking was easier, the land gently rolling with no steep slopes to climb. There was even, for a time, a slice of sun peeping through the clouds.

The spirits of the column rose imperceptibly.

Thomas Burke was not deceived by superficial improvements in their condition. The captain of mercenaries shaded his eyes with his hand and surveyed the surrounding territory again and again, watching. Waiting. He mistrusted every dip in the ground that might hide an enemy. The pattern of the march was set now. He knew, from long experience, that it would continue as it had begun, with fighting to be expected at any time. They would not be allowed to escape to the north unchallenged.

"Keep yourselves ready," he warned his men.

At the rear of the column, Ronan Hurley was giving the same order. He resented being kept at the back, since horsemen by tradition rode in the van, but he understood the necessity. Besides, being behind the others gave him an unparalleled opportunity to watch both Donal Cam and the baggage animals. The whole line of march was clearly visible to him from the back of his horse.

He could see the camp followers assisting the litter bearers with the wounded, whose number had been reduced by the freezing conditions of the night before. Ronan's sister Grella felt his eyes on her, turned, and waved to him. She dropped back to walk beside his horse. There was a question in her eyes as she looked up at him.

"Not now," he told her in a low voice. "We are out in the open here. We need some place where there is cover, and we need a lot of confusion. Did you find out about the gold?"

She nodded. "There are leather purses in one of the packs."

"How much, could you tell?"

"I did not have time. I had just found them when Orla Ni Donoghue came up to me and asked what I was doing. I told her I was helping adjust the baggage on the horse's back; the pack was slipping, I said."

"Did she believe you?"

Grella frowned. "I cannot be certain. She is so suspicious of anything that might be a threat to her precious Donal Cam. She looked at me very hard and I made myself busy doing something else. She may be watching me, now."

"Let her watch," said Ronan. "She cannot be on guard all the time."

"She tries to be. She gives herself great airs. In the year since Kinsale she has scarcely let Donal Cam out of her sight, and claims that all her instructions come from him. I daresay she runs to him with every tale told in the camps and every whisper there is against him."

"We have been fighting constantly since Kinsale," Ronan pointed out, "so how could the woman be anywhere but close to Donal Cam? Her husband is captain of his recruits."

"And there is another who gives himself airs. Do you recall how critical he was of our cavalry after the battle? As if he and his foot soldiers had not been the ones to give way!"

Ronan scowled. The subject was a sore one. Everyone had given way, not just the cavalry. The horsemen had merely been the first to do so, but the memory was painful enough.

Against the smaller, more maneuverable companies of Mountjoy's men, the three massive columns Hugh O'Neill had organized had proved both inefficient and unwieldy. They had been formed into huge hollow squares of buannachta and mercenaries, with musketeers and arquebusiers on the four corners. They had been told to stand firm under enemy fire, filling in gaps as they occurred. This was a pattern developed by the Spanish and much admired by The O'Neill.

But the formation did not make sense to Gaelic warriors. Their fighting tradition was to attack in a broad line. Then, if resistance proved overwhelming, their custom was to fall back and resume the attack from some more advantageous position.

When the horsemen in the lead were scattered by Mountjoy's charge, the following columns had abandoned the plan to stand firm and reverted to their familiar pattern. They had turned and run, expecting the enemy to follow until they could trap him somewhere. But the awkwardness of the columnar formation did not allow for this. Besides, Mountjoy, anticipating their action, had a number of small companies organized to fall upon them from unexpected directions, creating havoc.

Ronan Hurley remembered that havoc. He also remembered that he had been one of the few who did not panic, but kept his place, fighting a fear-crazed horse, and yelled for others to do the same. Yelled to no avail. And was never even thanked for it.

"What makes me angry," he told Grella now, "is that The O'Sullivan did not stand up for his own men. He accepted the criticisms being voiced afterward without a word of denial on our behalf. Some of us stood and fought, at risk of our lives. He should have outshouted O'Neill and O'Donnell and claimed honor for his army, no matter what was said of the others. He should have; he was our chieftain."

"Why did he not?"

"Those who are blindly loyal to him say it is because he is fair and just and the criticisms were honest. But I discount that argument. I think he simply wanted to curry favor with the princes of the north so he would be left in command of the resistance in Munster when they went home again. And so he was, which proves my theory. He had played a shrewd game. O'Sullivan Beare has always played a shrewd game, I give him that much."

"He was not so shrewd after Kinsale," Grella argued. "He fought all over Munster for a year and what did it get him? He lost Dunboy and he lost Dursey and he lost countless fine warriors. In the end he lost everything."

"But his life," her brother reminded her. "He deserves to lose that, for all who died following his standard. Our brothers, Grella. It is only by accident, and the fact that I had a fast horse, that I was chosen to go to Ardea with him and not left with Michael and Eoin and the defenders of Dunboy."

Grella's eyes glinted. "Will you slip a knife between his ribs before we go? For Michael and Eoin?"

He ached to say he would. But what if he was prevented; what if he failed? He chose not to answer, but stared off into space as if looking for . . .

"Horsemen coming!" he shouted abruptly.

It was not a company of English cavalry now appearing in pursuit of them, however, but a mixed mob of people mounted and afoot, topping a rise no more than a half mile away. A swift glance revealed a great number of them, a hundred or more, with the riders in front and men running behind with the speed of the fresh and well-fed.

There was the sharp bark of a caliver as someone fired an excited shot long before the targets were in range.

Ronan's warning was yelled up the line. Donal Cam wheeled his horse around and stared back. For a long moment he weighed the size of the pursuing crowd against the number of his own warriors.

"Who are they?" The O'Connor called to him.

"I will not know until they are closer—but I want them no closer," Donal Cam decided. "Keep moving at the best speed you can, all of you. We will fight on the run."

On the run it was, with the pursuers more able for speed than Donal Cam's weary refugees. As the enemy narrowed the distance between, they became recognizable. Some were local rabble hot for sport, or to ingratiate themselves with the conquerors. Others were professional warriors who had come from as far away as Limerick city, mercenaries hired by the White Knight, head of the Fitzgibbons family. A branch of the Geraldines, the Fitzgibbons were Old Foreigners who had long been loyal to the Catholic faith, but had formally submitted to Elizabeth in May 1600 in order to be allowed to keep their lands.

Now the White Knight's mercenaries howled for the head of Donal Cam O'Sullivan Beare.

Run and fight, shoot and pause to reload if you had a gun, run and fight again. Thud of pikes, clang of steel on steel, acrid scorched odor of gunpowder. Bullets flying so thick they seemed to warm the winter air. Skirmishing with Ronan's cavalry, the harassing mob savaged the flanks of the column.

By now even the weakest member of the column was a soldier, fighting to survive. Joan Ni Sweney had supplied her woolen stocking with a new stone in the toe and a number of women followed her example. The children no longer looked like children, but wore the hard, hating faces of old men as they hurled rocks and defiance at the enemy.

The day became a recurring cycle of assault, regroup, and renewed attack across an endless plain. O'Sullivan's dead were left where they fell because no one dared stop for them. The living, furious and frantic, dragged or carried the wounded for a time, but often had to drop them too, to save themselves.

They prayed for nightfall that might bring a respite. Some sort of a respite, somewhere.

Day Five

January 4, 1603. *Sulchoid*, the Place of the Sallow Trees

The wolf skinner had been out since before dawn, checking his snares. He was too poor to afford any sort of gun with which he might have shot the duck and snipe and pheasant that frequented the low, marshy woodland near his cabin. But with snares and traps he was able to catch enough small game to feed his family and he accounted himself a fortunate man. Others, people whose names he knew, were starving in Munster.

He was not really a wolf skinner, not anymore. In his youth, when he still possessed a pack of fearless hounds, he had hunted the great gray wolf in the foothills of Slieve Felim, and sold the luxurious pelts to chieftains of the region for their robes and blankets. But almost a dozen years ago the Sasanach soldiers had taken his hounds, exclaiming over their size and strength.

Sent back to England, they were, to breed more of their kind for the English people, who must not have any decent dogs of their own or surely they would not steal a poor man's livelihood.

Sometimes on winter nights like the one just past, he still heard the wolves singing in the hills. His heart sang with them then, and his eyes filled with tears.

No luck this night, nothing in his snares. A chill was all he had gotten for his efforts, and he was tramping back toward his cabin in a dark humor. Suddenly he stopped. His skin prickled with alarm. He gazed wildly around for some sort of weapon with which to defend himself. A stone, a stick . . .

Ahead of him, gradually visible in the seeping light of winter dawn, was an army.

Sasanach! was his first thought. They have come to kill all the game just to deny it to us. Come to fill their bags for themselves and leave the rest to rot on the ground. And my children to starve. It was happening elsewhere, he knew. Anger scalded his belly. If he was going to die a slow death of hunger, he might as well die a quick one in front of their guns.

He started forward with curses of defiance on his lips, then stopped again, staring.

No enemy army lay spread before him. Instead, piled haphazardly together, were hundreds of men and women and children in ragged clothes, taking what shelter they could from an old earth-banked enclosure that perhaps once penned cattle. Standing guard over them was a handful of red-eyed sentries staring back at the wolf skinner as he emerged from a stand of sallow trees, the low-growing willows of the region.

The wolf skinner had seen refugees before. For years, the dispossessed had ranged across Munster, seeking a safety they could not find. But never had he encountered so large a number. As many as six hundred were encamped before him like a huge herd penned for the shambles.

The nearest sentry called a challenge, though the wolf skinner looked in no way threatening. Still. Any man in Ireland might be the enemy, now.

He lifted his handgun, a battered caliver, with both hands to show that he was armed. He braced himself. "What want you?" he demanded to know.

The wolf skinner stopped and held out his hands, palm up, to show he was weaponless. "I mean no harm. Who are all these people?" he asked wonderingly.

The question had been innocent, but the reply was hostile and instantly suspicious. "Why do you want to know? What business is it of yours?" the sentry snarled.

The wolf skinner felt his mouth go dry. He had stumbled across something very big and very terrible.

Seeing the dismay on the man's face, the sentry realized the question had been harmless. This wizened fellow was surely no English spy, seeking Donal Cam for the price on his head. The English paid their spies well; none of them would have been out in this weather with no more than a single coarse mantle to keep him warm, belted with a piece of rope and falling to a ragged hem midshank, above bare legs.

The wolf skinner's eyes had taken on that wary, hunted look the sentry knew all too well. The man was darting glances to the left and to the right, looking for an escape route.

Taking pity on him, the sentry said in a more kindly tone, "We are from the south, where our lands have been despoiled and taken from us. We mean you no harm. We are only passing through on our way northward. Just simple folk seeking food, and some place of safety."

The wolf skinner was nodding, somewhat dubiously, until beyond the sentry he saw a man get shakily to his feet; a man whose face was covered with blood.

Violence had been done recently.

The wolf skinner turned and fled.

The sentry watched the man running but made no move to stop him. The blood-bathed figure—one of Burke's mercenaries—came to stand at his shoulder. "Who was that?"

"Some local who stumbled on us by accident. He has just had the fright of his life, I should say."

"Unh. He should have been with us yesterday. Will he spread word of us, do you think?"

The sentry heaved a weary sigh. "How can I say? And what difference would it make? The entire country seems to know of us already."

The mercenary realized for the first time that his face felt stiff and sticky. Touching it, he recognized dried blood. His fingers worked their way upward cautiously.

"You have a gaping hole in your hairline," the sentry observed.

"Unh. Indeed. I am just beginning to feel it. Yesterday . . ."

"There was no time for feeling, yesterday. Go find one of the women to tend it for you. But go swiftly, for we will be moving soon. The light is coming up. Jesus and Mary know I would rather just curl up here and sleep," the sentry added with passion.

"Do it," the other advised. "I could join you myself."

For a moment, both meant it. The will to act flickered between them. Then the sentry shrugged one shoulder. "We would just freeze to death here. We might as well go on. It may be better somewhere ahead."

"Do you think so?"

"I pray so," was the answer.

The camp was dragging itself into the day. Each person's first thought on waking was not fear, but hunger.

Hunger had tormented every belly at some time during the night. Whatever fleshy reserves anyone had were exhausted, and there was nothing to replenish them.

A girl on the edge of puberty dug into the mud nearest her sleeping place, using bare fingers as tools. A root, a nut, a sleeping seed . . . she felt a sharp edge. Her hand jerked back, then curiosity made her dig again. A bronze spear point, green with the centuries, was lodged in the mud. She lifted it out and peered at it, then tossed it aside and dug again, looking for something of real value. Something to eat.

It was getting harder every morning to make people stand up and walk. Some moaned piteously when they tried to move. Orla and her women had a few remaining pots of mallow ointment to rub swollen joints, and these were rationed among the most afflicted, but there was not enough for everyone.

Everyone. Not everyone is with us this morning, thought Donal Cam. Once more he looked for the missing faces. In the running battle of the day before, they had not only been unable to stop and bury their dead, they had not even been allowed to gather up the badly injured.

But at least, he thought with a sense of amazement, they had not lost any horses. He counted, then counted again. All the cavalry animals were still with them, as were the dozen saddle nags once used by officers and nobility and now assigned to carry small children, weak women, and the grievously wounded.

And two packhorses.

One of the camp followers was loitering near the baggage. Donal Cam beckoned to her. "Ask quietly, but find out how many people feel they can go no farther. We are in easy land here, but we are heading toward the uplands again. If some want to stay behind and try to find safe haven for themselves here, I shall do what I can to help them."

Grella stared at him. "Do you mean it?"

"I do of course. You saw what happened yesterday and the day before. It will happen again tomorrow. We are going to be hunted as long as we are within Carew's reach and perhaps even longer. I cannot force people to endure it. Those who wish to leave now, bring them to me before we set out."

Grella ran first to her brother. "The O'Sullivan has given us permission to leave, Ronan!"

"What are you talking about?"

She told him. Ronan stood listening, frowning, hands on hips. When she finished he said, "I am not leaving without the gold."

"But would he not pay you the wages due you?"

"I want more than that pittance! I want all he is hoarding for himself, and you and I shall stay until we can get our hands on it, Grella," he vowed grimly.

Weariness was wearing his sister down. The idea of falling out of the column was increasingly appealing. But she dare not do it without her brother.

She elbowed her way into the edge of the group she subsequently gathered for Donal Cam. She watched as he questioned them, trying to assess whether or not they would be able to survive if left on their own.

There were some two dozen, women mostly, but a scattering of husbands and brothers among them, and a few children with huge staring eyes and skins gray with hunger. Donal Cam told the group, "We are near the village of Sulchoid, and this land has enough cover to shelter game, so there should be food if you have the strength to hunt for it. I do not know if the villagers would be hostile to you, nor do I mean to go there and ask. I am going to leave you with a dowry; you will not be deserted without resources. Act cautiously, but try to find someone who will take pity on you and sell you provisions. I do not intend to leave you here to starve."

"Sulchoid?" someone said. "I seem to recall the name . . ."

Father Collins was unable to resist speaking up. "Brian Boru won a great victory here against the Northmen six hundred years ago. He crushed the foreigners."

Those who still had enough strength to use their imaginations turned slowly, looking around as if in hopes some ghostly Gaelic army would materialize from the clumps of willow and come to their aid now.

A rising wind mocked them, singing through emptiness.

"This has been the site of many famous battles since ancient times," Father Collins went on, but no one was listening anymore.

Digging into one of his packs, Donal Cam took out several small leather purses. These he distributed among the men who were leaving the column. "Your dowry," he said gravely. They accepted with equal gravity. They all understood the gold had no worth but what it would buy.

He left them weapons as well, and a little of his precious ammunition for the one gun he dared spare to the group.

Even that single gun was resented by the soldiers remaining with him. He knew it.

Grella returned sour-faced to her brother. "He gave some of the gold to them, Ronan. I told you we should go."

"Some of the gold. I want more than some. Look sharp, now, we are moving out!"

The dark mass stirred sluggishly and began to move forward, flowing like some viscid stream through the willow marshes. The group that had elected to stay behind huddled together and watched them go.

The last that was heard of the two dozen was one man's voice, exhorting the others to start cutting osiers and building shelters.

"Will they be all right?" Maire asked some time later. She was walking beside Niall again. Sharing his shaggy cloak had become a habit, though during the running battle of the day before she had lost his company for a time. Her relief at seeing him alive when they finally made camp had been so intense it surprised her.

"Will who be all right?"

"The people we left behind."

"At Doire na Fola?"

"This morning."

'Ah. Them. I suppose they will. If any of us are. Who can know?"

"Perhaps I should have stayed with them," Maire said in a small voice. "I do not think I am able for this. I should not be here at all, in fact. After Kinsale, the English captured my clan's stronghold at Castle Haven, but by that time I was with my betrothed at Dunboy. Then when The O'Sullivan left Dunboy for Ardea, my Richard insisted I join the party as one of Honora's attendants. Dunboy fell shortly after, you know, and my . . . my Richard . . . if he had known that half a year later I would be fleeing the length of Ireland, starving and terrified . . . he would not have wanted this for me."

"He would have wanted life for you," Niall assured her, "and your best chance is to escape Munster with us."

"But I did not choose life!" she replied vehemently. "I only wanted to be with my Richard!"

Niall wished she would stop saying "my Richard" as if

the dead man were a physical part of her, like her hand or her foot.

How does one fight a dead man? he wondered.

As they put Sulchoid behind them they were spared snow, but soon engulfed by wind and rain. Trees groaned with the strain of the gale. Rain stabbed through layers of clothing, straight to the heart.

Father James Archer walked with his head bowed. The cold was a solid wall to him; he forced himself through it with an act of will. Like Father Collins, he had long since discarded clerical garb in favor of more practical layers of wool and leather and a heavy woven cloak bordered with colorful fringe, which he had taken from a captain fallen at Kinsale after administering the last rites.

At the time he had thought it ghoulish to take a dead man's cloak. Yet he had done so. All around him, men were snatching what they could.

Or had that been Kinsale? he asked himself. Perhaps it had been some other battle. There had been so many battles, so many dead men.

Father Archer had never left Donal Cam since the disaster at Kinsale. The hard months of fighting that followed had taken their toll on both men as O'Sullivan struggled, with increasing desperation, to hold back the English tide flowing over Munster.

He would have been destroyed long ago without me, Father Archer told himself.

"Make me Your instrument, Lord," the priest murmured, folding his hands in a prayerful attitude in front of his body even though—or perhaps because—it made walking more difficult. "Make me Your instrument."

He paced on, chanting his litany.

Nearby one of the buannachta matched him step for

step, though they were oblivious to one another. "Warm and dry," the recruit was muttering to himself. "Warm and dry. Warm and dry. Warm and dry."

One step after another.

Many of the column were thinking of food when they heard the first gunfire. Like the child who had found the spearhead, they had crammed their mouths with dead leaves and twigs that morning, but their bellies were not deceived. Only the reappearance of some of the White Knight's men was enough to make them forget their hunger and struggle to run again.

With an angry oath, Donal Cam dispatched soldiers to guard the sides of the column and try to keep people together. Shouting at Rory O'Sullivan to replace him at the head of the march, he galloped back down the line to be certain his cavalry was holding the rear.

Ronan Hurley told him encouragingly, "There are not as many of them as there were yesterday. They are making a dreadful amount of noise, but staying out of range. I think they do not want to engage us again, they merely mean to frighten us. See there? Some are already falling back."

Donal Cam squinted, following the direction of Ronan's pointing finger. "So they are. On a day like this they probably prefer their hearth fires to the sport of slaughtering us."

"I would prefer it myself . . . if I had a hearth fire and a hearth for it to burn on. I would go there right now."

Donal Cam's lips twitched. "At this moment I think I would go with you."

After following them for a mile or so, their pursuers gave up the chase. It was as if each region through which they passed felt obliged to torment them before allowing them to go on to the next.

When the last curses and gunshots ceased, Donal Cam

rode slowly along the column, observing the condition of his people. None dead. None wounded.

They could hardly believe it. Like people reprieved from the gallows, they smiled shakily at one another. "No harm done, Commander," one of the musketeers called. He waved to Donal Cam, making the bottles of powder that hung from his shoulder belt rattle merrily. "No harm at all, they were afraid to fight us again!"

At his words, a wave of bravado swept through the crowd. They were alive. Starving and giddy, but alive.

Alive, Honora! Donal Cam exulted.

Looking around, he saw that they had halted on a rising track that led past a recently abandoned farmstead. Already the wattle-and-daub cabin was being obliterated by hazel scrub. The area was too open, they must not linger to give thanks for their deliverance.

With a crisp command, Donal Cam ordered the column forward once more.

The trackway led to a succession of hills, and soon they were climbing again, through a region all but cleared of the Gael since English policy began to bite deep.

Then from atop his horse Donal Cam began to catch glimpses of occupied, and prosperous, habitation: an occasional freestanding stone house with a slate roof, or a walled manor unchanged since medieval times, possessing in good repair barns and cow byre and threshing floor, and a long, low house, limewashed, with its reed thatching worn snugly pulled down to the tops of deep-set windows.

"Keep a sharp watch now," he called to his captains. "We will find no friends here, but there may be food." He leaned down from the saddle to ask Thomas Burke, "Do you know the name of this place?"

The Connacht man shrugged, but Dermod O'Sullivan

said, "We are approaching the Multeen river, I think. I was entertained most hospitably in this region some years ago."

"You have done a great amount of traveling," The O'Connor commented.

"A Kerry man would think so. Your people never leave their land, it is well known."

"Why would anyone want to leave Kerry? We have everything."

"Barren mountains and thin soil that will grow nothing."

"It grew me," retorted The O'Connor. Born of a tribe famous for its size, he was, even in his old age, a mighty man, towering above Dermod O'Sullivan as they resumed the friendly rivalry that had become one of their chief pastimes. The argument about whose homeland was better had become abstract; neither was certain he would ever see home again.

Donal Cam interrupted by saying, "The chieftain of the region, uncle—do you know him?"

"The O'Dwyer? I do indeed know him, he was my host."

"Could we expect hospitality from him now?"

Dermod frowned. "I doubt it. I should think the Earl of Ormond would have already forbidden any aid being given to the Munster rebels. I do not recall The O'Dwyers having offered assistance to The O'Neill."

Thomas Burke put his hand on the hilt of his sword. "What they do not give, we can take," he promised grimly.

The captain of the mercenaries possessed a short sword badly nicked from tip to hilt, a dagger rusted with bloodstains, a half-pike stained dark by sweaty palms, a helmet with its strap burst in a skirmish, and a mighty hunger. The light in his eyes promised death to anyone who stood between him and food.

The O'Connor nudged Dermod O'Sullivan. "If that man eats, we will."

Dermod gave him a critical look. "Are you limping, Sean?"

"Me? Limping? Never!" The O'Connor threw back his shoulders and strode forward to show his friend how excessively fit he was. Dermod at once stretched his legs to match him stride for stride. The two set off with such a burst of speed that Donal Cam's horse broke into a jog to catch up with them.

The day had improved. The rain ceased, and the prevailing wind swung around to blow at their backs, urging them forward.

Ahead lay Donohill, *Dun Eochaille*, the Fort of the Yew. For centuries this had been the site of a large milling operation, and a market and ancient fair were nearby. As the column advanced Donal Cam could see a man-made hill surrounded by a palisade, with some sort of stone building inside.

"There lies the storehouse of the O'Dwyers," he surmised. "If this region is under Sasanach protection, it should be quite full."

"Not for long!" shouted Thomas Burke.

The warriors surged forward, with the civilians hurrying behind them.

At the first sign of their approach the guards on duty at the storehouse had sent for reinforcements. But there were not enough to deny six hundred famished people access to food, though a pitched battle erupted.

O'Sullivan's followers had come less than five miles since awakening. What little strength their night's sleep had given them they summoned to the surface. They were the survivors, the hardiest of the thousand, for those weaker than they were gone. Knowing there was food for the taking, they fought with a ferocity O'Dwyer's men could not match.

The guards turned and ran.

It was the work of a moment to lift the heavy bar from the double doors and swing them wide. People all but trampled each other squeezing through. Then they stopped and stared as a newcomer might stare at the treasures of heaven.

Wooden shelves lined the interior as high as a man could reach, holding bottles and boxes and jugs. Crocks of butter and lard stood to the right of the doorway. Otherwise, the ground floor area of the storehouse was filled with sacks of barley, beans, oats, and ground meal.

Only a few months ago, many of Donal Cam's followers had been accustomed to taking their meals at a table spread with linen, while servants poured wine into blown glassware imported from the Continent and musicians played the favored music of the day on harp and pipe and lute.

Now these same people tore open sacks with their broken fingernails and crammed raw meal into their mouths with both hands, making frantic gobbling noises, choking, spewing, elbowing others aside to get to the next precious mouthful. The sound of their own chewing was the sweetest music they had ever heard.

Posting guards around the perimeter in case the O'Dwyers returned, Donal Cam gave his people time to exhaust their first wild greed. Much of what they ate was wasted, vomited by stomachs that could not accept sudden large quantities of coarse food.

Donal Cam scooped a handful of butter out of a crock. With an effort he restrained himself from gobbling, eating from his palm in measured bites. The richest pudding had never tasted so good.

They dared not linger long, he knew. When the first wild gorging had subsided, he instructed people to carry away what they could on their backs and set his soldiers to organizing them for the next stage of the march. He meant to get over the highest part of the mountains before they camped again.

A tremendous effort was required to push, pull, and drag some of the people away from the storehouse. "Our rest has been as short as an ass's gallop," observed Dermod O'Sullivan. He and The O'Connor were watching the operation from a position of comfort, sitting on the grass with their backs against a wall and their legs stretched out in front of them.

"We have to move, though," said The O'Connor. "The word has doubtless been spread and Ormond or someone else will come raging in here after us soon enough." He drew up one leg and began gingerly running an exploratory finger around the inside of his boot. His expression was tense.

"Are you certain you can walk?"

"I am of course!" was the quick answer. "We Kerry men are the best walkers in the land. It is yourself who will need help, Dermod," he predicted, standing up and brushing off the seat of his trousers.

"Not a bit of it." Dermod stood up as energetically, and brushed himself off as briskly. "I shall still be walking when you are laid in your tomb, old man."

"Old man? *Old man?*" The O'Connor inflated his chest in mock fury. As the two struck off across the grass, each watched his companion out of the corner of his eye, looking for weakness. Neither allowed himself to show any.

As the refugees headed north toward the vast, curving

slopes of the Slieve Felim mountains, so different from the wild crags and abrupt pinnacles of the southern mountains, a heatless sun unexpectedly broke through the clouds.

A strange euphoria seized the walkers. For the first time in days, they began thinking about the future.

"Do you know where it is we are going?" Maire Ni Driscoll asked Niall O'Mahony.

"To Leitrim, I heard, to The O'Rourke of Breffni. The commander says he will feed and shelter us and help us get resettled, then the commander will go to join The O'Neill and continue the war, I suppose."

"Resettled? In the north? But I do not want to live in the north, I want to go home!"

"Munster is not safe," Niall reminded her.

"But I do not want to live in Ulster, I know nothing about Ulster."

"Leitrim may not be in Ulster," the pikeman said uncertainly. "Connacht, perhaps . . . But even if it is Ulster, you should be glad. That is the safest part of Ireland now, Maire. I have heard our leaders say that the chieftains of Ulster will hold their lands as the last stronghold of the Gael, no matter what the Sasanach do to the rest of this island."

Niall spoke with the confidence he sensed she needed. It was his nature to tell people what they wanted to hear. His doubt he kept to himself, though he knew full well that with Red Hugh O'Donnell dead in Spain, Donegal, *Dun na nGall*, the Fort of the Strangers, had lost not only its prince but its stoutest defender. As for Hugh O'Neill, after the massive defeat at Kinsale his influence would be much reduced in Ulster. How long could even The O'Neill hold Tyrone? *Tir Eoghain*, the Land of Owen, might be no safer than Donegal.

Or perhaps The O'Neill could hold it all together. Perhaps Kinsale would be the last defeat. There was always the possibility.

With the sun shining on his head and a gentle woman at his side, Niall allowed his spirits to rise for the first time in many days. The old, irrepressible merriment that had once characterized him began to return.

"Would you like me to play for you?" he asked Maire. His eyes were sparkling. "When we next make camp?"

"Play . . . ?"

"My harp."

She hesitated, then smiled a smile so tiny he would have missed it if he had not been watching very closely.

"Here," he said, "you wear the mantle." He spread the full weight of the garment across her shoulders and shrugged the pack from his own. The pack was large and irregular in shape, with lumpy protrusions where he had recently stuffed beans and meal into the bag. With difficulty Niall extricated the chief contents of the pack. Maire's eyes widened.

Maire Ni Driscoll was no chieftain's daughter. Her father was only a distant cousin of the chieftain. But with her family she had sometimes visited the strongholds of the clan. Her earliest memory was of listening, enchanted, as The O'Driscoll's harper played for his noble patron in the Fort of Jewels. Maire knew that a common soldier was as unlikely to possess a harp as he was to own a sailing ship.

So she was astonished to see Niall's boast made good.

He held the harp bag for her inspection before showing her the instrument it contained. The otterskin bag was very old, decorated with coral and lined with roebuck skin so soft with age it was like silk to the touch. When Niall pulled the harp out partway, she could see that it was willow wood, glossy and black, with traces of gilding lingering in the deeply carved Celtic designs on its curving neck.

She could not resist touching the carving with two careful fingers.

"Tonight I shall play for you," Niall said huskily. "And for The O'Sullivan, of course!"

He lovingly tucked the harp back into the otterskin bag, then with Maire's help fitted the bag into his pack once more. His was the smallest of bardic harps, but carrying it had meant he had little room for supplies and was chronically short of food or footgear or leather for emergency repairs. Yet he had never once considered leaving the harp behind. As easy to abandon his soul.

As they walked on together, Niall stole darting glances at Maire. Was she impressed? Was she stealing glances at him, too?

Fueled by the food they had eaten, the column—a term of convenience only, for it had never been other than a shifting, shapeless mass—moved swiftly toward the mountains. In the lead, Donal Cam rode with the reins gathered in one hand and the other hand resting at ease on his thigh. The sun gave little warmth but at least it was shining.

Alive, Honora! he rejoiced. *They have not killed me. Carew, Mountjoy, Wilmot—they have not killed me.*

In the crisp, cold air his field of vision was so acute that the sight of a formation of birds scared his retinas with the stark contrast of their dark pattern against a pale sky.

As so often before, his thoughts went back to Kinsale. Formations. Patterns. Battle plans. In the end, however, winning was about dominance. The Sasanach understood. The man who won was the man who could control and dominate the opposition on a given day, as much through the force of his will and personality as through the force of arms.

Both O'Neill and O'Donnell had possessed strong wills and powerful personalities, but Donal Cam knew that the ability to dominate was unreliable. On some mornings he felt that he could shake the heavens. On other days he was aware of a subtle diminution of power, a failure of energy or concentration that might result in submission to a more certain strength if he were challenged then.

Counting the Spanish, he told himself for the hundredth time, our numbers at Kinsale were greater than Mountjoy's. And his men were weakened by disease. We should have won.

We should have won. The knowledge was a scourge.

"You are troubled," said a voice at his knee. He looked down to see the balding head of Father Archer as the priest walked beside his horse.

"Not troubled, merely thinking."

"You are tormenting yourself," the priest contradicted. "I know that look."

When did I begin resenting my confessor's preoccupation with my inmost thoughts? Donal Cam wondered. But I do resent it.

He invades me.

He replied with a lie. "I was simply considering the best place to camp for the night. The people seem stronger than they have in days, so I think we should push on over the mountains and reach some inhabited region on the northern slopes where we can forage for more supplies. The little we are carrying will be gone soon enough, I daresay they are cramming it into their mouths as they walk. It is something I must think about, but certainly not a torment to me," he added coldly.

The Jesuit recognized the rebuke. He credited it to the

burdens of leadership, which he alone could appreciate and share. But if he was not needed at the moment . . . he veered off to walk with Father Collins.

Noticing the two priests together, Thomas Burke remarked to his second-in-command, "Look at those two. If anyone is to blame for the current situation, it is men like those who think God Himself puts the words in their mouths."

The man he addressed was Daniel O'Malley, a Connacht man who prided himself on kinship with the woman who had led his clan as a male chieftain might for four decades. *Granuaille*. Grania. Grace O'Malley, as the English called her. The Irishwoman who had defied the worst Elizabeth could throw at her and somehow survived, making of that survival a triumph.

It did not sit well with her kinsman to be part of an army defeated by the English. He was interested in knowing of anyone who could be blamed. But . . . "Priests? Men of the Church?"

Burke said flatly, "In my opinion priests are more self-serving and less honest than mercenaries. We earn our pay in a straightforward way. When a man hires us he gets value for money, and our loyalty is his as long as he pays us.

"But who knows where the loyalty of priests really lies? And what do we actually get from them? They are accountable only to the pope and to God, and we never hear from either except through them. Do this, do not do that, it is God's will, they say, never explaining why. And people follow them like sheep, though they tell fables as truth—fables no lad of twelve would credit from anyone else.

"If a priest gives bad advice, who pays for it? Those who followed his advice are the ones who suffer. I mistrust all Roman clerics and that Father Archer most of all.

I happened to be with Donal Cam at Ardea when Archer advised the commander to . . ."

An awful idea had occurred to Daniel O'Malley. He interrupted to ask, "Are you a convert to the Tudor heresy?" A devout Catholic, he was appalled to think he might have been following a heretic all these months; perhaps even a spy!

But before Burke could answer, a new trouble overtook them.

The yelling and the gunfire had begun again.

As soon as the Earl of Ormond had learned of the looting of the Donohill storehouse, he had sent a company of O'Dwyer men and members of an allied clan, the Ryans, to head off the fugitives.

By following byways only locals could know they caught up with the column before it reached the safety of the mountains. Ormond's men were a large company, well armed. If they had encountered the dispirited refugees of the previous day they might have slaughtered them.

But today was different.

At the first sign of attack, Donal Cam let out such a bellow of rage his stallion almost shied out from under him. His men took up the roar. They turned and attacked Ormond's company with a martial joy they had almost forgotten.

The Ryans and O'Dwyers held their ground at first, but O'Sullivan's men had the cumulative frustration of many days to spend upon them. Soon they were forced to break ranks and run. The warriors returned to the column wearing grins of satisfaction. It was the best time they had had in months.

The civilians cheered them and pounded them on their backs. Women threw their arms around men who were neither husband nor brother, and kissed them passionately. The few surviving children, gaunt little figures with old faces, stared in open-mouthed admiration at the conquering heroes.

The march resumed.

The brief belt of English-supported prosperity fell behind them as they entered the foothills of the Slieve Felim mountains. Grassland gave way to furze and heather and the terrain was scored with streams, many hemmed with ice. There were no more fine houses to be seen, only an occasional mud-walled cabin containing people no better nourished than themselves.

"Be on your guard," Rory O'Sullivan warned his men. "The natives may try to attack us for what we have." His scarred face twisted in his best approximation of a smile, at the irony.

They followed the valley of the Multeen river toward its source among the hills. The Slieve Felim peaks were broad and gently curved, unlike the rugged crags of west Cork; the ascent was less difficult than it had appeared from a distance.

The sun deserted them. A few snowflakes fell. From behind an apparently deserted cabin a small dog ran out to fire a salvo of defiant barks at the strangers. The dog was a shaggy brindle bitch of indeterminate breed, with sharply pointed ears and a sharply pointed face.

She was also hungry.

Maire Ni Driscoll dropped to her knees. "The poor creature! She has been abandoned to fend for herself. Look, Niall." She twisted around to peer over her shoulder at him. "Can we not take her with us?"

The pikeman was nonplussed. Wanting a dog for its own sake was outside his experience. Dogs hunted or herded; pets were an affectation of ladies in great houses.

"We can hardly find enough to keep ourselves alive. Why should we take on another mouth?"

Maire was holding out her fingers for the dog to lick. By this time the small animal had ceased barking and was wriggling madly, making small pleading noises.

"Aaahhh," soothed Maire. "Aaahhh there. Come to me now. Come to me." She tried to pick up the dog but it drew back, wary of the smell of the shaggy mantle. Realizing the cause of its timidity, Maire flung the garment aside and renewed her coaxing of the dog.

Niall, watching, shook his head.

When Maire stood up with the little brindle bitch in her arms, the expression on her face was like that of a mother protecting a child.

"Bring the creature, then," said Niall resignedly. He picked up the mantle and tried to wrap it around Maire, but the dog growled, showing tiny white teeth. "My guardian," Maire said.

Niall sheltered beneath the mantle by himself.

As they advanced farther into the mountains, snow gave way to another cold rain. Water ran down the slopes in muddy rivulets, dark red in one place, yellow and clayey in another.

Dermod O'Sullivan remarked to The O'Connor, "Red Hugh came this very way from Donegal, did he not?"

"He did. To avoid Carew he led his warriors across these mountains when they were covered with more ice and frost than had ever been seen before. Ah, to be young!"

"You *are* limping."

"I am not limping!" The Kerry chieftain gritted his teeth. The steady, increasingly steep climb was not bothering him as much as the pain in his feet. The last time he had a moment to himself without Dermod looking over his shoulder he had eased his feet out of his boots for a thorough examination. He found blisters forming between his toes, translucent bags of fluid bulging on either side of gnarled joints. A large raw patch on his right heel was oozing blood. The ball of his left foot burned as if he had been walking on hot coals.

"I am not limping," he reiterated now. "Up, chin! Swing, arms!" He strode off at top speed, forcing Dermod to hurry to catch up with him.

The winding watercourse they were following led them ever higher into the mountains. The rain alternated with a thick mist that seemed to bleed up out of the earth. At one point it thinned enough to give them a view back the way they had come. To their right, seen through rain and mist, a succession of little fields glistened like new.

One man slowed, stopped, made his way to the edge of the slope and stared back.

The column moved past him.

The man who had stopped was of indeterminate age behind his brown beard, but his shoulders were broad and his legs long. He wore a loosely cut tweed coat with a slight flare below the waist, a garment the greenish-brown color of bog water. On his head was a woolen cap pulled down to cover his ears and nape, and fastened with two horn buttons under his chin. His boots were made of sturdy felt, soaked through. A rope around his waist held up his trousers, now that he had grown thin; on the seat and legs of the trousers were sewn the reinforcing patches emblematic of a horse rider.

Once he had been a breeder of horses, a man of importance whose proudest boast was that he supplied saddle animals to the nobility of Beare. The brown stallion that had died in a boghole, Donal Cam's favorite mount, had been bred and raised in this man's pastures.

His wife and two half-grown sons came up behind

him. "What are you doing? Come along, everyone is leaving us."

"This is not the worst place I ever saw," the man said dreamily. "Look down there. Our horses would thrive in such mountainy meadows."

"What horses? Are you mad? We have no horses now. Come with me, do." His wife tugged at his arm.

He turned toward her but did not move his feet. "You stay with me instead. We have a bit of meal and beans left, and tomorrow the lads and I can fish, or trap game. We can stay in these mountains and be done with walking and warring forever. No one will care, no one will even notice."

"You are mad!" His family crowded around him, arguing. The column moved on, leaving them behind in a gathering twilight.

No one noticed.

Night falls quickly in the mountains, in winter. The early burst of energy had long since been exhausted, but Donal Cam kept leading his people on, even after darkness fell. Taking advantage of their brief strength he had brought them a cruel long way and meant to take them still farther before they rested. They were on the downslope now; he would push them as far as they could go.

Somewhere ahead lay the Nenagh river. A well-known ford gave access to the land beyond, the tiny village of Latteragh and a chain of others leading all the way to the Shannon. This was the route in Donal Cam's mind.

Before they reached the river valley, however, his eye was attracted by the wink of fires off to his left. "Look there," he said to Thomas Burke, who had moved up to walk in the front rank. "Fires. Farmsteads? Perhaps we could supply ourselves with more provisions. I would not like to take food forcibly from some village where we mean to rest, so take your men and make a detour in that direction. See what you can find; we shall meet you below."

Burke set off at once, accompanied by Daniel O'Malley and sixty mercenaries. The weather had changed yet again. The sky was clear and filled with stars as hard and bright as chips of mica, while a full moon illuminated the countryside.

"Night is the ideal time for foraging," Burke remarked to O'Malley as they proceeded toward the fires. "Whoever it is, we shall take them by surprise."

"What if they are some of O'Donnell's men? We are losing people every day; surely he lost some when he came along here."

"If those are Red Hugh's men we shall find allies who will be glad to help us."

But they did not find allies. Instead they rounded a huge mass of holly bushes to find themselves, clearly visible in the moonlight, facing a military encampment. One startled glance was enough to reveal that the warriors were well clothed and well equipped.

"Sasanach!" O'Malley hissed.

There was one startled moment of mutual recognition, then the men leapt up from around their campfires and ran toward Burke's band. The element of surprise was equal on both sides, but the mercenaries had just made a long march through mountains. They were not at their best for the skirmish that followed.

At the first sound of gunfire echoing among the hills, Donal Cam shouted, "Our men are in trouble! Rory! Bring the buannachta and follow me!"

With a frantic scurrying, the recruits set off behind Donal Cam and their captain.

Niall alone hesitated. If there was danger, he did not want to leave Maire unprotected. And someone must stay behind to defend the column. But the habit of obedience was strong in him. After a brief delay he pressed his knife into Maire's hand, then ran off after the others.

Suddenly finding themselves alone in a hostile night, the civilians huddled together.

The stars overhead looked very cold.

Donal Cam drove his horse at a headlong pace, heedless of the dangers of the night and the unfamiliar ground. The sound of musket fire was his beacon; that, and the cries of mortally injured men as he drew nearer the scene of conflict.

Thomas Burke came staggering toward him out of the gloom. The face of the mercenary captain was bathed in blood and all his weapons were lost, though his helmet was still on his head. He was swaying from side to side; Donal Cam leaned down out of the saddle and caught him just as he fell.

"Can you pull yourself up behind me, Thomas?"

The other man grunted something unintelligible, heaved his body upward, fell short. When his weight came on one leg he gasped with pain. Donal Cam dropped the reins on his horse's neck, reached down with both hands and by brute force managed to drag Thomas Burke onto the horse, heaving him across the animal's rump.

The stallion skittered sideways. Donal Cam released his captain and grabbed the reins to control his horse once more, leaving Burke to struggle into a sitting position as best he could and wrap his arms around his commander's body. By the time the horse was under control the buannachta had caught up with them and were mingling with the mercenaries streaming back from the skirmish.

"Shall we go forward and fight?" Rory O'Sullivan asked.

"Too many," Burke muttered. "Go back."

"Will they follow?"

"Not in the dark." Burke slumped against Donal Cam, his iron helmet banging against the other man's shoulder.

"We go back," Donal Cam said.

When they rejoined the main body of the column, a head count revealed that twenty mercenaries, Daniel O'Malley among them, were missing and must be presumed dead. It was not possible to go back for them.

Donal Cam led the refugees on toward the river and the village beyond. Now they were certain of a number of enemy soldiers in the area, it was doubly important that they find some place of sanctuary. A Catholic church was no longer safe from Protestant soldiers, but Donal Cam sought sacral sites as campsites whenever possible anyway. In hope.

In the sixth century, St. Odhran had founded a monastic school in the village they were approaching. "Odhran was a pious man known for his kindness to travelers," Father Archer claimed. When the exhausted column, still wet from having forded the river, straggled into the settlement of Latteragh, they found the village dark, its doors barred against travelers. But Donal Cam succeeded in rousing the priest and persuading him to grant them access to the local church. The man reluctantly led the way out of the village and up a steep climb to a level place where stood the stone church with its walled enclosure and graveyard.

"Do not tell the English I helped you!" the priest pleaded. "You have done a most dangerous thing, there is a fort hard by with an English garrison, you could almost throw a stone and hit them."

"Go back to your bed," Donal Cam told the frightened man. "I have never seen you. We broke in here on our own and will be gone by daybreak."

His eyeballs felt as if they were packed with sand, but

he dared not sleep. There were too many suspicious night noises; the enemy was too close. So while the rest of the fugitives tossed and mumbled in fitful slumbers, Donal Cam stood watch with the sentries. Propped against the gateway of the church, he waited, sword in hand, for the dawn.

In the soughing of the night wind he fancied he could hear the enemy breathing.

Day Six

January 5, 1603. Latteragh. *Leatracha*, the Wet Hillside

When Niall realized he was awake, his first thought was one of regret. He had not kept his promise. He had not played his harp for Maire Ni Driscoll.

Not that she would have expected it, or even wanted it, the night before. They must have reached the church sometime after midnight, unable to do more than collapse on the ground and fall asleep in the building itself or the walled churchyard.

Niall sat up. His head was full of fog. He rubbed his eyes. When he opened them he could see bulky shapes all around him, vaguely discernible in the dim light filtering through an open doorway. Donal Cam stood in that doorway, peering into the small church. "Get up now," he was saying. "The light is coming, we must go. Rouse yourselves, hurry!"

"We just got here," someone growled. Someone else cursed under his breath; cursed Donal Cam, the English, the Irish, the weather, the day . . .

Niall dragged himself to his feet. He would go back for

Maire in a moment, but first he wanted to take a breath of fresh air to clear his head. Within the crowded building the atmosphere was fetid with sleep and sweat and mud and misery.

Donal Cam nodded to him at the doorway. "My bard. Are you well?"

"I have been better, Commander."

"I see you are with Maire Ni Driscoll. Is there something between you?" The commander's voice was husky with fatigue, but kindly.

"I . . . ah . . . I am merely trying to take care of her."

Donal Cam raised one eyebrow, elegantly mocking. "Take care of her indeed. And who would blame you?" Leaving Niall wordless, he set off across the churchyard, weaving his way amid a tangle of gravestones to find his captains.

Rory O'Sullivan was on his feet and proclaimed himself ready to march. But Thomas Burke was sprawled with his back propped against a headstone, while one of Orla's women applied a vile-smelling tincture of sloes to his swollen face. An ugly wound in his thigh had already been cleansed with extract of hypericum, both taken from the assortment of herbal remedies the camp followers carried on their persons, in tiny vials and boxes and purses tucked into pocket or waistband or bosom.

The woman looked up as Donal Cam bent over her. "His nose is badly broken," she reported, "but the worse wound is the one in his leg. He was struck by a musket ball, I think. The bone is not shattered but the wound is deep and painful."

"Can he walk?"

"Not today," she replied with conviction.

"Thomas?"

The mercenary groaned. "She tells the truth, Commander. By tomorrow, surely, but today . . ." His voice was rueful but it was impossible to read any expression in his face, which was a swollen, grotesque mass of purple and green flesh.

"Can you ride a horse?"

The big mercenary managed a shrug. Like Rory O'Sullivan he was a foot soldier, in spite of the rank he had inherited with the departure of his cousin William. The nobility and the cavalry rode, but other Gaelic warriors were justly famed for their stamina and fleetness of foot. Their captains fought on the ground beside their men. "In truth, I never sat on a horse in my life," Thomas Burke said. "But if you want me to, I can."

"Good man yourself, Thomas. I warn you it will not be comfortable for you, but we cannot afford to leave you behind, even if there were a safe place to leave you."

"No need. There is plenty of fighting left in me, just find me some sort of nag who will not dump me on the ground and break my good leg, will you?"

Donal Cam nodded. "You have it."

He raised his head and gazed around the area in the dim gray light of approaching dawn, looking for Ronan Hurley. Orla Ni Donoghue, standing nearby, thought he looked very tired, the lines in his face deeper than she had ever seen them. A strand of dark hair fell across his forehead. She longed to brush it back.

But he never allowed intimate gestures in public.

When Donal Cam ordered one of the cavalry horses to be given to Thomas Burke, Ronan Hurley was furious. "We have none to spare, I barely have a reserve for myself!"

"Then you had better acquire some more. I have to have one for Burke. Need I remind you that the Connacht mercenaries will only follow one of their own? Now tell me, which is your easiest-gaited horse?"

When Donal Cam left him Ronan said under his

breath, "If you are so anxious about Burke's welfare why not give him your own horse?" But he did not speak loudly enough for the commander to hear.

Inside the shelter of the church, Maire Ni Driscoll waited until the last moment before she made herself stand up and prepare to walk again. The little brindle dog was in her arms, its small body warming her chest. From time to time it licked her throat and chin, pleading for food. The day before she had given it tidbits from the Donohill loot, but that was gone now.

Niall took her elbow. "We must go now. Are you going to carry that dog?"

"I am not, she will follow me. She did yesterday. It is just comforting to have something warm to hold."

You could hold me, Niall thought. He watched her walk away from him, out the door of the church.

There still had been nothing sexual between them, but he was young and strong and in spite of their hardships, his body kept asserting itself. The constant threat under which they were living made life more precious. Niall knew full well that those of the buannachta who had wives with them, or women among the camp followers, went to them in the night if they had the energy. Or even if they did not.

Whether it was love or lust he felt for Maire Ni Driscoll he did not ask himself. He felt, that was what mattered. After a terrible year of loss piled upon loss, he felt the forgotten sensation of happiness just by being near the woman.

In the churchyard, two strong gallowglasses were lifting Thomas Burke onto a rawboned gray horse. "Hold on to the mane," someone advised. Burke at once took a death grip on the coarse black hair. "I am promoted to the cavalry," he said, though he did not dare smile as he said it for fear his swollen face would split open.

Donal Cam sent a whispered order for quiet down the line. Five hundred people, more or less—the number diminished every day, he thought, watching them gather themselves—crept from their brief sanctuary and headed in the general direction of the northeast, toward the distant Shannon that marked the boundary of Munster.

The priest of St. Odhran's hid behind the stone churchyard wall, peering around the corner to watch them go. Only when the last straggler had disappeared did he enter his church.

He found a purse of gold Spanish ducats waiting for him on the altar.

With a gasp, the priest dropped to his knees and bowed his head over his clasped hands.

The day proved as bitter as any the column had endured. Rain lashed them as soon as they left Latteragh, alternating with sleet. The wind blew in fierce gusts.

Thomas Burke sat swaying on his horse, clutching the reins with one hand and the mane with the other, listening to the ice ring like shot on his iron helmet. His wounded leg was tightly bound, but as it hung unsupported from the saddle it began to throb. He shifted, trying to ease himself. His broken nose was clogged with blood, forcing him to breathe the cold air through his open mouth, chilling his throat.

He wondered what it would feel like if the horse broke into a trot. The idea filled him with horror.

As if reading his mind, the gray took a few jigging steps. Burke gave the reins a violent jerk. His heart was hammering in his half-frozen throat. His leg felt as if it were being pounded by fists. He suddenly wished he had thought to urinate before they lifted him on the horse.

As the march moved out, Dermod O'Sullivan had told his wife, "God be with you," and gone to take his accustomed place with The O'Connor Kerry in the fore of the column. Joan was content to walk with other women of similar rank, though by now all were so bedraggled it was hard to tell who was married to a landowner and who to a tenant.

As they walked together, one Anne Ni Kelly remarked to Joan, "I see your husband is at the front again. A mighty man."

Joan sniffed, secretly flattered. "As mighty as a thrush's ankle. If it were not for competing with Sean O'Connor he would be moaning and demanding my sympathy and attention every moment."

"Men. My husband was the same."

"Was? Is he not still with us? I thought I saw him at . . ."

"At Ardskeagh," Anne said in a tight, toneless voice. "He had been wounded. He did not wake up that morning."

"May God have mercy on him! I am sorry, Anne. You are brave to go on."

Anne gave Joan a tremulous smile. "I must. Whatever life he still has is in me, in my memories of him."

The first shot of the day hit Anne Ni Kelly in the back of the head. She fell on her face without a sound, kicked spasmodically, and died.

Joan screamed.

Red-hot balls laced the cold air. Armed men came pounding after the column, yelling imprecations. While Ronan Hurley and his fistful of horsemen hastily spread out to form a wide curve designed to guard the rear of the column from attack, the kernes and gallowglasses engaged in yet another running battle along the flanks of the march.

From atop his horse, Thomas Burke shouted commands to his mercenaries. Every yell sent waves of yellow pain pulsing from his broken nose, but he yelled anyway.

If he had been a trained horseman and not weakened by wounds he would have led a charge. He was a professional warrior.

Up to a point, the skirmish followed the pattern of the one the day before by Ormond's men. When Donal Cam's soldiers turned to attack, the enemy gave ground.

When the column resumed the march, however, the enemy came after them.

Up through a defile, across hills and valleys, running, walking, stumbling, finding the briefest of respites, they fought and fled. Bodies were left lying in the heather. People who had had enough broke away from the column and disappeared. The wind blew, the rain pelted down, the earth was a sea of mud.

Through it all, Donal Cam found himself observing and analyzing patterns, watching for successful maneuvers that could be used in future battles. The next time the armies of the Gael went to war in their thousands against the Sasanach.

Weary, discouraged, and depressed as he was, he had to keep believing there would be a next time.

And a victory to outweigh the defeat of Kinsale.

If he had not believed that, he knew, he might as well have stayed in Beare and fought to the death, trapped like a rat as Carew's net tightened. Others had stayed, choosing to surrender their lives rather than their land. Others who had expected that the chief of the clan would stay and do likewise.

After Kinsale, Hugh O'Neill had returned to his stronghold in Ulster to regroup while Red Hugh O'Donnell had sailed for Spain to arrange for a fresh Spanish expedition to come and fight the English. Donal Cam had been left to continue the war in Munster against increasingly overwhelming odds. A year after Kinsale, six months after the loss of Dunboy, he had been driven to take refuge in the rugged wilderness around Gleann Garbh. There he had gathered not only his remaining warriors but his most loyal followers and a number of ordinary civilians who sought his protection.

Then two disasters struck, one hard upon the other. Their creaght was seized, and a messenger arrived to tell Donal Cam that Red Hugh had died in Spain. The promised Spanish expedition was countermanded.

The last hope gone, Donal Cam had chosen to save what he could. To save what remained of his army so he could join The O'Neill in Ulster and prepare to take up the battle on another front.

Some people had accused Donal Cam of deserting his homeland to save his own skin. He knew that.

It was not the first time such an accusation had been made against him. He knew that too. His defense would be to prove the wisdom of his decision by living to fight and fighting to win . . .

A shot whizzed past his ear. Snatched back to the present, he realized his thoughts had been wandering dangerously. An excellent way to get yourself killed, he rebuked himself.

The fighting and running would continue intermittently throughout the long, cold, hard-pressed day.

After the first company of soldiers, O'Sullivan's assailants were mostly local people who were using this method of demonstrating their loyalty to the English. Not many of them had guns. The majority were armed with darts, the Gaelic light spear, or cudgels and leather slings for hurling stones. They did damage with these missiles, however, and damage was done in return by Donal Cam's men, who no longer cared if the foe they faced was English or Gaelic.

Kill the man who is trying to kill you. That had become the only imperative.

The terrain gradually began dropping toward the distant valley of the Shannon. Behind them now were the slopes of Slieve Felim, and *Mauherslieve*, Mother Mountain. The column was making its way along a track through gently rolling woodlands when they found themselves alone again—for a while.

Donal Cam drew rein. "There is a stream here," he called out. "Water the horses and drink, but do not fill your bellies so full you cannot run again if you must."

He noticed Thomas Burke slumped in his saddle. Donal Cam rode over to him. "How goes it with you, Thomas?"

The mercenary captain raised his head. His face looked like an overripe plum about to burst. "I pissed myself back there a while ago," he admitted.

"Is that all? No one will notice, we are all soaking wet."

"I was afraid I was going to fall off. Now I do not think I could get off if I wanted to. My hand seems to be locked on this wretched animal's mane."

"Do you want a drink of water?"

"One of the women already brought me a cup, though I scarcely needed it. Every time I open my mouth the rain pours in."

At that moment one of Burke's mercenaries remarked, "I think I know just where we are."

"Where?" Donal Cam asked eagerly. He was relying on his companions as guides now. Common folks knew nothing beyond their birthplaces, as a rule, but among the warriors and the nobles were a number who had traveled and recognized landmarks or, like Father Archer, were familiar with the religious sites.

"We are in the land of the Kennedys," said the mercenary. "I fought in this very area some years ago as a kerne in the service of a Thomond chieftain. Not the earl!" he added hastily. "I never fought for any man who took English gold."

One of his fellow mercenaries snorted. "You would take gold from a corpse's arsehole. You fight for hire like the rest of us."

Thomas Burke cleared his throat. "We fight for The O'Sullivan now," he said sternly, making a point.

The O'Connor said, "I heard somewhere that the Kennedys sided with Hugh O'Neill, at least at one time. Do you think they would give us provisions now?"

"People have changed sides all over Ireland," Dermod reminded him.

The kerne scratched his head. "They have strongholds all around here, one just a few miles ahead. When they see us approaching we will know what side they are on now, I suspect."

The march set off again. Soon enough the dark, square, truncated shape of a small stone tower house appeared on the skyline. At a signal from their captains the warriors prepared their weapons, the musketeers loaded and braced their guns. But nothing much happened beyond the emergence of a small group of men from the ground floor of the tower, the armory level. They stood in front of the stronghold to watch the refugees pass. They called no greetings. Neither did they fire on the column. They merely stood, arms folded, in silence, as if observing some peculiar pageant that had no meaning for them.

"Clan Kennedy neither helped nor hindered," Father Collins remarked to himself, committing the incident to memory.

Rory O'Sullivan put his hand on Donal Cam's knee and asked in a low, urgent voice, "Shall we storm the castle and take whatever they have to eat?"

"I think not. It is a small place, their stores cannot be great, not enough to make any difference to us. And if they are not our avowed enemies I would not want to make them so."

He led the march away, over the crest of a hill and out of sight of the men who stood with folded arms, staring after them.

"There would have been enough to eat for some of us," Ronan Hurley said angrily to his horsemen. "We could go back."

The others exchanged glances. He was their captain, but if they disobeyed Donal Cam they might well be on their own. In unfamiliar territory. With many hands raised against them.

"I can wait a little longer for my meal," one of them said in measured tones. The others nodded.

Looking from face to face, Ronan felt rebellion in them. He had not endeared himself to these men. He had no gift for leadership, he had only been promoted to captain because he was senior among the survivors.

Ronan knew to the marrow of his bones that every one of the horsemen with him was as bitter as he was. They must be. Yet when he spoke aloud what the others were surely feeling, they rejected him. The cowards.

"If we were not all here to see it O'Sullivan Beare would go back and take their food for himself," Ronan said angrily. "He would. You know it. He left Dunboy when it became obvious that Carew meant to seize it at all costs. He fled to Ardea to save himself, leaving others to die in his place. You know it. So why should we not do something for ourselves? Why should we not ride back and kill those few men we saw and take their supples?"

They stared at him with hard, flat eyes. Every man was making his own calculations of survival and necessity and loyalty.

Ronan saw them decide against him; he knew it because nothing changed in their faces.

"Very well, fools," he said irritably, as if it were of no consequence. "We ride on." He trotted forward and they fell in behind him, not because he was leading but because he was going in the same direction they intended to go.

Some distance farther on they were assailed by yet another band of locals, who whooped and cursed and chased the column. The cavalry defended the rear, as before, while Ronan shouted orders.

When the latest pursuers gave up the column was still moving forward.

The sudden death of Anne Ni Kelly had shocked Joan more than she wanted to admit, even to herself. Throughout the day she kept seeing, over and over again, the moment when the shape of the other woman's skull had changed hideously, flattening and then bulging, blood spraying. She rubbed her eyes with her hands but the vision kept coming back to her, as if it were painted on the inside of her eyelids.

Her beleaguered mind sought for something to distract itself.

Patrick O'Byrne was keeping his eyes on the road—or what passed for road, a cuppy and mired trackway so torn up by the marchers in front of him that every step must be carefully planned. He had been a cooper in Bantry, one of those who sided with Donal Cam O'Sullivan instead of Owen O'Sullivan in the family feud. He was a round-shouldered man with large hands and a philosophic turn of mind, and was just musing on where he might have been this day if he had chosen to follow Owen when the woman walking next to him said in a peculiar voice, "I had three attendants of my own at Dursey, can you imagine? I had one woman who did nothing but mend my shifts and keep my gloves in good repair. I was vain of my hands when I was younger."

She held out a pair of chapped hands whose tendons stood up like cords leading to the thin fingers. It had been a while since gloves protected those hands, O'Byrne told himself.

"Anh-hah," he said aloud, noncommittally.

"All my children were educated," she went on. "No son of mine but knew his letters. And no traveler ever called to our door to be turned away. We had both beer and ale in the cellars, and spirits from France as well, for the nobility. My household was the pride of my husband's family. I saw to it that a man could be a guest in our hall for a day or a year and never put his hand on an empty cup, nor have less than three meats at a meal. Seven on feast days."

"Anh-hah," Byrne repeated, rolling his eyes toward her. Was she losing her mind? If so, what should he do?

"On the day I married Dermod I wore a gown embroidered with pearl wire and sequined with flakes of mica dipped in silver," Joan said, staring into a space and time that was safe.

O'Byrne began edging away from her. "Shall I summon your husband for you?" he asked nervously.

Joan gave a start, shook herself, seemed to notice him for the first time. "Were you speaking to me?"

"You were speaking to me. Talking about your household and your gowns."

She glared at him with the expression of an eagle disturbed on her nest. "I was talking to myself! It had nothing to do with you. I like to talk to myself. When I hear my voice I know where I am."

Mumbling something meant to placate her, O'Byrne dropped back to walk with the next tier of people. The wife of the erstwhile lord of Dursey might indeed be los-

ing her mind, he decided, bu
done about it. He almost envied

The leaders of the column topp
saw ahead of them a hill standing out
ing meadows with an eerie and singular
sentinel in the gloom of the day. The kerne
region said, in a voice hushed with awe, ksheegowna." *Cnoc Sidhe Gamhna*, the Hill of the Fairy Calf.

The priests immediately signed the Cross in the air, erecting their invisible shields against an ancient enemy. A shiver rippled along the march, like wind disturbing a river.

A few of the boldest stared curiously at the hill, recalling wild, disturbing tales. More prudent souls averted their eyes and murmured the immemorial Gaelic incantations meant to ward off the attentions of the Good People. The Good People: so called because it was dangerous to use any name that might offend the supernatural beings, the Sidhe, whose land this still was. They were not really fairies, which was a Spenserian image to beguile English children. The Sidhe was that lost race that had never surrendered Ireland, even to the conquering Gael five hundred years before Christ. And would not surrender to the English, either. The Sidhe would remain.

A whipping wind circled the base of Knocksheegowna, moaning.

Someone else called attention to an oblique view of the notched mountain known as The Devil's Bit. "The Devil himself took a bite out of it," he reported as fact, and as fact it was accepted.

Ireland was filled with mysteries.

Another long slope, another long way down, another climb. From a patch of woodland outlaws set upon them and another skirmish had to be fought. This latest band were roughs of the lowest class, the sort who now roam side, taking advantage of the disruptions of no traveler was safe from them, and neither Cross nor incantation would ward them off.

Fight and run and fight. Only the fading of the light put an end to it.

Donal Cam drew rein and looked back along the exhausted line. Grateful for any halt, people were collapsing in heaps. They would resent having to get up again, but this was no place for camping; their most recent assailants might return in the night.

Donal Cam rode over to the kerne who knew the area. "Is there a place called Lackeen somewhere near here?"

"Not too far, Commander. We could make it, right enough. There is an old monastery there with another Kennedy castle close by."

"So Father Archer says," Donal Cam confirmed. "And you can lead us to it?"

"I can."

"Then we shall make camp at Lackeen for the night, and since we have done clan Kennedy no harm so far we shall pray they do not molest us now. Tell me one thing more. How far is it to the Shannon?"

The kerne looked up at Donal Cam in the swift-gathering darkness. "A dozen miles or so."

A dozen miles. A dozen miles and they would have reached the border of Munster.

Reluctantly straggling after Donal Cam, the column wound its way down to a boggy valley and a pile of gray stone, the deserted monastery of an order recently fled. There was the familiar forest of gravestones, most of them no more than rough slabs harvested from one piece of earth and set upright in another. Many were splotched with lichens whose phosphorescent glow stood out eerily from the gray rock. A few headstones had been finely dressed, embellished with Celtic crosses, mitred bishops, wheels, spirals, animals, and faces wearing expressions that might have been rapture or madness. The age of a burial could be estimated by the degree to which its headstone had canted to one side or the other, or sunk back into the earth.

The women began preparing a camp which included the walled churchyard. Sleeping on a burial ground no longer bothered the people. Churchyards meant shelter and rest, and graves were merely the shelters of those whose rest would last longer, those whose sleep was more deep.

Donal Cam had just given the chestnut stallion to a horse boy for care when Father Archer came up to him. "Tomorrow is the Feast of the Epiphany," the priest reminded him. "What arrangements do you propose for celebrating the Mass? The door of the church is locked, you will observe."

"Rub his back well with grass," Donal Cam said first to the horse boy. "I thought I felt a bump rising just behind the withers. Ah, Father . . . the . . . Feast?" He gazed distractedly at the Jesuit, trying to gather his thoughts.

"The Feast of the Epiphany," Farther Archer repeated sternly. "You cannot have forgotten."

"Ah. Of course." Donal Cam closed his eyes for a heartbeat and massaged his aching temples. A holy day. Mass. When they were so near the Shannon! When, if they departed at first light, they might actually be out of Munster by midday. Boats! He must send someone ahead to arrange for boats . . .

Father Archer cleared his throat imperiously. "Donal Cam!"

O'Sullivan started to speak; bit off his words. Resentful

words born of weariness and irritation. Do not make me resent my faith, he thought with a flash of anger. Not that, sweet Jesus, not that!

"You shall have your Mass," he assured the Jesuit. More abruptly than he meant to, he turned away from Father Archer and crossed the churchyard to issue orders for the gathering of firewood.

Orla smiled as he approached her. "We have made it this far," she said, smoothing her wild hair with her hands.

"This far," he echoed. "The Kennedys have shown no signs of hostility, so we should take advantage of the opportunity and build fires to warm ourselves and dry our clothes as much as we can. I should think roving bands will not bother us here, so close to a Kennedy keep."

"Could we send someone to them to ask for food?"

Donal Cam stared off into space. "We might as well. But not a soldier, I think—no one threatening. Take several of the women with you—take my uncle's wife, she has a good head on her—and carry a torch so they can see you are only unarmed women."

"Unarmed? I always have a knife in my girdle."

"Keep it there. You are not afraid?" he asked suddenly, his tone perhaps one shade softer.

Orla gave him a sardonic smile. "We are all of us afraid, all day and every day. What does it matter?"

Orla gathered several women of her own station to make up the party. The only civilian was to be Joan Ni Sweney, whose more educated accents would identify her as a woman of rank and entitled to request the hospitality of the local nobility.

Grella Hurley was one of the women Orla asked. Her reply was swift and scathing, born of exhaustion. "Has O'Sullivan taken to sacrificing women openly now?"

The sound of Orla's hand across her face was like a gunshot. Grella staggered backward and sat down, hard.

"Now I know what you are," Orla hissed.

Grella ran to her brother. Ronan was less than sympathetic. "You are a fool. You have brought yourself under suspicion and that was the last thing we needed. Until we make our break I wanted the commander to keep thinking we are as blindly devoted to him as the rest of his people."

"Even his clan are not all loyal to him. Look at his cousin Owen. Or the O'Sullivans who stayed in Beare when he left."

"Clans are rarely loyal to one another," Ronan reminded her. "They roil with feuds and jealousies. But followers by choice have always been a chieftain's treasures and the recipients of his bounty, and I wanted O'Sullivan to keep thinking that way about us . . . at least as long as he still had gold. Now he will wonder."

"Perhaps Orla will say nothing," Grella said hopefully.

"You are doubly a fool. She tells him everything, did you not realize that long ago? I only wish she had hit you harder, knocked some sense into you."

Grella gathered her hurt feelings around herself like a mantle and went to sit alone in a corner of the churchyard, watching with angry, resentful eyes as the fires were built up, and Orla's small party set out for the nearby keep.

"Follow them at a distance, but keep out of sight," Donal Cam quietly ordered Rory O'Sullivan. "And take the musketeers with you."

Joan still felt dazed, as she had since the death of Anne Ni Kelly. Things were happening but she could not make her mind close down on them, understand them. She had been told the purpose of their mission, had agreed to go, even realized that it might be dangerous, but none of it meant anything to her. None of it was real. She walked as in a dream through the darkness, following the smoldering torch Orla held high.

A winding footpath led them to the Kennedy tower house. A lone sentry stood by the door, a gallowglass wearing a mail shirt and holding a halberd at an angle across his chest, the heavy axhead against his shoulder. "What do you want?" he called out as they approached.

"Now, Joan," Orla said in a loud whisper.

Joan Ni Sweney felt her tongue clinging to the roof of her mouth. She was not afraid. She felt nothing. She was simply not present.

"*Now,*" Orla insisted.

"What am I to say?"

"Let your belly speak for you!"

As if responding to Orla's words, Joan's belly awoke and writhed in hunger, dispelling the fog of shock that had cushioned her for hours. "We request food!" she cried out. "We request the hospitality of clan Kennedy, and vow that anyone of that name shall in return request hospitality of clan O'Sullivan whenever they have need!"

The sentry listened impassively to this formal speech. When it was over he said, "Go back where you came from."

"Can you not help us?"

"I have no orders to help you."

"Give us admission, then. Let me speak to your lord."

"He is not here."

"The lady of the . . ."

"She is not here. Go away."

"Is there no one who . . ."

The massive oaken door creaked open a hand's breadth. From inside, a gruff voice called out, "There are nine armed men here. Go away."

Joan's shoulders slumped. She turned to Orla, her face seamed with defeat in the torchlight. "We cannot force them."

Narrowing her eyes, Orla gazed for a long moment at the small castle. "Donal Cam would never have refused aid to people in distress. He did not have to be here, suffering this. The English once accepted him almost as one of theirs, he could have kept his lands and his revenues, but instead . . . ah, no matter. Come. We shall go back."

The wavering torchlight marked their progress back to the abandoned monastery. As they walked, one of the women asked another, "Why did The O'Sullivan give up his security to join the rebellion of the northern princes?"

"I cannot tell you" was the reply, "but I daresay Orla can. Ask her sometime."

In the encampment, people were preparing for the night. Those who had packs or purses searched frantically in the bottoms, along the seams, looking for some crumb of food that might have escaped earlier searches. A bit of overlooked bacon rind was wealth beyond measure.

When Ronan Hurley discovered the bit of rind at the very bottom of the pack tied to his saddle, his first thought was to share it with his sister. Then he remembered how angry he was with Grella. Good enough. The more for me. Turning his back so others would not see what he was doing, he measured the thin strip of meat against his thumb. Almost as long. Wonder of wonders!

His tongue ran over his lips in anticipation. Should he gobble it all down at once, or nibble tiny bites, making it last? He was considering the question with great seriousness when a tiny sound in the vicinity of his ankles made him look down.

A little brindle dog was sitting there, gazing up at him as if he were a god.

"Where did this come from?" Ronan inquired, looking around. But no one claimed the animal; no one seemed to notice it in the firelit dark.

The dog whined and pawed at his leg. Ronan crouched on his heels. "I had a puppy once," he said.

The dog cocked its head.

"Are you a stray like the rest of us?"

The dog cocked its head the other way.

I will hate myself for this, Ronan thought, tearing off a fragment of the rind. He held it out and the dog leaned forward yearningly but did not snatch the morsel. It waited with agonizing patience until it was certain the bite was a gift, then a pink tongue flicked out.

The rind disappeared.

For the first time in days, Ronan Hurley felt warm. Still using his back as a screen to hide his actions, he shared the rind with the dog, bite for bite, until it was gone. Then he held his fingers down for the animal to lick. The dog looked into his face again, wagged its tail, and trotted away.

"If you find anything, remember to share it with me," Ronan called softly after it.

The large campfires cast orange light on the stones, on the trees that stood beyond the churchyard. Most of the refugees were stretched in sleep. Some of the warriors, more accustomed to the rigors of long marches, were still awake, gathered around one of the fires and distracting themselves from the emptiness of their bellies by gambling. Rory O'Sullivan owned his own set of dice, and even a board and some gaming pieces. Others whittled the necessaries from bits of wood. Several games proceeded at once, with the players wagering their shoes, their belts, even themselves, a loser promising to be bondservant to a winner for a specified length of time until the debt was paid.

Niall O'Mahony watched for a while, then looked over to the place where Maire Ni Driscoll lay wrapped in his shaggy mantle. Her head was turned toward him. He could see the sparkle of her eyes in the firelight. He got up and went over to her.

"Can you not sleep?"

"I think I must be too tired to sleep."

"Where is your dog?"

"She went away for a time, but she is back now. Here, under the mantle with me." Maire turned back an edge of the covering to show a pair of bright eyes and two pricked ears peeping out.

"I could play my harp for you, if you would like," Niall said diffidently. "It might help you sleep."

"You did promise," she remembered. "Will it disturb the others?"

The mere question shocked him. "Who is ever disturbed by the harp?"

He took the instrument from its bag while she watched. He found a fallen stone to sit upon as he played, and pressed the harp into his left shoulder. Running experimental fingers over the strings, he listened, pained, to the various discords, then began tuning. The vicissitudes of war and travel had done their damage. Three of the brass strings were missing, and damp and cold and jolting had done damage that could never be undone. But it was still a harp. It had a soul.

At the first sounds, people fell silent. Those who were near sleep opened their eyes. Those who had wandered deeper into oblivion sensed something calling them and hesitated on their way, listening. The gamblers did not stop their games, but even they dispensed with the challenges and insults of their play, and listened.

Some of the refugees, those of the lower classes, had never heard a bardic harp before, though everyone was familiar with the pipe and the bodhran, the goatskin drum. Harps and lutes and recorders made music for the nobility.

Noble survivors no matter what their social station, the remaining followers of O'Sullivan Beare lay at their ease in Lackeen churchyard and listened to Niall play.

Superhuman effort was necessary for a warrior to keep the long fingernails needed for harp playing, but Niall still had most of his. As they plucked the strings the voice of the harp came sweet and clear, bell-like, yet with an added richness reminiscent of the lute. To impress Maire with his lively fingering Niall began with a sprightly air. His head drooped forward, his eyes closed to see the shape of the music.

As he played, Niall was no longer a fugitive being led to an uncertain fate by a man with a price on his head. The harp transported both harper and audience to a different world, where women were as fair as swans and men had the faces of eagles, a place illumined by exquisite craftsmanship and bardic competitions and just judgments and ferocious, stylized battles between celebrated heroes. Theirs was a time shaped by the leisurely rhythms of pastoral existence, a time of abundance and freedom. The savage gentle lazy vigorous wild uniquely civilized world of the Gael, now lost forever yet still trapped in the strings of a harp.

The listeners sat transfixed as Niall played one melody after another, gay dances and stately slow airs. Then one melody sweeter than the rest seduced a sleeping voice.

Maire Ni Driscoll closed her eyes and began to sing. "The Blackbird of Beare," someone whispered.

Her voice was purer than the harp. The faces of her audience were naked with emotion as Maire filled the valley with a lament for Richard Mac Geoghegan.

Niall played on, supporting her with his harp. No one noticed the tears seeping from beneath his eyelids.

Listening to their music, suddenly Donal Cam remembered the smell of his wife's hair.

Day Seven

January 6, 1603. *Baile Achadh Caoin*, Town of the Smooth
Field, also known as Lackeen, Small Stones

The day dawned gray and bitterly cold, but dry. The
air smelled of the night's campfires. Donal Cam
opened his eyes. Time to be up and moving, he thought.
In just one more minute. His eyes drifted shut again.

For no particular reason he found himself thinking of
summer nights, of languorous warmth as palpable as a
weight pressing against his body. Of moist air scented
green, and random lust heavy and hot. The flesh of
women was luminous in summer moonlight. Their eyes
had reflected only him.

Apple-bosomed women. Light-footed women. Orla
when she was young, a sturdy doorful of a woman, rak-
ing his back with her fingernails.

This ash-smelling morning he could not imagine lying
with a woman. It was as if the sap and semen had dried
up in him.

He arose with an effort. The O'Connor Kerry had occupied the tent alone last night. Donal Cam had chosen

to sleep under the sky, for no reason he could name. He was, in retrospect, surprised. How long has it been, he wondered, since I did something out of impulse?

Moving quietly, he slipped away to relieve himself and rinse his face in a rivulet beyond the monastery walls. As he returned he could hear the murmur of voices; the two Jesuits preparing for the Mass. Epiphany.

Feast of the Manifestation of Christ.

Christ appear to me now. Please. Give me some sign that I have done the right thing!

His personal necessities were in a pack tied by thongs to the rounded cantle of his padded saddle. Taking one of his razors from its gilded leather case, he tested the blade against his thumb. Dull. And no attendant hovering at his elbow with a sharpening stone and a basin of heated water. With a barely repressed sigh he fumbled deeper in the pack, found a small stropping leather, and applied it vigorously while staring off into space with unfocused eyes.

For Donal Cam the act of shaving had become a ritual of extraordinary significance, the symbol of still having some control over his life and his person. On the day they left Doire na Fola he had arisen and shaved at three in the morning, when he was no longer able to lie still and pretend to himself that he could sleep.

The razor dragged across his bony face, leaving his cheeks bare without nicking his narrow mustache, or the small beard that hid the cleft in his chin. His toilet completed, he arranged his face in lines of authority and prepared to meet whatever the day might bring. Donal Cam O'Sullivan Beare, Lord Commander of the Munster Irish Field and Garrison Forces since the departure of Hugh O'Neill for Ulster.

His first orders of the new day were addressed to Ronan Hurley. "Take two fast horses and your best man, and ride to the Shannon. I need you there and back as soon as possible, so start while we attend Mass. Arrange boats for us with every ferryman you can find."

Carefully keeping his voice uninflected, Ronan replied, "I shall need gold to pay them, Commander."

For a moment he thought Donal Cam would give it to him. In his mind he was already telling Grella, sneaking a horse away for her, arranging to lose his companion and meet her . . .

"I think not," said Donal Cam. "The land is crawling with outlaws, you could be robbed on the way. Tell the ferrymen we will pay them handsomely when we arrive, and an additional payment on the other side of the river. Go now. That kerne of Burke's can tell you the best way, and we shall follow your tracks as soon as we can."

A muscle twitched at the corner of Ronan's left eye. He dared not betray himself with a second request for gold. But once the column reached the river there would undoubtedly be mass confusion, loading the boats. He and Grella could make their break then . . .

Orla stood at a distance, watching Donal Cam talk to his captain of cavalry. Her brow was furrowed.

A few paces farther on, her husband watched her. Then Donal Cam looked up and met his eyes. Rory O'Sullivan went to the commander for his own orders.

"We must move out directly after Mass," Donal Cam told him. "Advise your men to be particularly watchful. We are losing more people every day. Give the buannachta orders to watch for any who leave the group for whatever reason. If they are civilians and genuinely want to go, let them, but try to ascertain how they intend to survive on their own."

"We cannot give them supplies, we have no food left ourselves."

"We will forage again when we can, but right now I just want to get out of Munster. Give your orders to your men now, even before they go to Mass."

Rory hurried away.

Unquestioning obedience had served him well. His father had been a very minor O'Sullivan, a poor relation on the outer fringes of Owen O'Sullivan's circle. Rory in his youth had been witness to the final stages of the feud that tore the clan apart. His family had observed it with obsessive interest, not only as a source of gossip and drama but also because self-interest lay in supporting the eventual winner.

The seeds of dissension had been sown as early as 1549, when *Diarmuid Ua Suileabhain*, Dermod O'Sullivan, then chieftain of Beare and Bantry, had been blown up in a gunpowder explosion. As the first of his race to die in this spectacular fashion he was posthumously entitled Dermod of the Powder. Under English law, succession passed to the eldest son. But Gaelic law was different. Life in Ireland was often violent, and no chieftain could be certain of living long enough to pass his title to a grown son. Therefore a younger brother or some other suitable clan member was appointed as their *tanaiste*, or successor.

The tanaiste of Dermod of the Powder was his brother *Amlaibh*, Awley. Unfortunately Awley was not a popular choice, and he was slain while attempting to take control of Dunboy after Dermod's death. At that time Dermod's eldest son, a boy of twelve called Donal, was in Waterford, where he was held hostage by the English to guarantee the obedience of his father to the Crown. Upon learning of Awley's death the English released young Donal to become head of clan O'Sullivan, because he had been under their influence long enough to become

Anglicized. His mastery of written and spoken English was exemplary. They felt they could control him.

This Donal, however, died abruptly before reaching the age of thirty. He had not yet named his tanaiste. His young son, Donal Cam, was only three, so a hurried conference of clan elders appointed Donal Cam's uncle Owen as chieftain.

While Donal Cam was growing to manhood, and following in his father's footsteps as a scholar of English, Owen O'Sullivan ruled Beare and Bantry. When the sparks of the Desmond Rebellion flared, he refused to take sides as the Old Foreigners rose against the New Foreigners. The New Foreigners promptly seized Owen and jailed him in Dublin as a man of questionable loyalty to the Crown.

Young Donal Cam took advantage of the vacuum in leadership to press his own claims, not under the Gaelic law of tanistry, but under the English law of succession. As he pointed out in English court, he was the eldest son of Donal who had been eldest son of Dermod of the Powder.

After two years he won his case. He also won the undying enmity of Owen O'Sullivan.

Now the son of that Owen, another Owen O'Sullivan, was fighting on the English side. He had been one of those who captured and destroyed Dunboy, in fact. Now Carew was calling him Lord of Beare and Bantry, though in truth power in Munster resided with the Crown since Kinsale.

Rory O'Sullivan's father had remained loyal to the line of Owen throughout this increasingly bitter dispute. But young Rory had been impressed by the dashing Donal Cam, who in his English velvets and plumed hats had looked like someone from a superior species altogether. Running away from home, Rory had presented himself to Donal Cam and offered his hand and sword in unswerving obedience.

His eventual rewards had been the leadership of the O'Sullivan buannachta and the hand of Orla Ni Donoghue.

The intent of this second reward was open to question. In the years since his marriage, Rory had often wondered whether Donal Cam had given him Orla to get rid of her or to keep her close.

He could never decide.

Three of her brothers and a number of her cousins served under him, but they would not have told him even if his pride had allowed him to ask them. They were as devoted to Orla as she was to Donal Cam.

"Are you not coming to Mass?" Joan Ni Sweney asked Orla, noticing the woman standing apart from the river of people flowing toward the carved wooden altar within the abandoned monastery church. There was a time when a woman of Joan's rank would not have spoken to a soldier's woman, but the trials the refugees had shared had long since broken down social distinctions.

"I shall be in soon; you go ahead," Orla replied, her eyes searching the crowd.

"Come now, it will be a hasty service, I fear. A pity. I used to so enjoy *Nollaig na mBan*." The Women's Christmas, a name applied to the Epiphany because its festive meal was traditionally of daintier foods than those served on Christmas Day.

Orla watched Joan hurry into the church. The most devout, which included the women, crowded as close as they could to the altar, leaving an overflow that remained in the churchyard beyond, able to hear the service through the open doorway. Everyone attended, though as usual, not everyone paid attention to the service. The usual percentage of men stood with folded arms and blank eyes, waiting with the stolidity of oxen until their duty was done.

Orla stood with them; like them. But her eyes were not blank. Once Donal Cam entered the church, she kept them fixed on the doorway waiting for him to emerge again.

"No feast tonight," a gallowglass standing near her remarked under his breath. "We had no Christmas feast either."

"More than we will have today, though," said a pikeman on his left. "We do not even have the oats for the candles, or we could eat those." He referred to the Epiphany custom of setting a dozen lit candles in a sieve of oats, with a larger candle burning in the center, to represent Christ and his apostles bringing light to the world.

"I could even eat the candles," a third man chimed in. No one laughed; they knew he meant what he said.

Lackeen was behind them; the Shannon lay ahead. The column moved sluggishly through the thick, cold air of a freezing January day. In the lead, two of Rory O'Sullivan's best scouts were following the hoofprints of the cavalry horses that had departed at a hard gallop even before Mass.

On the fringes of the column, two horse boys walked together. They had been in charge of pack animals, when there were pack animals. More recently Ronan had preempted them as cavalry attendants. Once a Gaelic cavalry boasted almost as many foot soldiers as horsemen. Riders were of the noble class, they must have servants and attendants to lead their extra horses and shield bearers on hand with extra weapons.

O'Sullivan's cavalry was fortunate merely to have a dozen horses left and enough men to ride them. Nor was Ronan happy about the quality of the two lads he had impressed into his service. Baggage boys were a distinctly lower class than the attendants he had enjoyed.

The lads were no more fond of him than he of them. "Did you see the way he galloped off?" Thady Cooney inquired of Peadar O'Coughlan. "Lashing that horse already, he was. The next time we see it the beast will be so jaded it will look fit to die. Who will be blamed? We will."

Peadar nodded agreement. "Last night he accused me in front of everyone of letting the horses lose flesh. Lose flesh! And the weight falling off them from the hard going, not from the feeding. As if we had any grain to give them."

"Horses arc bound to lose flesh when they can only eat what grass they can snatch in winter," Thady observed. "My old fellow would weep to see the condition of these animals."

"Your father was a good man with a horse, would you say?"

"He was that. Responsible for the entire stables of Mac Carthy Mor, he was. Once."

Peadar had heard this story before. He grunted noncommittally to show that he was listening and let his friend think he was believing what he heard.

"Why, none of the Mac Carthys would so much as sit on a horse without getting my old fellow's opinion of its quality," Thady went on, expanding on his theme. "A fine rider himself, he was. Taught me everything I know."

"Is that a fact." Peadar contrived to sound impressed. As he knew full well, Thady had never been on a horse in his life. Neither of them had. Being horse boy to a baggage animal placed one firmly on the lowest rung of society.

"If your father was a favorite of the Mac Carthys, why are you with The O'Sullivan now?" Peadar could not resist asking.

"Ah. Indeed. The wars, you know." Thady gave an expressive shrug and rolled his eyes. He was sixteen, with jug-handle ears and a bony, freckled face.

"Mmmm." Peadar knew. He was also sixteen, equally bony, distinguished only by a mop of Norse-silver hair. "War and war. I suppose there was something else sometime, but I do not remember it."

"War and war," Thady echoed. "My old fellow had a cabin built of sods. Warm enough it was, when the good smoke filled it. We had a pig. Sometimes a cow. Then the English came through. Killed the cow, stole the pig, pulled our cabin down. Burned the woods so we could not hide in them. Killed my old fellow, God have mercy on his soul."

"God have mercy on his soul," Peadar responded automatically. His own story was not very different.

"Why do they do it, do you suppose?" Thady asked.

"Who? The English?"

"Indeed."

"I could not be telling you. But I am not one to understand the ways of great lords."

"Are they great lords, the English?"

"They say they are."

"As great as The O'Sullivan, do you think?"

A light leapt in the eyes below the mop of silvery hair. "No one is as great as The O'Sullivan, Thady. No one save only The Lord Christ Himself and His Blessed Mother, may She pray for us.

"When all my family was killed except for me and my baby sister, The O'Sullivan found us, fed us, gave me work to do so I could hold up my head like a man. I would call him great before anyone, so I would."

"Where is your sister now?"

"After Kinsale, when we knew the English were killing

women and children, The O'Sullivan himself came to me." Peadar knew that sounded like Thady's bragging, but in his case it was the truth. "He told me he was sending some children out of Munster to safety, on a boat. He wanted to know if I would like to send my little sister with them. I said I did, and he took her. She is alive now, somewhere, beyond the reach of the English. And I would fight for that man with the last drop of blood that's in me."

Thady said, "A pity it is he could not send all the children out of Munster."

"A pity indeed," his companion agreed. "But I suppose there were not enough boats. How many people can you put on a boat?"

"Thousands. Thousands and thousands. My old fellow told me. He knew boats. Did I ever tell you about how he sailed for the O'Driscolls?"

"You did," Peadar assured Thady. "But I can always hear it again. We have a long day ahead of us."

To accompany him on his mission, Ronan had taken Liam O'Donoghue, a son of O'Donoghue of the Glen. Liam was an able horseman and a bold fighter; at Kinsale he had been one of the last of the Gaelic cavalry to give way to the English.

Riding hard, the two men saw within an hour the broad expanse of the Shannon, gray and sullen in the distance under lowering skies. Ronan drew rein. "There it is. Now which way did that Connachtman say to go from here?"

"North. Before long we should be able to see some sort of smoke from the settlement on the riverbank where the ferryboats are kept."

They soon saw the smoke, but as they galloped toward

it, they could see no boats. Even at a distance it was obvious that the shoreline was empty of them. Ronan cursed under his breath and pushed his horse harder. It was starting to rain again.

They thundered into the tiny village that had grown up around the ferry. Before they could even dismount, armed men emerged from the houses and sheds. "Are you O'Sullivan's men?" one of them called. His tone was not welcoming.

Ronan darted a quick glance at Liam, and saw the other man's face tighten in anticipation of trouble. "We are. I am Ronan Hurley, captain of the cavalry of Munster, and . . ."

"We know who you are. We have instructions about you."

"From whom?"

"From the lord president of Munster. Give no aid to the fugitive rebels and O'Sullivan Beare, we were told."

"But . . ."

"There is a price on his head, you know," the man went on. "Is he with you?"

"I never said we were with him," Ronan retorted.

"You are, though."

"You leap to a conclusion. We are two men looking for a boat across the river."

"We have no boats."

"But you are a ferryman, are you not? And that shed is a boatbuilding shed?"

"I am, it is. We have no boats. They have all been sent to the other side of the river, beyond your reach."

Ronan ground his teeth together in frustration. "We could pay you well!"

"Show me your gold!" a second man called out, but the first who had spoken to them rounded on him.

"Gold will not buy us, it would be worth our lives to help them. Remember what happened to those people at Doire na Fola?"

Ronan felt a cold chill run down his spine. "What people at Doire na Fola?"

The ferryman turned back to him. "A bloody tale, that is. We just heard it ourselves, from the same messenger who brought us our orders. That is his horse over there, gaunted from the gallop."

"I am not interested in your gaunted horses," Ronan growled. "Tell me about Doire na Fola."

The ferryman, whose bulbous, blue-veined nose looked like an overfed rodent peering over the brush of his mustache, gazed at Ronan with the satisfaction of a man delivering bad news. "As I am sure you know, O'Sullivan left the wounded and weak in a forest while he made his escape. It was a ruse to convince the English he was still there himself, but after four days the English officer in charge became suspicious and stormed the forest. When he realized how he had been tricked he killed everyone O'Sullivan had left behind. Chopped them and sliced them," the ferryman elaborated with evident relish.

"If you think we would help you after hearing that," he went on, "you are mad. Ride back to wherever O'Sullivan is hiding and tell him there are no boats for him anywhere on this river, the word has gone out. Donncha MacEgan, the queen's sheriff at Redwood Castle, issued the order himself. You will find no one willing to defy him, not for a tribe of southerners who are nothing to us."

The man squinted up at Ronan. "You could save yourselves, though. There is said to be a reward for anyone willing to desert O'Sullivan and tell the English of his plans."

Ronan regretted that he had not come alone. He could feel Liam's eyes on him.

"We are honorable men," Liam said after a moment, "and loyal. Donal Cam has given up everything, fighting for us, and we will not betray him."

The ferryman looked at him almost pityingly. "You are dead and do not know it. O'Sullivan has no chance, and if you stay with him, neither do you. Give up now and be done with it."

"We are fighting for you too!" Liam cried. "Do you not understand? Do you want to be no more than a vassal to the Sasanach?"

"What difference does it make? I have been what you call a vassal all my life anyway, at the service of whoever has the gold or the power. What difference does it make to me if the hand holding the purse is Gaelic or English?"

Ronan found himself losing his temper. He had never expected to agree with Donal Cam, not after all that had happened, but he shouted at the ferryman, "The English are taking our *land*, you fool. Our *land*! Does *that* not matter?"

The ferryman gave him a blank look. "I own no land. What I have, I rent. The only thing that is mine is the river, because no man can own a river."

"Liam," Ronan said in a clipped tone. When O'Donoghue met his eyes, he gave the briefest of nods in the direction they had come, then reined his horse around and set off at a gallop.

Liam followed at once.

Over the pounding of their horses' hooves they heard the ferryman shouting after them, "You are fools! You are dead men!"

At one time the chestnut stallion Donal Cam was riding had been sleek and well-muscled. Now he was thin, with deep hollows between his ribs and hipbones as sharp as Muskerry peaks. He was covering more ground than any other horse on the march as Donal Cam rode up and down the column, trying to keep his people together. Without constant herding they soon straggled out over a mile or more, easy prey to whoever might attack them next.

Donal Cam appreciated fine horses and had habitually treated them well. When he allowed himself to think of An Cearc, he still felt a swift spasm of grief. But he could no longer afford kindness. Had it been his beloved An Cearc beneath him he would have driven the animal as hard. Everything had become subservient to the desperate need to escape Munster and Carew; to reach the north.

At the point where he intended to cross the Shannon they would enter the southeast corner of Connacht. The province of Connacht had endured several changes of governorship under Elizabeth. Bingham, Conyers, and now Lambert had served in turn, each struggling to subdue the wild west.

But as every Irish person knew, the true ruler of Connacht—at least of its heart—was the female pirate, Grace O'Malley.

Grace 'Malley, *Granuaille*, had been a friend to Red Hugh O'Donnell early in his rebellion against the English. She had run guns for him and supplied him with fighting men. Their friendship had curdled, however, when The O'Donnell failed to support the political aims of her son, Theobald Burke, who sought to succeed to his father's title as chieftain of the Burkes of Mayo.

Now Theobald fought with the English, though it was said Granuaille remained unshakably Gaelic. She was an old woman, the same age as Elizabeth Tudor, and had devoted her life to defending Connacht against English domination. In her territory Donal Cam hoped to find some fresh support. Had he stayed east of the Shannon, on a more direct route to O'Rourke in Leitrim, he would have been leading his followers into some of the best-fortified English holdings in Ireland.

An tSionainn. The Shannon. The river had become a mighty symbol to him. Donal Cam had waited with barely concealed impatience through Mass that Epiphany morning, all his concentration on the Shannon. The west. The Gaelic west.

"I can almost smell the river already," he remarked now to his uncle, who was walking near him.

"It smells wet," said Dermod. "But everything smells wet. The rain is bucketing down."

It was indeed; so hard that at first Donal Cam did not hear the rattle of gunfire behind him. When he did he groaned audibly, spun his horse on its haunches, and galloped back to find yet another skirmish, another small but wearying battle to be fought with another band of local people anxious to do the refugees some injury they could boast of afterward, to court the favor of the Sasanach.

In Ronan Hurley's absence Donal Cam commanded his few cavalrymen himself and soon drove the attackers away. But the effort told on him. Every effort told on him now. He could feel it not only in the cumulative weariness of his body, but in the increasing depression of his spirit.

I cannot give in, he kept saying to himself. What will become of us if I give in?

The Shannon, the Shannon. Somehow it will be better once we cross the Shannon.

Then he saw Ronan and Liam riding toward him through the rain. Their exhausted horses were giving off clouds of steam.

"Have we boats arranged?" he asked eagerly, trotting forward to meet them.

"Boats!" Ronan drew rein, worked his mouth trying to make enough saliva to spit, gave up the effort. "There are no boats. By order of the queen's sheriff they have been removed, and any aid to us is forbidden."

Donal Cam looked at Ronan as if he did not understand. He was, in fact, trying not to understand. "No boats?" he repeated numbly.

"I said that. I told you."

Liam O'Donoghue urged his horse closer to Donal Cam's. "That is not the worst of it, Commander," he said softly, not wanting others to hear.

"What could be worse?"

"Doire na Fola."

Donal Cam went rigid on his horse. *I do not want to hear this. Take me somewhere else. Strike me dead with lightning, but do not make me listen to what this man is about to say.*

"Wilmot killed them all," Liam reported, his voice choked with emotion. "He cut them down as soon as he found them."

"The . . . the men who had been wounded defending our creaght? Those . . . those brave warriors?"

"Everybody. Sick, weak, everybody." Liam bowed his head, his throat closed with grief.

"Wilmot waited four days," Ronan added. "So with their lives they bought us four days. That was your plan, was it not, Commander? To spend other people's lives to save your own?"

Looking with dazed eyes at Ronan Hurley, Donal Cam recognized the expression on the other man's face.

He hates me.

The realization was like a cold hand squeezing his heart.

Then the other image cut through, obliterating everything else. Doire na Fola. Of all the terrors, and all the horrors, this was the worst . . .

He could see it. As clearly as if he stood in the Oakwood of Blood, he could see the slaughter Wilmot had perpetrated there.

With all the strength he had, he tried to keep his face impassive. Do not admit the pain, he warned himself. Do not let it take root in you or it will break you . . .

There was a stone in his throat like an unborn sob, choking him.

Everyone was looking at him. He could feel sweat spurting on his forehead in spite of the cold. The promise of pain twisted in his gut, trying to tear loose and devour him.

Do not break. You must not break. If you are broken you cannot help them, cannot get anyone to safety, cannot . . .

Cannot . . .

Doire na Fola. The old and the wounded, weltering in their own blood.

Donal Cam clenched his fists so hard the nails cut through his palms, leaving bleeding stigmata, but the pain was not enough to offset the other pain. Pains. All the griefs, losses, tragedies that rose up like an army of ghosts in his mind and gibbered at him. A man tumbling down a mountainside, too weak to save himself, dying, gone . . . a wizened, emaciated child frowning its way into death . . . a burned-out cabin, a bloody battlefield . . . a people destroyed because someone else wanted their land.

His people, destroyed.

As so often before, Donal Cam's mind addressed its maker, the God who was supposed to be watching and ordering the universe.

I am just a man, Donal Cam reminded that listening omnipotence. I made the best decision I could.

I have done my best! he longed to howl at the heavens in tortured protest against the blind injustice that kept a man's best from being good enough.

But he could not allow himself to howl publicly at the heavens. He could not even sit crying on his horse, like Liam O'Donoghue. People were watching their commander. They would take strength—or weakness—from him. Donal Cam must lock his emotions behind a rigidly controlled face, clinging to that control as the only surety he possessed, his only armor against chaos.

People were watching him. How many like Ronan blamed him? How many hated him? How many might be watching for a chance to exact retribution? For a moment he could almost feel a knife in his back.

Nothing he might say or do would ever mitigate Doira na Fola. Yet there had been no option.

There have always been few choices, he thought wearily; few choices and a terrible inevitability. We have been driven like cattle who, no matter which way they turn, have but one destiny. The slaughter pen. So far I have avoided the slaughter pen, at least for some of us—but for how much longer?

Only one decision of mine ever really made a difference. That first one, to join the rebellion. To sacrifice the security of English support and take up arms to chase the chimera of Gaelic freedom.

Chimera—was it a chimera, a mythic dream? Was it lost long before we ever began? Was it lost when Dermot MacMurrough invited the first English warriors into Ireland? From that moment were we doomed to eternal domination?

"No!" he cried aloud. Only when he heard the echoes of his voice did Donal Cam realize his thoughts had surfaced on their own. People really were staring at him now.

"You said something, Commander?" Ronan Hurley asked with the coldness of perfect hatred.

Donal Cam scrabbled frantically inside his head, seeking an explanation. "I said no, Ronan. It was never my intention to spend anyone else's life to save my own."

With his mask stripped from him, Ronan plunged on. "What about Dunboy? You knew Carew meant to mount a massive attack on Dunboy, yet you left at the last moment. Left others to die while you were safe at Ardea. I had brothers who died for you!"

With a mighty effort, Donal Cam kept his face as set as stone. It was hard to move his lips enough to speak. "I will not justify myself to you, Hurley. You do not know everything. And this is neither the time nor the place to have this conversation."

"You do not want it brought out in the open, do you? You are afraid of what . . ."

"I am afraid of what will happen to these people if we do not get out of Munster," Donal Cam interrupted him. "That is my only consideration now. Every moment you waste shouting at me could be costing lives. If you want to make a formal accusation against me, do it when we reach Leitrim. I shall make it easy for you. We can have a Brehon judge in the hall of O'Rourke's castle and you can put me on trial before him if that is what you want."

"Gaelic law. I should think you would want English law, it served you well before," Ronan replied contemptuously.

Without even realizing he was doing it Donal Cam hurled himself from his horse. He had a sensation of flying through the air, and then his fingers were clamped like iron on Ronan Hurley's body and he was dragging the other man off his horse. They hit the ground with a bone-jarring thud, Donal Cam on top.

Donal Cam was older, thinner, worn by his days, but his explosion of rage gave him a strength Ronan Hurley could not match. When the nearest men recovered from their astonishment long enough to pull the two fighters apart, Ronan had obviously got the worst of it. His eyes were unfocused, blood was trickling from a bitten tongue, and he kept pressing his hands to his belly.

Panting, Donal Cam stepped back and shook off the restraining hands. "I will not hit him again. I would not touch him for Patrick's own crozier."

His hands were shaking and he could feel tremors running up the long muscles inside his thighs. He walked over to his horse and, unaided, mounted, though it cost him an effort. He did not look in Ronan's direction again. He turned the horse's head toward the west and called out, in as strong a voice as he could manage, "We are going on to the Shannon now!"

There was nothing else to be done. There was no choice.

Even though they were going toward the river, the column still seemed to be climbing. It was as if their entire journey was an endless struggle uphill. Some were praying. Some were weeping.

The dead of Doire na Fola walked with them.

The rain eased and the clouds temporarily lifted, allowing a pallid sun to give a spurious impression of warmth. The refugees slogged their way across wet fields fringed with alder and hazel. In this region much of the primeval forest had vanished. Land had been parceled out in huge blocks to various favorites of the queen, and the timber felled to provide an endless stream of raw material for the English manufacture of ships, houses, barrel staves, charcoal. The remaining Gaelic population was learning the painful lessons of reduced subsistence on minimal resources.

The column wound past a neglected farmyard where one scrawny rooster was crowing valiantly, though his hens had long since gone into the cooking pot. One of the kernes caught Rory O'Sullivan's eye. "Shall we take him?"

Rory gave the creature a pitying look. "Leave him be," he ordered, though he could not have said why.

Rory's wife walked to one side of the column, among the buannachta. Orla preferred the company of men. She was currently walking beside Con O'Murrough, one of the ablest of O'Sullivan's musketeers—a man whose condition Orla was assessing with a professional eye.

Musketeers need not be as tall as pikemen, but were strongly built and affected a certain swagger befitting their status. O'Murrough had lost his swagger on the march. He had also lost his *giolla*, or attendant, in an early skirmish. In an army at full strength the attendants carried the heavy weaponry for their warriors. Now, like many others, O'Murrough had to struggle on his own beneath the weight of musket, ammunition, mail shirt, backpack, dagger and shortsword, and the wooden support upon which the musket was braced when firing. The support was being pressed into service as a makeshift crutch. O'Murrough's feet were badly swollen and blood was seeping through the dirty cloths wrapped around them.

"I told you," Orla was saying, "that you should not cut off your boots."

"I had to, I could not walk otherwise."

"When we reach the river I shall put some salve on your feet."

The musketeer summoned a ghost of a grin. "Make it something with enough grease in it to allow me to walk on water. That is the only way we can get across the Shannon."

"We will get across," she assured him.

"You heard what they said. No boats."

"Do you think the commander brought us this far to be turned back so easily? You should know him better than that, Con. He will find boats," Orla insisted with a confidence she did not feel.

Her last glimpse of Donal Cam had shown her a man with the life seemingly drained out of him; a husk of a man with burning eyes. The news of Doire na Fola had shattered him. His indomitable will had brought them this far; what if his will was failing now?

Orla gave the musketeer a last pat on the arm to keep him going, then slanted across the line of march, lengthening her stride to get nearer the front of the column. Donal Cam rode in the lead, slouched in the saddle, the reins dangling from his fingers. No one was walking beside him. He occupied the center of empty space, as if shunned.

Her heart went out to him. With an effort Orla lengthened her stride again, came abreast of the chestnut stallion. She looked up at Donal Cam and willed him to notice her, but he did not. He was staring ahead, his thoughts far away.

An unaccustomed impulse made Orla run her fingers through her wild hair, trying to smooth it. Her fingertips grazed her chapped cheeks, then moved upward, exploring the deep wrinkles fanning out from the corners of her eyes; the vertical lines carved deep between her eyebrows.

Badges of service, she thought. In every weather. Squinting through the rain or the gunsmoke, watching for him. Frowning with worry about him. Honora has no lines in her face. Never in that woman's life has her forehead been furrowed by a thought, Orla assured herself with contempt.

"Commander?" she said formally.

Donal Cam pulled himself back from whatever far realm he occupied and looked down at Orla. She was hardly recognizable as a woman, filthy as they all were, clothed in an assortment of genderless rags. He knew her by her untamed hair and her untamable eyes. "What is it, Orla?"

"I just thought . . ." she hesitated. "I just thought I would be proud to walk with you a while."

Her face, like his, gave nothing away; did not acknowledge loneliness or ostracism or the desperation of their situation. Orla's eyes simply assured Donal Cam that she was with him.

He resumed gazing ahead. Orla fell into step beside his horse, which was not difficult since the animal was barely plodding along. Out of the corner of her eye she observed that Donal Cam was sitting unevenly in the saddle with one shoulder higher than the other. More than anything, this told her his state of mind. Usually he held himself as erect as a pine tree, determinedly giving the lie to the nickname he had borne since childhood: Donal *Cam*, Donal the Crooked. He must be beyond weariness to allow a slight natural curvature of the spine to overcome his iron self-discipline.

He needs me, she told herself.

As if he heard her thoughts, the man on the horse said in a low voice meant only for Orla's ears, "You still believe in me?"

"Of course."

"Why?"

Startled by the bluntness of the question, she looked up and met his dark eyes. In them she read an anguished need to find some reason to believe in himself.

At that moment Orla regretted not being an educated woman like Honora, with a polished tongue and clever phrases at her command. But Honora was not here. Orla was. Honora could not help her husband now. Orla could. Would. Somehow. She knotted her fists with the effort to organize her thoughts while searching her knowledge of the man to determine what he most needed to hear. An affirmation of blind faith would be no good to him, might even put more pressure on him.

"I believe in you," Orla said slowly, "because you are the most intelligent man I ever met."

His eyes held and searched hers. Betrayal, or the expectation of betrayal, had become a constant; if he had seen the slightest indication of mockery on Orla's face or heard it in her words . . . but there was none. He found only sincerity.

Orla saw something deep inside him relax; that very relaxation conversely straightened his spine.

She looked away from him then, fixing her gaze on the muddy track winding toward the unseen river. Somewhere above her head she heard Donal Cam say, as if making a discovery, "*What* you believe is not as important as the fact that you *do* believe."

They went on toward the Shannon. No further words passed between them.

Some paces back, Rory O'Sullivan observed his wife walking beside the commander's horse. So did his second-in-command, his cousin, Maurice O'Sullivan. Maurice nudged the man walking next to him and indicated the pair with a surreptitious nod. Rory noticed the gesture out of the corner of his eye and frowned. He felt like a man who had received a thousand tiny cuts from a thousand tiny knives. Each one stung; none by itself was sufficient to kill him.

Father John Collins also observed Orla and Donal Cam together, her shoulder almost touching his thigh as he rode, a space separating them from everyone else. The

Jesuit pursed his lips thoughtfully, speculating on human nature. Passions did not interest him except as they applied to his own passion, history. But each item he discovered about the circumstances surrounding the recent tumultuous events and the participants in those events was being fitted into an elaborate pattern in his mind. The construction of that pattern had become the lifeline to which he clung through progressively more dreadful days.

"A mosaic," he now mused aloud.

"What?" Father Archer, walking nearby, gave him a quizzical look.

Flustered, Father Collins said hastily, "I was thinking of history, James. Thinking of it as being one huge picture made of thousands of tiny colored tiles, like the mosaics one finds in Spanish palaces. Each little piece is necessary to the whole, to an understanding of what it means. I enjoy putting the bits together to see how they fit."

Father Archer said coldly, "To what purpose?"

"Why . . . to satisfy my own curiosity, I suppose."

"An honest answer, but it does you no credit to admit mere selfish gratification. If you intended to teach history, or to write a book . . ."

"I would like to teach," Father Collins asserted. "The children of these very people around us are losing their patrimony, James. Someday those who survive will want to know why, and how it happened. I could tell them. The O'Sullivan children—those now safely in Spain and those who may someday shelter there—I could explain to them . . ."

The other Jesuit's voice cut across his. "I shall explain to the O'Sullivan children anything they may need to know." His words were rimed with frost, and the icy stare Father Archer turned upon Father Collins was a warning of territory not to be invaded.

Father Collins accepted the verbal chastisement without responding. A flash of inspiration revealed the older man's possessiveness to be an important theme in the mosaic: the desire to control.

Some men, discovering that the larger events were beyond their ability to dictate, became obsessively concerned with the pettier details of existence. How would a man like Father Archer—proud, authoritarian, convinced of his own rightness—cope with the relentless destruction of Catholic Gaelic Ireland? He would, Father Collins saw, fight like a tiger to maintain control over his own diminishing patch. He might say anything, do anything, to maintain for himself the illusion of still being in control of something . . . of someone . . .

Ah. Once again Father Collins pursed his lips thoughtfully. Another piece of the mosaic slipped into place in his mind. Someday, he told himself, I must ask someone who was there—though not Father Archer, obviously—about what happened at . . .

The priest's reverie was interrupted by shouts, curses, gunfire, a groan of despair, and then the fugitives were running again, stumbling again, fighting again, struggling on and on, endlessly persecuted.

Toward the Shannon.

Day Eight

January 7, 1603. *Poll na gCapaill*, the Hollow of the Horses

Dermod O'Sullivan came awake abruptly to find himself lying on wet leaves beside an old woman who snored. He lay awhile wondering where they were. Then he remembered.

The last pursuers of yesterday had driven the refugees into one of the few remaining stands of forest on the east bank of the Shannon that was large enough to hide them. In a loop of land between the Shannon and the Brosna river, a wet cold place that smelled of rotting wood and diluvial mud, they had at last found shelter.

A few people were reluctantly stirring, a sentry coughed and hawked phlegm, but for the most part the camp was still asleep. The lack of wind told Dermod it was the hour before dawn. His mouth tasted of fear and hunger.

"Joan?" He put one hand on her shoulder and was shocked by her boniness.

"Mmmm. Mmmm?"

"Stay here, I shall come back for you." Dermod tried to

get up but his legs refused. He sat for a moment, listening to the hammering of his heart and exploring his remaining teeth with his tongue. He was not encouraged to discover that most of his teeth rocked in his shrinking gums.

He tried once more to stand up, and this time succeeded by dint of clambering onto all fours first, like an infant.

When he put out one hand it touched a tree less than a pace in front of him. Dense woodland, the fugitive's friend. It had become a war of frontier and forest, with the New English determined to "tame" the frontier and destroy the Irish forest as fast as they could.

Dermod made his way among the trees like a blind man, relying upon touch as much as upon sight. When his groping fingers encountered the groping fingers of someone coming the other way through the underbrush he jumped back with a cry of surprise.

"O'Sullivan of Dursey?" asked a voice he knew.

Peering through the gloom, Dermod recognized a man with whom he had once done considerable business. "O'Houlihan. How goes it with you?"

"I survive. But my wife . . ."

"I heard."

The two men lowered their eyes in respect. Sheer repetition had robbed death of its power to awe; now it was granted no more than a simple acknowledgment. A person was alive or dead; what more was there to say?

"Do you know where we are?" O'Houlihan inquired before the silence became unendurable to him.

"That last lot who chased us yesterday were yelling the war cry of the Mac Egans, so we must have reached Mac Egan territory, which would mean this is Kiltaroe." *Coillte Ruadh*, the Red Woods.

"Are not the Mac Egans the hereditary Brehons of clan Kennedy?"

"They are, an irony that is not lost on my nephew. He is being hounded to the death for his defense of Gaelic Ireland, while those who should be its chief supporters, the most learned family in the land when it comes to Gaelic law, now lick the boots of the Sasanach and howl for O'Sullivan blood."

"You sound very bitter."

"Do I? And why should I be bitter? Are you, O'Houlihan? Your sons are killed in battle, your wife is dead of this march, your property is confiscated by Carew . . . are you bitter?"

The other man replied slowly, "I am a pillar of salt."

Dermod wandered on. He had set out with the intention of joining The O'Connor Kerry, but instead found himself rambling aimlessly through the soggy woods, brooding on a fate that was out of his hands. He was aware their location spelled doom. They were trapped deep in Mac Egan territory on a loop of land bordered to the west by the Shannon and to the north by the Brosna, both in winter flood. Unfordable. Uncrossable without boats. To the east the land was controlled by English sympathizers. To the south were Carew and Wilmot and dying Munster.

Death all around. No way out.

Life all around too, making the situation more bitter. As he walked, Dermod's feet trampled dormant wild orchids and blue-eyed grass and forget-me-nots that would bloom again in the spring.

When he was dead.

He heard the first notes of the dawn chorus and thought of redwing and lapwing and lark, all of which would skim across the flood on brave wings.

When we are dead.

He was increasingly angry. This was unbearable, someone must do something. Someone must. Someone . . .

After the capture of Dursey, its lord had suffered through one of those dire three-o'clock-in-the-morning confrontations with himself that can strip away a man's last pretenses. At its conclusion he had finally admitted to himself that he was old.

Old and getting older.

The good times behind him. Gone with Dursey.

As Joan lay unaware beside him he had traveled the immeasurable distance from resentment to anger to acceptance, and at last to a grudging thankfulness he would never admit to anyone.

I am old, and I can expect nothing more of life. But neither can anything more be expected of me.

It was a great relief.

Thereafter he had been content to follow his nephew's leadership in all matters. He never questioned, he never argued; he went where he was told and did as he was told. He found this freedom from responsibility left him able to enjoy many small pleasures, such as his rivalry with The O'Connor Kerry. During the long march he had taken pride in his ability to persevere and savored this unexpected late blooming of manhood.

But he did not want to die on a muddy floodplain, trapped like vermin. He very much did not want to end that way, with birds singing all around him.

Someone must do something.

He turned and made his way back to Joan.

He found her awake, searching for some edible fragment on the ground or among the bushes. The look of glazed distraction she had worn since the woman was shot dead beside her had disappeared. She was herself again, though dirty and weary and gaunt.

It will take more than shock to destroy my Joan, Dermod thought proudly. She still seemed to him a fine figure of a woman. Lean. But graceful. She did not move like an old woman, and when she smiled at him he remembered the way she had smiled at him many years ago.

He very much did not want to die yet.

He joined Joan in the search for something to eat. Their best efforts yielded some half-frozen roots. As Dermod's teeth proved unequal to the task Joan chewed them for him, then gave him the resultant paste on her fingers. Once he would have been humiliated. But now, he reminded himself, I am old. I can accept this and live that much longer. He ate gratefully. As he was swallowing the last bit, he remarked, "Who do you suppose I met in the woods a while ago?"

Meanwhile, Niall O'Mahony was trying to find food for Maire. He had tentatively suggested they might be forced to eat the dog, but she responded with horror. "This dog is my friend! I would rather die than betray the trust of an innocent creature, and you are a monster to even suggest it!"

The little dog looked up at Niall and whined. He said nothing more, but he knew if they did not eat the dog sooner or later someone else would. He encouraged Maire to keep it out of sight as best she could, but more than once he caught someone giving the animal a long, hungry look.

As the morning advanced, the camp prepared itself for the eventual certainty of attack. Scouts brought back reports of a sizable castle recently built by the Mac Egans under English patronage at no great distance from their hiding place. Cairbre Mac Egan, head of the clan, and his eldest son, Flann, were away at the time, but the younger son, Donncha, who was the queen's sheriff, was very much in evidence.

Donal Cam accepted this information glumly. He ordered his captains, "Assign your strongest men to digging a trench and throwing up a bank. Cut saplings to make a palisade, we must fortify our position as best we can." It was something to do, but he knew it for a futile gesture. There was no escape.

Yet there must be some way. There must. He tried to think. It was like swimming through lead. He had asked too much of himself for too long; he was drained.

Orla has faith in my wits, he reminded himself, but even that did not help, not when his skull felt scooped out and empty. His eyes watched the men beginning their pathetic attempts at fortification but his thoughts were elsewhere, wandering among ruins.

He was unaware that Dermod had returned until the older man repeated, "Did you hear me?"

"I . . . what?"

"I said, listen to me, I have an idea."

Donal Cam seized his uncle's shoulder with both hands in a grip as urgent as it was painful. "Tell me!"

"I ran into Dermod O'Houlihan a little while ago," Dermod O'Sullivan said, then watched his nephew's face for a reaction.

Donal Cam looked blank. "So? We see him every day, he has been with us since the beginning."

"Do you not understand? Think, man! Later I mentioned seeing him to my wife, and Joan said . . . listen to this . . . Joan said, 'Ah, indeed. The man who used to make currachs for our fishermen.'"

Donal Cam's eyes widened. "*Currachs*. Hide-covered boats."

"Precisely."

"But we have no hides, Dermod. Even if O'Houlihan built frames, what would we use to cover them?"

"We have horses."

Donal Cam swallowed hard enough to hear. "Your idea is to kill our horses for their hides?"

"And to eat the meat. It would be a godsend."

"But . . . the few horses we have left carry the weakest people. The packs. The cavalry . . ."

"No one will need to be carried anywhere if we wait here until the queen's sheriff can surround us and massacre us. We need boats right now a lot more than we need horses."

Donal Cam gave a deep sigh and began massaging his temples with his long, graceful fingers. "You are right. I should have thought of it myself."

"How could you? You are too fond of horses to think of slaughtering them. Whereas I like them well enough, but not as much as I like myself. And I have learned it is not necessary for me to have one to ride. In my old age I have become a mighty walker."

"And a mighty thinker, when ideas are in short supply. I am more grateful than I can say, Dermod."

"You sound more pained than grateful, and I do not blame you. Believe me, I wish there was another way. But time is short and so are ideas, as you said yourself. If you have a better one . . ."

"I have no better one," Donal Cam told him. His tone of voice reminded Dermod of O'Houlihan saying, "I am a pillar of salt."

Leaving his uncle, Donal Cam walked off among the trees to be alone, to absorb and accept. *I wonder how much a man can absorb and accept,* he thought. *What is the limit?*

When he told Ronan Hurley the plan, the captain of cavalry gave a howl of protest. "Absolutely not! Under no circumstances! You cannot take everything away from me just because you realize I am no longer one of your bedazzled admirers."

"This is not personal, Ronan. We are going to use the horses because they are our only hope. If we can get our people across the river before Mac Egan collects enough men at arms to surround the woods, we may yet reach Leitrim and safety."

Ronan bared his teeth like a dog with a bone. "You cannot have my horses."

"They are my horses," Donal Cam reminded him. "And if you refuse to obey my orders I shall have to put some other man in charge of this company."

"Do it then, and be damned!"

Not a muscle twitched in Donal Cam's face. He looked around calmly, caught the eye of Rory's second-in-command, and waved him over. "You are now captain of this company," he informed Maurice O'Sullivan. "And they have just become foot soldiers."

Red-faced and incoherent with rage, Ronan stormed off in search of his sister. Donal Cam began issuing orders to his captains. The most dexterous of the soldiers were to be assigned to boat building.

Most of Thomas Burke's Connacht men were O'Malleys who had been born and raised around Clew Bay. They had definite ideas about what constituted a good currach and insisted on crafting their own vessel. Rory O'Sullivan's hand-picked recruits, Niall O'Mahony among them, were put to work under the supervision of Dermod O'Houlihan. His first instruction was to begin cutting osiers, and they fell to the task gladly. None of them cared to think about what was happening elsewhere.

The horse boys led the doomed animals to a large natural hollow screened by buckthorn and whitebeam. A small crew of former farmers skilled in butchery followed them, equipped with the sharpest knives in the encampment.

Donal Cam had given the order, his was the responsibility. Therefore he made himself watch, biting the inside of his cheek. It was worse than the death of An Cearc. So many more horses were dying this time, and when the first throat was cut the others panicked. The sobbing, cursing horse boys could hardly hold them. The hollow became a charnel house ringing with the screams of the horses and pungent with the thick hot smell of fresh blood.

The living creatures were transformed into mounds of cooling flesh, seeming more massive in death than in life.

As he watched, Donal Cam found himself trying to fix in his memory forever the elegance of the slim legs, the strength of the taut muscles, the nobility of the sculptured heads.

All that grace, gone. A pain twisted through him. For a moment he feared it would tear him apart.

In the dead horses, Donal Cam could see Ireland.

Young Thady Cooney came up behind him to ask fearfully, "What of your own horse, Commander? We have him here. You said to hold back the strongest."

Turning, Donal Cam saw a few other horse boys among the trees with the last of their charges.

"Spare them for now, Thady. But if it turns out we do not have enough hides . . ." He put his head down and walked rapidly away from the hollow.

Thady gave a sigh of relief and patted the stallion's neck. The horse could smell the blood and was trembling, but he lowered his head for the boy's caress.

Niall was cutting osiers when Maire Ni Driscoll found him. "Do you know what they are doing? They are killing the poor horses!" she cried indignantly.

"I know. It must be done. We are to make boats from the hides and eat the meat."

"I had rather starve than eat those horses."

"Without their meat, you will starve."

"I cannot believe you would ever eat one," she told him.

"I will and so will you, even if I have to force the meat between your teeth myself. We are talking about survival, Maire."

She gave him a look of utter loathing. "If you ever try to do such a thing I shall never forgive you." She turned on her heel and left him, her slender back rigid.

Niall looked after her for a long time before going back to his work.

Dermod O'Houlihan's design was for a long currach capable of carrying thirty people at a time. The finished boat would be twenty-six feet in length, six feet in width at the center, and have an elevated prow to stem the river flood. For the basic framework, two rows of osiers were to be stuck into the earth with the thickest ends down, then curved to meet at the top and fastened together with horsehair. Orla's women cut off manes and tails for this purpose while they were skinning the horses and cleaning the hides.

The O'Malley boat was very different, with a round bottom like a shield and high sides. It would hold only ten at a time, and O'Houlihan's contingent claimed it would be unstable, which caused an argument. If both sides had had any energy to spare there would have been a fight.

The weakness of even the strongest men meant the work went slowly. Donal Cam spent the remainder of the day moving between the area where the boats were being built and the outer perimeters of the camp.

At any moment he expected some form of attack. The hastily erected ditch and palisade which traversed the most vulnerable stretch of land mocked him; it was the play fort of a child.

The brief winter day was quickly fading. While the osier frameworks were taking shape other men cut timber and began fashioning crossbeams and seats, or carving oars. Neither currach was ready for its horsehide covering, but when the hides from the horses already slaughtered had been cut and measured O'Houlihan announced that no more need be killed. Donal Cam's stallion was spared, together with three or four others.

Late in the day the man working beside Niall lifted his head. "Smell that!"

Niall sniffed the air. His stomach leapt at the smell of roasting meat.

"They need not cook it for me," said his companion. "I could eat a horse raw. Alive, even."

The fragrance was maddening. By the time the women began distributing food, it was all Niall could do to keep from jumping up and snatching the meat out of some woman's hands. His own hands shook as he held them out to receive his share of the steaming, blackened horseflesh.

The meat was stringy and tough, but saliva flooded his mouth and he gobbled as avidly as anyone.

A few people refused the meat. When it was offered to Maire O'Driscoll she covered her face with her hands. Her small dog, who was not burdened with such sensibilities, slipped away from her for a while to beg for scraps. Since those from whom it begged already had meat, no one grabbed the little creature to make a meal of it.

Grella Ni Hurley was one of the women distributing cooked horsemeat. She took a large joint to her brother, who was sitting on a fallen log with his chin on his fist. He wore the expression of a hornet looking for someone to sting.

"Stop scowling and eat this," she advised him.

He did not stop scowling. "You served everyone else first."

"I did not." Smoke-blackened and bloody to the elbows, Grella sat down beside her brother. "I put aside the best portion for us," she said placatingly, her eyes on the meat as she gave it to him.

He began eating at once without offering her any. As he tore the flesh from the bone with his teeth, red juices ran down his chin. Grella's eyes followed them hungrily.

Ronan was vaguely aware that she was watching him intently but his mind was not on his sister. He was imagining tearing Donal Cam's flesh with his teeth. Grella had to get up and start walking away before he paid any attention to her.

"Where are you going?" he asked around a mouthful of meat.

"To get something for myself, since it seems I must."

Her sarcasm was lost on him. "Then bring back more for me as well."

She turned to face him. "I cannot give you more, Ronan. We are only to give each person one portion so there will be some left for tomorrow."

"Are you an idiot? That is what I meant. Bring me some more to take with me when we make our escape."

She drew in a sharp breath. "Has the time come, then? Is this as far as we go with O'Sullivan?"

He nodded. "Whenever the boats are launched, we can take advantage of the confusion. The O'Malleys are determined to be the first across, and I want us to go with them, apart from the buannachta. Flirt with one of the Connacht men, get him to give us places in their boat. That way we shall already be on the far side when O'Sullivan's packs come across in the O'Halloran boat. He will probably split them up, sending them in several different boatloads, but you know where the gold is. Watch for it, and when you see some about to come ashore, give me a sign. At the moment the boat arrives I shall seize it."

"But how? The packs will not be left unattended."

"As the boat reaches the bank I want you to stumble and fall into the river. Do so much screeching and splashing that everyone hurries to rescue you. In that moment I can seize the gold, and perhaps even one of the horses which will be swimming across behind the boats. By the time you are pulled from the river I can be well away. If you make enough of a fuss I may not even be noticed leaving."

"But what about me? There I am, wet and freezing, screeching and screaming, and there you are running away with the gold. What happens to me?"

He made an ambiguous gesture with one hand. His fingers gleamed with grease. "I told you, I hope to get a horse. Watch for your chance and then follow the way I have gone. I shall be waiting for you at a safe distance. It is a perfect plan, Grella; these people are too dazed and disorganized to interfere with it."

Grella narrowed her eyes. She could envision the stratagem working—up to a point. There would doubtless be a lot of confusion, and she knew Ronan was adroit enough to seize a pack of gold and make off with it when everyone was looking the other way. But as for his waiting for her, how could she be sure?

A brother who would not think to share his meat with his sister might not be willing to share his gold.

"You have changed," she remarked.

"Why? Because I make my own plans now instead of marching to someone else's orders?"

"That is not what I meant. But you used to be . . . such a merry boy. Lighthearted, you were. And considerate, I remember that about you, when we were children together."

"And our brothers were alive," he added sourly. "I suppose I have changed since then. I hope so. I was a fool then. Wiser now." He resumed chewing, then waved the gnawed bone at Grella to make a point. "We have all changed, you know, how could we help it after what we have suffered? None of the people you remember from childhood are the same now, I promise you. Not just me.

"Think about Doire na Fola, Grella. Horrible? Indeed. A massacre. But it was not just Englishmen killing those people. Fully half of Wilmot's force is made up of Gaelic recruits from the area, tenants of the English who fight on their side as a condition of their tenancy on lands they once held outright. When you and I were children, some of those people would have been our friends. Now we consider them monsters.

"I have changed, but so have we all, Grella. So have we all."

She knew that what he said was true, but his reference to Doire na Fola had been unfortunate. Ronan accused Donal Cam of sacrificing those people—when he said he had grown "wiser" did he mean he would follow that example and sacrifice his sister? Grella did not find it difficult to imagine the Ronan Hurley sitting before her as a man who could ride away without bothering to look back.

I must be careful, Grella cautioned herself. I must be very, very careful.

Throughout the day, the mood of the refugees underwent a sea change. Most had begun with a sense of entrapment and hopelessness. They had said little, done less. Merely waited. There seemed nothing else to do.

Then came the horror of the Hollow of the Horses, as the place was already being called. Defenseless animals who had served them faithfully and shared their hardships were being rewarded with death, and people who had not cried since the march began wept openly. Many seemed unable to avoid the site, but returned again and again long after the bodies had been skinned and cut up for roasting.

Then, as if Poll na gCapaill provided a strange cathartic, the atmosphere began to lift. Out of blood and death a new hope was emerging. People wiped away their tears, ate the meat, felt strength return to their bodies, shook off the worst of their despair.

Father Collins observed an interesting phenomenon. After his last conversation with Father Archer he was reluctant to discuss it with his fellow Jesuit, so he sought out The O'Connor Kerry. He found the old man working as hard as he was able, sitting on damp ground with his blistered feet propped on a mossy stone while he diligently carved an oar for one of the currachs.

Everyone now seemed to be busy doing something.

Father Collins sat down beside The O'Connor. "Have you an extra knife? I could help with that."

"I doubt if there is an extra knife in the camp now, they are all employed. We are busier than a crossroads."

Father Collins smiled. "It feels good to be doing something. People are relieved to be able to help themselves. I have been watching them . . . and I have noticed something . . . strange."

"What?" The O'Connor raised his eyebrows but did not look up from his work.

"They are beginning to speak of the sacrifice of the horses as if it were a religious ritual. That same tone of awe, you know? And . . . this is the strangest part . . . I have seen several go to the hollow and actually dip their fingers into the puddles of congealed blood." A tiny shiver ran through the priest.

The O'Connor looked up at him then. "That bothers you, does it?"

"I cannot say, it just . . . yes. Yes, I suppose it does bother me. In the bizarre actions of these poor, exhausted people I see as in a distorted mirror a familiar symbolism."

The O'Connor Kerry put down his knife, lifted the oar, and sighted critically along it, examining his handiwork. Then he set it aside and turned to the priest. "I have never been particularly devout, as you know," he said to his confessor.

Father Collins's eyes twinkled like a frosty morning. "I do know indeed, better than anyone." What he knew was that the old man enjoyed being considered a rogue.

"Perhaps," The O'Connor continued, "you need someone like me to remind you that our people practiced blood sacrifice long before they embraced Christianity and the old responses are still there, just under the skin."

"The civilizing influences of the Church should have expunged those tendencies long ago," replied the Jesuit, settling himself for the sort of conversation he had enjoyed in better days.

"Do not be sanctimonious with me," The O'Connor replied. "You know better than that and so do I. We are all savages, not just the Gael but the Saxon and the Spaniard and the Frenchman. Every man who walks on two hind legs is a beast in clothing. What we have seen in the last few years is all the proof you need of it."

"I refuse to believe it, Sean. If what you say is true then the last sixteen hundred years have accomplished nothing."

"On the contrary, they have accomplished much. My own wife—the last one, for as you know my wives have a habit of dying in childbed—my wife was a great one for her faith and it made a lovely woman of her. If for no other reason I would be grateful to the Church for the qualities it taught her. But I am thinking it is easier to civilize women than men, Father. Tell me: Who did you see dipping their fingers in horses' blood? Women or men?"

With considerable relish the Jesuit replied, "I hate to shatter your fine theory, Sean, but they were almost all women."

The O'Connor had a quick mind. He blinked only once before replying, "That just proves my theory! Women are more civilized, and civilized people draw on everything available to them, including ancient lore. Those women instinctively sought blood to reinforce the connection with life."

Father Collins could not suppress a smile. "You would have argued the other point just as easily. Our Order would have had a fine Jesuit in you."

"Instead I recruited you for my order," the old scoundrel replied, pleased. "When I needed a new confessor my only requirement was that he be someone who could keep my wits sharpened. I let nothing wear out through lack of use; nothing!" he added with a hearty laugh.

Father Collins regarded The O'Connor fondly. A wasted giant of a man with an inextinguishable flame. I hope some of his grandchildren, scattered throughout Munster as they are, survive this, the priest thought. I should like to teach them someday about the root that nourished them.

Night and cold and the smell of ashes. With the setting of the sun the large fires had been extinguished so their glow would not draw attention as far away as Redwood

Castle. There was no point in reminding Donncha Mac Egan of their presence and showing him their exact location. Even the smoke of the day's cooking fires had been dispersed by flapping cloths so no smoky pillar could serve as an unwanted beacon.

Yet Mac Egan must know. Donal Cam was certain. Some of the sheriff's followers had chased them into these woods. What was the man waiting for? Was he torturing them on purpose as a cat tortures a rodent?

Similar worries were plaguing Thomas Burke. In spite of his injured leg he was prowling the encampment, checking the perimeters and conferring with sentries. He ignored the pain of the wound. It was neither his first wound nor his worst, and as a sailor marks the turn of the tide, he had marked the moment when the pain began to lessen and he knew the leg would heal. From that time he ceased to give in to it.

But when Joan Ni Sweney saw him limping past in the faint light of a partial moon, she called out to him. "You should rest yourself," she advised.

Burke was surprised. Noblewomen did not usually speak to mercenaries. He was uncertain how—or even if—he should respond.

Joan did not stand on ceremony. She came forward and took him by the arm to lead him to the space she had cleared for herself amid the undergrowth. A lean-to shelter of branches and a bed of moss and leaves offered the crudest shelter, but compared to Burke's usual sleeping arrangements it was luxurious indeed. Before he could think of a way to protest, Joan had him seated with a cup of water in his hand.

"With your wounds, you should not be stumbling around in the dark," she said severely. "I noticed earlier that you were looking very pale. You must take better care of yourself."

No woman had spoken to Burke in that tone since he left his mother's house a decade ago. The scolding was ridiculous under the circumstances, for none of them could take better care of themselves, but it brought such a rush of unaccustomed nostalgia to the toughened mercenary that for a moment his eyes stung and he had to blink them very hard.

Joan leaned forward and peered at him. "You poor lad, are you in much pain, then?" She touched his cheek.

Her sympathy had an astonishing effect. Acting upon the combined pain and tension and weariness of the man, they seemed to cut through as a sword cuts through a knot, reaching to his inner core and freeing from that core a great sob that struggled upward, was fought back, refused to be denied, and at last burst forth with a power that startled them both.

"Jesus Mary and Joseph," said Joan. Without hesitation she flung her arms around the dismayed mercenary and pressed him against her emaciated bosom. There, in spite of all he could do, he was racked with sobs like a beardless boy.

Joan bowed her head tenderly over his, an unexpected madonna holding a figure reclaimed from a cross. "There now, there now," she murmured. "I know. I know. It is very hard. You are nothing but grown-up boys, any of you, even my old Dermod. Grown-up boys killing and dying and afraid of the dark."

Thomas Burke buried his face between her flat breasts and howled. She muffled the sound as best she could by wrapping her arms around his head, and let the storm shake him until at last blew itself out.

A mercenary captain, the bemused Joan thought to herself. He will be horribly embarrassed when he recovers.

She said kindly, "This sort of thing happens to all of us,

you know. A friend of mine had her head blown off as she walked beside me. Until then I thought I was strong, but when that happened I just . . . went away. Somewhere. People spoke to me and I answered them, but I was not there. It was very strange and lasted for a long time. I cannot say how long, I was unaware of the passage of time. I was clenched inside myself, like a fist. The world went on around me but I did not know.

"Eventually I came back. Just like that, between one breath and the next. First I was far away, and the next moment I found myself watching an osprey winging westward toward the Shannon and wishing it was not so far away so our men could shoot it for us to eat.

"I was part of the world again, but for a while I had escaped. We are all desperate to escape for a while. We are all afraid of the dark."

Beneath her chin, Burke's head nodded agreement.

"Even bold brave men from Connacht," she said softly into his hair.

"Yes," he whispered.

She held him tightly until the feel of his body told her he too had returned from his brief escape. He drew a deep breath, and she released him.

When Thomas Burke left Joan Ni Sweney and limped off in search of some of his Connacht men, he barely avoided, in the dark, stepping on a huddled figure wrapped in a shaggy mantle.

"Niall?" Maire Ni Driscoll asked hopefully.

Burke did not hear her and passed on. Maire sank down in her bed again, wondering where the pikeman was. She had fully expected him to come to her sometime during the day and force her to eat the horsemeat. She had been prepared to fight him about it, but as the hours wore on and the smell of roast meat clung to the forest she began thinking of giving in. She would let him have his victory. Men liked to win, and he had been so good to her. She would not hold it against him that he wanted to keep her alive.

So she had waited, wrapped in his garment which he insisted on her wearing. "I never feel the cold," he had lied when he left her to go to work on the boats.

She had waited, but darkness fell and he did not come. He was angry then, she decided. What had she said to him? She tried to remember. But she was so hungry, faint with starvation, and her thoughts kept spinning. Sometimes she imagined she was waiting for Richard. She and Richard were going to sleep together in the shaggy mantle.

But Richard Mac Geoghegan did not wear the shaggy mantle, he was The O'Sullivan's constable with fine woolen cloaks, fur bordered. And he would never lie beside her at night without touching her, as Niall O'Mahony did.

Niall . . . she remembered. The first night he had persuaded her to share the warmth of the mantle with him he had whispered, "You are safe with me, Maire." True to his word he had never touched her intimately and never forced himself upon her in any way. At first she had been grateful. But as the days passed his restraint had begun to seem a reproach to her, a criticism, and she had tried to catch glimpses of her face in pools of water to see if she had grown ugly. She knew she was thin.

"Have I become a woman no man would want?" she had asked the little dog, but the creature's only reply was to wag its tail and try to lick her face. "I am Richard's, of course," she had told the dog, "but . . ."

But.

Time went by and Niall made no effort to claim her. They were desperate, harried, they might well be on their way to death, and she was alone. Alone, alone! She had a man's kindness and no more. In the face of such horrors as they were enduring, suddenly that was not enough. What life remained must be seized with both hands and devoured as she should have devoured the meat.

"If I have another chance . . ." she whispered to the dog in her arms. "If he comes back to me . . ."

But for once Niall was not thinking of Maire Ni Driscoll. Many people were awake and restless that night. Some were suffering the weight of the unaccustomed meat in their stomachs. Others were compelled to return to the clearing where the two half-built boats waited like the skeletons of grotesque aquatic beasts, awaiting birth at the hands of man and launching in their natural element.

Niall was among those who could not leave the boats alone. The night so close to the river was bitterly cold, and he thought with a brief and wistful longing of his shaggy mantle, then pushed it out of his mind. Maire was angry, she probably hated him. He had sought above his station. She spoke only of Mac Geoghegan and the past.

The boats were the future, and he was helping craft them. He spent the night standing watch over them as did a number of others who could not bear to leave them, Dermod O'Sullivan included.

Using his tinderbox and flints, Dermod had built a tiny watch fire hardly sufficient to warm a man's hands. Niall was among the score of men huddled around it, amused to observe that more kept coming to join them, even men who had not worked on the boats. People just seemed to want to see them and be assured of their reality.

They were being constructed in a clearing created by the felling of trees for the boats' planking. From time to time Niall, like the others, would get up and go over to the big boat and give it a touch, a measuring glance, pretend he had found some small thing that needed to be done, although in actuality the remainder of the work must be done by daylight.

"How much longer will it take?" one of the other men asked Dermod.

"O'Houlihan says another day, for ours. The Connacht men may have theirs done sooner," he added with a certain contempt for the smaller boat, which would be like a giant basket covered with horsehide. The O'Houlihan currach was a more splendid craft altogether, his tone intimated.

Niall asked the question uppermost in everyone's mind. "Do you think Mac Egan will attack before the boats are ready?"

Dermod scratched his jaw. "Our people are scattered all through this forest. The only way to attack successfully now would be to surround the entire woodland, and that would take a great lot of men. Donal Cam thinks we may be safe enough until the boats are finished, but of course once we leave the shelter of the woods and are in the open on the riverbank, anything could happen."

His words hung on the cold air.

Anything could happen.

Day Nine

January 8, 1603. *Poll na gCapaill*

Shortly after Dawn, Niall sought out Maire Ni Driscoll. He found her trying to scrub her face with a handful of wet moss. He stood shyly waiting until she completed her crude toilet, then said, "I just wanted to be certain you are all right."

"I am," she said coldly. She felt that he had abandoned her she would not offer him warmth.

"Did you eat?"

"I did not."

He marveled at her self-control. Compared to her he seemed a coarse creature, ravening over horseflesh. He was at once embarrassed and obscurely annoyed. "You should have eaten, it was foolish not to."

She would not look at him. She picked up the little dog and held it to her, prattling to it as if to a child. When she looked up, Niall was gone.

How could he leave me? she thought, feeling the tears come.

When Niall returned to the boats he found Donal

Cam already there, examining the work done so far. Dermod was showing off the large currach like a proud father while O'Houlihan stood to one side and let the old man enjoy his triumph.

"There is a lot still to be done before we put on the hides, of course," Dermod was saying.

"How long?"

When Dermod hesitated, O'Houlihan came to his rescue. "Normally, Commander, the osier frame would have been weighted with stones and given several days to set in its shape before the interior planking was affixed, but I gather we do not have that much time."

"We have no time," Donal Cam replied. "How soon can you get these boats in the water?"

"If we are diligent they can be completed by sundown," O'Houlihan replied, "though I will not trust either of them as I would trust a currach that was properly cured. However . . ."

"They will float?"

"I believe so. I mean, I am certain this one will. The Connacht men will have to speak for their own, I have no experience with round-bottomed coracles like theirs."

"We can carry them to the river's edge under cover of darkness, then," Donal Cam decided, "and start ferrying our people across at first light tomorrow. I would rather we could go today, but . . ."

"Planking to finish, hides to fit and fasten, it is not possible," O'Houlihan said.

"I see that. Do your best, just make certain the boat will carry us."

The workmen returned to their labors. Watching them, Donal Cam recalled the fine ships he had sailed upon, the Spanish vessels rising like small castles above their decks replete with chapels and treasure rooms, the bunks fitted with linen, the sea far below, hissing tamed beneath the bow.

These currachs were a different matter. He wondered how many of the refugees had ever been out in one. A currach was like a living creature, its flexible ribs giving with the motion of the water as if it were breathing. The water would seem very close; the brown, roiling water of the Shannon in flood. The fishermen among them might not be dismayed, but what of the others? Donal Cam was not thinking exclusively of women and children. Many of his stouthearted buannachta had never set foot on a boat.

For an island people, the Irish were curiously disinclined to seafaring.

As he remarked later to Father Archer, "The hardest part of this may be getting people to enter the boats."

"Not if we gather them first and kneel down and pray together. Once they have commended their souls to God they need have no fear."

Donal Cam gave the other man an incredulous look. "You think not?"

"Perfect faith casteth out fear."

"That is easy enough to quote in a dry chapel with a full belly and no enemy at the gates. It is something else entirely to try to convince a band of famished refugees who have been pursued and shot at day after day, and are facing a river that is dangerous at the best of times. How can you expect perfect faith of them?"

"I do expect perfect faith," the priest said quietly. "Of you, of everyone. I must, as God expects it of me. My assurance lies in the knowledge that He never asks more of us than we can give."

For a moment, Donal Cam was fiercely jealous of the man's blind faith. Only later, when he had left the priest, did he allow himself to wonder.

Was it possible for any human being to be that secure in his belief? Once he would have accepted it, but that was before the foundations of the world were shaken loose.

Once Donal Cam had assumed the priests had the answers. Now he was not even certain they knew the questions.

God may strike me down for such thoughts, he warned himself. If He is listening.

If He exists.

His own daring at even thinking that thought shocked him. Part of him fully expected to be struck down by a giant fist of thunder, like the monstrous, unnatural storms that had rolled across Munster for the month preceding the battle of Kinsale. God's handiwork, they had thought then, trying to find encouraging omens in the black clouds and leaping lightning.

Now Donal Cam wondered if God had sent those storms at all.

None erupted over his questioning head.

He felt a momentary defiant relief. But the old habit was deep in him. A voice embedded in his soul that might have come from God and might have come from conscience urged him to beware, do not tempt God.

I must be careful, Donal Cam said sternly to himself. I must avoid these dangerous thoughts, in case . . . When this is over I shall find a way of making propitiation for my lack of faith.

When this is over. The words hardly had any meaning in his mind.

The work on the boats continued. Niall was fascinated by the way the big boat grew. Laths running from stem to stern were fitted inside the osier framework, then reinforced with timber under O'Houlihan's watchful eyes. They had little in the way of tools, things had to be contrapted from whatever materials came to hand. Pegs were whittled to hold the laths in place, thongs were made of discarded strips of hide to lash the hides to the frame.

Even under the circumstances—or perhaps because of them—O'Houlihan demanded meticulous craftsmanship. "Our lives depend on it," he reminded them frequently, "so hurry slowly."

The day was dull and raw. As the boats grew, people kept crowding around to watch the work. More than once an irritable O'Houlihan drove the spectators back. "Would you come between a man and the light?" he demanded to know.

People who knew nothing of boats stood at a respectful distance, telling one another what was right and what was wrong about each detail of the construction. Unlike O'Houlihan, the Connacht men responded to this audience enthusiastically.

"Come over here and see a real boat made," they invited. "See how it is done on Clew Bay."

Thomas Burke found himself comparing the two groups. O'Houlihan's Cork and Kerry crew were working tight-faced, silently, with intense concentration. The Connacht men had begun singing some ballad about herrings running and a high sea following. They joked with the spectators and each other. They worked with a cheerful casualness that was meant to convey professional expertise.

Burke sauntered over to the round-bottomed Connacht coracle. The man in charge of its construction, Teig O'Malley, gave him a cheerful nod. A dark man with pale eyes, he stood with his hands on his hips, his legs planted wide in a supervisory stance. "We shall be done long before that other lot," he assured Burke.

"This is no race, Teig. What we want is a safe boat."

"Nothing is safer than a coracle, have no worries."

Burke pressed his lips together. Edging past O'Malley, he gave the boat a hard look, though he was no boat-builder. Still, he recognized a note of bravado in the other man's voice that worried him. Bravado was a substitute for confidence.

"Have you ever personally built a coracle before?" he wanted to know.

O'Malley began shifting weight from one foot to the other. "My people have fished Clew Bay since . . ."

"Have you ever built a boat yourself?" Burke repeated pointedly, wishing he had asked that particular question when the man volunteered to be in charge.

"Would I undertake this otherwise?" O'Malley replied with wide-eyed innocence.

Burke knew evasion when he heard it. Every Irish person knew how to talk in circles and spirals that flowed around the heart of a matter without ever coming to grips with it. "Answer me straight out, Teig!"

O'Malley gave him a look of withering contempt. "I know more about building boats than all your family together, Burke. My people are Gael. You have a Norman name."

"I am as good an Irishman as you are and my living body will be entrusted to that boat the same as yours!" Burke shot back. O'Malley was testing him. These were still his cousin William's men, though William Burke had long since abandoned Donal Cam. They considered the younger Thomas something of a usurper, untried. Among such men, loyalty once given was only very slowly transferred.

They had all stopped working on the round-bottomed boat and were staring at Thomas Burke, waiting to see what he would do.

We are all afraid of the dark, a voice inside him said, like an echo. But I am not afraid of this lot.

"Take yourself away, O'Malley," he said harshly. "Someone else can do the job as well as you." While Teig O'Malley glared he raised his voice and asked, "Who among you has actually shaped a coracle with his own hands? I am not talking about someone who has seen it done. Who has done it?"

They exchanged glances. "I have," one man said at last, a worn thin man with a diamond-shaped face and sea-colored eyes.

"Then you are in charge now. Mind you make a good fist of it if you ever hope to see Connacht again." Burke turned to Teig O'Malley. "I am your captain," he said, stressing each word carefully. "If you resent my leadership, you should have gone with William."

O'Malley met and held his eyes, then looked down. "I did not agree with William," he said in a low voice. "He did wrong, taking The O'Sullivan's gold and then deserting him when things got too hard."

Burke tardily regretted his handling of the man. "Your attitude does you credit. I feel the same myself."

Teig O'Malley looked at him hopefully, half expecting Burke would rescind the order and put him back in charge. But he was disappointed. Thomas Burke's model had become O'Sullivan Beare, a man not given to capricious turnarounds after an order was given.

The other Connacht men moved over to allow their former supervisor to take his place among them as they began fitting the horsehides to the frame. One of them remarked in an undertone, "I never yet got in trouble with my mouth closed."

"You are about to get in trouble with me," Teig warned him.

"Do you see what I mean?" the man laughed, elbowing his companions.

Thomas Burke watched for a few minutes to be sure

they were accepting the new arrangement, then went off to hear the reports of the perimeter sentries. Every eye and ear was alert for some threatening move from Mac Egan.

The horsehides being affixed to the two boats were fresh and raw. Before delivering them Orla's women pounded each one vigorously with stones but they were still far from supple. Damp, heavy, the colors of the coats still heartbreakingly recognizable, they were awkward to handle. The Connacht men lashed them to their boat's framework in doubled thickness to make up for any gaps, but the more thorough O'Houlihan insisted men chew the edges flat where they were to join, then stitch them, turn them and stitch again with improvised awls and needles made of slivers of bone. All this took time as the refugees waited with mounting anxiety.

Donal Cam ceaselessly patrolled the encampment, several times going as far as the river. After a careful survey of the area he decided to launch the boats just north of a long, narrow spit of land still visible above the flood. In a milder season the place was reputed to be a ford, though fording was impossible now. Water extended like a vast sheet across the low land on either side of the river, drowning reedy shallows and turning meadows into lakes.

He told Rory O'Sullivan, "We will be well out of the trees no matter where we put the boats into the water. That is what Mac Egan is waiting for, I suspect: to catch us in the open."

"Do you think he knows about the boats?"

"We must assume he does. Surely someone reported the sound of trees being cut. And the screams of the horses carried."

Rory's eyes were somber. "They carried into my

dreams. But if you think Mac Egan knows, why did you order us to be so careful with the fires?"

"You may have one leak in your boat, but that is no reason to allow others."

"I wish you had not said that about boats leaking."

Donal Cam's eyes glittered. "Are you afraid of the river?"

The captain of the buannachta threw back his shoulders and lifted his chin, setting his scarred face in brave lines. In spite of his long service to his prince, O'Sullivan Beare had never encouraged familiarity but kept that slight degree of aloofness necessary for leadership. It would not do to admit fear to him now. "The river is nothing to me," Rory said.

Donal Cam cast a grateful glance at his captain. Rory is one of the real ones, he thought to himself. Strong and able, loyal even when circumstances make loyalty most painful, uncorrupted by change, untainted by slackness of spirit. He and Orla are well matched.

Orla.

Honora.

He shook his head, warding off the competing images.

Misunderstanding, Rory O'Sullivan repeated with still more conviction, "I am not afraid of the crossing, Commander. My men and I are well able for it."

Donal Cam pulled himself back to the matter at hand. "Of course you are, I was casting no aspersions on your courage. I just want to be certain we are as prepared as possible for the crossing. Any fears we feel now must be dealt with and put aside, because fear is catching, and when we start herding civilians into the boats we will all be as busy as a piper's fingers encouraging and reassuring them. Right now, when the crossing is still many hours away, they think they are eager for it. When the time comes to entrust themselves to that river they may feel very differently, and I am counting on my buannachta to set the best possible example."

Rory O'Sullivan considered his words carefully before speaking. Was it possible O'Sullivan actually wanted him to speak frankly, on a personal level? Were the walls that separated commander from captain being set aside temporarily? "How does one deal with one's fears?" he asked, carefully avoiding using a more specific pronoun.

It was a serious question for a serious time, and one that Donal Cam had asked himself. On many a bitter night, at three o'clock in the morning.

"I shall give you the only answer I have," he replied. "Remember that the Gael are trees grown on kingly roots. Each one of our clans traces its direct descent from some particular warrior king, from some man celebrated in his own lifetime for his courage and nobility of spirit. Every Gaelic surname is proof of royal blood, even if the person bearing that name plows fields or tans hides or mends fishing nets for a living.

"Perhaps, living as we do on a small island, we are unique in that respect. We are all kings in a sense . . . and we have always known it.

"The New English are making every effort to strip that heritage from us. To my certain knowledge they have forged documents to persuade one Gaelic prince that another has gone over to their side, thus creating suspicion and anger. They have used our intense personal connection with the land as a weapon against us, seizing the land and then bartering part of it back to us in return for accepting Anglicization."

In Donal Cam's words Rory recognized the bitter sound of self-contempt.

His commander continued, however, by saying, "The Gaelic princes whom the English cannot subvert they mean to kill. When no one of them remains to inspire the people and remind them of their nobility, the New English intend to turn the surviving Gael into the sort of squalid, cringing peasantry that will best serve their needs.

"Our fear of that happening must be greater than any personal fear we have, Rory. The Ireland of tomorrow is being decided today. While there is breath in our bodies we must go on to the north, join The O'Neill, rally the Ulster men who are still free to fight, and hold Ireland for our children. Your sons and mine may be sent temporarily to places of safety elsewhere, but I promise you, they will come back some day. We shall bring them back to take their place on this island of kings.

"Weighed against that, what do our fears matter?"

Staring at Donal Cam, Rory O'Sullivan had not the slightest doubt as to why he followed the man. He would have followed him over the rim of the world, if the commander asked. There were those who thought Gaelic Ireland was already dead. If that was true, O'Sullivan Beare was struggling northward carrying its bleeding corpse. But he obviously was not anticipating a burial.

No, Donal Cam expected a resurrection, and to that end had dedicated himself and every human being who stayed with him.

Rory meant to stay with him to the end.

So fear, truly, did not matter.

Mist was rising from the trees. They bled vapor into the clouded sky. A sullen wind sang down the Shannon, troubling the water.

Donal Cam paced and worried, trying to anticipate the morrow.

A woman came to him, a member of clan O'Callaghan. She had once been a pale, pretty woman, with prominent blue eyes and a wealth of russet hair. Now she was a wraith. The hives caused by extreme cold had left her face reddened and misshapen with swelling, and the blue eyes were lost in granulated eyelids.

"Does everyone have to cross the river tomorrow?" she asked in a thready voice.

"They do of course."

"But some of us are so weak and tired. Could we not stay here? We could hide in the forest and after you have gone we could slip away somewhere."

Donal Cam tried to be kind. "We will do what we can to make it easier for you, but you must go with us," he said gently.

She began to cry. "We are too weak for any more of this. In the name of God"—she held out an imploring hand—"leave us."

"In the name of God, no!" An horrific vision of Doire na Fola had leapt full-colored into his mind.

Donal Cam's vehemence alarmed the woman. Putting one hand over her mouth, she scuttled away.

Catherine O'Callahan made her way back through the woods to her family. Once she had presided over a thriving brood of healthy children and a prosperous household. Now two adolescent sons, a daughter who had lost the power of speech, and her husband's steward remained to her. The rest were dead.

She envied her dead.

A pine marten broke from cover and darted past her. The shy creature had been badly disturbed by the intrusion of the refugees into its forest, but would not abandon the place to them. It stayed, fleeing from one tree to another. Chocolate-brown fur with a cream patch at its throat, the pine marten would eat almost anything and was fierce in the defense of its young. It hated these huge two-legs who had invaded its kingdom, and gave the woman a brief glare before whisking up the nearest tree out of her sight and reach.

As he made his ceaseless rounds, Donal Cam came upon a small glade where Orla Ni Donoghue was working over the last of the horsehides. She had pegged the skin to the earth with crudely whittled wooden stakes and was scraping the fleshy side with a piece of sharp stone. She was so intent on her work she did not notice him standing among the trees, watching her.

We have become very primitive, he mused. They have reduced us to this. She might be a woman of the Gael a thousand years ago.

Yet at this very moment, other women in silks and velvets hold pomanders to their noses to protect them from the stench of Dublin's cobbled streets. Their men lounge in taverns with glass windows, drinking fine whiskey and comparing the cut of their breeches. In great houses with well-furnished larders servants are pleating linen with Holland boxes, using a red-hot slub inserted into the metal to press the fabric smooth. The trappings of civilization. I know them well.

And there is Orla squatting on her haunches, using a rock and her bare hands to turn a stinking horsehide into a covering for a currach so we can survive another day.

He cleared his throat and she glanced up. When she saw him, she quickly ran the tip of her tongue over her chapped lips so she could smile. "Have you been there long?"

"A little while. Watching you."

"Not so much to see," she said diffidently. When Donal Cam looked at Orla he wished she were beautiful. At the same time, something perverse rose up in her so she flaunted her plainness, her wild hair, her unpainted skin with its true texture showing. This is me, she seemed to announce. This is what I am. Strong bones, strong heart. Durable and true, a full-blooded woman like the O'Donnell's celebrated Ineen Duv, of whom the poets said, "She joins a man's heart to a woman's thought."

See past my surface. See what is valuable.

See *me*.

Donal Cam's dark eyes were brilliant and opaque. Orla could not imagine what he might be seeing.

He said, "Is that the last hide? O'Houlihan needs it."

"I just had to take out a bit of stiffness." She gave a final dig with her stone, then patted the hide like a woman smoothing a quilt. "There now."

"I shall help you carry it." Donal Cam lifted one end while Orla took the other. There had been no time for drying the hides and this one was very heavy.

Donal Cam looked at it with narrowed eyes.

"Will it absorb much water in the river?" Orla asked as if she could read his thoughts.

"I could not tell you. I know little about boatbuilding and less about currachs, but O'Houlihan has confidence in them, so we can only hope."

"I went to look at the river first thing this morning," Orla confided. "Before anyone else was up. I wanted to know what we must face."

"And?"

"And the water is flowing so fast! Logs, branches, all sorts of debris whirl by. Anything might strike a boat in midcurrent, even the body of a drowned animal. I do not know what I expected, but I found the Shannon alarming."

"You have seen rivers in full flood before, countless times."

"None as wide or strong as this. It seemed like a living being as it roared past me, deliberately destroying everything it could seize."

Donal Cam half smiled at her imagery. He told her, "Our pagan ancestors believed the rivers were living beings, each with its own particular spirit and character."

She waited for him to say more but he did not, instead concentrating on guiding the bulky hide among the trees. Orla was disappointed. She wistfully recalled more leisurely occasions when he had given her the benefit of his education, quoting poetry, reciting bits of classical philosophy, awakening her mind to the beneficent sunlight of his.

"Be careful!" he said sharply as she stumbled.

They reached the boats, and several men came forward to take the hide from them. Donal Cam left Orla and went to confer with Dermod O'Houlihan.

"When this final hide is fastened, will the boats be ready to launch at dawn?"

"Ours will be ready," the currach maker assured Donal Cam. "I am not as certain of the other."

"Why not?"

"It is more of a coracle meant for sheltered bays than a vessel fit to cross a raging river."

"We have to trust it," Donal Cam replied. "Do you realize how long it would take to transport all our people if we only use the one boat?"

O'Houlihan shrugged and said nothing more. Command decisions were not his to make.

Donal Cam went over to take a long look at the Connacht boat. As far as his untrained eye could tell there was nothing wrong with it. He turned to one of the workmen. "Would you entrust your life to this coracle?" he wanted to know.

Teig O'Malley grinned, pleased to be singled out. "This coracle is as sturdy as a sea turtle and I would entrust myself to her ten times over," he boasted.

"I should think once will be enough." Donal Cam ran

a speculative finger along the seam where one horsehide
lay against another, then moved around to peer at the inside of the boat, looking for some obvious flaw but finding none.

From a distance, Ronan Hurley observed his inspection of the coracle. Since his removal as captain of the
cavalry Ronan had found himself with little to do. No
one asked for his help. No one but Grella even spoke to
him.

Hypocrites, he thought sourly. They are no more loyal
to O'Sullivan Beare than I am, they only pretend to be.
That old blind allegiance to the chieftain. What has it
ever gotten us?

Each man for himself, that is the way. O'Sullivan
surely practices it. Look at him over there. He wants to
satisfy himself as to which boat is best, and that is the one
he will ride in.

Ronan noted that Donal Cam was lingering over the
Connacht vessel. That was his choice, then. Ronan was
reassured, since he meant to cross the Shannon in that
same boat. Though not at the same time as Donal Cam.

He mentally reviewed his plans. Grella's importance to
the scheme was beginning to worry him. He was growing
increasingly uneasy about having his entire future depend on one woman's ability to distract a small army.
What if she failed and someone saw him snatch the pack
with the gold in it and run? One of those idiots who pre-
tended to be devoted to O'Sullivan Beare would be after
him in a trice and he would undoubtedly be shot without
mercy.

The more he thought about it, the more worried he
became. Any plan examined too long and too earnestly
reveals its flaws, and the flaws in this plan could cost his
life.

He walked farther through the woods, his brow furrowed. Dusk was falling. He thought himself alone until he heard a harsh voice challenge, "Name yourself!"

Ronan gave a start. One of Rory O'Sullivan's kernes came through the trees with a sword in his hand, repeating the sentries' traditional challenge.

"Ronan Hurley."

"Ah." The kerne sheathed his sword. "What are you doing here? This is the edge of the forest, there is nothing beyond but Redwood Castle."

"How far away?" Ronan wondered.

"If I yelled loud enough they could probably hear me. But then, I have good lungs."

"Has there been any sign of activity from them?"

The sentry backed against a tree and began rubbing his shoulders from side to side, scratching the itchy spot between them. "None so far. Mac Egan is there, one of the other sentries went close enough to the castle to make out his standard flying. But if he has called in more men-at-arms to attack us, they must be coming from the north. None has passed within our view, though surely there is already a garrison at the castle."

Ronan said, "Is it possible Mac Egan is taking his time because he thinks he has us trapped here, the way Wilmot thought he had us trapped at Doire na Fola?"

"Could be."

"He may not even know about the boats, then. We could be gone tomorrow before he realizes."

"Please God!" the sentry said fervently. "It is almost too much to hope for that the commander could bring off such an escape twice, but if anyone can do it, he can."

Idiot, thought Ronan.

He left the sentry and began to make his way back through the woods, his mind still turning over the problems of his own escape with a substantial amount of gold. What he needed, he decided, was a second distraction. One might be ignored, but not two.

Suddenly he stopped. His body prickled with the force of inspiration and a slow smile spread across his face.

Of course!

He turned back toward the north, carefully angling through the woods to avoid running into one of the sentries.

Each man for himself, thought Ronan Hurley as he headed toward Redwood Castle.

As night fell, Father Archer called the faithful to prayer. Most of the women and not a few of the men answered his summons, gathering in the clearing with the boats to prepare their souls for the trials to come.

"Acknowledge your every sin no matter how venial," the Jesuit exhorted his listeners. "We must not be weighed down by even the smallest transgression when we commit ourselves to God's mercy on the river tomorrow."

His congregation crowded around him in a circle, kneeling on the cold mud. The night was frigid. They could hear the roar of the flooding river beyond the forest.

Father Archer gazed down upon their bowed heads. In their faith and fragility they seemed particularly dear to him that night.

My humble and obedient flock, he thought. These are the true believers. Everything else has been taken from them to force them to acknowledge God's omnipotence. Wondrous are His ways. Like Job, they are driven to the ultimate extremity, where they have no will of their own but His will.

His will as I interpret it for them. If I tell them they

must kneel, they kneel. If I tell them they must confess, they confess.

An odd fancy came to him. He could imagine himself commanding them to lie down, stand up, follow him like an army. Like apostles. Anywhere he said to go. He could imagine himself, Father James Archer of the Society of Jesus, going down to the riverbank with these people behind him, and setting his foot upon the flood. Walking across the Shannon. Walking on the water. And these people following because he commanded them to do so. Walking on the water, buoyed up by their faith in him.

Father Archer stood before his congregation with his eyes closed, his rapt face turned upward toward the heavens.

"He looks like a saint," whispered Catherine O'Callaghan to the woman kneeling beside her.

Guiltily, Maire Ni Driscoll pulled her attention back to the priest. Instead of praying, she had been trying to make out Niall O'Mahony's face in the cluster of men on the far side of the clearing. But it was too dark to see him; she only knew that he was there somewhere, waiting with those who were to carry the boats down to the river under cover of darkness, as soon as the prayers were concluded.

A gallowglass called Gerald Ryan shifted his weight restlessly from foot to foot. "We should launch the boats tonight," he said under his breath, "and save the praying for tomorrow. There will be time for thanksgiving once we reach Connacht."

"You are no Connacht man," Niall reminded him.

"I am not, but I shall be glad enough to see the place. I mean to wipe the mud of Munster from my feet and never look back."

A third man wedged himself into the whispered conversation. "I am from Connacht, and I had as soon stay here if I could. There are plenty of the New English in Connacht, and they have lists with names on them. My name is surely on one or more of those lists."

"What did you do?"

"Ach, not so much myself as my father. I just clapped and cheered but that was enough. My father, may God have mercy on his soul, was on our roof mending the thatch when Sir Richard Bingham rode by with some of his men. Going to arrest Grace O'Malley he was, or some such mischief. Anyhow, the father reached down and untied one of the stones that keeps your roof from blowing away in our part of Connacht and hurled it at Bingham. Hit him on the side of his plumed hat and knocked it away. A horse trampled on it.

"I was down below but I saw the whole thing, and applauded. One of Bingham's men had a gun and shot my father off the roof. I ran clear away before they could shoot me, and have never been back since. But I have no doubt my name is on a list."

Ryan nodded. "If it was not on one before, it probably is now. I should think we are every one of us on a list somewhere. The Sasanach have a passion for recording the names of their enemies and forgetting the names of their friends."

"If what you say is true," Niall remarked, "then even if we get away this time we are not safe. As long as we are in Ireland they will be watching for us."

The gallowglass pressed his thumb against one nostril to pinch it shut and blew the other one violently into the air. That done, he reversed the process. Then he said, "Father Archer over there would tell you your only safety lies with God."

"Do you believe that?"

Gerald Ryan's teeth gleamed in the darkness. "I carry an ax," he said.

When those who had been kneeling at last got to their feet, Niall and his companions stepped forward to shoulder the boats. The man from Connacht went to the smaller one while Niall and the gallowglass took their place with the others assigned to O'Houlihan's currach. It was by far the heavier of the two, and there were several anxious moments as the hunger-weakened men lifted it and balanced it on their shoulders.

They made their way toward the river, cursing the dark, stumbling over roots, trying to steer their awkward burden between trees while avoiding the branches that reached out to snag them. With every step they took, the threatening roar of the flood grew louder.

The Shannon did not sleep. In high summer the river swept as stately as a queen through the heart of Ireland, wearing blue and silver, ornamented with reeds and fringed with flowers. In winter flood, however, she was untamed and untamable, a hellion devouring everything in her path. To make matters worse, the winter had brought unprecedented storms, swelling the river beyond all previous proportions.

Of O'Sullivan's original cavalcade, less than four hundred remained. The majority of these were soldiers, but there were still some frightened, weary noncombatants as well. Transporting all of them across the Shannon in two hide-covered boats was a daunting prospect.

"Listen to her," the man directly behind Niall muttered. "Listen to that bitch roaring and gobbling and licking her lips for a taste of us tomorrow."

They set the boats down on a muddy flat at the water's edge, and sentries were assigned to stand guard over them for what remained of the night. The other men returned to their various improvised shelters throughout the woods to take what rest they could.

Niall found Maire Ni Driscoll wrapped in his shaggy mantle, with her head pillowed on her arm. When he bent very close and peered at her she seemed to be asleep.

"Maire?"

No answer.

He was very cold and tired. He had saved some of his horsemeat for her, but now he was reluctant to offer it for fear of offending her still more. He wanted nothing so much as to pull the mantle over himself and snuggle close to her warmth, but if she was asleep he would wake her up and he did not want to do that either.

"Maire?" he asked again, very softly.

Her breathing was regular and deep. He waited a minute more, then turned and went in search of a fellow recruit who had shared his mantle with Niall the night before and probably would again.

After he had gone Maire opened her eyes.

"He abandoned me last night, and now he has left me again," she whispered to the little dog who lay curled against her. "He is not of the quality my Richard was. Richard would have been more audacious."

She lay in the dark and bit her lip to keep from crying because all the good men were dead.

Day Ten

January 9, 1603. *An tSioainn*, the Shannon, named for
  Sinann, a princess of the Tuatha de Danann and kinswoman of Lir, god of the sea

Well before first light, the refugees began gathering
their meager belongings to carry to the river's
edge. Some had no more than the clothes on their backs.
But all joined in the painstaking collection of every remaining shred of meat or gristle, and even odd bits of
bone that looked as if they could be made into some form
of tool on some later occasion, as if nothing better could
be found across the Shannon.

There was a sense of finality about this last day in
Munster.

A cold wind blew from the river, promising rain or
sleet or both. People tore up handfuls of moss to stuff into
their clothes for added warmth, but only Donal Cam
took the trouble to select a willow twig, fray one end with
his knife, and scrub his teeth until the gums bled. He prepared himself as methodically as he did every morning,

then set out to examine the boats one more time and cast a critical eye on the river.

Across the flood, a few lights twinkled as the last stars faded. Smallholders were already lighting their cabins with thick candles made of reeds and butter so they could begin the day's work. There was evidently a settlement on the opposite side of the river.

"The women are awake over there," Donal Cam guessed.

"We should be safe enough until their men get up," said Rory O'Sullivan.

Donal Cam had been joined by his captains and his uncle, as well as Dermond O'Houlihan, who had taken off his shoes and waded out among the reeds to test the strength of the flood. When he returned to shore he flung himself down with chattering teeth and began chafing his half-frozen legs. "That river is a bitch," he said with heartfelt feeling.

"It will do us no harm as long as the boats remain afloat," said Dermod O'Sullivan as optimistically as he could.

"My boat will float right enough, but I have never seen a river in worse spate."

Thomas Burke spoke up. "At least Mac Egan has not attacked, that is one blessing."

Donal Cam agreed. "The forest has hidden our activities from him so far. We may be across the river and away before he realizes we have boats."

"Across the river we may meet other men as well disposed toward the queen as Mac Egan himself," said Maurice O'Sullivan gloomily, scratching himself where mud had dried.

"We have to be prepared for every possibility," Donal Cam told them. "Since I could not sleep I spent last night planning the crossing, exactly how we will go and in what order. The order is extremely important, as I will explain. The buannachta are to go first, in case we meet a hostile reception on the other side, and . . ."

Thomas Burke cleared his throat. "There could be a problem, Commander. The O'Malleys have sworn to be the first across in the boat they built themselves."

"They will just have to wait. The safety of the column is more important than their pride."

"You know that and I know that, but . . ."

"You are their captain, Burke. Order them!"

"Yes sir," Thomas Burke replied obediently. His deceptively mild blue eyes were troubled, however. No one knew better than he how difficult it was to order an O'Malley to do anything. The members of clan O'Malley set their own sails and followed their own stars.

Folding his arms, Burke stood listening thoughtfully while Donal Cam explained the rest of his plan.

Rory O'Sullivan expressed some misgivings of his own. "If we leave all the baggage until last, what will my men do if they arrive on the other side and have to fight before the extra ammunition is brought across?"

"Your musketeers will be carrying their usual powder bottles and bullet bags on their belts, will they not? That should hold them until we are all across, no matter what happens."

"I suppose so," Rory said dubiously.

"It has to. We have to transport people first, then the baggage and supplies with the last two boatloads. I have no intention of having my people wait while inanimate objects are carried across the river ahead of them, do you understand?"

"Yes, Commander."

"What about the horses?" asked Maurice.

"Have horse boys waiting with them to swim them behind the last two boatloads. The boys will ride with the baggage, and as soon as they are across, we can strike off inland. I do not want to stop again until we are well away from the river."

"Very well, Commander."

Reminded by the exchange, Donal Cam asked abruptly, "Have any of you seen Ronan Hurley this morning?"

"I did not even see him last night," said Rory.

"He did not sleep with us," Maurice added.

"Burke?"

"I have not seen him either. He is still angry, Commander, so he has probably found himself some hole to simmer in. When we start loading the boats he will come along quickly enough."

The explanation was insufficient. A new fang of worry began to gnaw Donal Cam's brain. He mentally reviewed his plans for the crossing thoroughly, trying to be prepared for any eventuality . . . when he was satisfied, he dismissed his captains.

"Go and give your men their orders, and make it clear there is to be absolutely no deviation from them. Everything may depend on it. And Rory, I want your wife and her women to put the baggage together in one place and be prepared to help people into the boats."

When the captains had departed, Donal Cam remained with his uncle and O'Houlihan, watching the flood. "How long will it take to get everyone across?" he asked the currach maker.

"Ten to twelve trips, I should say. Thirty in one boat, ten in the other. But each crossing will take time. Not all of our men have experience with boats, and even for the best of them the going will be hard on the Shannon today."

"Where is the most dangerous place?"

"Midriver, where the normal channel lies. The current

will be strongest there, though it is dangerous everywhere. See how much debris there is? Uncured horsehide
can be easily torn, Commander."

"We shall just have to pray it is not," said Donal Cam.

Prayer was uppermost in the mind of the Jesuit, Father
Archer, as time drew near for the river crossing. He had
his flock of the devout only partially assembled to implore God's protection when Orla Ni Donoghue appeared and insisted they were to get off their knees and
down to the water's edge.

Father Archer was outraged. How dare the woman in-
terrupt devotions! "We always have time to pray," he told
her imperiously.

Orla shrugged. "Then you can pray in the boats."

"You insolent . . ." With an effort, the priest bit back
the epithet that sprang to his lips. Donal Cam was too
close, he might overhear.

She was the enemy. The ancient enemy, the creature
who had brought original sin to Adam and continued to
infect mankind. Father Archer had prayed interminably
over the problem she represented, and the battle was still
far from won.

But it would be, with God's grace.

Meanwhile there she stood, cause and harbinger of disaster, arrogantly assuming authority, denying the innocent their right to pray. Monster, he thought with
revulsion.

How difficult it was to destroy the licentious customs
that stubbornly survived the pagan Gael. In remoter
parts of Ireland chieftains still enjoyed their ancient privi-
leges in direct contravention of canon law, though they
did so quietly rather than openly, as in former times.

Before Christianity became preeminent in Ireland,
Gaelic chieftains had taken as many as four wives. Each
had legal status under the Brehon law, the elaborate cod-

ified system of social order and control that had survived intact from an age lost in antiquity. Each of a man's wives had legal status under the Brehon law—which did not recognize the concept of illegitimacy. A man's first marriage was for dynastic reasons, to unite powerful families. His second was to supply a head for his household, a woman to be in charge of his domestic arrangements. The third wife was chosen to be the companion of his spirit, his comrade and confidante. The fourth, if a chieftain could afford a fourth wife and the other three gave their permission, was often younger, an amusing child wife to spur an aging man's virility.

By dividing wifely duties among several women the chieftain not only assured himself of variety, but also gave his women a certain amount of personal freedom, as no one of them had to devote her entire time to him. As a result, some pagan women had assumed power on their own, taking part in the politics of the tribe and considering themselves the equal of the men.

Barbarous, thought Father Archer. Heathen, disgusting.

The Church had undertaken to put an end to such unnatural practices. But Father Archer saw a threat in the introduction of English Protestantism. Aside from its obvious heresy, the new religion espoused by Queen Elizabeth might encourage other females to seek personal power rather than accepting meek subservience to the male. Such submissiveness was their only proper attitude, of course: their fitting punishment for having inflicted the tyranny of sexual desire upon men.

Father Archer hated Protestantism almost as much as he hated women.

That hatred smoldered in his eyes as they watched Orla among the refugees, encouraging them to go down to the boats. The woman obviously considered herself one of O'Sullivan Beare's "wives," Father Archer thought. He had little doubt that Donal Cam had carnal relations with her, though they no longer discussed sexual matters in the confessional.

They no longer discussed anything in the confessional. Thanks to the evil influence of Orla Ni Donoghue, no doubt, Donal Cam had ceased giving his confessor any lever with which to pry the pagan rot from his soul.

How much longer could O'Sullivan Beare hold out against the righteous wrath of God?

As long as he keeps that woman with him, Father Archer told himself, his eyes following Orla.

"There is nothing to fear," she was saying for the tenth time to yet another frightened, dispirited woman who was afraid to get into a boat. "The boats are safe," Orla insisted, putting a comforting arm around the shivering woman's shoulders. "Did I not see your own husband working on them? Surely you trust him. Just put your trust in his handiwork as well and soon you will be safely across the river. Come now, you can do it . . ." She prodded her reluctant charge forward, glancing around for someone to help her.

In the dimness of approaching dawn she recognized Grella Ni Hurley coming toward her.

"Grella, where have you been? Come and help us get these people to the boats!"

Grella looked distracted and made random gestures with her hands. "Have you seen my brother? I need to find him."

"Is he not with the other recruits?"

"He is not. Someone said one of the sentries saw him last night, so I found that man and questioned him. At first he did not even remember, but then he told me he had seen Ronan almost as far upriver as Redwood Castle, at the very edge of the woods. No one has seen him since. I am afraid something terrible has happened to him."

A cold curl of presentiment traced its way up Orla's spine. Ronan Hurley . . . Redwood Castle . . . with a gasp, she caught her skirt in both hands and began running toward the river in search of Donal Cam.

She emerged from the trees just above the launching site. Both boats were already bobbing in the water. Men stood waiting among the reeds for the order to board.

Orla ran toward Donal Cam. "Ronan Hurley!" she cried out, panting.

"What about him?"

"He hates you, I know it. And his sister just told me he was seen last night near the Mac Egan castle."

Of course, thought Donal Cam. Why am I not surprised?

He turned toward the waiting men. "Into the boats, now! We may have very little time. It does not matter who crosses first, just get out onto the river.

"Go! Go!" Donal Cam waved his arms at them as if he would push them bodily into the boats.

His shout precipitated a mad scramble. The waiting men abandoned any discipline and floundered into the water, trying to get into the two boats. The men who were holding the boats fought back to keep them from being tipped over in the confusion. Meanwhile the boats themselves bobbed elusively atop the water, like horses refusing to be mounted.

Thomas Burke's O'Malley contingent interpreted Donal Cam's words to mean they could now go themselves. Ignoring their captain's shouted order to stand fast, they raced to the launching site and added to the chaos, making for the boat they had built and shoving aside those who were there ahead of them.

At this moment Ronan Hurley reappeared.

He came trotting innocently out of the woods as if he had been there all along, but his jaw dropped when he saw the O'Malleys attempting to seize and launch the first boat. Ronan had planned to be in that boat and was in no mood to be thwarted. With a yell of his own, he ran forward.

Grella reached water's edge in time to see her brother splashing through the reeds with some of the Connacht mercenaries. His officer's aura lingered; they did not refuse him. He was with them when they succeeded in claiming and boarding the coracle, and he helped them repel those who tried to stop them. The O'Malley men kept pulling their clansmen over the side until the little boat was jammed far past its carrying capacity. Then with one hard shove of the oars, they set themselves in motion. Everyone else stopped to watch as the coracle lurched and lunged into the belly of the flood.

Looking back toward Munster, Ronan Hurley was elated. The vessel bobbed sickeningly but he was too excited to be bothered. As for Grella, she could make her own way. He did not really need her now, he could recognize O'Sullivan's baggage and he had made other, better arrangements for a diversion. When the . . .

"Here, take an oar," a man demanded, thrusting one into his hands.

Ronan had never used an oar in his life. In more leisurely circumstances he would have chosen to be insulted. Here he was outnumbered, however, and his own safety was at stake, so he rose to clear the high sides of the coracle and took a mighty dig at the water.

He missed the surface altogether.

Misspent momentum sent him staggering backward. He dropped the oar on one man and stumbled over another, arms flailing. "Sit down!" someone yelled as several others jumped up to try to catch him. They were too late. He crashed heavily against the side of the coracle while the sudden movement of his would-be rescuers further unbalanced the boat.

From the river's edge, people watched in horror as the coracle heeled over. They could see what those clinging to the sides of the boat could not—a massive log being borne toward them on the flood. When the coracle was tilted almost over, the log struck with a boom like thunder.

The unbalanced, overloaded coracle was doomed.

One scream was lost in the roar of the Shannon. The boat disappeared as if it had never existed.

Not one swimmer surfaced to battle the current, though Grella watched until she thought her eyes would bulge from her head.

"My God," breathed Joan Ni Sweney, who was standing near her.

Donal Cam allowed his recruits no time for reflection, but began urging them into the remaining currach and out onto the river before they could lose their nerve. "Here you, climb in there, take up an oar. O'Houlihan, show him how. You too, right behind him, in with you now." He waded into the water with them, helping to steady the currach so they could scramble in.

The second boat was then launched onto the flood. White faces stared back at the land.

Seated in the prow, Rory O'Sullivan tried to pick out his wife's face from among the huddled mass at water's edge, but the only figure that stood out distinctly was that of Donal Cam, still up to his hips in brown water. He seemed to be intent upon propelling the boat across the Shannon through the sheer force of his own will, although its rowers were busily wielding their oars with varying degrees of efficiency.

No one made the mistake that had cost the first boat.

They were careful to move no more than was absolutely necessary in order to row. The sides of O'Houlihan's design were lower, making it possible for the oarsmen to sit on the plank seats, and the slightly elevated prow skimmed over the water. The men inside expected every moment to be their last, but in fact the currach handled the river very well. They crossed more than a quarter of a mile of the flooded Shannon without incident.

When the boat reached the shallows on the far side most of its occupants leapt out and ran to higher ground to take up positions while the oarsmen, with some difficulty, got the currach turned around and headed back for a second load.

They were already breathless from their first struggle with the river. The boat was lighter now, and therefore more subject to the whims of the Shannon. It was tossed from side to side, it leapt and plunged like an unbroken colt. Men turned green. One, not daring to take his hands from his oar, spewed vomit over his companions.

Suddenly the boat was caught in a giant eddy. It rotated wildly out of control. Dermod O'Houlihan was with them and his calm good sense saved them. In a voice that did not admit of any difficulty, he ordered the oarsmen with calm decisiveness until they were clear of the whirlpool and on their way again.

"Different men must row next time," said Donal Cam, watching from the river's edge. "It is enough to ask a man to make that journey twice."

"It is too much," his uncle agreed. "And too much for you to go wading into the river as you did. You could fall in a hole and be gone before anyone could get to you. Your recklessness has always worried me."

Father Collins was standing not far away, and he heard this last statement with interest. When Donal Cam, ignoring his uncle's injunction, waded out to meet the boat as it landed, Father Collins said in a low voice to Dermod O'Sullivan, "Is that true, what you said? Is O'Sullivan Beare indifferent to danger?"

"He always has been. He is an O'Sullivan, after all!" Dermod's weather-beaten face lit with pride.

"Then you would say he is not a man to act out of cowardice, out of fear for his personal safety?"

"What are you talking about? Of course not! He is the bravest of men, always has been, since boyhood."

"How can you be certain when you have not been with him every moment?"

"I was not with him at Kinsale because I was too old to march off behind his banner," the old man said with dignity, "but I heard from others how he acquitted himself. He was one of the last to leave the field. I did join him afterward at Ardea and have been with him ever since through the most terrible of times, and I can assure you that . . .

"You were at Ardea? When Dunboy fell, you were there then?"

"I just said so." Dermod was beginning to lose his temper.

"Aha! Then you can tell me . . ."

"Aha!" Dermod interrupted like an echo. "I see my wife. You must excuse me, Father." Without waiting for an answer he hurried toward Joan, who was looking the other way. When she began to turn toward him he slowed to a casual saunter, pretending not to notice his wife until he was right in front of her. For her part, Joan immediately began scolding him about something, Father Collins noticed—all the while giving him surreptitious little touches and pats.

Their mutual concern for one another surrounded them like a magic circle.

The Jesuit felt a lump rise in his throat.

Two old people in the midst of death and horror, and they are happy just to be together.

Perhaps I should have married, he thought enviously. How wonderful it must be to have your roots buried that deeply in another human soul!

Joan was asking her husband, "When are you going across?"

"When The O'Connor does, I expect."

"And when will that be?"

"Why, do you want me to go with you?"

She shrugged. "I am quite capable of being rowed across a river without needing you to hold my hand."

"I know that."

They watched the scene before them as another boatload of recruits headed across the flood toward the distant shore. "It will take a long time with just the one boat," Joan said.

"Too long. Damn Hurley." Dermod had a proprietary interest in the boats. He felt as if he had just watched a child of his lost in the flood. In spite of himself, his voice trembled.

Joan shot him a quick look out of the corner of her eye. No nuance of his speech or change of his posture was ever lost on her. But her glance reassured her that Dermod was all right. He will hold, she thought. My old fool. My dear fool. He is strong, and he will hold.

Maire Ni Driscoll was not feeling strong. Every boatload that made it across successfully brought her own time of passage that much nearer, and she was terrified. When Richard died she thought she wanted to go with him, but the months since had been filled with the fight to survive, and now she could not imagine how it had felt to want to die. Death waited on the river, death for the taking, and she shrank from it in terror.

The little dog in her arms felt her trembling. They

were submerged in Niall's shaggy mantle. Maire wondered if he would ask to take it back before he boarded the boat. He was a recruit; he would go across before she did. She could not expect they would let him stay with her, even if he wanted to, which he probably did not.

Her eyes sought and found him at the edge of the flood with several other members of the buannachta, talking in tense voices and eyeing the water.

If his arms were around me I would not be afraid to cross the river, Maire thought. She wondered if the thought was a betrayal of Richard Mac Geoghegan. Perhaps. Perhaps not. Hard to know.

Hard, in the desolate dawn, to care. She shivered again. The little dog in her arms whined, twisting around and trying to lick her throat.

Niall and the others were discussing Ronan Hurley.

"Where do you suppose he was?" Gerald Ryan was wondering. "He came running up in a mighty hurry."

"He did that," another gallowglass affirmed. "He ran like he had a girl's father after him."

There was a snort of nervous laughter. "You would feel sorry for any lass who opened her arms to him," someone said. "He was a surly bit of business, there toward the end."

Gerald Ryan remarked, "We are none of us rainbows."

They looked up at Maurice O'Sullivan's approach. "You are the next to go, so be ready," he told them. "Leave your packs here, they go with the baggage at the end. Right now the commander wants to save all the space for people."

"My harp is in my pack!" Niall protested. "Surely you cannot expect me to leave that?"

Maurice looked sympathetic. "Sorry, you must. Orders. Flesh and blood first, the commander says."

"What about his own baggage?"

"That must wait with the rest."

"Men will be needed to row the women and children," Niall pointed out. "Could I not wait here and be one of those?"

Maurice O'Sullivan could not help smiling. He had large eyes and a pointy face; when he smiled he looked like a satyr. "You do not want to be separated too long from your harp, is that it?" he asked mischievously. "Very well, O'Mahony. You can wait here and help row the civilians, but do not try to sneak that harp into the boat with you. I mean it. It stays with the baggage."

Niall felt a wash of relief. He looked toward the women. His eyes found her instantly. The shaggy mantle was her standard. Leaving the other men, not caring what they said to his back, he made his way toward Maire.

"I am going to be one of your oarsmen," he told her as casually as he could. "So I shall wait here with you . . . and the others . . . until it is your turn to board the boat."

He watched her face, trying to read her expression. She was watching his for the same reason.

Neither could tell what the other might be thinking.

The little dog popped its head out of the mantle and looked at Niall with eyes like polished jet. He scratched it behind the ears ostentatiously, currying favor.

The dog yawned and looked away.

The silence threatened to become awkward. "Did you ever eat?" Niall asked. He knew it was a dangerous question but he felt compelled to ask because she looked so pale and fragile.

"I did not," she said with downcast eyes.

His heart went out to her. "Neither did the commander," he told her gently. "He could not bring himself to eat his horses either. You are in good company."

She looked up at him through her dark eyelashes and

managed a small, grateful smile. "I am glad I am in good company."

Niall O'Mahony suddenly felt seven feet tall.

He waited with her, watching, as boatload after boatload made its way across the river, ferrying the buannachta. When the big currach discharged its last load of them and started back for the first load of civilians, Niall was aware of a perceptible division taking place among those waiting around him. Some were eagerly moving closer to the flood, anxious for the boat. Others were shrinking back, spiritually if not physically, trying to postpone the moment they must commit themselves to the turbulent water. A few were even edging toward the trees as if they meant to slip away when no one was looking.

He was about to go after them when he felt that prickling at the base of his spine that every soldier knows and respects. He whirled around, looking upriver toward the area where the dark woodland met the water.

There were shadows moving among the trees. Shadows that should not be there, and were advancing swiftly toward the launching site.

Niall felt a thrill of horror. He turned back toward the river, staring across in the direction of Donal Cam, who had crossed together with his uncle and The O'Connor Kerry in the last boatload of soldiers.

"Attack!" Niall screamed. He began jumping up and down and waving his arms frantically, trying to draw the attention of those on the other side of the river.

Donal Cam noticed, and in the next moment saw the movement at the edge of the forest, and men running.

"Mac Egan," he said in a tight voice, pointing.

Dermod O'Sullivan craned his thin neck forward as if to narrow the distance and see better. *"Where is my wife?"* His fists clenched.

"Sweet jumping Jesus," breathed The O'Connor Kerry.

When Donncha Mac Egan broke from cover the first thing he saw was a crowd of women and children and a pile of baggage. With a hoarse shout, he waved his men forward. There was a rumble of running feet behind him as the white faced civilians, crouched at the edge of the flood, turned toward him in horror.

"Kill them all!" he cried to his men.

The night before, a disaffected follower of O'Sullivan Beare had appeared unexpectedly at Redwood Castle. At first the suspicious sentries refused him admittance, but eventually he was taken into the presence of the queen's sheriff. Mac Egan had listened with interest to Ronan Hurley's words.

"O'Sullivan Beare is more ingenious than I expected," the sheriff remarked to his own captains. "I thought we could wait for reinforcements to surround him, but apparently it is too late. The men I have sent for have not arrived and O'Sullivan is about to slip away from us, damn his eyes. We are going to have to attack them with this garrison alone."

"Counting his buannachta and mercenaries, O'Sullivan still has two hundred and fifty soldiers," Ronan had warned.

Mac Egan, fair and stout and powerfully built, had frowned in thought. "Then perhaps we should hold off until he has ferried some of them across, eh? We can attack when the odds are more in our favor. And what of you, Hurley? Will you take the queen's coin and formally forswear O'Sullivan?"

"Absolutely," Ronan assured him. "But I do think I should go back to the camp, at least put in an appearance in the morning so no one gets suspicious. Will you give me some food and a dry bed in the meantime?"

"Agreed. You can sleep in the armory and leave before first light. When my attack comes, be sure to stand well aside."

"Oh, I shall be across the Shannon by then," Ronan said blithely. "I am going over in the first boat."

That night as he slept on dry straw with meat in his belly and ale on his breath, Ronan dreamed of Spanish gold. In the confusion of Mac Egan's attack no one would be watching the baggage.

Donncha Mac Egan had also slept soundly, dreaming of the glowing reports he would send to Her Majesty's authorities after he had slaughtered a number of the rebels.

But with morning came delays. There was an argument over the assignment of weaponry, bits of equipment were broken, a few of the garrison were late in reporting to their leaders. The sun was well up when the attack force set out from Redwood Castle behind Donncha Mac Egan. Only Ronan had got away early; he no doubt was already on the opposite shore.

In fact, by the time Mac Egan and his men arrived it appeared Donal Cam had ferried his entire army across the river. Only civilians were waiting at the edge of the water, with a pile of baggage. A boat was beating its way back toward them but making slow headway against the flood.

Donncha Mac Egan grinned in anticipation of an easy triumph.

One recruit had not crossed the river. Waiting with Maire, Niall O'Mahony found himself the sole visible warrior standing between Mac Egan and the refugees.

He thrust Maire behind him and snatched up his pike. At that moment he was nearly tripped by the dog, who leapt out of Maire's arms and ran forward, yapping furiously, to sink its teeth into the leg of the foremost of Mac Egan's men.

Watching from the far shore, Donal Cam cupped his mouth with his hands and yelled with all his might, "Spare my people! We can talk, wait for me! Mac Egan! *You are one of our own!*"

By a trick of the wind, his voice carried across the river. Donncha Mac Egan understood every word. For one moment the queen's sheriff paused and looked across the flood, assessing the size of the force on the opposite shore. Then he shook his head and repeated the order to attack.

Pinned on the riverbank, the refugees sought desperately for any weapon they might use in their own defense. Joan Ni Sweney had no time to make herself another stocking-and-stone skull basher before the first man reached her, so she contented herself with giving him a brutal kick in the genitals.

A year ago I could not have kicked that high, she thought with satisfaction as he doubled over, gasping. *The march has done me good!*

Some of Mac Egan's men cut off one group of women and drove them into the water, where they meant to drown them while others were seizing the baggage and making off into the woods with whatever loot they could. Men were shouting, women were screaming, children were shrieking, one little dog was barking frantically as she darted from one pair of legs to another, slashing and nipping and running away before she could be hurt.

Donal Cam watched from the other side of the river, impotently beating one fist against the open palm of his other hand. He said to Rory, "It is taking an unconscionably long time for . . ."

Then Thomas Burke's men broke out of concealment

in the forest and swarmed over the Mac Egans, screaming Connacht war cries.

They did not strike the first fatal blow, however. The honor of bringing down the queen's sheriff, blighted fruit of a noble tree, went to Niall O'Mahony, who struck Donncha Mac Egan a killing blow to the temple with his pike.

Mac Egan staggered sideway and fell like a tree. Maire's little dog ran up and bit his nose savagely, trying to worry it off his face, but he never felt the pain—nor did he feel it when Niall bent over him and thrust a dagger into his heart, just to be sure.

Too late Mac Egan's followers realized the trap they were in. Twenty musketeers and as many kernes—all that remained of Thomas Burke's mercenaries since the O'Malleys were lost—were attacking them with no more mercy than they had meant to show the refugees. Burke's company killed with professional ease. After the first volley, the musketeers did not take time for reloading and repositioning but used their guns as clubs, while the kernes with the skill of long practice used sword and spear and pike to telling effect.

The shock of surprise was as effective as the weaponry.

Donncha Mac Egan had been the first to fall, and the loss of the chieftain traditionally had a disheartening effect on Gaelic warriors. Their loyalty was to the man rather than to whatever cause he espoused. When they realized Mac Egan was dead his followers began scattering and trying to save their own lives rather than continuing the attack.

Those who ran fastest reached the safety of the forest. But by the time the skirmish was over fifteen of the sheriff's finest lay slain by the riverbank . . . and the O'Houlihan currach was just pulling into the shallows.

Niall flung down his pike and gathered Maire into his

arms. The little dog came prancing up to them, tail a-wag, with a volley of barking that boasted of valorous deeds.

The attack had come so swiftly and ended so suddenly that reaction did not set in until it was over. Then some of the people collapsed crying on the cold mud. Others who could truly bear no more simply crept away into the woods. Perhaps they found their way to Redwood Castle and took the queen's coin, giving Mac Egan a posthumous success. Or they may have run until they could run no longer, then found shelter—or died.

Watching from across the water, Donal Cam let out a breath he had not known he was holding. His heart was hammering; lights swam behind his eyes. Around him he heard murmured prayers as some of the buannachta gave thanks for the rescue of the women.

Donal Cam's lips also moved in prayer. He strained his eyes with the futile effort to recognize individuals on the far shore.

Dermod O'Sullivan clawed at him. "Your eyes are younger than mine, do you see her? Do you see my wife?"

Sometimes, thought Donal Cam, a lie is mandatory. "I do, of course. She is there on the shore, I am certain she will be in the first boatload across."

Dermod made a sound like a sob suppressed with difficulty. "She could have been killed."

"That is why I left a rear guard, uncle, to be certain the civilians were protected. Burke was in time, you could see that." But even as he spoke he knew some people had been killed; his keen eyes had told him that much. The horse boys had fought to hold on to their charges as well as to protect the baggage, and they had taken the brunt of the assault. They . . . and how many more? He stared across the water.

The loaded currach approached with what seemed agonizing slowness.

Even before it reached midriver Dermod had waded into the shallows, calling his wife's name. Donal Cam went after him and had to drag him back to the land. "You told me yourself the shallows are dangerous, uncle!"

"I say a lot of things. Now let go of me. You were right, I can see her, she is in the first boat. Let go of me, I say!" Dermod gave a mighty tug and freed himself from Donal Cam's restraining hand. He promptly waded back into the water, holding out both hands toward the distant boat. "Joan, Joan!"

"Rory!" Donal Cam shouted. "Help me, quickly!"

Rory O'Sullivan splashed into the water and the two of them succeeded in recapturing the old man and returning him to dry land a second time, for which he did not thank them. He was shaking with equal parts of chill and indignation.

"Hold on to him," Donal Cam commanded his captain of buannachta, "until the boat carrying his wife reaches this side and my aunt is safely ashore, do you understand?"

"I do, Commander." Trying to be respectful and firm at the same time, Rory took a grip on Dermod's arm and braced his feet. Beneath his fingers, the other man's wiry muscles felt like overtaut bowstrings. "Your wife is all right," he reiterated soothingly, holding on. He was relieved to see that Joan really was in the approaching boat.

But where was Orla? Rory's gaze moved past the boat and scanned the far shore, searching.

Donal Cam was doing the same thing. It was impossible to recognize anyone among the tiny dark figures waiting, they were specks in the distance, yet he tried.

He tried, his lips moving silently.

As the currach came breasting through the reeds men ran to help its passengers clamber out. After the terror of the attack, the crossing had left them numb. Some did not seem to realize they had arrived. They sat in the bottom of the boat like lumps of clay wrapped in rags, and men had to reach in and drag them out bodily.

Joan Ni Sweney got out of the currach under her own power, though her legs were trembling. She stepped into knee-deep water and felt slippery mud beneath her feet as she started for shore.

Rory O'Sullivan did not release Dermod until Joan had actually emerged from the water and was on comparatively dry land. Then he opened his hands and stepped back, and the old man stumbled forward a step or two, then stopped and stood with his head up, proudly, waiting for his wife to come to him.

"You old fool," was her greeting. "Was it yourself I heard yelling at me?"

"It was myself. I wanted to know if you brought my things with you?"

"How could I bring your pack? They told us to leave all the baggage behind until last, and then those wretched men came out of the woods and made off with it."

"Did they take everything?" Dermod asked, trying to sound as if that was what mattered.

She shrugged. "They took enough, I cannot say how much. The soldiers' women will know what is missing."

The soldiers' women. Staring across the river, Rory heard those words with a pang.

So did Donal Cam. For no particular reason an image came back to him from Poll na gCapaill. The grass white and tufted and stiff with frost. The dead horses lying so still.

"Were any of the civilians killed?" Donal Cam asked one of the oarsmen from the boat, who was watching as fresh men took his place and got the currach turned around for its next trip.

"A couple of women were driven into the river by the enemy and drowned, and at least one man was shot. In addition to that, Commander, several of our horse boys were killed. So there are bodies. Shall we bring them over in the last boat—now that there's not much baggage to carry?"

"Who were the women?"

"I honestly cannot say, I did not wait to find out. We just loaded the boat and came away. I think their bodies may still be in the water. I did not hear anyone name them."

Donal Cam cupped his hands around his mouth and shouted to the departing boat, "Have our dead brought back with the last load!" He turned toward the men around him. "We can at least bury them here before we . . ."

"Look there!" someone cried, pointing downriver.

Attracted by the sound of gunfire, locals were approaching the crossing site along both banks of the Shannon.

Experience had taught Donal Cam to fear the worst. "Make haste!" he shouted urgently after the departing boat.

At first only a few people approached the scene, and they stood warily at a distance, watching curiously while Donal Cam and his buannachta watched them, alert to any sign of hostility. Meanwhile the currach crossed the flood, reloaded, and started back.

Orla was not in this load either, Rory saw, although Father Archer was very much in evidence in the prow.

Donal Cam came striding to meet him. "Who was killed?"

"Two women were drowned when Mac Egan's men

drove some of them into the water. A good and pious widow, and one of the camp followers. Also some of the attendants were . . ."

"Name the women." Donal Cam's voice was suddenly harsh.

Father Archer raised his eyebrows. "The widow was one of the O'Callaghans. She panicked in the water and her steward was shot while trying to save her."

"And the other woman? Who was she?"

Donal Cam's eyes were like a stormy night. For once the priest could not meet them. Instead he looked down, only to observe that Donal Cam's clenched fists were being held rigidly at his sides. This was no time for a confrontation.

"I honestly do not know who she was. I did not see her face, nor get anywhere near her. I was busy administering the last rites to . . ."

But Donal Cam had walked away, fists still clenched.

There was no time for him to imagine the worst. The local people were gradually edging closer, and in their wariness he read a warning. They did not intend to welcome the refugees warmly. Donal Cam began issuing orders to strengthen their defensive position until the crossing was completed.

"I do not think the natives are friendly," he said ruefully to Rory and Maurice O'Sullivan.

On the eastern side of the flood, Thomas Burke held the same opinion. By the time the boat returned he had the next load of passengers already in the shallows, waiting to climb into the currach. Dermod O'Houlihan was valiantly making these final trips across himself, both to help with the rowing and to keep an eye on the condition of the boat.

He was increasingly concerned about the currach. Well-built though it was, it was sheathed in uncured leather. Worse, there had been neither time nor materials for waterproofing. Tar or even many coats of rancid tallow would have sealed the currach, but without such treatment the hides were absorbing water. They were growing heavier with each trip, swelling and straining at their bindings.

Dermod O'Houlihan was afraid the currach would not stay afloat for very much longer. "Send the other priest in this next trip," he advised Thomas Burke.

Burke rightly interpreted the anxiety in his voice and asked Father Collins to join the next load of civilians in the boat. He also assigned Niall and Maire to this group, but Niall hesitated.

Maire tugged at his arm. "Come now, we must go."

Niall was staring toward the place where the baggage had been piled.

"My harp."

At first she did not understand. Survival had preempted other considerations. Then the misery on Niall's face jogged her memory. "Oh, Niall. It was with the baggage, in your pack."

"It was," he said in an agonized voice, "and someone carried it away."

"Did you see it taken?"

"I was fighting for our lives," he reminded her. "Until just now, I did not realize it was gone."

"Perhaps you could catch up with whoever took it and make him give it back," Maire suggested because she could not bear the pain in his eyes.

"How would I find him? The sheriff's men scattered in every direction, taking their loot with them." Niall's body stiffened abruptly. He stared, drew in a sharp breath, then darted forward so swiftly he carried Maire along in his wake like a blown leaf in a whirlwind.

Little remained of the heap of baggage: some ripped

and torn packs, a few broken bits of boxes, some parcels of cooked horsemeat that had been dropped when the mercenaries appeared.

And one scrap of color that gleamed like a beacon in the sea of trampled mud.

Niall squatted on his heels, hardly daring to hope. With infinite gentleness he began working something free from the muck. Maire bent over him. "Be careful. Ah . . . there."

Together they looked at the empty harp bag.

The bosses of coral ornamentation still flaunted their color, and the soft otterskin, in spite of being muddy and trampled, still hinted at the shape of the harp.

But the harp itself was gone.

Niall crouched on his heels for what seemed an eternity, not moving, not speaking. He felt as if shutters were closing in his head. Shutters that when open had let him look through wide windows into the bright past. One by one they closed, and he fancied that with each one he could hear, ever more faintly, the last sweet strains of a music that would not come again.

On the bank of the Shannon, Niall O'Mahony bowed his head over an empty harp bag and cried.

"Oh Niall! Oh please stop! Do not cry!" Maire's hands fluttered like butterflies around his head and shoulders, powerless to help. Seeing him weep terrified her.

The little dog crept forward and tried to lick Niall's face. There was no comfort for him in the warm pink tongue. He pushed the animal aside but it came back, whimpering, to assault him from a different angle.

Niall twisted away and almost collided with Maire's legs. He drew back abruptly and the dog saw its opportunity. It flung itself into the opening and swarmed up him, licking every bit of skin its tongue could reach and whimpering and wriggling in an ecstasy of sympathy.

It was irresistible. Caught between tears and laughter, Niall hugged the dog to his bosom. "Ah, you creature!"

"Come away now," Maire said gently. "The boat has gone but we can be in the next boatload."

Still holding the dog, Niall got slowly to his feet. The muddy harp bag dangled from his fingers. Maire took it from him and left him with the living dog instead.

Thomas Burke had filled the boat as fast as he could and helped shove it clear of the reeds. Now he stood at water's edge, watching its progress anxiously. From time to time he turned his head to see how near the local people had dared to come. At the edge of the trees he saw one, doubtless a farmer, holding a pitchfork at the ready.

"Spectators do not come armed with pitchforks," he said in a low voice to one of his musketeers. "Reload now, but turn your back so they do not see what you are doing. I want you to be ready, pass the word."

The currach stayed afloat, crossed the river, returned. Niall and Maire were in the next boatload, with the dog. Burke gave the dog a hard look as it was lifted in, but said nothing.

"It takes up no space," Niall assured him, giving it to Maire to hold while he manned an oar.

Someone joked, "Just do not let it add to the water in the bottom of the boat."

It was scarcely a joke; the seams were leaking. Those who were not going to row were expected to bail out the currach with their cupped hands or in any other way they could.

Maire sat with her feet in the cold water because there was nowhere else to put them. She set the dog on the plank seat beside her, then did as several other women were doing, pulling off her underskirt and using it to sop up water, then wringing it out over the side. This did not help much but at least it was a distraction.

When the full force of the river took hold of the currach, the boat shuddered throughout its length. Several people gasped. Maire forgot about bailing and clung to the gunwale with both hands, her rigid stare fixed on the swirling water. The boat felt to her like a living creature gone out of control. She had no faith in the human beings who were pretending to row it, they were merely performing a ritual in the presence of an elemental deity. The river. The hungry, roaring river.

An tSionainn.

The Shannon paid no more attention to the currach than to any other debris. The sea was waiting.

Father and mother and child, source and destination of the river. The sea was waiting and the Shannon was hurrying toward the rendezvous. The circle of life must continue, river to sea to vapor to cloud to rain to stream to river. Change and transformation.

The Shannon sang on her way.

Maire clung to the side of the currach and heard the voice of the river. At first it frightened her, but she dared not turn loose of the side of the boat, so she could not cover her ears with her hands. She had to listen.

The deadly flood sang to her of the thin bright trickle of water at its source, hidden among reeds and cresses. It sang of rain and ice and energy, of rushing and seeking, of being inexorably driven like a refugee across the heart of Ireland, of carrying stinking mud to enrich new land farther downriver, of growing and changing and forcing its way through or around or over. It sang of drowned cattle and gliding swans. Most particularly it sang of indifference to death and a total commitment to life, because death meant nothing to the spirit that was the Shannon.

The Shannon sang of life and Maire listened.

By the time they reached midriver Niall thought he

could feel blisters rising on his hands. The oar was crudely, hastily carved, there had been no time for smoothing. In spite of the cold he could feel sweat puddling in his armpits. His face was wet too, though not because of his tears. Everyone in the currach was soaked; a thin rain was falling, adding to the spray from the river as gusts of wind slanted across the water.

"At least the wind is at our backs right now," said the man rowing behind him. "I feel sorry for the lads returning who must face into it."

"You will not go back yourself?" Niall called over his shoulder.

"Not me. There is only one more boatload to bring over anyway, let fresh men do it."

He was correct. The last civilians were with Niall and Maire, as well as some of the mercenaries. One more load would bring the rest over. The dreaded crossing was almost completed.

Niall dared risk a glance at Maire. She was holding onto the edge of the boat and watching the river. Even when the currach gave a lurch and settled more deeply into the water she did not react. Her thoughts were obviously far away.

I suppose she is thinking of Richard Mac Geoghegan, Niall said to himself.

The indefatigable Dermod O'Houlihan called the stroke and his crew bent to their oars. Dermod did not like the way the currach was settling. "She is too heavy," he remarked several times.

It would be better, he thought, to put fewer people in the next load and divide the crossing into two more trips instead of one. But he was not certain the boat would last for two more trips back and forth.

The currach was increasingly sluggish; it might not last for one more trip.

They made worryingly slow progress toward the opposite shore. Donal Cam's distinctive figure was waiting for them at water's edge. Beyond him O'Houlihan could see the main body of the buannachta drawn up into a defensive square. And beyond them, the local people. Watching. Tense.

As the boat reached shore, Niall dropped his oar and stood up to go to Maire. His unplanned movement made the currach rock dangerously. "You left-footed limb of Satan!" O'Houlihan swore at him, "get out of my boat before you sink her!"

Niall was glad to comply. He helped Maire out of the currach and the little dog leapt out after them, bounding into the water without hesitation and paddling ashore with its head held high, obviously considering itself the hero of the day.

When they were clear of the flood and trying to wring it out of their sodden clothing, Niall murmured as if surprised, "We made it!"

"So we did," Maire said. "We are going to live."

"Are you so certain?"

"I am certain. The river told me."

He gave her a startled glance. She had been through so much—was her mind broken?

Just then Rory O'Sullivan trotted up to him. "Join the other kernes over there in case of attack. Go quickly, and put that woman in the center of the square. Hurry now!"

On the far side of the river Thomas Burke waited tensely for the return of the boat. He could sense danger closing in, feel its aura crawling up his spine. Waiting with him were the remainder of his mercenaries, two horse boys and their charges, and the last of the soldiers' women.

The dead also waited. Burke had made a command decision to leave them behind. He preferred to get everyone into the boat and be done with it, which allowed no room for corpses. The currach was built to hold thirty but had taken a few more on every trip. It must do so one final time.

The natives were coming closer, emboldened by the reduction in numbers of those on the shore.

"Hurry for the sake of God!" Burke called hoarsely to the oarsmen as the currach at last approached.

As if that was a signal, one of the locals shouted, "Break some skulls for the queen before the rebels escape!" and ran forward, brandishing a club. The others streamed after him.

The boat was in the reeds by now. Burke and the rest ran for it. The cold water felt good on Burke's wounded leg, but the violent exertion sent an unexpected stab of pain through him. He gritted his teeth and ignored it.

When he caught hold of the side of the currach Dermod O'Houlihan was scowling down at him.

"You have too many people here, some of them are going to have to wait for another crossing."

"We cannot wait, man! Look behind us!" Burke lunged upward, scrambling over the side. The others were doing the same; the boat rocked wildly. Burke hooked his good leg over the gunwale, gave a heave, and fell in, dragging the wounded leg after him. It responded with a flare of pain that made him nauseous.

The locals were arriving in great numbers now, thirsty for excitement. Someone hurled a spear. One of the mercenaries who was just climbing over the side of the currach grunted and fell back into the water with a splash.

"Hurry, hurry!" Burke urged as he reached out in spite of his pain to catch a woman's outstretched hands and pull her over the side.

From among the trees came the unmistakable bark of a caliver. Either some of the natives had handguns, or Mac Egan's men were returning.

The frightened oarsmen tried to push the currach clear of the reeds while people were still floundering toward it. They caught hold of its sides and fought one another to get in. The overstressed boat groaned like a creature in pain. "Turn loose, damn you!" O'Houlihan screamed, trying to pry a man's fingers from the gunwale. But it was too late. The currach had cleared the reeds, but was sinking by the time it reached open water.

When Thomas Burke felt the boat go down he thought he was a dead man. But it did not sink far. They were over what was, except in times of flood, dry land. The currach went down in four feet of water, leaving its startled passengers standing in the flood up to their shoulders.

As the boat began to sink some people who had not yet been able to get into it plunged on into the river to try to swim across instead. Driven by their desire to survive, they did not wait to see what became of the boat. The current caught them, carried them as it chose, and eventually deposited a few of them alive on the western side of the Shannon.

Meanwhile Burke and O'Houlihan got everyone out of the sunken boat. Men held their breath, ducked beneath the surface to pull it free of the mud, and hoisted it onto their shoulders. O'Houlihan directed the tipping of the currach to empty it of water while the musket barked again, then the boat was refloated and the reboarding began under a fire of missiles and taunts from the shore.

A few who had not got into the boat, and were unable to attempt to swim the river, ran toward the woods as if they no longer cared who waited there or what happened to them.

The second attempt saw the currach loaded, and out on the river. The survivors sat dazed; it was a few moments before any coherent effort was made to begin rowing.

Thomas Burke let the pain take him. He looked at those around him with glazed eyes. He did not bother to count them and he made no effort even to recognize them. He consigned himself to the river's mercy; it must surely be kinder than man's.

For the last time, Donal Cam waded into the shallows to meet the final boatload. Their faces were anguished and several of them were bloody. His eyes sought one face in particular; sought and held one pair of eyes, just for a moment.

Watching from the shore with his men, Rory O'Sullivan saw his commander catch hold of the side of the boat nearest Orla, and reach up to help her get out. There was blood on her clothing.

"Is that someone else's blood?" Even as Donal Cam asked the question, he knew the answer. Orla's weatherbeaten face was far too pale.

"A glancing blow, it is nothing." She brushed past him and walked ashore under her own power. He had turned back to help the rest disembark when he was alerted by a commotion behind him. Whirling around, he saw Orla lying facedown on the ground. People were running toward her.

Rory O'Sullivan was running toward her.

Donal Cam stayed where he was. He assisted the last man in getting out of the currach, and Thomas Burke limped ashore leaning on his commander's shoulder.

Farther downriver, others were coming ashore. Between

them, Peadar O'Coughlan and Thady Cooney had managed to save four horses—or the horses saved them. During the final attack on the currach and its sinking, no one had bothered about horse boys and swimming animals behind the boat. Peadar and Thady had decided between them to trust horses rather than men or boats. Tying the lead ropes of two animals apiece around their waists, they dared the flood, keeping their heads above water by keeping their fingers firmly tangled in the manes of two of the horses.

The boys crawled up onto the bank and lay panting. The horses stood beside them, heads hanging, sides heaving, water streaming off of them.

"Are we dead?" Peadar asked without opening his eyes.

"I am," said Thady.

They lay awhile longer. Peadar at last said, reluctantly, "The commander will be wanting these horses, they are all we have left."

"He will that," agreed Thady, flinging his forearm across his eyes. "We should tether them so they do not stray."

"I hurt all over," moaned Peadar.

They lay a while longer without moving. The horses began cropping the frosty weeds along the shore.

At the landing site, Orla had opened her eyes to find her husband bending over her. "Where are you hurt?"

"My . . . back, I think. I was . . . shot . . ."

He said something in reply, but his voice faded away. The last thing Orla saw before a soft grayness folded around her was the scar on his anguished face.

They carried her to the defensive square and laid her in its center. She was eased onto her side and the back of her gown torn open. The blood-soaked cloth pulled away to reveal a crater just under her shoulder blade where the bullet had entered. There was no exit wound; it was still embedded deep in her body.

Donal Cam pushed his way through the crowd around her. "How badly is she hurt?"

"A bullet in the back, Commander," Rory told him. "It might have entered the lung, but there is no bloody froth from her nose or mouth. She is a strong woman, the wound may not be fatal, please God."

He is telling me what I want to hear, thought Donal Cam. It is our way; we always tell people what they want to hear.

"Prepare a litter and organize bearers for her," he ordered brusquely, as if unmoved. "Riding a horse would be im . . . the horses! What happened to the horses?" He was astonished to realize that he had, in all the confusion of crossing, forgotten them. Hold on! he warned his mind.

He found Thomas Burke with his men, counting the survivors. "What became of the horses and horse boys, Burke?"

The big mercenary captain had also forgotten them until that moment, his face plainly said. "I . . . ah . . ."

"They swam for it, Commander," a Connacht gallowglass volunteered.

"Did they make it? Did anyone see?"

No one could answer him.

"We were under fire, Commander," Burke explained. "Our attention was elsewhere."

"Who was shooting at you, local people?"

"Possibly, though I am more inclined to think some of Mac Egan's men came back."

Donal Cam slitted his eyes and gazed across the river. "If they did, I want no boat left behind to ferry them across the Shannon so they can pursue us. You told me

Mac Egan was killed, so they may well seek revenge. Have some of your men smash that currach to bits before we leave this place so no sympathetic local person can take it over to them."

"What are the locals likely to do to us?" Burke wondered.

"Hard to say. Unlike those on the opposite side, they have been content to watch from a distance—so far. But I think the sooner we leave here, the better."

"You are in the west now, Commander," said one of the Connacht men. "These folks will not hurt you."

Donal Cam snorted. His faith in his fellow man was not what it used to be.

He ordered the buannachta held in their defensive position while the boat was destroyed and the remainder of the column prepared to get under way once more. The column, he observed, was considerably diminished. Donal Cam did not take a head count, but he suspected there were not many more than three hundred altogether now. Dead, defected, lost . . .

He would have liked to allow them to rest after the ordeal of the crossing, but he did not dare. Not with those people in the distance watching, like black crows on a tree limb.

The breaking up of the currach distressed his uncle. O'Houlihan accepted it pragmatically, but to Dermod the boat was his idea made manifest, almost like a child of his siring. Watching as the gallowglasses smashed it with axes, he flinched at every blow.

Meanwhile Maurice O'Sullivan began shouldering responsibility for the ordering of the buannachta, leaving Rory O'Sullivan to be with his wife.

Under other conditions Rory would not have relinquished any portion of his command to any man. But he could not leave Orla. She was his wife, the mother of his children.

And there was a deeper, atavistic reason that compelled him to remain beside his fallen mate. An instinct he could not name and perhaps did not even recognize told him this was the time to stake his claim on Orla irrevocably. She did not belong to the commander. She was his. Now that she was wounded, his was the right to stand beside her. Even if Donal Cam ordered him to he would not leave her.

But Donal Cam did not ask him to leave her. He busied himself going from one knot of people to another, assessing their condition and getting them ready to resume the cavalcade.

He hesitated beside The O'Connor Kerry, who was sitting on wet ground rubbing his feet. "We must walk again soon, Sean," Donal Cam said as gently as he could.

"I know it. I preferred the currach, it asked nothing of my feet."

"Can you walk at all? We have no horse for you."

"Ah, the loss of the horses is worse for you than for me. That lot watching us from the distance would be more impressed if you at least were sitting tall on a horse, glaring back at them. We would look more like an army then."

"We are an army, Sean, no matter how we look. An army making a strategic withdrawal so it can gather its forces to fight again."

The O'Connor tilted his head back and squinted up at the resolute face of O'Sullivan Beare. "If you say so."

"I say so."

The old man sighed. "Then I march with you," he announced, dragging himself painfully to his feet.

When they were ready to move out Donal Cam went

to the water's edge one last time and stared across the brown flood, filling his eyes with Munster.

Then he turned his back on the Shannon and gave the order to march on Connacht.

Day Eleven

January 10, 1603. *Cill Iomair*, the Church of St. Iomar

Riding O'Sullivan Beare's horses through the darkness in a strange land would have been a grand adventure under ordinary circumstances. But Thady Cooney and Peadar O'Coughlan had not experienced ordinary circumstances for many months. Now they were only weary and frightened.

Exhausted by their swim across the Shannon, they had been unable to rouse themselves until the fading of the light warned them they must do something. They were still groggy, but as their realized their predicament their senses sharpened to near panic.

"We have to catch up with the column, Thady!"

"And do I not know that? Do you take me for an idiot? Which way did they go, do you suppose?"

Peadar looked blank. "To Connacht."

"We crossed the queen of rivers, so we must be in Connacht now."

"Oh." Peadar scratched his head, wondering if the river had drowned his lice. "To Leitrim, then."

"Do you know where Leitrim is?"

"I do not, but the commander is surely somewhere between here and there and we had better follow and find him."

Thady pointed out, "Any number of people have stopped following him along the way."

"We are not that sort," Peadar replied with dignity. "Besides, where would we go? From my observation, everyone wants to kill us no matter where we are. Our only safety is with the commander."

"Then we must get to him," Thady agreed. "But how?"

They stood close together in the dusk of a cold winter's day, looking to the left and right as if inspiration might come floating toward them. Then Peadar's eyes fixed on the chestnut stallion, tethered as he had been all afternoon to a stunted tree near the water's edge.

The animal was shaking his heavy crest and pawing the earth. His keen ears had long since told him the column was leaving. An old war-horse, he hated being left behind and had waited with growing impatience. Now as the darkness closed in he was on the point of breaking his tether and going where he knew he belonged.

The other three horses, similarly tethered, were watching him with interest.

"At least we had the sense to tie them up, or we would have lost them all by now," Thady remarked.

"Do you not see? The stallion knows which way the column went! Look at him!"

"You may be right."

"I am of course. One of us can ride him, the other ride one of the others, and each lead a horse. That way we can cover ground quickly, and if we give the stallion his head he will follow the column!"

"You think he can do that?"

"Do you have a better idea?"

The boys looked at each other. One of them, if he was brave enough, could sit on the back where O'Sullivan Beare customarily sat.

But they were horse boys: attendants on foot. Horse riding was the preserve of the nobility and the cavalry. All either knew of riding was from their dreams, their flights of fancy.

"If your father was chief of Mac Carthy's stables you should ride the stallion, Thady," Peadar said.

"Ah no, it was your idea, you deserve to ride him. I can take the gray myself, so I can."

The gray was the gentlest of the lot. "He is too dull a mount for a lad like you, Thady. Leave him to me and mount the chestnut."

"Perhaps," Thady said cannily, "neither of us should ride the commander's horse. It would be a sort of . . . sacrilege. We can lead him on a long line so he can go ahead of us a few steps and show the way."

The plan delighted them both. They set about tying the lead ropes of two of the horses into reins, and extending that of the stallion with their own rope belts. When the stallion realized they were actually leaving he half reared and whinnied eagerly. He was worn with privation, but his spirit was undiminished.

Each boy was secretly glad not to be on his back.

They set off through the gathering darkness, guided by the eager stallion. In the distance they caught occasional glimpses of light from isolated habitations, but these soon fell behind them and they were alone in the night. A night of stars and silence. The sky had cleared, ushering in a bone-chilling cold.

The stallion resented being held to a walk but Peadar, who was leading him, managed to restrain him. It was bad enough to be riding over unfamiliar terrain in the dark without going at a jolting trot and risking a fall. They had no saddles; the horses' gear had been stolen by the Mac Egans as it lay waiting with the baggage.

They traveled across bleak moorland, thin soil pierced by sudden outcroppings of rock that loomed out of the darkness. Frequent expanses of bog forced the boys to dismount and pick their way step-by-step across the treacherous surface. The memory of An Cearc dying in a bog pool was clear in both their minds. They made slow progress, but they continued to follow the chestnut stallion as sailors followed the stars.

It seemed they had been riding for a very long time when they stopped to relieve themselves and Thady made a discovery.

"Look here, Peadar. Here, in the mud. Do you see how the ground is trampled and torn? A lot of people came this way, and recently. The mud has not dried." Crouching down, Thady fingered the earth, tracing the footmarks.

"God bless and preserve us!" Peadar said thankfully. "We are on the trail of the column for sure."

Their minds as relieved as their bladders, the two boys hurried on.

Some eight or nine miles from the Shannon they came upon a hollow shielded by the shoulder of a low hill. As they approached a voice challenged them from the darkness.

"It is ourselves with four horses!" Peadar called.

A sentry came forward cautiously, sword in hand. "Name yourselves or . . . is that the commander's horse?" he asked in surprise.

"It is, and we have brought him," Thady said.

Donal Cam was swiftly summoned. The boys glowed in the warmth of his praise. "Give these lads all the food they want," he instructed, "and find a dry place for them to sleep. Later we will decide on a proper reward for their valor."

"Food?" Thady asked incredulously. "All we want?"

The sentry who had first challenged them replied, "While you were taking your ease we had a busy time of it. Come with me and I shall get you something to eat, but do not wake the whole camp. Most folks are sleeping."

He led the boys to a small fire beside which the surviving soldiers' women had made their beds, and showed them a small store of food. Several sacks of wheat and barley, some loaves of bread wrapped up in a woman's apron, a basket of beans. The women had cooked a gruel and one of them spooned out portions for Thady and Peadar, which they devoured with a quantity of bread.

The sentry went back to his station and Grella watched, dull-eyed, as the boys finished their meal. They seem so alive, she thought. Ronan lay like a bruise in her mind.

"Where did this come from?" Peadar wanted to know as he reached for another chunk of bread.

"We came upon a small village, no more than a few huts, really, not long after the battle . . ."

"What battle?"

"After the river," she said patiently.

Evidently, Peadar and Thady had missed a lot.

"Did the sheriff's men come after you?" Thady asked around a mouthful of food. He was eyeing the cooking pots the women had contrapted using helmets propped on forked sticks.

"Not them," Grella told him, reading his glance and reaching for another pot of gruel for him. "This was another crowd altogether. They began gathering when the first boatload came ashore, but they did not attack until we moved out. I am surprised you did not hear the gun-fire, at least."

"I suspect we were too far downriver," Peadar told her, "and anyway, we were probably asleep. We could not seem to wake up for the longest time. Who were these people?"

"Members of clan Madden, someone said. More Eng-lish sympathizers—or perhaps they were just afraid of the Mac Egans and wanted to curry favor. At any rate, they followed us from the river crossing on to the plain, and there they opened fire."

Peadar put down the bread. "Damn their eyes. Does it never stop? Are we vermin to be hunted to the earth and destroyed?"

Grella could not answer his question, but because she could not sleep anyway and talking was better than think-ing about Ronan, she went on. "The commander ordered us to fight on the run. He divided his soldiers into two groups and had them take turns guarding the rear and fighting off our attackers, while we made all possible haste at the front with the weak and wounded. Rory O'Sullivan was with us; his wife was carried on a litter. She was badly wounded during the crossing.

"Thomas Burke and Maurice O'Sullivan managed to fight off the Maddens at last. Being ahead, I did not see any of it, but I understand it was a fierce skirmish. We kept hearing gunfire behind us."

"Where was the commander? Did he lead you?"

"I told you, Rory O'Sullivan led us. The commander was somewhere back with the buannachta, fighting."

"On foot like a common soldier, because we had his horse," commented Thady.

Grella smiled faintly. Her face in the firelight looked a thousand years old, with dark circles under her eyes and deep lines scoring her skin, though she was not yet thirty. The battles she had seen were carved on her face.

"We got some more horses," she said surprisingly.

"Where?"

"The same place we got the food. Shortly after the Maddens fell back we came to a village, little more than a huddle of huts, but they had their winter's supplies laid in and even a few old plow animals in a pen. We relieved them of everything," she added. "There were more of us than there were of them."

Once Grella would have been reluctant to take part in looting a miserable little settlement in a land on the edge of starvation, as most of Ireland was now on the edge of starvation. But such scruples were far behind her. Like the rest of the refugees, she had fought for her share of the corn. The frightened villagers had abandoned the place to the horde from Munster, who had been overjoyed to discover a few casks of beer and a small store of uisce beatha.

This they had drunk on the spot. Grella could remember vividly the crisp, bitter goodness of the barley brew in her parched mouth and throat. She remembered too the way Donal Cam had insisted on taking the whiskey to Orla and trying to get her to drink some of it while Rory O'Sullivan stood watching them with unreadable eyes and a muscle twitching in his jaw.

"So now we have more food and horses," she summed up, "and they say we are out of Munster."

"How far are we from our destination, then?"

"That depends on what your destination is," she replied after a pause.

Peadar was certain of his. "I am going wherever the commander goes," he said proudly. "He promised us a reward, and I shall ask to be taken into his cavalry when he forms a new army with The O'Neill. Thady and I . . ."

"Speak for yourself," said Thady Cooney, whose tail-bone ached from the ride. The only destination he was interested in was a bed on the ground; something that did not move.

Both boys fell asleep soon enough. Grella stayed awake, sitting staring at the fire. Around them slept the small remnant of the band of camp followers.

What remained of the night ended all too soon.

Before sunrise Donal Cam was on his feet, preparing for the day. A day with snow, he feared; the smell of it was in the air. The exceptional bitterness of the winter seemed oddly appropriate. It matched the exceptional bitterness of the march.

He was still sharing his sleeping accommodations with The O'Connor Kerry. When he heard Donal Cam stirring the old man rolled onto his side but made no attempt to get up. "Are we moving out soon?" he asked.

"Soon enough. Are you all right, Sean?"

"Right enough."

"How are your feet?"

The O'Connor laughed. It was meant to be a laugh, but it sounded more like the grating of rusty chain mail, a noise to make the listener wince. "My feet are grand."

"I want you to sit on one of those horses we took yesterday."

"Is your uncle riding?"

"If needs be."

"If he does not ride, neither shall I."

Donal Cam sighed.

He found Dermod O'Sullivan with Joan, the two of them making a meal from remnants of yesterday's feast. "I want you to ride a horse today, uncle," Donal Cam began without preamble.

"Is Sean riding?"

"He is."

Dermod squinted up at his nephew. "I know a lie when I hear it. Your tongue is too straight for your own good, lad. If The O'Connor Kerry can walk, so can I."

"I do not want either one of you to walk! We have the new horses, plus the four that a pair of our horse boys brought back to us in the night. We can mount you, Dermod; the both of you."

But when Donal Cam went to examine the animals, his heart sank. His stallion knew him, and nickered a welcome. The three other horses who had swum the river stood with hanging heads, however, obviously the worse for their ordeal. The horses taken from the village the day before were starving beasts with hipbones sticking out like stags' antlers. None of them looked fit to go any farther, much less carry weight.

But the time for mercy was long past.

Donal Cam told Maurice O'Sullivan, "Put the weakest who are still able to sit on a horse onto these animals, saving two for my uncle and The O'Connor Kerry." But when the two old men saw the condition of their prospective mounts they rebelled. That is, Dermod rebelled, and the moment he refused to ride The O'Connor joined him. Each claimed—with one eye on the other—that he was perfectly able to walk.

"Oh, let them do it!" Donal Cam snapped, his temper fraying.

Joan had overheard the exchange. She said aloud, to no one, "Old people are so stubborn."

She was not the only person who talked to herself by now.

Orla was to be carried on a litter again. The women had bound her wound as best they could. They could find no fresh hypericum to cleanse it with, nor woundwort to control the seepage, but they had stuffed moss into the hole and packed more around it, and wrapped the whole thing with torn clothing.

"It will do until we find a physician to take out the ball," one of them told Rory.

"We may not find a sympathetic physician until we reach O'Rourke's stronghold. Can one of you not take it out now? Surely you have done as much before."

"Orla is the only one still with us who is experienced in delving for lead," they told him. "She is the one who usually cut out anything lodged in a wound after a battle."

"But surely one of you . . ."

"Ah no, ah no." They held up their hands; they backed away.

Rory bent over his wife. She was awake and her eyes were open, but her face was the color of cheese in a pot and her breathing was labored. "We must get you to Leitrim," he told her. "Can you make it?"

She tried to speak, licked her cracked lips, tried again. "I . . . cannot . . ."

"You have to!" He grabbed her hand and squeezed so hard she gasped, which brought on a fit of coughing. Her women glared at him. Orla closed her eyes and turned her face from him.

Aware of a presence looming over them, Rory glanced up. Donal Cam sat on his chestnut horse, looking fixedly at Orla. "How is she?"

"Not well, Commander."

"Stay with her again today. Maurice is handling the buannachta capably enough, I had rather you were looking after her."

"In your place?" Rory asked before he could stop himself.

Anger flared in Donal Cam's eyes. "In a husband's place!" Before he said something that might make the situation worse he reined the chestnut around and trotted off.

Fighting back his emotions, he devoted himself to ordering the day's march. Eighty men-at-arms, under Burke's command, were to be the advance guard. People incapable of fighting were to follow close behind them. Bringing up the rear would be the remaining soldiers and the surviving male civilians who could offer some defense. Donal Cam would stay with them; the rear had proved to be the place of most danger. Besides, now that they were in Connacht he thought it prudent to have men with Connacht accents in the lead.

As the column arranged itself, Donal Cam revised his previous estimate of numbers. Most of the noncombatants were gone. Including civilians who could fight to some degree, he had a total army of less than three hundred, plus the few remaining women and a very few exhausted children.

Out of a thousand, he thought grimly. Two thirds lost, and a long way still to go.

Thady Cooney and Peadar O'Coughlan took their assigned places at the rear. They marched with three seasoned warriors, Con O'Murrough, Hugh O'Flynn, and the former cavalryman Liam O'Donoghue. Liam entertained the party with war stories for the first hour or so until the morning flush of energy faded and they walked in dogged silence, staring at their feet.

Niall O'Mahony was also at the rear. He could not catch a glimpse of Maire ahead, though he was always aware of her general location. His marching companions were another former horse boy and a dour gallowglass with a racking cough.

Donal Cam rode close enough to his uncle and The O'Connor to keep an eye on both men. Sooner or later they would have to ride, and he did not want to wait until they collapsed on their faces before forcing them to it.

He noticed Father Collins fall back to walk a while beside Dermod. The priest was, sensibly, carrying a blackthorn stick, that stout walking aid and path clearer that was also one of the primary weapons in any countryman's arsenal.

Father Collins was among those physically able to fight, and had resolved to give a good account of himself the rest of the way. Deep in his soul was an unchristian itch to break a few skulls. He had seen too much to feel otherwise.

He matched his stride to Dermod O'Sullivan's. None of the column was walking briskly anymore, each step was a deliberate effort, and every change of grade forced a conscious lifting of the knees. Father Collins's legs and back had ached for so long he could not remember them feeling any other way, and he marveled that men like Dermod and The O'Connor were able to keep going after all.

He made the customary derogatory comment on the weather, and Dermod grunted agreement. Then seemingly by accident the priest edged the older man to one side of the line of march, out of earshot of the others. In a quiet undertone more appropriate to the confessional, he remarked, "I seem to remember your telling me you were at Ardea with The O'Sullivan when Dunboy was captured?"

Dermod grunted again. Perhaps, thought Father Collins, he is too tired to talk. But his curiosity overrode his compassion. They were marching with a constant sense of doom and disaster. Anything might happen, he might never have another chance to ask the questions burning in his brain.

"Do you remember much of that time?" he asked Dermod.

"Of course I remember," the old man snapped. "My mind is as clear as a trout pool."

"I have long wondered," said Father Collins casually, "why your nephew left Dunboy and stayed away as long as he did when he knew Carew meant to take it."

Dermod gave him a stony look. "What are you implying?"

"I am implying nothing, merely wondering aloud."

The old man gave a humorless smile, exposing his rotting teeth. "More than that, I think. You are trying to find a subtle way of saying something others have said more openly. Do you think we have not heard the accusations? Some believe Donal Cam ran away from Dunboy, knowing it was sure to fall to the English, in order to save his own skin. Some believe my nephew is a consummate coward."

The bald words hung on the cold air, making Father Collins uncomfortable. But he could not abandon the conversation; his mind worried at the topic as a dog worries a bone.

Dunboy, he thought. Doire na Fola.

"Have you questioned my nephew's confessor?" Dermod asked abruptly.

"I would never ask another priest to betray the secrets of the confessional!"

"I am not talking about what Archer might have heard in confession. I am talking about the advice he has given my nephew over the months and years in a purely secular capacity. You should talk to him. He knows better than anyone why The O'Sullivan was not present at the siege and fall of Dunboy." Dermod clenched his fists. "I tell you honestly and from my own knowledge," he added,

"James Archer of the Society of Jesus is directly, willfully responsible for the loss of Dunboy Castle."

Father Collins was taken aback. At first he thought Dermod's mind was wandering. The rigors of the last months would have been enough to addle the wits of a much younger man. But when he looked closely at Dermod he saw lucid eyes and an expression of such rationality that he was forced to take the man seriously. "On what grounds do you base your accusation?"

"I told you before; I was there. At Ardea, with my nephew, at his invitation. Which was just as well, or my wife and I would have been slaughtered when Carew's men plundered Dursey. So if Donal Cam was saving his own life he saved ours as well, but I do not think he had any such intention at the time.

"Archer was the one who had informed him of a fleet of ships—a fleet, not just one—due to arrive at Ardea with gold and munitions and most important, soldiers. Soldiers to add to our own forces, Spanish fighting men of courage and skill. Archer assured my nephew that the Spanish ships were bringing enough men to allow us to hold Beare against the worst Carew might attempt. All we had to do was go to Ardea, meet the ships as they arrived, then march back to defend our territory at the head of an invincible army. Or so Archer said.

"My nephew believed him. He wanted to believe him. Saving Dunboy had become his foremost concern. In camp at Kinsale he had written a letter to Philip of Spain in which he said, among other things, that Dunboy was 'the only key of mine inheritance, whereupon the living of many thousand persons doth rest.' He had a great sense of responsibility, you see.

"So of course he hurried to Ardea, expecting salvation to arrive on the tide.

"One ship did arrive. The *Santiguillo*, out of Cadiz, sailed into the mouth of the Kenmare river laden with envoys and go-betweens and a fortune in gold, but no soldiers. Archer assured us it was the forerunner of many to come, and the priests aboard the *Santiguillo* agreed with him. Fourteen thousand fresh Spanish soldiers would arrive to aid us any day now. My devout nephew believed the promises; what man would doubt his confessor? And so he was held immobilized at Ardea day after day, waiting, while Dunboy was besieged and fell."

"But when no more ships appeared, surely . . ."

"Ah, my nephew wanted to return to Dunboy, wanted it desperately. But Archer was not the only one pleading with him to wait. The gold on that first ship had been apportioned to our allies to help with the struggle, you see; chieftains who claimed to be loyal. They expected more; they insisted on waiting for it, and Donal Cam had to wait with them. They were his principal supporters, or so he thought. He could not refuse. And so they were, as long as they thought more gold was coming.

"Once it became obvious there were no more ships, however, a number of those same men took their gold and vanished," Dermod went on bitterly. "They did not even wait until Tyrell arrived with news of the assault on Dunboy. James Archer had claimed a share of the gold too, incidentally, though he did not desert afterward. He took the gold for the Church, he said.

"The *Church*." Dermod made the word sound like an epithet. When he saw Father Collins's shocked expression he said, "I have learned a lot about the Church, I can tell you. Don Juan Aguila volunteered to bring a fleet to Ireland on the grounds that ours was a religious war. He said he would stand with us for the sake of the true faith. In light of his later actions, however, I think he was just another adventurer like Elizabeth's pirates, hoping to be on the winning side and claim the spoils of war. At any rate, he wrote glowing letters supporting the Gaelic cause; he even directly addressed Irish Catholics, telling them the pope was ordering them to take up arms in defense of their faith."

"That was not true," Father Collins said. "Pope Clement gave no such instruction. He refused to recognize this as a religious war even though the Gaelic princes had written to him complaining about the Protestant oppressors abusing their people. Nor would the pope excommunicate the Irish who refused to join the rebellion with O'Neill and O'Donnell."

"You see?" crowed Dermod. "Rome turned its back on us. We have suffered more from the Church we loved than from the Sasanach. The only English pope, Adrian, once actually *gave* Ireland—which was not his to give—to Henry the Second of England, who sent the Normans to attempt to conquer us.

"Now the Church has cast us adrift again when we needed Her most. Who are our friends? Not Spain, with whom we have our faith in common. Not the Church, that takes its share of the gold and gives nothing in return but pious prayers and injunctions to offer our suffering as penance for our sins. *What* sins? The desire to stay alive and free?"

The Jesuit could think of no rebuttal. As he well knew, Ireland was a pawn in a larger political game. Ireland, which had never sought to become an empire, could only lose by being a secondary battleground for giants. England. Spain. Religion.

But he felt he must try to defend his fellow priest. In a soothing tone he said, "I cannot believe you think that Seamus Archer"—he deliberately Gaelicized the name in hopes of mollifying Dermod—"would knowingly mislead and deceive your nephew, or anyone else."

"I know what I saw. *James* Archer kept The O'Sullivan at Ardea long enough for Carew and his allies to destroy my castle and Dunboy, and seize the entire kingdom of Beare. That is a fact, one as impossible to overlook as a rotten fish on the pillow."

We are in dangerous waters here, thought Father Collins. Suddenly he regretted his compulsion to unravel mysteries. "Are you actually accusing Father Archer of collusion with the enemy? And if so, to what purpose?" Even as he spoke, it occurred to Father Collins that such a thing was not impossible. Priests, even Jesuit men of the cloth, were men. Archer was a respected and learned man, with a wide-ranging reputation, but that did not mean he was incapable of playing the sort of elaborate political games so many were playing at the dawn of the seventeenth century. In fact, from what Father Collins knew of the man Archer might even enjoy being up to his neck in intrigue.

But Dermod would not go so far as to accuse him of being a traitor. A tardy caution asserted itself; the old man blinked, hawked, spat phlegm, considered before answering. "I am making no such accusation. I am merely telling you what happened. On the one hand, Archer seemed loyal; he even wrote to Dunboy from Ardea with detailed instructions for strengthening the fortifications. On the other hand, he kept us there while brave men died. And for that I curse him; I curse him from a height."

"Surely Father Archer cannot bear all the responsibility for the disasters that have befallen us since Kinsale."

"Ah, he cannot, not at all. I grant you that. Much more of it belongs to Don Juan Aguila, I should say; that noble Spaniard who was so eager to involve himself in the Irish cause. As long as it looked profitable to him, that is.

"But then he lost his nerve. When we had the enemy outnumbered at Kinsale and could have won, if he and his men had joined with us, what did he do? He stayed safe behind the walls. So much for his heroism.

"He showed his true nature when, after surrendering Kinsale to the English without a struggle, he then offered them himself and his men as well. He stated that he no longer wanted any connection with the Gaelic cause because the Irish were, he said, 'unable in themselves.' Meaning we had not won the day. Aguila therefore elected to side with the victors, seeing more opportunity for himself there."

"By doing so he undoubtedly spared the lives of his own men," Father Collins felt obligated to say.

"Everyone always has a justification," Dermod replied with a contemptuous snort. "The English no doubt think Aguila a fine fellow indeed, now. Carew and the others agreed to his offer—which included a payment of gold to him, I understand—and began assigning Spaniards to occupy the Gaelic fortresses they were seizing. As it happened, there were already Spaniards garrisoned at Dunboy, because in his letter to the king of Spain Donal Cam had given Dunboy into the king's safekeeping, promising to hold it as an allied fortress for Spain in return for Spanish support against the English.

"When Aguila went over to Carew, the Spaniards at Dunboy began flying the English colors from the ramparts. By the time a weary and heartsick Donal Cam reached home after the defeat at Kinsale and the counsels that followed, his own gates were barred against him. You can imagine his feelings! But he recaptured Dunboy that time, Father. And such was his nobility that he did not execute the Spaniards who had betrayed him, although they had killed three of his best men before surrendering the castle to him. Because they had been allies, he spared them.

"That is the quality of the man. I assure you, if he *had*

been at Dunboy during the final siege he would somehow have held it against Carew and Thomond and the Devil himself!"

At that moment Donal Cam rode past, ingathering the column. Father Collins shot a sideway look at the haggard face with its finely modeled features and resolute mouth.

Dermod O'Sullivan followed his gaze. "You are seeing a prince of the Gael," the old man said proudly.

I am seeing Ireland, the Jesuit thought. Robbed, deceived, betrayed repeatedly. Fighting enemies on every side, and the worst of them those who should have been your friends.

He watched O'Sullivan Beare ride away up the column. The man's spine was still straight, his head still held high.

What is the truth of him? Father Collins wondered. And then, because he was beginning to feel he knew the truth, he asked himself, What will happen to Ireland when men like O'Sullivan Beare are gone?

They were traveling through a bleak landscape, a barren plain relieved only by bog and stone and clumps of sallow trees. The lushness of Munster was behind them. This was Connacht, pitiless beneath a pitiless sky.

One of the exhausted horses gave a groan and sank to its knees, then toppled over. People gathered around the stricken animal. Donal Cam rode up and dismounted, bending over to look into the dazed eyes. The horse obviously could go no farther.

"Leave the poor brute behind," he ordered.

One of his most faithful gallowglasses, a ruddy giant called Lorcan Mac Sweney, prodded the horse's haunch with a toe. "We could cook it," he suggested, "and use the hide to wrap our feet. Our shoes are destroyed from the walking." He hefted his ax suggestively.

Donal Cam glanced at the line of marchers continuing to straggle past them, but his mind was elsewhere. For a moment he heard again the screams of the horses at Poll na gCapaill. "Leave it, I said!" he commanded sharply. "Take off its gear. Perhaps after it has rested the animal may recover enough to get up and graze. It may even survive. We are going to give it that chance." He swung aboard his own horse and trotted away.

As they were carrying her past on her litter, Orla heard his voice. Donal Cam . . . she roused, tried to call out to him, but dizziness swept through her in waves. There was a ringing in her ears she mistook for music. She thought it was the woman singing in the fields of high summer as they "saved the hay." She thought she was a girl again, running down to the seashore. Gulls were wheeling overhead, and the strand was littered with seaweed drying in the sun. Its pungent ammoniac smell filled her nostrils. Like blood, not seaweed . . . the smell of blood . . . "I am bleeding again," she said faintly.

Instantly Rory was bending over her. Her face frightened him, it was so pale. The color was even bled out of her chapped cheeks. He took her hand in his and found it cold, the bones like a bundle of tiny sticks. He could have crushed them with one squeeze. "How is it with you?" he asked in a low, urgent voice.

"I am bleeding again," she repeated. "Perhaps you should leave me behind."

"He would never allow it," Rory said. They both knew whom he meant.

Orla twitched her lips in an effort to smile. "He would not," she agreed. She meant to say something more, but the music was rising again. Was it singing? Or a war chant? She thought she heard the skirling of the war pipe, and the beat of the bodhran. She fell silent to listen, her legs twitching under the ragged blanket that covered her as if she thought she was marching along behind the buannachta.

"Be gentle, do not jostle her so," Rory ordered the bearers.

Exhausted and long beyond patience, one of them snapped back, "Had you rather carry her yourself?"

He meant to reply in the affirmative, but his eye was drawn just then to one of Burke's mercenaries, trotting back down the column to intercept Donal Cam.

Trouble, thought Rory.

Gerald Ryan fell into step beside Donal Cam's horse and looked up, squinting, into a sky glaring with snow waiting to fall. "My captain bids me tell you there is an army waiting for us up ahead. Five companies of men and two troops of horse."

Donal Cam's long fingers tightened on the reins. He gave the stallion such a kick in the ribs the animal expelled its breath with a huge grunt. Galloping to the head of the column, he drew rein beside Thomas Burke.

"Who is it, Burke? Kellys? This is Kelly clan land, someone said."

"My scouts recognized Sir Henry Malby, together with Clanrickard's brother and a number of other Burkes who have gone over to the queen, damn their eyes. It is not local people but a Royalist force, well armed and ready for us, Commander."

Donal Cam, who had lost members of his own clan to the queen's side, sympathized with Burke's simmering anger. "What is the land like ahead?" he wanted to know.

"Not enough cover to allow us to get around them. They are drawn up across our way at Aughrim, in front of the fort on the high ground there. If we mean to keep going, we must fight."

Donal Cam nodded. "Fight. Fight Malby. An English opponent at last." He sounded almost relieved. Wilmot's army, which had so harassed and pursued him in Munster after Dunboy fell, had been predominantly Irish. Fully four fifths of them were native tenants on land now in English hands, men who had no choice but to follow the queen's flag if they wanted to keep their homes and their lives.

Men doing what The O'Sullivan might also have done.

"We go forward," he said tersely to Thomas Burke. He reined the stallion around and rode back along the column to issue the same order to Maurice O'Sullivan and the buannachta.

Looking down at faces as he rode past them, the thought struck him that, in their emaciation, they appeared sexless. Where were the women, the children? He searched in vain for a child's face. Had they all been killed or died of sickness? Had they fallen away from the march unnoticed?

I was not aware when the last of them left us, he thought sadly. And who is it for, if not for the children. His mind ran back to the moment that had decided him to abandon safety and rebel against the English, throwing in his lot with Hugh O'Neill.

The children . . .

He stared more intently at faces and found at least two women. Orla on her litter would make three, and there was Mac Geoghegan's Maire somewhere. He located her with difficulty, dragging along with her head down, her face shadowed by Niall O'Mahony's shaggy mantle.

Four women remaining. No children. Out of all those families he had once hoped he could save.

Did they think I could save them? he wondered. Or did they only come because there was no alternative?

His brooding gaze lingered on the plodding people, worn to the bone, wrapped in rags, their eyes sunken into dark hollows. Male and female, soldier and civilian, the march had distilled them into one consolidated unit of suffering.

An army of ghosts, thought Donal Cam.

The Connacht men in the vanguard emerged from a thin stand of sallow trees to see in the distance a sight that chilled their blood. Ranged across the face of the rise were the enemy; well fed, well rested, warmly clothed, armor gleaming, unfaded standards blowing in the wind, sleek horses pawing the earth with excess energy. A drumroll and the braying of trumpets signaled a symphony of slaughter.

The mercenaries panicked. They broke and ran back through the sallow stand. At first Thomas Burke yelled furiously at them to hold, but when he found himself abandoned he ran after them, cursing. They burst upon the following column like water from a ruptured dam.

At a glance Donal Cam realized what had happened. He had only moments before the entire column fled the scene; the fear of the mercenaries was infectious. It was Kinsale all over again.

Now, he thought. If ever, now!

He wheeled his horse and galloped in a wide circle, herding his people like sheep, bunching them, holding them, forcing their attention on to him. The trees provided a partial screen to shield from them the sight of the advancing enemy. When he had them gathered, he turned his horse so his back was toward those trees and raised his arm commandingly, silently thanking God he still had a horse to sit on.

O'Sullivan Beare drew a deep breath. "Since on this day," he shouted, "our desperate circumstance and unhappy fate have left us with neither wealth nor country, nor children nor wives to fight for, the struggle with our enemies is for the life that alone remains to us.

"Which of you, I ask in God's eternal Name, would

not rather fall gloriously in battle, avenging your blood, than, like cattle who have no sense of honor, perish in cowardly flight?

"Let us follow in the footsteps of our ancestors, who would never flee to avoid an honorable death. There is no other salvation for us. The plain stretches on either side of us with no adequate place of concealment. The neighboring people are no protection, they would not come to our aid. Our enemy blocks the roads and passes. Whatever chance we have is only in our courage and strength of arms.

"Remember that each time our enemies have attacked us, we have survived through divine mercy. Let us believe, then, that Christ our Lord will be with His servants in their most dire need.

"Up, then, and attack the enemy, whom you excel in spirit! Fear not such a worthless mob, they are not men of such fame as we are! When they see us defy them, I pray they will turn tail and run from our faith and courage!"

His people stood as if rooted, their minds absorbing his despairing eloquence. In a low voice, Dermod O'Sullivan said to Father Collins, who stood beside him, "Is that the man you would accuse of cowardice?"

Donal Cam turned his horse and started forward, north again, on the way to Leitrim.

At first in ones and twos, and then in a mass, his men broke into a trot and ran beside his horse, cheering him.

A great lump rose in his throat. The column was under way again; his army of ghosts.

They emerged from the sallow trees to find two companies of Royalist horse charging toward them at full gallop, lances at the ready and standards whipping in the wind. Foot soldiers followed them at the run.

Donal Cam's mind ran faster. Looking to his left, he saw a vast expanse of deep red bog, with another thin stand of trees beyond. He turned and galloped toward it and his army of ghosts ran after him.

"They think to escape! Catch them!" an English voice cried. Lances were hurled; a few people fell, but the column hurried on, apparently panicked into flight.

Reaching the bog, Donal Cam abruptly halted and shouted orders to his twenty surviving musketeers to stop, turn around, and form a defensive line as the rest of the column poured past on to the marshy surface that could destroy a horse's legs.

The momentum of Malby's charge carried the Royalists to within a spear's throw of the unexpected line before they could stop. Sir Henry Malby, in the lead, sawed desperately at his reins. "Deploy in a wide circle and surround them!" he shouted. But his men were confused by Donal Cam's sudden halting. They misunderstood Malby's order; the cavalry wheeled in a circle where they were . . . directly in front of O'Sullivan's muskets.

With iron control, Donal Cam waited for the perfect moment. When he shouted "Fire!" twenty guns barked in unison. Eleven of Malby's finest tumbled from their horses.

The Royalists were shocked. Instead of attacking fleeing refugees, they found themselves facing disciplined warriors.

After one volley the muskets had to be reloaded, but there was no time to reload. Donal Cam shouted another order. His men attacked. Some of Malby's men had begun to dismount already. Others were dragged from their horses. The musketeers used their heavy weapons as clubs. Gallowglass and kerne joined them with ax and pike, sword and spear. Heads were butted into bellies, stiffened fingers thrust into eyes. The combat intensified as the Royalist foot soldiers caught up with their cavalry and began to join the fray.

Maurice O'Sullivan felt an invigorating burst of pure hatred when directly in front of him he saw one of the queen's Burkes in the finery of a Royalist officer. "Traitor to your people!" Maurice yelled, drawing his sword. But Richard Burke, larger and heavier, pressed him backward over the rough terrain until he lost his footing and fell, dropping the sword. Burke raised his own for the fatal thrust. Fortunately, the leader of the buannachta still wore the better part of a rusted coat of mail, the last remaining to the recruits. The links deflected the sword with a hideous screech. Maurice rolled over and up onto his feet with an agility that surprised both of them. At the same time, someone pressed a short spear into his hand. "Kill him!" yelled Hugh O'Flynn.

Maurice gladly complied, driving the spear into his enemy's throat so a great gout of blood burst from him. O'Flynn and another recruit joined him, hacking off Burke's hand as he fell.

Blind fury energized the column. Even the weakest now joined the fighting. It was not enough to kill; they lusted to maim and mutilate. When a Royalist fell his assailant continued to hack madly at him. The savagery had a powerful effect on Malby's men. The cavalrymen in the forefront of the fighting fell back, unwilling to face madmen. The foot soldiers behind them briefly blocked their way, then the impulse for retreat spread to them and a general scramble to the rear began, with men shoving and pushing and yelling in growing panic.

Thomas Burke, brother of the earl of Clanrickard and namesake of the captain of O'Sullivan's mercenaries, was appalled by the unexpected massacre taking place. He had ridden in the front rank and dismounted to fight, but now he wanted only to get back on his horse and escape. He was burdened by armor, however, and his horse was as frightened as he was. It would not stand for him to mount. When he jerked the reins angrily it pulled free and trotted away, leaving Burke clanking along behind, yelling for attendants to catch the animal and help him get on again.

Con O'Murrough hurled a spear that narrowly missed his eye when Burke glanced backward.

As he fought, Donal Cam felt the tatters of refinement and civilized behavior fall from him like rotten rags. Kinsale, he kept thinking. This was how it should have been at Kinsale.

A recognizably Gaelic face appeared before him and he checked his sword a moment before driving the man through, moved by some obscure impulse not to slaughter his own race. The next moment he saw a recognizably English face, however.

O'Sullivan Beare had found Sir Henry Malby.

The English captain had anticipated an easy victory with considerable honor accruing. He was young and ambitious, he expected to be well rewarded for delivering the head of the rebel O'Sullivan on a pikestaff to the queen's agents.

Too late he realized he had underestimated the Gaelic leader and his ragged army. O'Sullivan's quick thinking in using the terrain to his advantage, and employing the tactic of surprise, had changed the shape of the battle. But Malby had no intention of letting his prize escape him. From the moment the two sides clashed he had been looking for O'Sullivan Beare.

When the gaunt, dark-haired man came toward him, Malby believed providence was on his side. O'Sullivan was easy enough to recognize in spite of his thinness and rags; he still had that noble carriage that would always identify him. Malby grinned. He would take the rebel's head personally. He gripped his sword with both hands and turned the blade sideways for a decapitating swing.

It was never struck.

Donal Cam's eyes followed the movement and his hands mirrored it. For one incredibly brief moment the thought flashed through his mind that he could spare the young Englishman. He could show a mercy to Malby that he and his kind had not shown to the Irish.

But even as he thought the thought, his shoulders were turning into the swing.

Joyously freeing himself of all conscience and all regret, Donal Cam O'Sullivan Beare swung his sword in a shimmering arc through the cold air. Henry Malby's head, yellow curls bouncing and astonished blue eyes staring, bounded away like a ball and rolled over and over in the trampled red mud.

Con O'Murrough and Dermod O'Houlihan ran past Donal Cam and eagerly attacked Malby with their own weapons, hacking at the helpless body and screaming. They had hurried forward to protect their commander in such excitement they did not yet realize what had happened.

Breathing heavily, Donal Cam stepped back. He wiped his sword on his sleeve, leaving a smear of Malby's blood on the caked mud and grime.

O'Murrough and O'Houlihan continued to attack the fallen body, then gained control of themselves enough to realize Malby was not only dead, but headless. They turned toward Donal Cam.

"I thank you for coming to save me," he said graciously.

The two men exchanged glances but there was no time to say anything more. The battle closed around them again, carrying them on its cresting wave.

By now every member of O'Sullivan's column who was capable of raising a hand against the enemy had joined in the fighting. Everyone except Maire Ni Driscoll.

Maire's beauty survived only in memory. The long march had burned away her flesh, destroyed her complexion, turned her dark glossy curls to lank strings. She was unaware of the change. It had been a long time since she thought about her looks. The loss of beauty was nothing compared to the other losses she had endured.

Maire's only thought now was of Niall O'Mahony. He had gone to fight with the rest of the buannachta, leaving her. Leaving her almost but not quite alone, for the little dog was still with her. As she waited, cringing, in the bog, hearing every blow that was being struck, it pressed against her bony ankle and whimpered.

"Ssshhh," she said absently. "Ssshhh. The English will hear you and eat you."

Although her eyes watched, she could not follow the battle. To her it was nothing more than a muddle of men trying to kill each other for some reason she could not recall. Her sole thought was of Niall. He had left her. He must come back.

Niall. Niall. The fabric of her dazed mind would support no other thought.

To her vast regret, Joan Ni Sweney's woolen stockings now had so many holes she could no longer keep a rock in them. She tore off a strip of her skirt instead and made a sort of sling with that and hurled missiles at Malby's men. She was unskilled and inaccurate, but the doing was enough. That, and the satisfaction of seeing the enemy run away after Malby fell.

A man ran past her, pursuing them. Ran was an inexact description. The O'Connor Kerry limped, lurched, swayed, and hobbled, but he went forward at all possible speed, waving his sword unsteadily and shouting, "*Abu! Abu!* To the victory!"

"You are wonderful entirely, Sean!" Joan shouted after him.

Her husband heard her voice. Checking himself as he also hurried after the enemy, he irritably demanded of empty air, "What is that old man doing trying to impress my wife?"

It was true; the charge of the Royalists was destroyed and the survivors were hastily retreating toward the fort atop Aughrim hill. Donal Cam let his men pursue them as close as he dared, then shouted the order to fall back. He did not want to risk facing cannon fire from the fort.

They fell back reluctantly. The taste of victory was heady. People who had thought themselves so exhausted they could scarcely set one foot in front of the other were now walking with spring in their step. They exchanged smiles, cracking chapped lips that had all but forgotten how to smile. Some of the men made obscene gestures in the direction of the fort on the hill. One saw Father Archer looking at him and repeated the gesture defiantly.

The Jesuit looked away, lips tightly compressed with disapproval.

In the heat of battle Rory O'Sullivan had left his wife on her litter and joined his men, but now he was among the first returning to the bog where she lay. Grella was already crouching beside her. The woman turned her head and looked up at his approach.

"How is my wife?"

"Thirsty. She keeps licking her lips."

"I shall find water for her." Rory hurried off, looking for a clear bog pool or at least someone with a filled waterskin.

When he was gone Orla opened her eyes. Yellowish matter glued the lashes together; she rubbed at them feebly. "Where is he?"

"Do you mean your husband? Or the commander?" Grella could not resist asking. But even as she spoke she was sorry. They had moved beyond meanness and pettiness, or should have; surely all that was dross long since burned out of them. Surely whatever was bitter in herself had drowned in the river with Ronan, she thought.

Fortunately Orla had not understood the intent behind her question. She had not even heard it; she had settled back into a cobwebbed grayness. But even as it closed over her she made one more effort. "Are we not winning?" she asked in a whisper. "I think I hear the pipes . . ."

Grella looked down at her. "We are winning," she said. "You imagine the pipes, but we are winning." There was wonder in her voice.

Donal Cam surveyed the plain before Aughrim hill. It was littered with bodies. He sent Thomas Burke and Maurice O'Sullivan to do a body count. They reported over a hundred Royalists dead, and a total of fourteen slain from the column.

Seriously injured, but surviving, was Niall O'Mahony, whose arm had been all but severed.

"Right arm or left?" Donal Cam asked.

They thought he was concerned about the man's weapon's hand. He was, however, thinking about the harp.

"Right, Commander. It is a grievous wound."

"Will he live?"

"He will, probably. But he will never have full use of it again, the tendon is destroyed. Grella Ni Hurley is with him now, she has stopped the bleeding, but nothing else is to be done."

"Even by The O'Rourke's physician in Leitrim?"

Maurice O'Sullivan shook his head. "I fear not, Commander."

Donal Cam went to Niall. He found the pikeman lying on the ground not far from Orla's litter. Two women crouched over him: Grella and Maire Ni Driscoll.

Maire looked so fragile he was embarrassed for looming over her. Crossing his legs, Donal Cam sat down beside her.

He wondered if he would have the strength to get up again. With the battle over, the flush of exhilaration was waning. Soon they would all be weary again, hungry again. Struggling again.

"He will live," Donal Cam assured Maire in response to her pleading look.

"How long? Until the next battle?"

He heard despair in her voice. Looking beyond her at Grella, and beyond her again to where Joan Ni Sweney stood engaged in some sort of argument with her husband, Donal Cam thought of the female members of his army of ghosts. How many of them had any future?

This one. Perhaps.

"There will be no more battles for O'Mahony, nor for you either," he said.

"But wherever you go . . ."

"You will not go with me," he interrupted. "No farther. Once we are safely past Aughrim, you and O'Mahony are to leave our company and find some refuge for yourselves. I have a few gold coins left, here and there . . . enough to give you some for your support. Find a remote valley where the only sounds from one season to the next will be birdsong and the ring of O'Mahony's ax cutting wood when he is strong again."

"He will never leave you," Maire said. "He is loyal."

"And I am loyal to my people," Donal Cam replied. "I have asked enough of them; too much. This is an order I give you both, and I will not allow you to disobey me."

A small form squirmed out from under Maire's skirt and stood with cocked head and beady eyes, looking at Donal Cam.

He almost smiled. "You still have that dog?"

"You knew about it?"

"Of course. Did I not issue an order that it was not to be harmed? Anyone who ate it would answer to me, I told the soldiers."

Maire swallowed hard. "Oh."

"Take it with you. I want all three of you to survive."

Niall forced himself to sit up. "I hear what you say, Commander, but I think . . ." His voice was weak with loss of blood, but as he spoke it grew stronger.

"What you think does not matter," Donal Cam interrupted him briskly. "A bard does not dictate to a prince. Do as I tell you. Leave the column once we reach some safe place, and make a new home for yourselves. There will be no more fighting for you, there is no point in forcing yourself to go farther." Something shifted deep in his eyes. "Make a home for yourselves, and have children," he added. "That too is an order. Have children. Keep them alive and safe, and . . . and . . ." His face worked. He broke off abruptly and stood up, making a great show of brushing off his clothing.

O'Sullivan Beare hurried away to prepare the column to move out.

Niall turned toward Maire. "Did you hear? He orders us to . . . you and me . . . to . . ."

"Have children." She finished for him. "For that, we must be . . ."

"We must," Niall agreed. His head was spinning, but he was definitely feeling stronger.

Donal Cam issued orders to get people moving as soon as possible, before the Royalists recovered themselves enough to mount a counterattack. It was too much to hope that they would remain hiding in the fort indefinitely. They had lost Malby, several of the queen's Burkes, other senior officers, and many prominent Royalist supporters, but the loss would not be permanently crippling. As soon as they realized the full extent of their humiliation at being routed by a smaller and much-despised force, they would come swarming out of the fort like hornets, hot for revenge.

By then Donal Cam wanted his people to be far away.

In addition, the inevitable locals were gathering like ravens to scavenge discarded weaponry on the battlefield and plunder whatever they could from the pitiful remnants of the column's possessions.

It was time to go.

Donal Cam shouted to Thomas Burke, "Drive away that clan Kelly rabble and take any lost weapons or armor for yourselves! And bring the fallen English standards as well!"

"Trample them in the mud!" someone cried. But Burke's mercenaries were obedient; they gathered the enemy's flags and delivered them, dirty and torn, to Donal Cam. He accepted them with grave dignity, as his right.

While Peadar held his horse in readiness, he walked among his followers, congratulating them on their success. The most timid among them had held back until the battle was won, but even they had finally darted forward and struck a blow or two, and were now delighted with themselves.

They had not fled like cattle with no sense of honor.

In his mind, a balance had shifted. Aughrim had eased some of the rage and frustration that had been tormenting him ever since Kinsale.

This time we won, he thought to himself. This time we stood together, we held our ground. And won.

The knowledge blew through his spirit like a clean wind.

Day Twelve

January 11, 1603. From *Eachdhruim, Aughrim*, the Ridge of the Horse

Donal Cam kept the column moving throughout the night, exploiting the exhilaration of victory to put Aughrim as far behind as possible. Until darkness they were still at risk from locals, but having won a battle against an organized Royalist force they were in no mood to be intimidated by civilians. They defended themselves briskly and gave no quarter, and by sundown they were alone.

Alone in a frozen world. The snow that had begun falling some hours earlier now blanketed the earth to a surprising depth, reminding them that the weather of this winter was unprecedented. The snowfall diminished with the dying of the day, but a paralyzing cold set in. The only defense against it was to keep moving.

Niall O'Mahony, weakened by his wound, was not ready to think of leaving the column yet. He forced himself to keep walking for Maire's sake, trying to ignore the throbbing pain of his arm. Midnight arrived unnoticed.

The survivors of O'Sullivan's thousand began the twelfth day of their ordeal in icy darkness.

Father John Collins was walking with The O'Connor Kerry. The old man's enthusiasm at Aughrim had cost him dearly. Now he could barely hobble along, leaning heavily on his confessor's shoulder. But he kept going, and sometimes he even made jokes.

At first neither man noticed that a third had joined them. Niall cleared his throat several times. Finally the priest turned toward him. "What is it?" Father Collins asked more irritably than he intended. Helping The O'Connor was sapping his own slim reservoir of strength.

Nervously, Niall replied, "I have a favor to ask of you."

"Now?"

"Ah . . . not now. In the morning, perhaps. You see, the commander has asked me to . . . I mean, has requested that we . . . Maire Ni Driscoll and I, that is . . . that we . . ."

"That you *what*?" The O'Connor demanded to know, bending forward to peer around Father Collins. Niall saw his face as a gray oval floating in darkness.

"Have children," Niall mumbled.

The other two stopped walking. "Did I hear aright?" The O'Connor wanted to know. "Or is there snow in my ears?"

"The commander wants us to have children," Niall said hastily before his nerve could desert him altogether. "So we need you to marry us."

The O'Connor said in an amazed voice, "How absolutely extraordinary. The man's raving, of course."

Niall was indignant. "I am telling the truth! Father, will you marry us tomorrow?"

The Jesuit struggled to overcome his own astonishment and order his thoughts. "If you are certain this is what you want . . ."

"It is. It is."

"And the young woman? Is she agreeable?"

"She is of course or I would not be asking you."

"Ah."

"A clear case of the daft marrying the daft, then," The O'Connor interjected. "Ludicrous to be talking of marriage in our situation."

Father Collins said gently, "I would rather be marrying people than burying them, Sean."

"Ah well. There is that. And marrying is easier, with the ground too frozen to bury anyone in anyway."

"Are you willing to marry us?" Niall burst out, unable to bear any more of this. "Please, Father!"

The Jesuit turned toward him. "I will of course, did you not understand?"

With a mumbled thanks Niall left them, returning to Maire to tell her the news.

"Absolutely extraordinary," The O'Connor said again. "What do you make of it?"

"It was the last thing I expected," the Jesuit replied. "We are all of us struggling just to stay alive, and here this young couple wants to be wed—when they might be dead tomorrow—but perhaps that is not so extraordinary. Life and the desire to continue life seem to assert themselves in the most antithetical circumstances."

"Anti . . . mmm. Jesuit sort of word."

"It means . . ."

"I know what it means," the old man interrupted. "Am I not a Kerry man with a great amount of reading done? It means the pair of them will have a poor enough marriage night."

"I doubt if they are in any condition to take advantage of their marriage night."

"Not now, perhaps, but you heard what he said. They

intend to have children—at Donal Cam's request! Now what do you suppose that is all about?"

Father Collins was wondering the same thing.

The woman who might have enlightened them lay on a litter with the life slowly ebbing from her. Most of the time she was unaware of her husband, who was now taking his turn carrying one end of the litter.

He walked behind her so he could watch her. In the night she was no more than a pale shape before him, but he kept his eyes fixed on her rather than on the litter bearer at the front.

My wife, he thought. My. Mine.

An ice-ringed moon appeared through a break in the clouds to cast its bluish light on Orla's face. She seemed carved in marble.

She should have a marble tomb, Rory thought. A queen's tomb.

He became aware of someone walking beside him. "How is she?" asked Joan Ni Sweney.

"Nothing stops the bleeding, it keeps oozing out of her."

"If we had a physician for her . . ."

"I doubt it would make any difference."

"But she is still alive, so there is hope."

"She is still alive because she is so strong. It is taking her a terrible long time to die."

Joan felt a deep pity for him, though she knew he did not want pity. Rory O'Sullivan had never wanted pity. He had taken what life gave him, rejoiced in its blessings as best he could, and, according to Joan's observation, borne its burdens with fortitude.

She had little to offer him, but at least she could express her admiration.

"You have been both a good husband and a loyal captain," she said. "It cannot always have been easy."

"The commander is head of my clan. There was never any question of my loyalty."

"Of course not. Still . . . a more spiteful man might have gone over to the side of Owen O'Sullivan when . . ." Joan caught herself, bit her lip. Tactless woman, she thought. You have always been too blunt.

Rory showed no sign of offense, however. He merely finished her words for her. "When he realized he had been given one of his leader's cast-off women?"

Joan was embarrassed. "I did not mean . . ."

"I know what you meant. It does not matter."

In spite of herself, Joan could not resist asking, "But have you never wondered if they are not still . . ."

"I have not," Rory said firmly. Lying.

"You are a most decent man," Joan told him.

He responded with a bitter laugh. "If you think that, then you are a very poor judge of character."

She did not know how to respond. She busied herself by trying to scrape dried mud off her sleeve as if it were important to do so, and waited for him to say something else.

But he seemed to have forgotten her. He lowered his head and walked on, shoulders hunched, staring at the ground, obviously in no mood for conversation.

Joan edged away from him and let herself drift among the walkers until she found her husband. Dermod was stumping along by himself, swinging his arms violently to keep warm.

"You are not with The O'Connor, then?" his wife inquired.

"I am not. There is room with him for you."

"What does that mean?"

"Whatever you want it to mean."

"What are you talking about, old man?"

"Old man! Shall I tell you who is an old man? The O'Connor is donkey's years older than I am."

"So?"

"So." Dermod slammed his feet as hard as he could against the frozen earth. "I heard you. You called him wonderful entirely."

"You are jealous!"

"Not a bit of it. Why would I be jealous of an old man like that?"

Dermod trudged on. Beside him, his wife tried to smile with amusement at the childishness of old men, and the flattery of jealousy. But her face was too chapped and cracked, the effort made her lips bleed.

The night march was taking its toll. A man stumbled, fell, could not get up. Donal Cam dismounted and had the man lifted onto the chestnut stallion. They had not gone much farther before someone else fell, and the stallion was forced to carry double, as were the few other surviving horses. Only the stallion was able for it. The others began collapsing like the people they carried.

By the time the first gray light showed in the east, only the chestnut stallion and one bony bay mare remained with the column.

They were fighting their way through knee-deep snow, an effort more exhausting than anything they had yet done. People groaned aloud. They were making dreadfully slow progress, but by now Donal Cam did not dare let them stop because they would freeze to death out in the open if they did not keep moving.

A rise of land in the distance was pointed out to him by one of the Connacht men as Mount Mary. "We will be out of the wind in the lee of that hill," Thomas Burke said. "We could rest there for a little while, Commander."

Coming from the mercenary captain, the suggestion was a telling admission.

Donal Cam peered through the dim dawn light. To one side of Mount Mary he could make out, shrouded in snow, the outlines of some huge and long-abandoned ring-fort.

"We can halt there just long enough to melt snow for drinking water, and catch our breath," he decided. "But then we must press on. We are still in O'Kelly territory and they have proven themselves hostile."

Dermod asked his nephew, "Do you seriously think these people can keep on walking?"

"They have to," was the grim reply.

The ring-fort, though badly damaged by weather and neglect, was a welcome sight, providing at least an illusion of shelter. The column stumbled gratefully toward it.

While several men lit a fire, the rest stood in groups like cattle, head down and stolid. Knowing the halt would be brief, they did not sit. It was too hard to get up again. They contented themselves with stamping their feet in the snow and blowing on their frozen fingers.

"I think we have just time enough for a wedding," a smiling Father Collins remarked.

His fellow Jesuit was incredulous. "Who could possibly want to marry under these conditions?"

"One of the buannachta. And Maire Ni Driscoll."

"She is Richard Mac Geoghegan's betrothed . . ."

"Was. He is dead."

". . . and a kinswoman of The O'Driscoll. She has noble blood, John," Father Archer pointed out. "Therefore I should be the one to give her the wedding sacrament."

"But the young man asked me."

"Nonsense. If they were both common folk it would not matter, but given her station. I am sure you agree I am the appropriate priest. Probably the young man was merely too shy to ask me." Father Archer began to smooth and order his filthy, tattered garments, preparing himself to officiate as if no further discussion was necessary.

Father Collins was irked. Why should the other priest blithely assume . . . ah well. It was not worth causing hard feelings over, he told himself. If Father Archer felt that strongly, let him marry them.

He glanced regretfully in the direction of Niall and Maire, who were standing some distance away and had not heard the priests' conversation.

I will do something else for them, he thought. Make some other contribution . . . find some substitute for a chapel, perhaps? He gazed around at the snow-covered desolation, then his eyes lit up. The very place! On the eastern side of the ring-fort a section of tumbled wall formed a rough half circle like embracing stone arms. He hurried over to examine it more closely. The bit of wall broke the wind; there was a snowy hush that seemed almost reverential.

Pleased, he went to assemble the remaining female members of the march. Any wedding, no matter how poor, was the province of women. Unfortunately, there were only four left. The bride was one and Orla on her litter made two, which meant there were only two more to carry out all those offices that should have been distributed among chattering dozens. He thought of other weddings he had attended: of flowers perfuming the air, the music of harp and lute and recorder, a lavish feast spread over many tables, a nuptial bed awaiting with linen sheets and rose petals scattered . . .

Ah well. Make do, he told himself.

Joan Ni Sweney held the same philosophy. When Father Collins told her about the wedding she replied, "I have a few shreds of horsemeat saved; we can give them that. Just the pair of them, mind—I have not enough for anyone else, I meant to save it for my old man. But if he has gotten this far on an empty belly he can go a little farther."

She fumbled in her clothing and produced a pitiful scrap of dry, stringy meat: the wedding feast.

"What shall we do for music?" the priest wondered aloud.

Grella Ni Hurley folded her arms and considered. "The bridegroom was a harper, but he has lost his harp and the use of his arm."

"We could not ask a man to play the harp at his own wedding anyway," said Joan.

"We could if he was the only musician we had. Which he is."

"One of the kernes is still carrying a bodhran."

"Would you have him beat the war drum at a wedding?" Father Collins asked, scandalized at the idea.

Joan gave him a look of mingled amusement and cynicism. "For this wedding, I should say it would be singularly appropriate."

The priest would not hear of it, however. They would do without instruments; perhaps someone would sing.

"The bride is our singer," Joan pointed out. "We cannot ask her to . . ."

"I know, I know." But Father Collins refused to be defeated. He was determined to make a wedding of this hurried and pitiful event. He began canvassing the buannachta, the mercenaries, even the surviving attendants in search of a singer.

The two women turned their thoughts to more urgent matters. "She has no proper gown," Joan said disapprovingly.

Grella sneered, "I suppose you expect her to have some brocade tucked away in her baggage somewhere?"

"I do not, but it hurts the heart of me to see the girl stand up in those rags. Surely between us . . . is your shift in one piece?"

Grella folded her hands across her body defensively. "It is not, it would not do at all."

Donal Cam approached, looking tense. "We are still in O'Kelly land," he reminded them. "I would like to move on."

"As soon as we have those two married," Joan said firmly. "Which we cannot do until the bride is properly dressed."

Donal Cam realized she was eyeing what remained of his shirt. Once it had been beautiful, a traditional Gaelic garment of soft linen with bell-shaped sleeves formed into scores of tiny pleats. He had done his best to maintain himself, but the shirt, like everyone else's clothing, was in tatters.

Joan did not see the tatters. She saw the finest garment, no matter what its condition, that remained to any of them. And in her face Donal Cam saw grim determination.

With a few minutes he had lost his shirt and Maire Ni Driscoll was arrayed in a strange costume with pleated sleeves, an overskirt made of a blanket that retained a trace of its original vivid crimson, and a headdress fashioned from Grella's shift.

Joan and Grella stood back to survey their handiwork.

"The girl is too thin to do it justice," was Joan's verdict.

Maire Ni Driscoll felt as if she were drifting through a dream. None of this was real. The O'Sullivan's aunt could not be dressing her in a blanket; one of the camp followers was not possibly adjusting her headdress.

And . . . was that Richard standing waiting, with a bemused expression?

It was not . . . she did not even remember what Richard had looked like. This was a different man, emaciated, one arm wrapped in bandages, but with a light in his eyes and a most tender curve to his chapped lips.

Maire squared her shoulders. "I am ready," she said.

Father Collins led the bridal party to his makeshift chapel. The remainder of the column trailed after them, except for Rory, who remained beside Orla as she lay on her litter on the ground. He followed with his eyes, however. Remembering.

When they stood amid the encircling stones Father Collins moved aside to make way for Father Archer. Maire's eyes widened. "What is this?"

"I am going to perform the marriage rite," Father Archer told her, smiling benevolently. "You see?" He fumbled among his garments. "I still have a Missal. We shall celebrate this sacrament togeth—"

"We will not!" Maire cried shrilly. "You are not going to marry us! Tell him, Niall. Tell him you asked the other priest."

"I did, but . . ."

"We cannot change now. It would bring us bad luck, bad luck entirely. Tell him!"

Father Collins laid a placating hand on her arm. "Ah, child, what does it matter? Father Archer is my brother in Christ, he can dispense the sacrament as well as I."

Maire was trembling violently. "Bad luck, bad luck, bad luck to change priests for a wedding!" She was on the verge of hysteria.

Over her head, Donal Cam said to Father Archer, "She is fixed in her idea. Give her her way in this, we have no time."

The Jesuit drew himself up into a tower of affronted

dignity. "If I am not wanted, I shall withdraw." Giving Maire and Niall a withering look, he left the circle.

John Collins was acutely embarrassed. He was aware of Niall's eyes pleading with him, and Donal Cam shifting his weight impatiently from one foot to the other.

Awkwardly, Father Collins took the other priest's place and began reciting the marriage service. He had not performed a wedding in a long time, and his brain was numbed with fatigue and hunger. He stumbled over the phrases and forgot words, but it did not matter.

What mattered was the expression on the two starved faces watching him, making a commitment to the future.

The incongruous celebration was soon over. There was no Nuptial Mass, for there was no wine, no consecrated Host. There were only the vows and the tumbled stones and the snow, the silvery silence of a winter's dawn. The spectators stood with hands folded in prayer.

Gerald Ryan and Lorcan Mac Sweney both had to turn away and knuckle their eyes.

The rising sun broke through the clouds just long enough to give Maire's pale face a momentary glow, and Niall thought her beautiful.

So, for that brief time, did they all.

Afterward, Donal Cam pressed a small leather purse into Maire's cold fingers. "It is not much," he apologized. "Most of our gold has been lost along the way with the baggage. But there is a little left. And this was sewn into the lining of my cloak. Take it."

"You are too generous, Commander," Niall said.

"Not at all. Once I expected to . . ." He did not finish. Maire met his eyes, knowing they were both thinking the same thing. He had once expected to give a much more lavish wedding gift to the constable of Dunboy and his bride.

"Thank you," Maire said simply.

The little dog pressed against her ankles. Holding Donal Cam's purse in one hand, she bent down and gathered the small creature into her arms, pressing her cheek against the top of its head.

Father Collins craned his neck until he found Thady Cooney in the crowd. A prearranged signal in the form of a nod passed between them. Thady turned to two of his companions and said something in a low voice.

Three horse boys began to sing as the Jesuit had requested. The three knew no wedding songs; such music was the province of women. The only song Father Collins had learned they knew in common was a Christmas hymn, but the discovery had delighted him because the final line was so appropriate. Huskily, wearily, with voices untrained but sincere, the boys sang,

> "Jesus, good above all other,
> Gentle child of gentle mother . . .
> Give us grace to persevere."

"Please God!" someone cried in heartfelt echo.

In her semiconsciousness, Orla heard the singing. "Angels," she murmured. Her fingers scrabbled at the edge of her blanket.

As soon as the hymn was over Donal Cam began moving them out. Niall wrapped his shaggy cloak around his new wife. Having the use of only one arm made him awkward. Maire put down the dog and thrust the purse into the bosom of her gown so she could help him.

Grella Ni Hurley noticed the gesture.

Always gold for the privileged, she thought; never any for me. The old bitterness surfaced.

She narrowed her eyes, watching Niall and Maire.

Donal Cam walked over to Father Archer, who was

still standing as he had throughout the wedding, with his back turned on the bridal couple.

"That was ungracious of you," Donal Cam said behind him.

The priest whirled around. "Ungracious? They were the ones who were ungracious. They insulted me, giving in to peasant superstition. His influence, no doubt; she should know better, she is well-bred and educated. But she let him persuade her to petty behavior that was quite beneath . . ."

"On their wedding day," Donal Cam said evenly, "they should have things the way they want them. We have little enough to give them."

"Ridiculous."

"Ridiculous to see an insult to yourself where none was intended. Is pride less a sin than superstition?"

Father Archer's wounded temper got the best of him and he raised his voice. "How dare you speak to me of pride! You, who never fail to shave your face every day of your life, no matter what disasters befall us. You, with your peacock's vanity."

The other man shook his head. "We shall not move this on to a battlefield of your choosing, Father. Indeed, we are not going to argue at all. I am in no mood to have you yapping at me."

Keeping his back straight and his shoulders square— with an effort—Donal Cam turned and strode away to give the order to move out.

The priest glowered after him. *How dare he speak like that to me? The Devil put those words in his mouth. But I know you, Satan; I know where you lurk and the face you wear. I am on guard against you!*

The column trudged off toward the summit of Mount Mary. It was not snowing, but the absence of snowfall allowed the temperature to go even lower. The air through which they forced themselves was so cold it felt solid. People dragged themselves up the slope with great difficulty. Every step required a conscious act of will.

"Bend, knees," The O'Connor Kerry muttered. Beside him, Father Collins was silently issuing the same order to his legs.

Toward the rear of the column, Niall O'Mahony walked proudly beside his new wife. He could not resist glancing at her again and again. Only the strongest of the thousand who had begun the long march were still going forward, and Niall marveled that the delicate-seeming Maire had somehow kept up with them. She is a queen, he thought, a queen from one of the ancient poems.

She felt his eyes on her. "How is your arm, Niall?"

"A little sore, but I have been hurt much worse." Niall shrugged his good shoulder in a gesture of bravado, courting her admiration.

"I do not like to think of my . . . my husband in pain," Maire said softly.

The glow that suffused Niall made him forget all about his arm.

As he climbed, Donal Cam absentmindedly rubbed his fingers along his jaw. They felt rough stubble.

I did not shave today, he mused. Nor, come to think of it, did I shave yesterday. My set of razors was lost somehow when we crossed the Shannon.

Yet Father Archer still sees me as shaven. He looked right at me and told me I am shaving every day.

Reaching the summit, he gazed out across a desert of snow. His eyes sought in vain for some relief, some interruption to the glaring desolation.

His captains came up beside him. "Which way, Thomas?"

The mercenary scratched himself in the armpit. "Leitrim and O'Rourke are to the northeast, but if we go in a straight line we will encounter at least one English garrison. They probably already know about the battle at Aughrim, someone on a fast horse will have warned them. They will be watching for us."

"Ah. Then what if we . . . go to the northwest in a wide circle, gradually turning back when we are clear of them? What lies that way?"

"Rough country, broken, boggy, hilly. Thinly peopled. But we could get back to the Curlew mountains, I think, without meeting an enemy patrol. If we circle wide as you said, along that line . . ." He extended a forefinger and traced a route in the air.

"What about the local clans?"

"The English may think they have Connacht subdued, Commander, but they will never conquer the west. You are in friendly territory now."

"Friendly?" Donal Cam rolled the word across his tongue as if he had never heard it before.

"Indeed. Oliver Lambert, who became president of Connacht after Red Hugh's men killed Sir Clifford Conyers, has made a lot of enemies here. There are clans that will help you just to spite him."

Donal Cam looked deep into Burke's childlike blue eyes. His thoughts turned to other men he had trusted, men allied to him by blood or heritage or supposedly common interest. Men who had betrayed him.

Here stood Thomas Burke, bearing a name that belonged to some of the most rabid of the Royalists. A Connacht man, and Connacht and Munster had feuded since the dawn of time. In addition, Burke was a mercenary, a man who admittedly sold his loyalty to the highest bidder.

Donal Cam stood unmoving, reading his eyes. Then he gave an abrupt nod. "Very well, Burke. You guide us. Northwest, then around to the Curlew mountains and Leitrim beyond."

Maurice O'Sullivan protested. "Going that way adds too much to our journey, Commander. We are exhausted enough as it is, how can you ask this of us?"

"Look behind us," Donal Cam suggested. "Do you see those three women back there? If they can still walk, then so can you and the others. A few more miles can make the difference between reaching Leitrim alive or being cut down by an English garrison—had you rather have that happen?"

Turning, Maurice O'Sullivan found Joan Ni Sweney almost on his heels. Her eyes challenged him.

He clamped his mouth shut and did not protest again.

Slowly, the column made its way down the northern face of Mount Mary. "We are entering Mac Davitt clan land," Burke told Donal Cam. "There is a village up ahead."

"Would they give us provisions? Are they one of the friendly clans you mentioned?"

"Ah . . . not exactly. I think they have truly submitted to the queen. But we might be able to overpower them and take their food."

"Us?" Maurice gave a scornful snort. "Have you looked at us lately? Do we look as if we could overpower anyone?"

"We did at Aughrim."

"Since then we have marched a day and a night without sleep. There is hardly a full company left, we are . . ."

"A company!" Donal Cam cried, inspired. The others looked at him. "Where are those English standards?" he asked them.

Peadar O'Coughlan spoke up. "I have them, Commander."

"Bring them to me. And the bodhran—do we still have a war drum?"

"One. We do."

Signaling a halt, Donal Cam formed his followers into something resembling a military formation. He put the biggest men in the front, and had the horse boys go before them, carrying the captured English flags on pikes, like banners. Bits and pieces of English armor that had been found on the battlefield were parceled out among the soldiers, until those in the front line bore at least a passing resemblance to Her Majesty's men.

"We will never fool anyone who looks at us closely," Dermod warned his nephew.

"Perhaps not, but we may surprise them enough to keep them from looking too closely."

They proceeded on toward the village. When the first cabin was in sight, Donal Cam called, "Beat the drum! Wave those flags!"

"Why are we doing this?" asked Thady Cooney, who was carrying one of the banners. "I feel a proper idiot with English colors."

"You are a proper idiot if you cannot see the cleverness of it," Peadar told him. "The commander is hoping we will be taken for Royalists and allowed food."

"Pray God it will work, then!" Thady began waving his banner wildly.

If the villagers had been unprepared, the ruse might have worked. But The Mac Davitt Burke, in nearby Glinsk Castle, had been warned of the approach of the refugees. One of his men had spotted them six miles away at Mount Mary and ridden at the gallop to give warning. Mac Davitt had at once gone to Glinsk village and had all possible foodstuffs carried away so there would be nothing for the rebels. Flocks and herds had been hidden; grain and bacon put into souterrains underground. Women had concealed loaves of bread in their clothing and children had poured buttermilk onto the ground rather than have it aid O'Sullivan's people.

As Donal Cam led the column into the village, a sullen householder appeared in his front doorway to shake his fist at them and yell abuse.

With a despairing wail, Thady Cooney dropped his banner and ran from a hail of stones. Peadar pounded after him. People were emerging from every doorway, throwing whatever came to hand at the refugees, clods and rubbish and household items and burning brands from the hearth.

Donal Cam shouted frantic, unheard orders, trying to keep his people together and get them to the open fields beyond the village.

"No more, no more," Thady was sobbing as he stumbled over the frozen ground.

Joan Ni Sweney cast one swift glance to see that Dermod was all right, then gathered her skirts in her hands and ran. Grella Ni Hurley passed her, but fell to her knees when she was hit in the back of the head by a hurled pot. Joan paused long enough to help her to her feet and the two women ran on.

Niall felt a sudden wild impulse to stand where he was and make a glorious fight of it, going down doomed but undaunted, letting his life and his weariness end together. His existence had reached its apex, the Blackbird of Beare was his wife. He could hope for nothing more. Better to die now . . .

Maire grabbed his arm and pulled him after her. "Run!" she screamed in his ear. "Run, Richard!"

Niall ran. The small dog ran after them.

The two bearers who were carrying Orla's litter panicked. They dropped the litter onto the ground and abandoned it. Rory, who had been walking beside, screamed at them uselessly, then scooped his wife into his arms and ran, carrying her.

She weighed almost nothing. Her head bobbed against his shoulder. He prayed that she was unconscious.

Had it been the day before, the refugees, fresh from victory at Aughrim, would have fought back. But sleeplessness had not only eroded their strength; it had sapped their confidence. They fled like chaff before the wind, scattering.

Donal Cam forced his horse to a faltering trot and tried to herd people together, shouting at them in syllables indistinguishable from the curses he was shouting at Mac Davitt's men.

"Merciful hour, how does he expect me to *run?*" gasped The O'Connor. The other surviving horse broke loose from its horse boy and trotted past. The O'Connor flung himself toward it and clutched its mane with both hands, allowing the animal to pull him along. His blistered feet were dragged across the ground. "Jesu, Jesu, Jesu," sobbed the old man. But he hung on.

Once the refugees were clear of the village, most of their pursuers fell back. But Donal Cam's people were scattered in every direction, hiding in copses, cowering in hollows, stumbling lost along cow paths winding through scrub and brambles. It took O'Sullivan and his officers more than an hour to gather them again.

A few were never found.

A small number of Mac Davitt's followers continued to hound them in desultory fashion for some time, but did no great damage. They were poorly organized, and when at last they seemed to have given up Donal Cam gratefully signaled a brief halt. "Who is still with us?" he wanted to know.

"My wife, for one," Dermod told him. "Over there, see her? A mighty woman."

"She is that," his nephew agreed absentmindedly, his attention elsewhere. Scanning the huddle of people around him, he realized that two in particular were missing.

"Wait here and keep everyone together," he ordered Maurice O'Sullivan. When he tried to ride back the way they had just come, his weary stallion balked. Hardening his heart, Donal Cam hit the animal a cruel blow across its haunches with the flat of his sword. The stallion snorted and laid back its ears in anger, but moved forward.

Donal Cam found Rory half lying against a stone outcropping with Orla across his lap. He slid off his horse and bent over them. The stallion dropped its head and stood unmoving, eyes half closed.

"Rory? Rory!"

The other man roused himself. "Commander?" His speech was slurred with fatigue.

"Can you walk?"

"I think . . ." Rory broke off, coughing.

"What about her?"

"Her?" As if he had forgotten her, Rory looked first at his wife, then back to Donal Cam. "Her?" he said again dazedly.

Donal Cam put one hand to either side of Orla's face and shouted down at her, "Orla! I command you to speak to me!"

He could not be certain she was even alive. Her skin felt heatless and clammy.

Her eyes opened, but they did not focus on him. They

were lusterless; dull stones pressed too deeply into the pallid wax of her face.

"Her litter bearers dropped her," Rory said slowly, remembering. "I carried her myself. For miles. Until . . . I must have fainted."

"Are you wounded?" Donal Cam asked, keeping his eyes fixed on Orla's face.

"I think not. Just tired to the death."

"We shall put you both on the horse, then. Can you help me with her?"

Rory made a strange sound that might have been a laugh, hollow with irony. "Can I help you? With my wife?"

Donal Cam gave him a sharp look, refusing to read anything into his words. "That is what I said. Take hold of her there, we are going to have to lift her up because obviously she cannot do it herself."

Inch by slow inch, Rory dragged himself to his feet. His body felt like a bag of skin filled with broken glass, the shards grinding together when he moved. He coughed again, stood with feet wide-planted to keep from swaying. When he tried to do any more his body failed to respond.

"I do not think I can lift my arms," he said. "My strength is gone." He stared helplessly at Donal Cam.

"So is mine," said O'Sullivan Beare quietly.

He had never made such an admission before. It seemed the ultimate defeat of manhood and the two of them were suffering it together, with Orla on the ground between them.

She moaned faintly. Donal Cam's jaw muscles worked. "If we can somehow get her upright and prop her against the horse, Rory, the two of us together can push her up onto him."

Rory nodded uncertainly.

Between them they fumbled Orla into a vertical position and leaned her against the horse, who still stood with head hanging. The stallion did not seem aware of the woman, nor she of him. They silently endured.

Holding Orla pinned against the horse's shoulder, Donal Cam then bent and put his shoulder into her midsection. With Rory's hands guiding, her upper body was folded across his so that when he straightened she would be lifted high enough to be pushed across the horse's back.

But he could not straighten. He felt the long muscles in his thighs trembling violently. When he demanded that his body obey him, it rebelled.

"Commander?" Rory said.

Donal Cam ground his teeth together and tried again. Sweat spurted from his forehead, running into his eyes and stinging them. He forced his body to straighten, but then Orla began sliding sideways.

Both men grabbed for her, heaved, got her halfway up, felt her begin to fall back. At the last moment Donal Cam thrust his hands into her crotch and pushed violently upward against the pelvic girdle.

With a groan, Orla slid on her back across the saddle. Rory caught one of her feet to keep her from going clear over and falling off the other side.

"You can take your hands off my wife now," he said coldly. "I have her."

Donal Cam forced himself to step back. "Turn her over so she lies on her stomach. Protect her wound as much as you can. Then you get on behind her. Here, step into my hands."

He cupped his hands like a horse boy to form a step and Rory put one foot into it, then swung the other leg across the stallion's back. The animal's knees promptly buckled.

"Get off!" Donal Cam shouted. Rory obeyed. The two of them stood looking at the horse, who had recovered its balance but was obviously spent.

"He cannot carry you both, Rory. I am afraid you will have to walk."

They set off, Donal Cam leading the horse and Rory walking beside his wife, holding her on. She hung head down, arms swinging limply. When the weary horse stumbled she grunted with pain.

They made slow progress. The horse threatened to collapse at any time.

Orla muttered something. "I think she wants a drink, Commander." Rory fumbled behind Donal Cam's saddle but found no waterskin tied there. Something else lost along the way.

"We can get water for her at the next stream," Donal Cam assured him, looking around.

They were in a scrubby woodland broken by meandering animal trails, the sorts of paths that inevitably led to water. Donal Cam left Rory with the horse and followed the nearest.

The sheltered pocket of woodland was warmer than elsewhere. Some of the snow had melted. He could smell mud . . . and something else. His nostrils flared.

Ahead lay a small river fringed with brittle brown reeds. A bulky shape was bobbing gently in the shallow water.

Donal Cam picked his way down the slippery riverbank. A stench rose to meet him on the warming air; a miasma of death and rot.

A man lay facedown in the shallows. He could have been Gael or Sasanach; it no longer mattered. He was merely a man who had met a violent death in a land and time where violent death was commonplace.

He lay at peace in the river now, fouling the air.

Donal Cam waded into the water and gingerly turned the bloated body over. The face had been shot away. A huge pike poked its narrow snout from the rotting body cavity.

The great fish, as long as a man's arm, had somehow wedged itself into the corpse to feed. Disturbed, it glared at Donal Cam with soulless eyes. Its gaze was as cold as winter, and the predatory head with its long jaw and formidable teeth seemed an embodiment of indifferent evil.

Donal Cam shuddered and drew back. With a strong arching of its body, the pike leaped past him into deeper water and disappeared.

Sickened, Donal Cam left the river and made his way back to Rory. "Did you find water, Commander?" the other asked hopefully.

"Nothing we could drink," Donal Cam said shortly. "There will be other streams." He took the stallion's reins and began walking again, his face closed.

Rory asked him some question but he did not hear. His feet moved automatically. His brain was preoccupied with the terrible vision of life ending in both serenity and horror; the glittering fish nourishing itself on the rotting corpse.

When at last they reached the remainder of the column Donal Cam's captains came forward to report to him while other men helped Rory ease his wife from her horse and organize new litter bearers.

"Some of Mac Davitt's people may still be following us after all," Thomas Burke said, frowning.

"Why do you think so?"

Maurice O'Sullivan said, "We catch glimpses of men in the distance, trying to conceal themselves among the trees. We thought they had given up, but . . ."

"But." Donal Cam rubbed his aching eyes. "But we have to keep moving. Guard our rear."

Their way lay across an endless plain of scrub forest and bogland. The brief warming spell ended with a change of wind. A gale howled down on them from the north. Deep drifts of snow remaining in low areas trapped the unwary, who found themselves floundering up to their hips or even armpits.

Then it began to rain.

Rain was worse than snow. Their clothes turned sodden, adding an unbearable weight that must be borne by the weary refugees. The wind strengthened; ice began to form on lashes and eyebrows.

One person and then another fell away from the column to sleep, to die, surrendering almost gratefully to the elements. Those who plodded on were so intent on placing one foot in front of the other that they hardly noticed.

Grella Ni Hurley longed to lie down and not get up again. The temptation was constant and almost irresistible. Almost. She would have surrendered to it if she had not been able to see Niall and Maire just ahead of her. Maire was still on her feet, still walking. Still carrying O'Sullivan's gold in her bosom.

Grimly, Grella followed them.

The rain seemed to grow colder and colder. Maire could not stop her teeth from chattering. Niall kept his good arm around her, but his body gave off no warmth. His shaggy mantle was keeping their bodies relatively dry, but as it grew more and more sodden it was more of a burden than a blessing.

Niall had hoped that somewhere today he would find a place where he and Maire could stop and seek a haven for themselves. There was no such place on this dreary plain, however, and the possible threat of Mac Davitts still following them meant they dare not risk setting off on their own.

We will walk until we die, he thought. No emotion stirred in him. The words seemed meaningless.

Eighteen miles across the plain brought the refugees to Slieve O'Flynn. In spite of its name it was not a mountain, merely a wooded rise in the level landscape. But it loomed out of the rain like a friend, a reminder of the highlands of Cork.

With one accord they headed for it.

The gentle slope was furred with pine trees, and generations of dead needles carpeted the earth. The pines accepted the rain on their unbowed heads, forming a shelter for the people beneath them.

"Ah," murmured Joan, closing her eyes. "Ah. Ah."

She stopped walking and stood still, enjoying the cessation of rain and the cushiony feeling of the earth beneath her feet.

Donal Cam did not have to give a signal to halt. They all halted as soon as they reached the pines. Those who had the strength began gathering deadwood for fires and making crude shelters among the trees. The sound of the rain changed; they heard the first pinging of sleet, but little of it reached them. They collapsed on the pine needles and lay as if dead.

They had come almost fifty miles without sleep since Aughrim.

The O'Connor Kerry sank to the ground with a moan and stretched out his legs, staring in the general direction of his feet. Father Collins sat down stiffly beside him. "I could not walk another step if it killed me," the Jesuit remarked.

"If I did walk another step it would kill me," his companion assured him.

They watched the sketchy camp being made around them. It was up to the men now, though Grella collected one or two dead branches for the fire. Burke's mercenaries did the bulk of the work. The fires caught quickly and burned hotly as they added resinous pine branches to them.

Once more we rely upon the trees, Donal Cam thought. Trees. The ancient druids held trees to be sacred . . .

He had a sense of his mind drifting.

Rivers. They thought rivers were sacred too. Trees and rivers.

Doire na Fola. The Shannon.

That river with the corpse and the pike . . .

He found Rory with Orla, who lay with closed eyes on a litter close to the fire.

Donal Cam crouched down beside his captain. "How is she?"

"Alive. I cannot understand how she holds on." Or why, Rory almost added, then thought better of it. "How much farther do we have to go to O'Rourke?" he asked instead.

"Two days, three at the most, I think."

"Will any of us make it?"

Donal Cam said harshly, "Every person who can stand and walk is going to make it."

"My wife can do neither. It would be kinder to let her die than to keep dragging her on like this."

"'Let her die'? How can we let her die? That is not up to us but to God."

Rory looked at his commander's face in the firelight. The lines were now so deeply carved that Donal Cam looked like a man twice his age, a figure hacked from stone in cruel caricature of himself. Rory raised one hand and felt the great scar twisting across his own features.

We are neither of us beautiful men, he thought. But one of us has always seemed beautiful to my wife.

"She will not die while you live, Commander," he said bluntly. "Not if she can help it."

"You are talking nonsense."

"I am talking truth. It is time the words were said between us. The only way Orla will die is if you set her free."

Donal Cam's body tensed but he managed to keep his words calm, unemotional—which was a great effort given his weariness. "I would not ask any of my followers to take their loyalty to me to such painful extremes, Rory."

"Loyalty? Is that what you call it?"

Donal Cam darted a swift glance around the campsite, but the only person close enough to overhear their conversation was Orla, who appeared to be asleep or unconscious. "You have both been unfailing in your loyalty to me," he said, "and I would . . ."

"I would call it love."

"What?"

"Love. What Orla feels for you."

"This is neither the time nor the place for . . ."

"Ah, but it is, Commander. We could all be dead tomorrow. If we do not say these things now we may never say them."

"Better so."

"I think not. I have lived with them too long."

"Your imagination, Rory."

"I did not imagine they way you brought Orla and me together and encouraged us to marry. That was just about the time you decided to marry a woman from clan Mac Carthy, was it not? A woman from a family even more powerful than yours, a proper dynastic marriage for a prince of the Gael? Something my Orla was not, of course. Orla was an inconvenience to you then, if you meant to follow the English style of one wife. One woman. A style," he added, "that you put on as easily as English clothing."

"I burned my English clothing," Donal Cam said in a tight voice.

"I know." Rory stared into the fire.

"And I love my wife."

"Did you ever say that to Orla?"

"I never discussed Honora with Orla."

"What about the other way around, Commander? Did you tell your wife that another woman bore you children, and the captain of your guard was expected to think they were his?"

Donal Cam waited a careful heartbeat, then replied evenly, "Of course Orla's children are yours, Rory."

"Are they? Then perhaps you could tell me just what gave you the right to put young Hugh and little Sinead on that ship to Spain with your son Donal, and Dermod's Philip?"

"I was saving them from Carew! There was no way I could put every youngster in Beare beyond his reach, but in the light of what had already happened to . . . I was doing the best I could for you as a reward for your loyalty, I thought you knew that . . . your son and daughter are safe in Spain, at least, no matter what happens to us now . . ."

"My son and daughter. Is that how you think of Hugh and Sinead? Is that how you thought of . . ."

He broke off, looking past Donal Cam. A cloaked figure had emerged from between the nearest trees and was coming toward them. Rory's hand automatically sought the short sword belted to his waist. Warned by the gesture, Donal Cam whirled around and looked behind him.

In a broad Connacht accent the newcomer said, "Would one of you be O'Sullivan of Beare?"

"I am," said Donal Cam warily, getting to his feet.

"Jesus Mary and Joseph, I am glad of the sight of you. I am called Felim O'Flynn, and you are in our clan land. I have been sent to warn you, as a friend, that The Mac Davitt Burke and some of his men have followed you into our territory. We have no specific quarrel with them, mind, but we think you should know they plan to surround you here and slaughter you in your sleep."

Day Thirteen

January 12, 1603. *Ros Comain*, Roscommon, Saint Comain's Wood

Daybreak revealed human figures struggling blindly
through a pocket of almost impenetrable woodland
near the river Suck. Caught in a lightless, densely packed
oak forest with undergrowth of holly intermingled with
birch, alder, and hazel, they had wandered directionless
through the night and advanced no more than four miles.

Before they realized how lost they were, one of Burke's
mercenaries had remarked, "I remember hearing that in
my father's time a man could walk on the tops of the
trees from Letterfrack to Galway." Someone else had
laughed.

Now it did not seem funny. They had begun to think
they were trapped forever in the dark purgatory of Saint
Comain's Wood.

When Felim O'Flynn delivered his warning the night
before, the refugees had just begun to settle themselves
for their first rest in two days. When Donal Cam tried to
get them back on their feet many flatly refused.

"Help me, Rory; these are your men. Order them."

Rory O'Sullivan looked stonily at his commander. "Have Maurice do it. My place is with my wife."

"Who will die as we all will die if we do not leave here! Is that what you want, to see your friends slaughtered like game? Help me with them!"

Their unfinished conversation hung like smoke in the air between Donal Cam and Rory O'Sullivan.

Rory hesitated a moment longer, shrugged, and issued the order to the buannachta to move out. For a time it seemed they would not obey him either, but Felim O'Flynn went from man to man, detailing the danger and giving graphic descriptions of the pains Mac Davitt's people meant to inflict.

Eventually the column was up and moving, though more than one man was cursing under his breath and two of the horse boys were crying with fatigue.

"What worked before must work again," Donal Cam decided. "Build up those fires as large as possible before we leave, so it will look as if we are here for the night." He was beginning to feel as if this was his only successful tactic. Like a sorcerer, he saved his people by creating an illusion.

Like a druid, he thought wearily. Among the trees.

They had not had enough time to dry their sodden clothes by the fire. The water-heavy garments weighed them down as they set off once more, heading northeast, or in the direction Thomas Burke assured Donal Cam must be northeast. The belt of pines that encircled Slieve O'Flynn soon gave way to ash and alder, and then to the oaks of Saint Comain's Wood. Donal Cam led the stumbling column forward into Stygian darkness and the trees closed around them.

It was hard enough for a person alone; the litter bearers with Orla had a desperate struggle to manipulate their burden through the dense woods. The horse boys who were leading the two surviving horses, neither of which was fit any longer to carry a person, had equal difficulty.

"We have been consigned to hell for our sins," Father Collins heard Father Archer say in the darkness, somewhere off to his right.

The O'Connor Kerry complained, "If I had known I was going to pay such a high price for my sins I would have taken care to enjoy them more at the time."

Incredibly, someone in the darkness chuckled. Father Collins found himself smiling too.

The wind was rising, stirring the trees.

Dermod O'Sullivan walked with Joan. They could not lean on one another, there was not enough space between the trees. But they talked in random snatches, saying whatever came into their heads, using their voices to keep them close together. Joan had begun reminiscing.

"The cliffs of Dursey Island are high to the north," she said almost dreamily. "Three miles from end to end and a mile wide, Dursey is. Pasturage and plowland."

"Fine land," Dermod agreed. "Keep talking. Remind me of it."

"Three hundred good people on Dursey. I see their faces still. Freckled, the children, with sea light in their eyes. Were there ever such beautiful children? Dead, now . . ." Her voice faded.

"The fish we used to catch!" Dermod said quickly. "The boats coming in and the women going down to meet them with their baskets, singing. Talk to me, wife!"

Joan's voice came again. "Blue. Blue is a color. Red. Yellow. Green. Speckled. Plaid. Nuts swelling in the hazel wood. Always open a boil with a silver needle. One, two, three, four, five . . . Five springs of water that never fail," she said more brightly, her mind returning to Dursey Island. "Hake and cod and ling in the sea, and black cattle

on the cliffs. Sweet berries, like honey on the tongue. Butterflies. Ah, do you remember the butterflies dancing?"

Others had begun following the cracked thread of her
voice as if it were a beacon. The wind rose, tearing
through the branches, and Joan raised her voice, tran-
scending the mounting tumult.

"Butterflies dancing, husband!" she called.

Someone's voice asked, "What sort of berries?"

"Sloes, briars, bilberries . . ."

The wind shrieked and howled, trying to drown out
the sound of human voices. The trees began to groan
piteously as their bare branches were whipped about.

A man's voice, gasping: "In my father's time it was
said you could walk from Letterfrack to Galway on the
tops of the trees."

"What?"

"I said . . ." But his voice was lost in the gibbering of
the triumphant wind.

Joan and Dermod gave up trying to talk to each other.
They struggled blindly through the lightless forest, with
no sense of east or west or up or down, stumbling, swearing, cut loose in time.

The first light seeped in among the trees so faintly that
at first no one was aware of it. Then Thomas Burke realized he could actually see his hand in front of his face; he
began trying to find a way out of the forest. Others followed him. The surviving refugees broke out of the
woodland at the same time Mac Davitt entered their
abandoned camp and found only dying fires.

He set off at once, aided by daylight, to find O'Sullivan
Beare.

Once clear of the trees, the remnant of the column had
slogged across an icy marshland, forded a river, then
struck out for the distant Curlew Mountains, skirting a

dark, melancholy lake on their way, a mirror of death and time.

Donal Cam's every instinct warned him of pursuit. They would never reach the Curlews before their enemy caught them. He instructed his captains to be on the lookout for any bit of high ground where they could make a stand if they must.

He also decided the chestnut stallion must bear his weight again, giving him an elevated vantage point. Sadly, the animal's strength was spent. There were great hollows above his eyes and his hipbones seemed about to burst through his hide.

"He is going to die, Commander," Peader told him in a tremulous voice.

Donal Cam put a hand on the horse boy's shoulder. "Every living thing dies, lad. Do not give your heart to a beast to break, because we outlive them. At least, I hope you and I both shall outlive this one. Now step me up."

Aware that Donal Cam had ignored his own advice and had given his heart to the lost An Cearc, Peadar merely nodded. He made a cup of his hands and the commander stepped into it, then swung a leg over the stallion's back and eased down as gently as he could.

From that height he counted the followers left him, those who might be capable of defending themselves. Sixty at the outside, excluding the two priests and the two old men.

And four women. One badly wounded.

Rory O'Sullivan was taking his turn carrying Orla's litter. It was easier on open ground, though the term was relative. Nothing was easy anymore. Even breathing was an effort. The cold air cut the lungs like knives, and his arms screamed with protest at the weight of the two litter poles.

A sky the color of dirty iron brooded overhead, sullen with cloud. Pools of black ice lurked amid the snow. Leafless trees clawed at the sky, seeking the absent sun. The region seemed desolate and empty.

But Donal Cam knew they were not alone. The back of his neck told him.

"Hurry," he urged his captains. "Push your men faster, I tell you our enemies are gaining on us."

Maurice O'Sullivan protested, "They cannot go any faster, Commander. It is a miracle of God that they can march at all."

"Then we need another miracle to give wings to their feet," Donal Cam replied. "If we are caught out here in the open we are dead."

A trick of wind carried the mention of God to Father Archer. He squinted at the leaders, then forced himself to move up and join them. Once he had been a portly man, strong and well nourished, and though the flesh was melted away he had reservoirs of strength not available to some of the others. God, he believed, succored him.

From somewhere in the region of his knee Donal Cam heard his confessor's voice ask, "Are you calling on Our Lord?"

He glanced down. "I am calling on my men for more speed," he said shortly.

"Let us implore the Almighty," the Jesuit said. "Draw rein. We shall kneel and pray together."

"There is no time," Donal Cam said gruffly.

Father Archer seized his thigh and held onto it with surprising strength. "No time for prayer? You never needed prayer more, I tell you."

"But we are being pursued, our lives are in danger."

"Your soul is in danger! Listen to me! Dismount and pray with me for your deliverance. Not only from your human enemies, they are nothing compared to the true adversary. Please, my son! Listen to me!"

He tugged violently as if he would pull Donal Cam from the horse.

It was imperative that O'Sullivan obey him now. So much had happened, so much order had been overthrown and needed to be reestablished. For months, the Jesuit had been brooding over the fact that Donal Cam, once the most devout of men, almost his acolyte, had paid less and less attention to him.

At least in the first days of the march Donal Cam had followed Father Archer's advice to the extent of seeking sacred sites for his camps, and leaving offerings at the shrines of the saints. Now he no longer even bothered with that.

As what the priest perceived to be Donal Cam's irreverence increased, so had their hardships. Obviously, God was sending His punishments down upon them. Their enemies multiplied, the weather grew more savage, yet still Donal Cam seemed less and less aware of his Christian obligations to his priest and his God. Who spoke through His priest.

"Dismount and kneel with me!" Father Archer cried commandingly, pulling the rider's leg with all his strength.

The motion was enough to unbalance the enfeebled stallion. He staggered sideways and almost fell. Donal Cam swore aloud. When Father Archer reached for him again he lost control and cried, "Let go of me, you whoreson!"

The priest fell back, mouth gaping.

At that moment Rory and the litter caught up with the halted leaders. Donal Cam's eyes fixed briefly on Orla's unconscious face. The skin at the corners of his dark eyes tightened as if in pain. Then with a cluck of his tongue and a kick to the horse's ribs he set the stallion in motion again, leaving Father Archer behind.

The Jesuit stood paralyzed by anger and disbelief. He swore at me. He swore at *me*! Called me a whoreson, the word whore in his mouth and his eyes on that woman of his, that demon . . .

The refugees flowed past him. He was no more aware of them than a rock in a riverbed is aware of water flowing around it. His mouth was working though no words came. When the last of the column had passed him he finally shook himself, looked around, and followed them.

His face was unreadable.

The captains were doing their utmost to keep the column from spreading out too thin and leaving the weakest behind, but it was impossible to keep them to any sort of formation. Donal Cam rode to the rear several times to encourage the stragglers. Several times he reluctantly held up the front of the column so they could catch up, though he was painfully aware that every halt gave their pursuers more opportunity to catch up as well.

"I cannot . . . not anymore . . ." Maire gasped, stumbling.

"You must," Niall told her. He tightened his grip around her waist and pulled her along, but she stumbled again.

He could not carry her, not with only one arm. He looked around frantically. Two of his fellow kernes were nearby; he called to them and they caught Maire between them and half carried, half dragged her.

The little dog ran after them.

About nine in the morning they reached high ground, a hill overlooking snow-dappled brown and purple bogland. From its summit Donal Cam and his captains saw, quite unmistakably, a band of men hurrying toward them along the way they had come.

There would not be much time to get ready for them.

Donal Cam ordered the women and the two old men into the center and formed a defensive circle around them with his soldiers. Without asking what place he should take, Father Collins stood with the buannachta.

Father Archer tried once more to convince Donal Cam to pray before battle was joined, but he might have been talking to one of the stones that studded the hillside. Donal Cam did not seem to hear him.

His confessor's voice fell on O'Sullivan's ears but did not reach his brain. What remained of his thought processes, dazed with hunger and muddled with fatigue, was spent on strategy. Two circles. Buannachta the inner circle, mercenaries the outer. Count the remaining muskets. Station the musketeers at intervals across the front, but put three on the other side. The enemy would probably try to surround the hill and come up behind them. Who had what weapons? Who was strongest? How many gallowglasses?

He forced his mind to work. It felt as sodden as his clothing. He could only think one very simple thought at a time, like a baby taking its first steps. But he must keep thinking. He must. One step at a time. They were depending on him.

He could see the enemy now; see them clearly, coming closer. Mac Davitt's people. Loyal to the English queen, now; their lord had received a knighthood from Elizabeth. Was he among them? O'Sullivan wondered.

He turned to Con O'Murrough, who was standing at the ready with a spear in his hand. Con was fighting back a yawn. "Are you prepared to fight?" Donal Cam asked.

Con gulped down the yawn. "I am that, Commander. I

would rather fight and die on this spot than go any farther without food or sleep."

"Good man yourself." They are all good men, Donal Cam thought. Brave men. They have accomplished the incredible already, and when I ask more of them, they do that too. A lump rose in his throat.

The enemy band halted at a safe distance, watching them. One figure, obviously the leader, was mounted, but the rest were on foot. Not a military company as such; Mac Davitt's loyal locals, anxious to stay in his good graces.

Anxious to claim the price on my head, Donal Cam thought suddenly. That is why they have dared pursue me through the clan land of the O'Flynns. For the money. The gold. They have no interest in killing a band of ragged refugees.

I could simply walk down that hill and surrender to them. Then they would probably let my people go unmolested.

Mac Davitt surrendered. Submitted to the English to keep his lands and his life; to gain a Sasanach title. Glinsk Castle stands and Dunboy is rubble.

I could surrender.

The thought dropped like a pebble into still water in his mind. Circles spread, widening. The outermost touched Con O'Murrough standing exhausted, yawning, weapon in hand, still ready to fight. Beyond him the kernes and gallowglasses, the mercenaries, the horse boys. The old men. The women.

"Fire at them," Donal Cam ordered in a deadly voice.

The distance was too great, the muskets were ineffective. But the burst of gunfire was startling in the cold morning air, and explicit in its meaning. The refugees had run but they would run no more.

Mac Davitt on his horse was nearly unseated when the

animal shied at the gunfire. He recovered, but the men with him were shaken. Unlike O'Sullivan's people, they had not been hardened through a fortnight's marching. They were farmers and herders and villagers who had set off at the order of their chieftain, but they had missed a night's sleep and their bellies were empty.

They had no taste for facing guns.

As Donal Cam shaded his eyes with his hand against the snowy glare, he saw them beginning to mill about uncertainly. The man on the horse rode a few steps forward, but they did not follow. He halted, looked back. Some sort of exchange was taking place. A few dark figures began returning the way they had come, then the whole pack set off after them.

Only the man on the horse remained, gazing toward the hill where Donal Cam waited, looking back at him. They faced each other across a gulf of air.

Then The Mac Davitt Burke turned his horse around and rode for home.

Home, thought Donal Cam, watching. Home to his castle, his hearth, his walls. His wife and children and storehouses and hounds stretched lazily in front of the fire . . .

He fought his way back from a dangerous mental precipice. Thomas Burke was looking at him, awaiting orders.

"We need to find a safe camp where we can get some hours' rest, Commander."

"We do indeed. An open hilltop in the dead of winter is no good. If we linger here, exposure will kill a score of us."

"It would," the mercenary captain agreed.

Maurice O'Sullivan added, "We must move out then, but could we, ah, take them on a bit more gently?"

Donal Cam almost smiled; would have smiled, if his

facial muscles had remembered how. "Gently. Very well, Maurice, I think we can take them on a bit more gently."

"I cannot go on at all," Maire told Niall.

"Just a way. Just a little way, they said, until we can find a place to make camp. Then we can sleep as long as we like, all this day and the night too."

"I cannot." Her voice was a mere thread. Tears welled into her eyes and spilled over onto her hollow cheeks, freezing as the cold wind of the hilltop struck them.

Niall approached Donal Cam. "Commander? My . . . my wife is too weak, she can go no farther."

"You cannot leave us here, there is nothing here for you."

"I know that. But she cannot walk anymore."

Donal Cam looked past him to the slight figure sitting on the cold earth, half fainting with fatigue. She looked not like a woman, but a child. A small child, helpless.

"Put her on one of the two horses we have left," Donal Cam ordered. "The stronger one is the stallion, I think."

"Are you not going to ride him anymore?"

Donal Cam shook his head. He helped lift Maire onto the horse and led the animal himself, while Niall walked beside them.

The stallion could hardly carry even such a negligible weight. Donal Cam kept his face turned away, unwilling to see the expression in the horse's eyes.

The refugees made their way down the hill and resumed the march.

They squelched across the bogland they had seen from the hill, falling into holes, trying to help one another out and being pulled in instead, falling into snowdrifts, gasping, struggling on, every thought and feeling sublimated to the necessity of lifting one foot, setting it down, and then lifting the other and setting it down just a little farther on.

The ground rose toward the Curlews; became rocky, more broken. Mountain land, and a mountain wind blowing down on them, savage with ice. They went on, into the wind.

There was no talking now. They had passed the point where such an added expenditure of energy was possible. Each person walked alone in his misery, unaware of those nearest. Some prayed silently. Some cursed silently. Step, swing the leg, step, swing the leg, step . . .

Peadar O'Coughlan plodded along with his eyes closed to slits against the wind. His mind wandered in a dream in which he was sitting on a horse again, feeling like a god again. Cantering through clouds. Effortlessly. He smiled in his dream.

Father Archer's thoughts were also on godhood. I walk in God's eye, he told himself reassuringly. Nothing happens to me that His all-seeing eye does not observe. He knows that I have ever been the instrument of His will. Though others oppose me, reject me, He is always with me. *Please God, make it so!*

The great dome of the gray winter sky, implacable, all-seeing, loomed over them like a glass bell trapping eternity within. An icy, changeless eternity with no hope and no escape. Walking, floundering, collapsing. Cold. So bitterly cold. On and on and . . . Dermod holding Joan's hand . . .

"Here," said Donal Cam hoarsely.

A kerne who was walking behind the chestnut stallion, letting its bulk break the wind, almost crashed into the horse's rump before his numbed mind recognized the cessation of forward movement. Some people halted abruptly. Others wandered on unaware, and had to be called back or physically caught.

"We can rest here for a little while," Donal Cam announced.

They had come to the edge of another woodland, a dark spill of trees pouring down through the folds of the mountains. Here, at the border of the forest, a tangle of holly and birch were locked in mortal combat, competing for light and life.

The refugees made their way in among the trees to a glade out of the wind. Those who could began gathering deadwood for a fire. Peadar O'Coughlan did what he could for the two ruined horses, which was not much.

He reported, "Neither one of them can go another step, Commander."

"We shall set them free, then," Donal Cam said softly.

Peadar's eyes widened in alarm. "Ah, Commander, if you turn them loose they will starve, they are too weak . . ."

"I did not mean to turn them loose," Donal Cam assured him.

He sought out Gerald Ryan, who was helping gather firewood. "We have to put the horses down," Donal Cam told the gallowglass. "Do you have your ax?"

The other man nodded silently.

Peadar went to each horse in turn, stroked their necks, whispered to them. Then he surrendered them to the gallowglass. Donal Cam took the horse boy by the arm and led him away.

When they heard the crash as the first horse fell, he put his arms around Peadar and let the boy bury his face against his chest.

Donal Cam ordered the horsemeat cut into chunks and distributed, tough and rank as it was. "It is better than nothing," he said, "and we can cook it over the fire. Cut it into small chunks so it will cook quickly."

But the instruction was wasted. People would not wait for the meat to be cooked. They snatched it and ate it in raw, bleeding gobbets which they crammed into their mouths with both hands. Then more often than not their bellies rejected it and the half-digested meat was spewed up again, to be replaced at once by more.

Even Maire ate the horsemeat this time. Niall took her a piece of liver, soft as velvet, offering her a bit between his fingers. She swallowed it like an obedient child and opened her mouth for more. "Is there any for the dog?"

There was. The two horses were stripped to the bone and every part of them devoured by people who thought they had never tasted anything as good.

With a curious sense of fitness, Ryan offered the stallion's brain to Donal Cam, who hesitated only a moment before accepting it. The other brain went to his uncle Dermod, who could not chew anything tougher.

Orla could not chew anything at all, but her eyes were open again, so Rory tried to pour a little of the blood down her throat. "Swallow," he urged. Her throat spasmed; perhaps some went down. Most of it ran down the side of her face.

Grella Ni Hurley seated herself on the ground close to the fire and to Niall and Maire. As he sucked the marrow from a bone, Father Archer noticed the way her eyes kept straying to Maire.

Evil desires to spread, he thought. There is another of them, hoping to contaminate a new bride with her own lewdness.

With returning strength his sense of mission rose strong in him.

Once there was food in his belly, The O'Connor Kerry returned his attention to his feet. The leather boots in which he had begun the long journey had disintegrated, leaving his bruises and blisters unprotected. He called across the fire to Donal Cam. "What are you going to do with the horsehides?"

"Why, do you want to eat them?"

The O'Connor grinned. "A while ago I thought I could, but now I would just like them to wrap around my feet. To make pampooties, you know; like islanders wear."

A clamor arose at once. Everyone wanted pampooties, the soft leather footgear that was wrapped around the foot and tied in place. Pampooties did not wear well, but while they lasted they were comfortable and gave purchase on stony ground.

"Do you know how to make them?" asked Lorcan Mac Sweney.

Even severe exhaustion could not destroy The O'Connor's sense of humor. Eyes twinkling, he assumed an exaggerated expression of insulted dignity and held out his great gnarled hands, the skin chapped and reddened, broken in places, the nails torn to the quick. "These are the hands of a chieftain," he announced pompously. "They do no common labor. They touch only butter and silk, as you can see."

"I know how to make pampooties," one of the Connacht men said. "If some of you who still have an edge to your blades will help me cut up the hides and make thongs from the guts, we can shoe those of you in most need of it."

Several men dragged themselves to their feet and set to work on the project while the rest just watched, sitting or lying as close to the fire as they could get.

Gesturing toward the workers, Father Collins remarked, "An hour ago they thought they were dying, and now look at them. Were there ever such people as these?"

"Never," said Donal Cam proudly.

The firelight flickered among the trees, lengthening the shadows to grotesque proportions. The light was changing. Donal Cam began to feel uneasy. He got up and left the fireside, walking to the edge of the trees to look back along the way they had come. He saw no one, merely an expanse of frozen, broken ground, desolate and empty.

But we have enemies everywhere, he warned himself. Never forget.

We are still too vulnerable here.

He returned to the fireside where Maurice O'Sullivan lay propped on one elbow, picking the last shreds of horsemeat from between his teeth with a sliver of bone.

Donal Cam paused beside him and looked down. "I think we should start moving out."

"What? Now?"

"Now. We need a safer place than this for a night camp, we are too close to the edge of the forest. I want to go deeper into the mountains and find a truly secure position on the high ground before I let these people sleep."

Thomas Burke spoke up. "We are safe enough here for that, Commander. This is friendly territory, as I told you, and the local folk are sympathetic to our cause even if they seem to accept English authority. We can stay here as long as . . ."

"Are you questioning the commander's judgment?" Maurice snapped.

"I am not, but . . ."

"We were not so safe when Mac Davitt attacked us."

"That was different, he had followed us a long way. But the O'Flynns helped us, remember. They warned us."

Maurice was skeptical. The farther they ventured from Munster, the more uncomfortable the buannachta became in what was for them alien territory. Old antagonisms against Connacht had begun to surface anew as they grew wearier and tempers grew shorter.

Added to this, Maurice was aware that his was only a temporary appointment as leader of the recruits. He resented what he saw as excessive trust being placed in

Thomas Burke. He glared at the big Connacht mercenary. "We have only your word that we are in friendly territory. I would not trust a Connacht man's word, myself."

Donal Cam turned on him with a flash of anger as quick and cold as a drawn sword flashing in winter sunlight. "Say nothing to divide us, Maurice, have you no sense? The English have done enough of that already, to our great cost. If Burke says we are safe here, then I believe he believes it.

"But the command decision is mine, and I say these people are not to sleep until we get them to some less exposed place, where enemies cannot creep up on us unaware."

The tension in their voices was attracting attention. With a groan, Dermod left his warm place by the fire to join them, as did the two Jesuits. Father Collins said, "You cannot make these people go any farther today, surely. Just look at them. They are dead on their feet."

"They are alive," Donal Cam contradicted, "and I mean to keep them that way."

"Can you not let them be until tomorrow morning? We have none of us slept in . . . what is it . . . two nights . . ."

"I think," began Father Archer, then realized Donal Cam was looking the other way. He raised his voice and tried again, "I think . . ."

"Can you get your men up and ready to go now?" Donal Cam interrupted, addressing his captains.

"I honestly doubt if some of them are able," Burke said doubtfully.

"When will they be able?"

"Another hour, perhaps two. When the horsemeat has done its work and the fire has thawed them a bit more."

"Too late in the day," Donal Cam objected. "We need to have a new camp before dark."

"In my opinion . . ." Father Archer attempted a third time, only to have Donal Cam inadvertently turn his back to him in order to say to his captains, "If they cannot all move yet, I suppose we could send a scouting party on ahead. They could blaze a trail to mark their way, find a campsite, and the others could follow as soon as possible. I am reluctant to split the group, but I am more reluctant to allow us all to sit here like deer awaiting the hunter."

"Who will go ahead?" Dermod asked.

"I shall lead the scouting party," Donal Cam decided, "since I know what sort of campsite I want."

Thomas Burke said, "Who will you take with you?"

"Ah." Donal Cam pursed his lips. The chapped skin broke and bled but he did not notice. Always another problem, he was thinking. He wanted the strongest men for the advance party, but he also had to leave some able men behind to defend the others if need be. If there was animosity between Thomas Burke and Maurice O'Sullivan, he should take one and leave the other. But which? Maurice would resent Burke's being chosen to go, he would take it as a sign of honor. But Burke was a native, this was land he knew . . .

Still, if it caused dissension . . .

I wish I were not so tired, Donal Cam said to himself. I wish I could think more clearly.

Out of old habit, and without really being aware he was doing it, he glanced around for Father Archer. His confessor responded to that turn of the head and the familiar, seeking look by taking a swift step forward. "My son?"

The response was too eager. The avidity glittering in

the priest's eyes made Donal Cam draw back. Ah no, he warned himself, seek no advice here.

But he had to say something. "You and Father Collins will stay here, of course, to rest and give comfort to the others. And . . . ah . . . Maurice and Thomas will each select five others from their companies and come with me, leaving the balance of the fighting men behind."

"But who will be in charge of them here?"

"Rory O'Sullivan, he will want to stay with his wife anyway. He will bring the others to the new campsite as soon as he can."

"What if his wife is not able to go any farther?" Father Collins asked. "I am very worried about her."

He did not notice the expression on the other priest's face.

"She will come," said Donal Cam succinctly.

He did not notice the expression on Father Archer's face either.

The refugees greeted the new plan with little reaction. Those who were staying behind felt only relief; those who would form the scouting party groaned and began gathering themselves. A few returned to the butchered horses, looking for last bits of meat to carry with them.

Donal Cam spoke quietly with Rory O'Sullivan. "Linger here no longer than you must. As soon as you think you can, have everyone up and moving again. If they protest, ignore them. Be cruel if you must, but shift them."

Rory looked around dubiously. "Not easy. And I do not think they will travel very fast in any case. What if darkness falls before we reach you?"

"We shall light fires you can see from a distance."

"If we can, so can anyone."

"I know it. There is an English garrison somewhere in the area, under Lambert's command. I think we have gone wide enough to avoid them but I cannot be sure. Just be careful, Rory." He looked down at Orla, lying on her litter.

"And take care of her," he added.

Rory's lips tightened over his teeth. "You need not tell me my responsibility, Commander."

Donal Cam bent over Orla, observing the barely perceptible rise and fall of her chest. Miraculously, she clung to life. Feeling Rory's eyes on him, he let his lips frame a silent command to the unconscious woman: live.

Then he straightened and beckoned to his men. Followed by a dozen equally divided between buannachta and mercenaries, he moved off into the forest.

Rory O'Sullivan stared after him. The scar on his face stood out lividly against his weather-beaten skin.

As the sounds of departure faded, those left behind began to stir. They seemed more aware of Donal Cam's absence than they had been of his presence. They began talking to one another in low voices, glancing nervously into the shadows between the trees.

Maire lay wrapped in the shaggy cloak, holding the little dog clasped in her arms for warmth. She had been dozing, but some disturbance in the atmosphere waked her. Her overtired brain began torturing her at once, imagining the walk ahead.

Niall sat down beside her, trying to flex the fingers of his injured arm.

"Those men who left," she said drowsily. "Where did they go?"

"To find a safer site for our night camp."

She came horribly awake. "Do you mean we have to go on?"

"The commander wishes it."

Tears began to leak from Maire's eyes. "I thought we would sleep here right on through the night. I thought . . .

I cannot go any farther. Niall. I cannot. There is no end to it. If I thought there was . . . but it is hopeless. I cannot go on."

"You will feel better soon," Niall tried to assure her.

"Never. It is too much. Too much. Niall . . . he said we could leave the column, remember? He said we should. Oh, please, let us do it now! Let them go on without us!"

Niall had been torn, seeing some of the buannachta go off without him, though loyalty to his new wife had compelled him to ask Maurice O'Sullivan for permission to stay with her. Faced with her demand, he realized just how much he hated being left behind.

I am The O'Sullivan's bard, he reminded himself. Harp or no harp, I should be with him. "Maire, we have to keep going. This is not place to spend the night, it is a dangerous wilderness."

A mercenary who had suffered a wound to his shoulder lay sprawled on the ground nearby, where he could hear every word of their conversation. "A wilderness surely," he agreed, "but there is a pleasant enough village not far to the northwest. I know the place well."

Niall turned toward him. "Royalists?"

"Ah no, though they submitted—on the surface at least—to save their lives. But underneath they remain second to none in their hatred of the Sasanach."

"Oh, Niall, could we go there?" Maire cried. "Would they give us shelter?"

"What do you think?" Niall asked the mercenary.

"They would if you had me to speak for you. Some of them are clanspeople of mine."

Maire said eagerly, "Would you? We could pay you, I have gold."

"Hunh." The man sat up, rubbing his shoulder. "You would not have to pay me to get me to leave the army. Though mind you, I would not say no to a coin or two."

"It is agreed, then. You will take us to this village and—"

"Now wait, Maire," Niall interrupted. "We must talk about this."

"Talk about what? Escaping with our lives while we have the chance? Is that not what The O'Sullivan wanted us to do?"

"We should wait until we see him again, to be sure."

"I am sure now."

"We should at least rejoin him long enough to bid him farewell," Niall temporized, suddenly feeling that he was being backed into a corner.

"How many others have bothered to say farewell? We have his blessing already, what more do we need? Think of it, Niall. We could be done with walking. You could build us a cabin, with a hearth . . . and a fire blazing all the time, even in summer! We could have a bit of earth to plant corn and kale. And buy a cow." Her pale face was alight. Her still-lovely voice spun a web that reached out to those beside the campfire and drew them into her dream.

Niall and the mercenary exchanged glances. "I should say she has you, right enough," the Connacht man remarked.

"I would like to go with you," said a Munster man, one of Orla's kinsmen from clan O'Donoghue.

"A strong fighting man like yourself? The commander still needs you, surely," Niall protested.

"When I cough, I cough blood. I will fight no more battles. But I might live a little longer if I stop here."

"Even the lice have left me, I am worse than you," said another Connacht man. "If I am about to die I want to do it in Connacht. Why should I go any farther than this?"

"I have kinsmen somewhere around here myself," said yet another mercenary. "I shall go and find them."

Afraid he was about to be responsible for a mass desertion, Niall argued, "None of us should leave the column, not now. We will reach Leitrim in a day or two. And the commander expects us to be with him tonight, he is finding a good campsite for us."

But Maire took hold of his good hand. Gently, she drew it to her tear-wet cheek. Her starved eyes pleaded.

From the corner of his eye, Niall noticed Father Collins get up and leave the fireside. "Wait here." Niall followed the priest among the trees and found him vomiting undigested horsemeat into a holly bush.

"You heard, Father? What should I do?"

Father Collins scraped a handful of icy snow from a branch and revolved it slowly in his mouth, cleansing away the foul taste. He spat several times, thoroughly. "Now," he said with satisfaction. "You wanted something, O'Mahony?"

"If I leave the commander, I will feel disloyal," Niall admitted. "He has been so good to me, and he is the best chieftain on the ridge of the world."

"He will not condemn you for leaving, and it is foolish for either of you to go any farther in your condition."

"Perhaps, but . . . what about the others?"

"You are not responsible for them. The choice is theirs."

"But . . ."

Too many buts, the priest told himself. "I suspect the truth is, lad, that you still hunger for adventure," he guessed.

"Adventure? You call this nightmare an adventure?"

"I do indeed, the greatest adventure either of us will ever have. And the need is on you, as it is on me, to see it through to its conclusion."

"I never thought a priest would feel that way."

"Did you not? Did you not know we are men like

yourselves, who hunger and thirst, dream and defecate, are frightened or exhilarated? Or curious?

"Besides, the closer we get to reaching The O'Rourke, the more I believe Donal Cam will succeed. Granted, he has not been able to save as many as he hoped, but unless something totally unforeseen happens I think he will deliver at least a hard core of soldiers to rise again with Hugh O'Neill, and I would like to see it."

"So would I," said Niall.

"But your situation is different. You have a wife now." Father Collins folded his arms across what had once been a pleasant little paunch, but had become an aching hollow. "You must think about what is most important to you."

Niall looked down at his feet in new pampooties. "The commander and my wife are equally important to me," he said in a low voice.

"Oh holy hour." Father Collins ran a hand through his thinning hair. "Poor lad, the hard decisions always come upon us when we are least prepared to make them. I wish I could help you with this one, but it is not my place."

"If we do leave the column now, Father, will you come with us?"

The Jesuit was startled. "Me? I have the same problem as yourself, I want to stay and see what happens. Besides, I am confessor to the chieftain of Kerry and cannot desert him. And I assure you he would never leave, destroyed though he is by the walking. I thank you for asking me, though."

Father Collins smiled a wistful smile. A vision flared in his mind. He saw a cabin thatched with golden straw. Children were romping outside an open doorway. An aging, avuncular man—himself with paunch restored—was watching them fondly. He saw Maire in all her loveliness emerge from the cabin to hand him a great slab of bread slathered thickly with butter, then linger, chatting with him, watching the children together . . .

"Take your wife and go," he said abruptly. His voice was harsh with urgency. "Listen to me. You wanted advice, now I am giving it. Forget about O'Sullivan Beare. *Life* is waiting for you. Seize it with both hands while you have the chance!"

Niall was taken aback by the priest's intensity. It was like hearing a command from God.

Catching his elbow, Father Collins hastily steered him back to the fire. Maire looked up at their approach. In her skeletal face was no trace of the beauty of the priest's vision, but he knew it would return. Her soul was beautiful, the sweet spirit of a gentle woman.

Priests can also feel envy, he said in his mind to Niall O'Mahony.

Under the stern eye of Father Collins, who allowed no second thoughts, Niall prepared to leave the column. With the Connacht man who knew the place as guide, they would strike out for the village lying to the northwest. At least one of the O'Donoghues, plus quite a few other Connacht men, were going with them.

Those who had chosen to remain did not blame them; they understood too well. There was a brief, terse leave-taking as men said farewell to companions they would not see again.

Throughout, Grella Ni Hurley had been sitting by the fire not far from Maire. She had busied herself making aimless circles on the frozen ground with a charred stick. When Maire had spoken of paying the mercenary, Grella's fingers had tightened spasmodically on the stick until it broke with a snap.

Now she called out to Niall, "Will you take another woman with you?"

Brooding in a solitary space on the far side of the fire,

Father Archer had been only peripherally aware of the proposed departure, and indifferent to it. But when Grella spoke his reaction was instantaneous. "Stop!" he shouted at her, scrambling to his feet. "I forbid you to go with them!"

"Father?" Grella was astonished. Donal Cam's confessor had never spoken personally to her before. He had seemed to inhabit a rarefied plain where only the nobility were human, and common folk were, preferably, invisible.

But now he was looking at her very hard indeed. He circled the fire and came toward her. "I said," he repeated, enunciating each syllable carefully as if she were stupid, "that you are to leave decent folk alone."

"Decent folk!" Grella shrilled. "I am decent folk!"

Father Archer scowled. "You are a . . ."

"James, please!" Father Collins laid a placating hand on the other Jesuit's arm.

Father Archer shook him off. "You are a Magdalene," he hissed at Grella. "An abomination put into this world by the Devil to tempt men. I will not have you insinuate your foulness between this man and his wife."

Father Collins was appalled. "James! You do not know what you are saying! These women are not . . . I mean . . . remember that Our Lord cherished the Magdalene, He forgave her and made her one of His most . . ."

"You are a whore!" Father Archer roared at Grella.

Orla was the one he longed to attack, but any overt attack on her would permanently alienate Donal Cam. Grella Ni Hurley had no such champion.

The confrontation was making Niall acutely uncomfortable. His wife was gently bred; she should not hear such things. "I think we had best leave now," he said to Maire in an undertone. Gathering the others with his eyes, he began to move his little party away from the fire.

When Grella tried to join them, Father Archer planted himself in front of her and held his upraised palm toward her. "You are not going, whore."

She tried to ease past him as inoffensively as possible. He caught her by the shoulders, digging his fingers in so deeply she gasped with pain. "You are the Devil's instrument but I am God's instrument, put on this earth to circumvent you and your kind!" the Jesuit screamed at her. He began shaking her violently, making her head snap back and forth. "I see your evil design!"

Grella was terrified. She thought he was talking about Maire's gold. How could he know? Was it true as the old ones claimed that the priests could see your thoughts and know your sins before you committed them?

She felt naked to his attack. Her only thought was escape.

He shook her harder. Her hair whipped around her face. Through its flying strands she caught a glimpse of Maire and the others leaving. The little dog was trotting behind them, its tail waving like a flag.

"Oh wait for me!" Grella called piteously. But the tangle of woods had already closed behind them.

Father Archer had lost all control of himself. Father Collins tugged ineffectually at him, trying to drag him away from his victim. Both Dermod and Rory O'Sullivan joined him, reluctant to lay hands on a priest but afraid he might do Grella some terrible harm if he continued.

"In the name of God, James, let her go!" Father Collins pleaded.

Dermod said, "Have mercy on her, let her go, she is almost the last woman left . . ."

"She is not!" Father Archer shouted at him, hanging on to Grella with fanatic strength. "The real whore is still with us also! He will not let *her* go! She is like a great tick burrowing under his skin, poisoning him. She is the one to blame for our every disaster. She is the one who caused him to involve himself in this ill-conceived rebellion in the first place. The Devil has brought destruction upon us through her, I tell you. I know it! In the confessional, O'Sullivan Beare . . ."

The man was raving, Father Collins realized. But he must not be allowed to betray secrets of the confessional.

Not knowing what else to do, Father Collins drew back his fist and hit the other priest the hardest blow he could, direct to the point of the man's jaw.

Father Archer staggered and released his hold on Grella. She staggered too, then broke and ran. In her panic she did not notice that she was going in the opposite direction to that taken by Niall and Maire. She was fleeing in mortal terror, expecting the judgment of God in the form of Father Archer to fall upon her at any moment.

She was swallowed up by the forest and they saw her no more.

Rory O'Sullivan's eyes blazed with anger. He shoved forward to face the Jesuit. There could be no mistaking the meaning of Father Archer's words. "And you call yourself a man of God!" he cried, doubling his own fists. "Take back what you said about my wife!"

The Jesuit was shaking his head, trying to clear it. His jaw ached mightily.

Father Collins's knuckles also ached mightily, but he pushed himself between Archer and the enraged captain. "My colleague does not know what he is saying," he told Rory. "Our long ordeal has mazed his wits."

"My wits are perfectly clear," Father Archer mumbled. With his fingers, he gingerly wagged his jaw. "You hit me!"

"You were about to tell things no priest may ever tell. There was no other way to stop you in time."

"You did not stop him soon enough," snarled Rory. "Now make him take back what he said about Orla or I shall hit him myself."

"You must not, he is a priest."

"He is a slanderer! I demand an apology!"

Somewhat recovered, Father Archer said more clearly, "I never apologize for speaking the truth."

"The truth is," interjected Joan Ni Sweney, who had come to stand at her husband's side, "that you are the sort of man who would attack a woman. You are no better than the worst of Carew's men."

Encouraged by his outspoken wife, Dermod added, "And if we are allotting blame at last, then it is you I blame for the loss of Dunboy. You and no other."

Joan Ni Sweney nodded in agreement. She had never liked James Archer anyway. She thought he gave himself airs. Any person as obsessed with the nobility as he was must be hiding a secret scorn for his own origins.

Eighteen months earlier, most people would have considered Father Archer to be above reproach, leonine in his dignity. As Joan shrewdly sensed, his background was humble, but he had cleverly obscured and long since forgotten it. Through a combination of personal diplomacy and political opportunism he had risen through the ranks of the clergy at a time when the Church was in turmoil. Being appointed confessor to the powerful prince of Beare, a man known to be devout, and yet possessing certain influence with the English authorities, had been a major step on the road which would, Father Archer firmly believed, take the Jesuit someday as far as Rome.

Fulfilling such an ambition required keeping a delicate balance between idealism and pragmatism. He had vigorously opposed Donal Cam's joining the rebellion. "You have the trust of the English now," he had argued. "You can use your influence, quietly, secretly, in high places, to defend the faith in this part of Munster. It is a matter of suggestion, of accommodation . . .

"But if you anger the English authorities by joining this insurrection we will lose everything. Carew will undoubtedly confiscate all Church property.

"Listen to me, my son. You have always heeded my advice before; heed it now. Be patient and keep your head down and we may yet ride out this crisis unscathed. When the heretics are overthrown, as they will be with the aid of Spain, we shall find ourselves on the winning side and have lost nothing."

"Lost nothing!" Donal Cam had echoed in astonishment. "Carew is putting Munster's Catholics to the sword, thousands have lost their lives already!"

"So why add your own to that number? You can do so much more for our cause by staying alive and working within the system. I know how such things are done, I will guide and instruct you. But you must not involve yourself in the slightest way with Hugh O'Neill and that wild young O'Donnell."

The priest's advice had fallen on deaf ears. Satan, as he soon discovered, was working on the other side.

Ignoring Father Archer's counsel, Donal Cam had thrown away his inestimable advantages and openly turned against the English.

Father Archer knew why. Orla Ni Donoghue. She, the whore, the serpent, had been with him the day the fateful decision was made. Pleading with him, seducing him. The priest had seen them himself, Donal Cam and the Devil's instrument, together.

That day. The beginning of the end, the shocking day that led inevitably to Kinsale and destruction because it was the Devil's handiwork.

Father Archer had done his best to try to counteract her evil. Surely, if the others knew the truth they would understand and approve.

He locked eyes with Dermod O'Sullivan. "Dunboy was only stone and mortar," he said. "Dunboy did not matter."

Two red spots flamed above the old man's sunken cheeks. "And the men who died trying to defend Dunboy—men who might have won and lived, with my nephew to lead them!—do they not matter?"

"Their deaths are regrettable and I myself pray for the repose of their souls, of course. But the greater good was served."

Dermod was mystified. "What greater good?"

"Are you so blinded by admiration for your nephew's military skills that you cannot see the truth? If he had gone back to Dunboy he would have died with the rest. He could not win. Even if he had had an army of five thousand men he could not have won. And why? Because Satan was in league with Carew against him! Had been from the beginning, had lured The O'Sullivan into the rebellion for the express purpose of destroying a great Catholic prince. His death at Dunboy would have given a mighty victory to the heretics and the Devil's minions.

"But I forestalled Satan. I held Donal Cam at Ardea by promising reinforcements I knew he would not get; by taking him every morning to watch for ships I knew were not coming. I blackened my immortal soul with lies, but I made the sacrifice gladly. Gladly!

"Do you not yet understand? A great mission was vouchsafed to me by God. I, James Archer . . . I saved the life of O'Sullivan Beare!"

Day Fourteen

January 13, 1603. *Diamhrach*, Bracklieve; Solitude, Mystery

High in a forested fastness, a fire blazed. The campsite was all but impregnable, backed up against a mountain's stony shoulder with ground falling sharply away on either side. In this same area Red Hugh O'Donnell had fought Sir Clifford Conyers, then lord president of Connacht, in 1598. Conyers had died at the hands of Brian Óg O'Rourke. Young Brian of the Battle Axes.

Donal Cam recalled listening to the reports of that victory breathlessly recounted by a messenger from the north as he sat warm and comfortable in the great hall at Dunboy.

A thousand years ago.

His dozen companions lay scattered about him like felled trees. He had kept watch through the dark hours alone, waiting with mounting anxiety for the remainder of the column to arrive.

The cold was glacial. The air smelled of black frost: piercing, metallic on the back of the throat.

No watch was ever lonelier. Thomas, Maurice, and the others had tried to stay awake with him but one by one they had been overpowered, falling asleep between one breath and the next. Lorcan Mac Sweney had been the last man on his feet, but now even he was snoring lustily.

O'Sullivan Beare sat facing outward, with his back to his fire. His knees were drawn up, his arms folded atop them. Occasionally he leaned forward to rest his forehead on his arms, but that put a strain on his aching back.

He could not remember how it felt to be comfortable.

So many memories had been submerged in the flood of events.

To keep himself awake, he began sorting among those that remained, trying to salvage some bright image.

Honora!

Honora as he had first seen her, standing slim and regal beside her father, who was brother-in-law to Florence Mac Carthy Mor. When he met Honora, Donal Cam had forgotten every other woman—for a while. She was perfect down to the smallest detail of her person. The carefully arranged waves of her hair were art. Her eyelashes, as she gazed at him through them, were like glossy black thorns, thick and curving and impossibly long.

He had realized he was staring, but he had not been able to help himself. Her every gesture had a studied grace that made the breath catch in his throat.

For company in his solitude, Donal Cam now summoned an image of Honora as she had been in her youthful perfection. But even as her face filled his mind it faded, replaced by another face.

A pallid face framed by wild red hair.

The death's-head that Orla Ni Donoghue had become looked back at him accusingly.

I thought you could do anything, the cracked lips said.

He closed his eyes and ground the heels of his palms into them, trying to press the vision away.

I did my best, Orla. You should not have expected so much of me, no man could live up to that.

Your worship put a terrible pressure on me.

Orla's worship was too flattering to resist, the cold small voice of truth whispered in his soul. Your wife, after the first flush of marriage wore off, saw you as a man.

Orla always saw you as a god.

Another voice rang in his ears: You, with your peacock's vanity, Father Archer said.

Donal Cam bowed his head to his arms again.

If my pride and vanity have brought us to this I will spend the rest of my life trying to expiate the sin, he vowed.

I did want the glory of defeating the English. I thrilled to the sound of the trumpet and the beat of the bodhran. I even, may God forgive me, nurtured the conceit of taking my army north to O'Neill to fight again, and having him put his arm around my shoulders and say, "Well done," as he did when Hugh O'Donnell arrived at Kinsale.

I am human. I wanted those things.

But it was not pride that brought me here, Donal Cam told himself, remembering. Pride alone would not have been enough.

Orla's face stared at him from inside his closed eyelids. Not as a death's-head now, but as a vibrant young woman, laughing at him, challenging him to a footrace and throwing a splat of mud at him as he flashed past her.

Orla comforting him the first time he and Honora quarreled. He had come upon her quite by accident, not looking for her, merely turning a corner in the village and there she was, with a basket balanced on her head, wearing the same smile she had always given him. Since they were youngsters together.

Orla had never been fashionably beautiful like Honora. She did not belong to the princely branch of clan O'Donoghue and so had never been petted and polished. Never even educated, which was a pity, because she had a fine mind.

Her father was a guard in the service of Donal Cam's father, one of those loyal O'Donoghues famed throughout Munster as bold fighting men. Orla had been bred and raised to be a warrior's woman, durable and sturdy.

A woman to bear strong sons.

A shudder ran through Donal Cam's body as he sat alone in the mountain night. He got up to put more wood on the fire.

"Where are you?" he whispered to the wind.

He heard something crashing through the undergrowth down below. In an instant he was on his feet, trying to see through the darkness. It was well after midnight but too early for the dawn. Only blackness met his straining eyes.

Then something moved, closer. A man came scrambling up the slope toward Donal Cam, sobbing for breath. "Commander! It is you!"

Donal Cam ran forward to take Peadar O'Coughlan's hands.

He led the shivering boy to the fire. "Where are the rest of them, lad? Are they right behind you?"

The horse boy's teeth were chattering so hard he could barely talk. "They were . . . some . . . not all . . . some left."

"Who came? Who is with you? And where?"

Peadar waved vaguely. "Back there."

Donal Cam wrapped his own cloak about the youth and left him crouched close to the flames. He backtracked down the dangerous slope, looking for the others.

A low, monotonous cursing led him to Father Collins, whose rags had snagged on a bush, holding the exhausted man fast. With Donal Cam's help he extricated himself. "My fingers are that cold, they will not bend," the Jesuit explained.

"No matter, they will be warm soon. There is a great fire blazing above."

"I saw it, it led me to you," the priest said gratefully.

"What of the others, where are they? Did some stay behind?"

"Ah they did. That young couple I married, they went off with some of the Connacht men in search of a village that might take them in. She could go no farther, the poor lass."

Donal Cam breathed softly, "God go with them."

"Indeed."

"And The O'Connor and my uncle? What of them?"

"We were together until darkness caught us. The others were ahead of us, but Sean O'Connor can hardly walk, as you know, so your uncle and aunt and I were all with him, encouraging him. And he putting a brave face on it and telling us to go ahead, not to wait for him."

"But you did not leave him."

"Of course we did not leave him. It was a strange thing, how we got separated. Dermod and Sean had rested enough to be joking between themselves, you know how they are, saying they were going to have a footrace. And Dermod's wife said she would kiss the winner, which seemed to make her husband angry. An old man like that! He sulked and she scolded him and they stopped in their tracks to have words about it. Sean dare not stop, he kept stumping along and I with him, both of us thinking the others would come up to us at any moment. They did not, and Sean began to worry. He said he would go back for them but I would not let him. I bade him wait for me while I went back for them myself. But when I got to where I thought they were, they were not there. And I had become confused. Dusk had fallen and nothing looked familiar. I could not be certain which direction led to Sean. I went the way I thought was the right one and did not find him either, so I just kept walking. Before long I knew I was lost."

Father Collins caught his breath with a little sob.

"Yet you are almost the first here!" Donal Cam told him.

"Am I?" The Jesuit was amazed.

"How did you find us, the fire?"

"I did not even see the fire for a very long time. I was in another forest, the trees hid its light, I suppose. I had become convinced I was going to die, if you want the truth of it.

"When a man is about to die there is only one thing to do, so I did it. I put myself in Our Lord's hands.

"And here I am."

His narrative had confirmed Donal Cam's worst fears. They had come too slowly, the darkness caught them and they could not follow the blazed trail. People had become separated and lost. Yet if Father Collins had eventually seen the fire and been able to follow its light, surely the others would.

Please God, surely they would!

"What about Rory O'Sullivan and his wife? What of them?"

Father Collins shook his head. "They were ahead of us

when I got lost, that is all I can tell you. Have they not arrived already?"

Donal Cam replied in a choked voice, "Not yet. You go on to the fire and warm yourself, and wake my men. Send them to me, we have people to search for."

The priest obediently set off up the slope, catching hold of protruding rocks and bits of brush to pull himself along, his eyes fixed on the welcoming flames. He did not want to think about the look on Donal Cam's face.

Half walking, half slithering, Donal Cam was making his way down, hoping every moment he would meet someone coming up. The hour must be well after midnight. They should have reached the new camp long ago. It had been a terrible mistake to divide the column, he saw that now; he should have seen it then.

When exhaustion could so distort a man's judgment that foolishness seemed like sense, how did anyone ever win a war, he wondered.

Perhaps God does intervene. Yet both sides claim Him . . .

God, if You are listening, if You led Father Collins, hear me now. Let me find them. Her. Let me find her. What ever fortune of mine is safe in Spain, that I will designate for Your work. Just let me find . . .

He froze. There were more sounds below; people approaching. It never occurred to him that they might be a Royalist patrol. Only one thought was in his mind now. "Here!" he cried as loudly as he could. "This way! We are here!" He began to run, risking a bad fall and not caring.

Con O'Murrough materialized out of the gloom. "I told you this must be our fire," he called over his shoulder to a second member of the buannachta. The two men stumbled wearily toward Donal Cam.

"Who else is with you?"

"There are a score of us, I think, strung out over a distance. We had to stop for the woman, but . . ."

"What woman? The one on the litter?"

"Ah no, the old one. Your uncle's wife, Commander. Herself and himself had gone astray somehow and she started calling. One of our lads with sharp ears heard her, a trick of the wind. We turned around and went looking for her, knowing you would not thank us for losing your uncle. Finally we found the both of them. They were in a bad way, so we waited with them until they had recovered themselves."

"Are they with you now?"

"Back there . . . somewhere . . ."

"And the woman on the litter?"

"Captain O'Sullivan and one of the O'Donoghues were carrying her, the last I saw. They were ahead of us, they did not turn back when we did. We thought they would be here by now."

"Not yet," said Donal Cam through clenched teeth.

By twos and threes, the stragglers arrived. When they reached the fire they threw themselves onto the ground and fell asleep where they were. Kerne and gallowglass, recruit and mercenary, they collapsed.

In an agony of impatience, Donal Cam waited, searching the face of each new arrival. Still among the missing were Dermod and Joan, Father Archer, The O'Connor Kerry.

And the litter carrying Orla.

He thought of sending his twelve rested men back along the route to look for them, but forced himself to discard the idea. If splitting the group had been a mistake in the first place, he must not repeat the error.

He paced the perimeter of the firelight, staring out into

nothingness. The montane wilderness was peopled with ghosts. He saw figures move, but when he focused upon them they were revealed as trees, bushes, tricks of firelight. Hallucinations of an exhausted mind.

He envied those who slept by the fire. I have forgotten how to sleep, he thought.

Ghosts. One in particular. A child . . .

He gave an inarticulate moan and lashed his head from side to side like a man in bondage.

"At last!" cried a voice he knew.

Dermod O'Sullivan came up the slope toward him, pulling himself up by rocks and bushes as Father Collins had done, holding one hand behind him for his wife.

Donal Cam threw himself toward them as if they were saving him.

With an arm around each, he brought them the last few steps of their journey. They were both frail and faltering, but their minds seemed clear and their relief was as palpable as his. He sat them close to the fire and chafed Joan's hands while Dermod recounted, in a weak voice, their story of being lost and found. He concluded by saying, "We never found Sean, though. Is he here?" He looked around hopefully, scanning the recumbent forms by the fire for one with the shape of The O'Connor.

"He will be along soon," Donal Cam lied.

"Ah, he will," Dermod agreed. "You could not kill him with an ax." But his concern showed in his eyes. "I . . . ah . . . I could go back down the trail and meet him," he suggested.

"Old fool!" Joan caught hold of his arm and held fast. "You stay right where you are. Here with me." She gave a tired sigh and let her head sink against his shoulder.

Dermod O'Sullivan forgot about The O'Connor. With one hand he smoothed his wife's gray hair. Over her head he looked at Donal Cam, and the younger man thought he saw a suspicious glint of tears in his uncle's eyes.

O'Sullivan Beare had never envied anyone as much as he envied Dermod and Joan at that moment.

Somewhere beyond the mountains, dawn was breaking.

Father Archer arrived with the light. Donal Cam greeted him with more warmth than the priest had honestly expected, given the recent coolness between them.

But Donal Cam was genuinely glad to see him. If he had made it, the others still might.

The Jesuit collapsed by the fire. Donal Cam sat down beside him. "Did you see anyone else?"

Father Archer knew who he meant. That woman. His warmth was spurious, then; his only interest was in her.

"No one," the priest said coldly. Pillowing his head on his arm, he closed his eyes.

Donal Cam's own eyes seemed full of sand, but whenever he tried to close them he saw ghosts. He kept his lonely vigil by the fire, letting the rest of his people sleep. This was a safe place; they could sleep as long as they liked, for once.

For the first time in a fortnight.

At last even Donal Cam's iron will failed. His head began to nod. He started, shook himself awake; nodded again.

He almost did not hear the footsteps.

When his dulled senses tardily registered a warning, Donal Cam scrambled to his feet so precipitately he lost his balance and nearly fell into the fire. He stumbled back, only to tread heavily on the outflung arm of a sprawled gallowglass.

"Mind yourself," the man growled without moving.

The O'Connor Kerry hobbled into the pool of firelight.

He was half draped over Thady Cooney, who had somehow managed to maneuver the older man up the slope in increments, scrambling and cursing. When he realized they had reached the top at last, Thady simply folded his legs and sat down where he was. The O'Connor staggered forward on his own to grasp Donal Cam's eagerly outstretched hands.

"I never thought we would make it," he panted. "If I had not had to carry that poor lad, of course, I would have been here long ago." He grinned and collapsed. Donal Cam barely caught him in time to keep him from hitting the ground very hard.

"Rest here, Sean," he said unnecessarily, easing the old chieftain to earth.

"Just for a moment" came the weak-voiced reply. "Just until I catch my breath. Tell me . . . am I here ahead of Dermod O'Sullivan?"

Before Donal Cam could answer, The O'Connor was asleep.

They were all asleep, even the twelve who had formed his advance party. Satisfied that most of the stragglers had arrived, the dozen had returned to their own positions beside the fire and surrendered to exhaustion gratefully.

Almost against his will, a wakeful Donal Cam found himself counting the prone figures as if the act of counting could magically multiply their number.

But though he painstakingly enumerated them twice, there were only thirty-six. Thirty-six left from a thousand. Including himself, eighteen of those could be classed as warriors. The remainder had begun the long march in a civilian capacity; most were horse boys or porters. Over the endless miles they had become warriors by default, having to fight for their lives with whatever came to hand until they were indistinguishable from the recruits and mercenaries.

My army, thought Donal Cam.

Aside from Father Archer, there was not one of the survivors who had not struck a blow at the enemy. Donal Cam smiled, recalling Joan with her woolen stocking and stone; The O'Connor Kerry, screaming a battle cry; a hundred other moments of valor too briefly glimpsed, never to be forgotten.

He felt a fierce pride in them, in each and every person. If he had only these to deliver to Hugh O'Neill, still he could boast of having brought the finest.

Except for . . .

He went again to the edge of the slope.

My two best soldiers are still out there, he thought.

The loss was insuperable.

He fleetingly considered pleading with God one more time, but he had offered God so many bargains over the past months. The fact that any of them were still alive was a miracle in itself. How dare he ask for more?

What could he offer in return? Could he say, Strike me down, Lord, but spare those I care for?

He had offered that bargain in the beginning when they were all trying to bargain with God. Yet here he was, still alive, when so many he had hoped to save were dead. It had come as a shock to realize that the prince of Beare was obviously poor coin for barter in the eyes of the Almighty.

So much for me and my peacock's vanity, he thought, glancing toward Father Archer, who had never understood him.

But how can one person know what is in the mind of

another? he asked himself. Except on rare occasions, a lightning flash of perception . . .

Orla.

Orla as she had been that day. *That day*. Opalescent sealight flooding the market square at Beare Haven; the same village square where the surviving defenders of Dunboy would be hanged the following June. Cold sea light, ushering in the winter that would culminate with Kinsale.

Himself and Orla bathed in that light, staring at one another with horror in their eyes.

The talk in Beare had all been of war that year, of O'Neill and O'Donnell in the north, of a Spanish invasion from the south to rout the heretic English. Of Carew, who since his appointment as lord president had been cutting a terrible swath through the land, carving his authority in blood across the face of Munster.

Seemingly out of deference to The O'Sullivan, Beare had been spared any serious incursions.

Until that day.

Orla's face had been startlingly white beneath its customary windburn. He had never seen her cry before, not even when he told her he was marrying Honora.

"They came right into the house," she had told him, "as if they had every right. Laughing and drunken, encouraging each other. Then one of them took out his . . . ah, does the English queen know what is being done in her name?" Her voice had shrilled in anguish.

Trying to be conciliatory, Donal Cam had replied, "I should think Elizabeth is unaware of such things, Orla. She gives a broad command; it is up to her deputies here to decide with what methods those commands are to be met."

Orla's face convulsed with hatred. "You hold her innocent? I think she knows. Perhaps she even enjoys reading the reports that are sent back to her, sitting there in her safe high place, herself who has never lain with a man nor borne a child. I tell you, she knows what is being done to us and does not care!"

Donal Cam had tried to calm her, glancing around for some place more private than the open square. He did not want the party accompanying him to witness a scene involving Orla.

But then she had told him the rest of it, and he forgot to care if anyone was watching.

Remembering now, he sat as if turned to stone.

Then he heard a cry for help.

With a soul-wrenching effort, Donal Cam dragged himself back from the marketplace at Beare Haven to the dawn forest of Bracklieve.

The voice he heard calling was Rory O'Sullivan's.

The litter was gone. The second litter bearer was gone. Alone, Rory was struggling up to the campsite, his breath tearing his throat. Donal Cam scrambled down to him. "Where is she?" was his greeting.

"Down below. I carried her as far as I could."

A shout summoned help. With Lorcan Mac Sweney and Maurice O'Sullivan following him, knuckling their bleary eyes, Donal Cam made his way down to the shelf of rock where Rory had left Orla.

She was wrapped in a blanket with one corner pulled over her face.

Perhaps it was meant to keep her warm. Perhaps not.

Donal Cam was afraid to turn back the blanket and find out.

Maurice O'Sullivan reached past him to bare her face.

In the dawn light, she was as colorless as water. Even her red hair was leeched of life.

"Orla?" Donal Cam whispered. Not a command this time, but an entreaty.

Her eyes opened.

He fell to his knees beside her. "Just a little farther, we have a fire, you will be warm . . ."

"Never again," she said so faintly he could hardly hear her. Her speech awakened an awful rattle in her throat.

Donal Cam knew that sound. He had heard it too many times. He fumbled under the blanket for her hand, found it and held it.

"I got this far anyway," she whispered.

"You are an incredible woman."

"The strongest?"

"The strongest." He bowed his head over her hand.

Orla stirred restlessly beneath the blanket; the last torn, filthy blanket left to them.

"Are you in pain?" he asked quickly.

She could not answer him, but he read the agony in her eyes.

Though Donal Cam did not notice, another man had joined them. Rory O'Sullivan had come back down the slope to his wife. Elbowing Maurice and Lorcan aside, he bent over the pair on the ground.

Orla was struggling to focus her eyes. Everything was gray. Could it be mist from the sea? The breakers rolling onto the beaches . . . Dimly she made out a face. Her glazing eyes tried to hold on to the face, but the mist got in the way. She ran her swollen tongue over her cracked lips.

"I love you," she whispered to the face.

Donal Cam made a strangled sound. His fingers tightened on hers. "Go now," he said, unable to see her suffer more. "Go now. Be free!"

He doubled over her in his own agony.

Rory O'Sullivan flung himself down beside the two of them, hesitated, then put his arms around them both, the living and the dead.

Maurice O'Sullivan buried his face in Lorcan Mac Sweney's shoulder.

After a while, they covered her face once more and carried her almost weightless body up to the camp. They laid her down beyond the firelight. The sleepers slept on, oblivious.

"This soil is too shallow to dig, so we shall erect a cairn over her," Donal Cam said. "Gather stones." Then he sought out Father Collins and shook the sleeping Jesuit's shoulder. "We need a priest, Father," he said in a low voice.

Lying nearby, Father Archer overhead and came awake at once. "What is it?"

"Nothing," Donal Cam said over his shoulder. "Go back to sleep."

But Father Archer was already getting to his feet. "If you need your priest, I am ready." Then he noticed the blanketed form lying some paces away, different in the quality of its stillness. "Did someone die? Who?"

"My wife," Rory O'Sullivan told him. "She needs the Last Rites."

The priest's face suffused with blood. "Her? And where will she receive them, hell? I give no sacraments to whores and demons."

He never saw what happened. Suddenly he found himself lying facedown on the ground, with one arm twisted excruciatingly behind his back. "Leave us," said Donal Cam in a deadly voice. The grip on the arm tightened.

The priest feared he would faint from pain. "But I am your confessor!" He was shocked beyond measure.

"Leave us, I said! I never want to see you again."

Hands dragged Father Archer to his feet. He was badly shaken. "Where would I go, what would I do?"

In that same deadly tone, Donal Cam replied, "The natives are friendly, I am told. Find them." With a nod, he signaled Maurice and Lorcan. They closed unquestioningly on Father Archer and began to force him physically away from the camp. He looked beseechingly toward Rory, but there was no help to be had there. Father Collins was on his feet by this time, but he made no move to intervene. He merely looked from one face to the other, wearing an intensely thoughtful expression.

"This is a terrible mistake," Father Archer protested. The two soldiers pressed him back relentlessly. When he held up his hands in an attempt to ward them off they brushed them aside.

Maurice and Lorcan had been relatively unaware of the increasing friction between their commander and his confessor, but the priest's attack on the dead woman was intolerable.

She had been a comrade-in-arms.

Glowering at Father Archer, they moved menacingly closer.

At last he gave up and began picking his way down the slope, trying not to fall and add further insult to his ruptured dignity.

Donal Cam stared after him until he disappeared. Then he turned to the others. "Now we can bury her," he said.

Father Collins gave Orla the Last Rites, trying not to let his mind be distracted by the scene he had just witnessed. It was a rebellion he had never envisioned.

They found a cleft in the rock that provided a partial tomb. When Orla's body was laid as far inside as it would go, they filled the opening with stone until it resembled a natural rockslide. No one would ever disturb her.

A cairn for a queen, Father Collins thought but did not say aloud. It would be too painful to say and too painful to hear.

Rory and Donal Cam worked side by side, piling stones on the cairn, but they did not look at one another. Each man was alone inside himself.

Each man was still hearing her last whispered words.

When there was nothing left to be done for Orla, they went back to the fire.

A ringing silence seemed to fill the forest. Perhaps I can sleep at last, thought Donal Cam. But even as he had the thought, he heard someone calling from below and was instantly on his guard again. Rory O'Sullivan, shattered as he was, came to stand shoulder to shoulder with him, sword in hand, peering down the slope. Maurice and Lorcan—and Father Collins as well, fully prepared to fight—were right behind them.

But it was not an enemy who approached. Smiling, cheerful, welcoming faces appeared below, looking up, waving.

Donal Cam could hardly believe his eyes.

A half dozen men approached, winding their way up the hill with the confidence of familiarity. "Natives surely," whispered Rory.

"Name yourselves," Donal Cam called out, still wary.

"Friends bringing you food!" was the astonishing reply.

The six men proved to be members of a local clan who had seen the signal of the fire and rightly surmised that it belonged to the fugitives from the south. "Your exploits precede you," their leader told Donal Cam.

He was an affable man with a head too large for his body and a nose too small for his face. "Colm Mac Donough," he introduced himself, dropping a large bundle into Donal Cam's astonished hands. "And that parcel contains bread and bacon."

"By the way," said a second man, stepping forward and bringing a familiar figure with him, "we found this member of your party down below. He appeared lost and you could not afford to lose a priest, so we have returned him to you." He smiled, obviously pleased with himself.

Father Archer and Donal Cam stared at each other.

Mac Donough and his party made straight for the fire. Each of them had brought some gift of food, and it did not take long to awaken even the soundest sleepers once that fact was known. People so groggy they could not have told their own names recovered themselves enough to claim a share of the feast.

"I told you we had entered friendly territory," Thomas Burke could not resist saying to Donal Cam as he tore a great loaf of bread apart.

Donal Cam had no appetite. Orla was like a vast chasm in his mind. He noticed that Rory O'Sullivan was not eating, either, although the rest of them were devouring every morsel and picking crumbs out of the dirt to eat.

As leader of the group, Colm Mac Donough took a seat by Donal Cam to engage the rebel chieftain in conversation. He had not met anyone so interesting since Red Hugh O'Donnell. There would be great tales to tell of this day.

Donal Cam was nonplussed. He had inured himself as best he could to hardship and hatred; he was unprepared for kindness. At first he could respond to Mac Donough's well-meant overtures only in the gruffest tones, reluctant to reveal anything of himself and his people.

But Mac Donough was persistent and Donal Cam was too tired to resist. Soon he found himself relating the details of the long march at some length, while his new friends listened avidly, making exclamations of wonder from time to time.

"You did!"

"How extraordinary!"

"And is it not remarkable that you escaped!"

Their warmth reached a cold core in his bones that the fire had not thawed.

"When we first noticed the blaze up here," Mac Donough told him, "we knew it had to be you. A dangerous thing, that, lighting such a beacon!"

"I have been putting everything that would burn into those flames all night," Donal Cam replied. "It was to guide my people to me."

"It could well have guided Lambert's men from the garrison. Fortunately, they believe this fire is the work of laborers taking stone from the mountains."

"Why should they think that?"

"Ah." Mac Donough smiled modestly. "Someone sent them a message to that effect. We have become experts at dissembling and at spreading false stories since Elizabeth's men have been here."

"Do you really think the English are so foolish as to believe we would be quarrying stone way up here in the dead of winter?"

Mac Donough laughed. "They will believe anything of us, they think all the Gael are mad. The more insane an action, the quicker they are to believe it of us."

"You and I must have a long talk about strategy sometime," Donal Cam said admiringly.

"Myself to teach O'Sullivan Beare strategy after what you have done? I could not," the other replied. "As soon teach a wild goose to fly."

"If I had more of a gift for strategy we might not find

ourselves in this desperate situation now," Donal Cam told Mac Donough.

"Not so desperate, you have almost reached O'Rourke's territory and certain safety. The queen's men are very wary of him, I can tell you, after what happened to Conyers at the hands of an O'Rourke. Do not blame yourself, O'Sullivan. These are the fortunes of war, but you have survived, you will fight again."

Donal Cam gave him a somber look. "That was my hope when we set out. But so much has happened since . . ."

"Ah, you only say that now because you are spent. Some sleep will make you feel different, and you will be ready to take up arms against Elizabeth's land grabbers again."

Donal Cam narrowed his eyes. "You did not call them heretics."

"And why should I? Do I know the truth of God's plans? I tell you, O'Sullivan, there are all sorts of paths winding up this mountain. You came by one and I another, yet here we are, both of us on top and safe and warm."

"Indeed." Donal Cam was nodding in agreement. "We all worship one God. It is only those who claim to speak for Him who lead us astray. When we hear hatred in their voices we know they are not speaking for the Almighty but for their own prejudices."

Detecting an angry undertone, Mac Donough guessed shrewdly, "Has something turned you against priests, O'Sullivan?"

Lying near them, Father Collins strained to hear the answer, but Donal Cam's reply was pitched so low he only made out the last few words: ". . . never want to see a priest again."

Ah the poor man, Father Collins thought. He closed his eyes in pity but it was a mistake. In another heartbeat he was asleep.

Donal Cam spoke long and earnestly with Mac Donough. Among other things, his new friend warned him that Lambert was aware of the refugees' arrival in his territory and would have set up a watch for them on the main routes into Leitrim. "If you are able for it," Mac Donough said, "one more night's march across the mountains would avoid the eyes of Lambert's men and put you within a half day of O'Rourke's castle."

Donal Cam was grateful for the advice, but before he could ask for a more specific set of directions sleep finally began to overtake even him. Noticing him fighting to keep his eyes open, Mac Donough and his men exchanged meaningful glances. It was broad daylight. The great fire Donal Cam had built upon his arrival had long since burned low. No Royalist patrol had arrived from the nearest garrison. Mac Donough decided it was safe to leave the refugees to their rest.

When Donal Cam's head nodded on his breast and his eyes closed, Mac Donough put a finger to his lips to signal silence, arose very quietly, and led his men away. He left behind what remained of his thoughtful gift of food, and an indelible impression of kindness.

The exhausted survivors slept through the day. Occasionally one or another roused enough to relieve themselves, but for the most part they lay as if dead, letting the food in their bellies work its restorative magic.

Father Archer awoke once, abruptly. The day had grown warmer. He cast an uneasy glance in the direction of Donal Cam, and was thankful to see that he was fast asleep.

When he awakes he will be more reasonable, the priest tried to tell himself.

But he did not believe it. He could not forget the fury on Donal Cam's face, or that cold and deadly voice.

I went too far, Father Archer admitted to himself. I let that demon win.

He clenched his fist and gnawed on the knuckles until they bled, but the penetential pain was not cleansing.

I have failed. I have failed.

James Archer had trained in many disciplines, but never in failure. Deep inside himself he felt a seismic shifting, an irreversible change.

Suddenly he was very hot. He sat up, panting. But the sensation soon faded and he found himself shivering, growing colder and colder out of all proportion to the temperature of the day. He lay down again and wrapped himself as tightly as he could in his rags.

His mind wandered away in a fevered dream.

There were many fevered dreams.

The O'Connor Kerry was increasingly aware of the pain in his feet and legs. He imagined he was walking through fire, with an angel leading him by the hand. He tried to explain to the angel that all his sins were venial—or he had intended them to be no more than venial—but the angel seemed to be drawing him deeper and deeper into the flames.

He awoke with a snort. "Ah. Annnhhh . . ." He tried to draw his legs up to his body so he could rub his calf muscles, but the legs were too stiff to bend at the knee. He levered himself with his arms until he was sitting up, staring resentfully at his feet.

His movement awakened Dermod O'Sullivan. "Are we going?" Dermod asked fuzzily.

"I hope not" was the sincere answer. "I think I would like to sit here until St. Stephen's Day. At the earliest."

One by one, people began to awake. Thady Cooney became aware of a cramp in his belly, the result of having eaten too much too fast. He whimpered under his breath and massaged his stomach. Had he imagined all that food? Surely not. A dream of food did not give a person a bellyache.

Thomas Burke floundered among images, listening to bells ring. Like Father Archer he was alternately hot and cold. As those around him began to move he tried to awaken himself and join them, but he could not seem to clear his head of those ringing bells.

Donal Cam stood up slowly, rubbing his eyes. The fire was dead.

His people—what remained of his valiant people—were alive.

Orla.

He thought then of Honora, holding out her arms to him; her graceful arms. "Come for us!" she had implored when he left her. "Come to us soon, and safe!"

"We had better be going," he announced groggily. "A night's march and part of a day will see us with Brian O'Rourke."

Maurice O'Sullivan grunted unintelligibly, but dragged himself to his feet. Rory O'Sullivan also looked up at his commander's words, but did not arise. He stayed where he was at the very edge of the camp, nearest the tomb.

"You go without me," he said loud enough for Donal Cam to hear.

At first, Donal Cam seemed to ignore him. He was going from one to the other, urging them to rise and prepare to move out. "I am staying here, Commander," Rory called more forcefully.

Donal Cam turned toward him, frowning. "You cannot stay here. We are on top of a mountain, for God's sake."

"Near here, then. In the valley below. I can build a shelter for myself, no one will bother a hermit alone."

"You are being foolish, Rory, going to extremes," Donal Cam said briskly, hoping to shake his resolve. "Of course you are coming with us, what would I do without my captain of recruits?"

"You have Maurice. He is very able."

"I need you."

"Do you, Commander?" Rory asked thoughtfully. "Am I so unique? I think not. In the days to come you will surely find other men to fight for you, you have always been good at inspiring others with your courage and defiance.

"But I am past the point of being inspired. I have given all I have to give."

Donal Cam argued desperately, "What of your children in Spain, do you not want to see them again?"

"My children?"

The two men looked long at one another.

"Take care of them," Rory said carefully.

Getting slowly to his feet, he wrapped his shaggy mantle around his shoulders and left the campsite, walking with even tread to the edge of the piled stones that marked Orla's cairn. There he stood, immovable, staking his final claim.

His eyes locked with Donal Cam's across the space between them.

Donal Cam lifted one hand in a salute, then turned away to give the order to move out.

Father Collins and Dermod O'Sullivan helped The O'Connor to his feet. In spite of himself, the old man gave a groan of pain. Joan reached toward him but he pushed her hand away. "I am grand," he said between clenched teeth.

Looking down at his swollen, horribly blistered feet, he addressed them sternly. "Have you not gone through the most difficult trials already? Why do you now shrink from one more march? Are not my head and my body precious to you? Why have you carried me so far, if you mean to desert me now, my delicate feet? Ho! You must shake off this sluggishness and obey me!"

He lifted one foot and stamped it violently against the ground, breaking blisters, causing a great outpouring of blood and pus. Then he did the same with the other. He found a bit of armor among his pitiful belongings and banged it against both feet mercilessly. Putrid material spurted out.

Strong men averted their eyes.

When The O'Connor Kerry had relieved the pressure in his ruined feet, he stood up and stepped out boldly. "Now, feet! We are friends again."

Thomas Burke was in worse condition. He was able to stand, but he was extremely feverish and his mind was wandering. When Donal Cam asked him how best to cross the mountains he replied with a stream of incoherent nonsense.

Donal Cam was dismayed. Mac Donough had gone; he was relying on Burke to guide them toward Leitrim. "Which of you knows how to get across these hills and into Leitrim without using the main roads?" he asked the other mercenaries.

They looked at each other and shrugged. "None of us," Gerald Ryan admitted. "I could make a guess only, I have never been here before."

"A guess is not good enough. We must not have a repetition of what happened before, these people are too weary to spend hours or days lost, trying to find their way." Donal Cam turned back to his captain of mercenaries. "Thomas, think. Please! Listen to me . . . can you understand what I am saying? What way to O'Rourke from here?"

Burke struggled to give an answer, but no one could make sense out of his rambling speech.

Joan put a hand to his face. "The poor man is burning with fever. He needs a physician—O'Rourke's physician."

So near! They were so near! They must not linger here and wait for death—or for the Royalist garrison to decide to investigate the source of that fire after all, which would also mean death. The old urgency gripped Donal Cam. They must march.

But along what route? The sky was overcast. In the misty grayness of evening there was no telling east from west, no hint of sunset to inform them. There would be no stars to follow, though the blanket of cloud would at least keep the temperature up.

March, thought Donal Cam, his own mind wandering. I persist in calling it a march because I would rather die than call it a retreat.

Would rather die . . . "We are going now!" he cried out as if in wild defiance of the universe.

Without attempting to choose any direction at all, he simply plunged off down the slope, dragging them behind him with the will that had dragged them this far already.

Father Archer, fearful of getting too close to Donal Cam, brought up the rear.

He could not relinquish his connection with O'Sullivan Beare. He could not afford to; there would inevitably be questions asked when all of this was over, and he must be able to say he stood firm. It would considerably enhance his reputation, actually. And Donal Cam had not thrown him out a second time, there was hope in that. Had looked at him with hard eyes, as if he were a stranger, but had not denied him as Peter denied Christ. There was hope, matters between them could be mended, he could . . .

He realized, through his own fevered senses, that the fading of the light was accompanied by the first flakes of fresh snow falling. The air was comparatively mild, there was no wind, merely the soft white flakes, very large, drifting down like . . .

. . . like feathers from molting angels, Father Collins mused, watching a flake float lazily past his face. How lovely. He had lost all sense of time and place. He had begun to live only in the Now, which meant a snowy wood, a hilly slope, dark trees looming, friends gathered around him, a journey to make to somewhere . . .

The food they had eaten and the hours of sleep had restored their bodies sufficiently to allow them to continue, but their minds were more damaged. If anything, the sleep had left them dazed. Many of them were feverish from wounds, and had unwittingly surrendered to fever in their sleep as they had not done while awake and moving. Now they could not shake it off. They followed Donal Cam almost witlessly, stumbling through the twilight.

The snow grew thicker.

They came to a narrow plateau above a slide of scree. Dermod O'Houlihan remarked to Donal Cam, "At least we did not come this way, so we are going in a new direction. But which way now?"

Two narrow trails led away from them, one to the left and one to the right, both circumventing the dangerous scree. But they seemed to go in opposite directions. Donal Cam stared at them, unable to make a decision.

My judgment is destroyed, he thought. I should never have brought these people away from a good campsite. We should have stayed where we were.

Only when O'Houlihan answered him did he realize he had spoken the last words aloud. "We could not stay there any longer," O'Houlihan said. "Look at this snow! It will only get heavier, it would have covered us and killed us, weak as we are. You were right to leave the camp. Just lead on, we shall follow you."

Still Donal Cam hesitated. His lack of ability to make a simple decision was unnerving him. Decisiveness had been one of his strengths. If that was taken from him by the rigors and exhaustion of the march—if his fine clear mind was clouded—he was helpless. Forsaken.

He stood in the falling snow, unmoving, and they gathered around him, waiting to be led. The silence of the mountains embraced them. A great hush settled over them.

A figure materialized from the snowflakes.

"A ghost," gasped one of the horse boys, sinking to his knees in fear.

The figure was very pale, wrapped in white. Its face was hidden by a cowl.

Different people saw different things. Joan thought the stranger wore a white wreath around his temples. To Father Collins, he appeared to carry some sort of long wand, tipped with an iron point. A druid's wand, the Jesuit thought wonderingly, trying to remember exactly what it was druids were supposed to carry. An ash stick? His thoughts rambled away.

The O'Connor Kerry gaped at what he perceived to be a man walking barefoot in the snow, with undamaged and unfrozen feet.

Father James Archer saw a woman. A woman with wild red hair.

His heart gave a huge leap and began thundering in his breast, threatening to shake him apart. He put up a hand to ward off the apparition. He tried to stand his ground and be brave.

Donal Cam squinted at the spectral figure half-hidden by the snow. He had seen worse things; much worse. "Name yourself," he challenged.

Ignoring his request, the stranger replied, "I know that you are poor Catholics. I know that you are lost. I can show you the way to Brian O'Rourke of Leitrim, it is not more than fifteen miles from here."

"Do not listen!" cried Father Archer. "The Devil has come to tempt you!"

A muscle twitched in Donal Cam's jaw.

"It is a ghost," Thady Cooney moaned.

Donal Cam continued to regard the strange figure which seemed no more than a man to him, strangely garbed but not menacing. "We shall test him," he decided. "Ghosts have no need for gold."

Raising his voice, he told the white-robed stranger, "You can have all the gold I still possess on my person if you will see us safely to O'Rourke."

The stranger seemed to smile. "Because of the goodwill I have toward you, I will accept your offer not as a regard, but as a pledge of faith between us. I would do you this service for nothing."

"Do not trust it! Do not listen!" Father Archer cried.

The figure turned toward him. He thought it advanced upon him.

Against his will, his feet began to back away. In his fevered mind the apparition loomed larger, coming straight toward him. He thought the figure was gazing directly at him. He thought he saw, in its hated face . . . pity.

Unbearable pity.

With a sob, Father Archer turned and stumbled away among the trees, fleeing his devils.

His departure went unnoticed. The attention of the others was fixed on the figure in the pale cloak.

"He could be an agent sent by Lambert to lead us into a trap," Maurice O'Sullivan whispered to Donal Cam. "Be careful, Commander."

Donal Cam continued to regard the white figure intently. Whatever he was seeing did not seem to frighten him. At last he nodded. "Lead us as you will," he said.

The figure turned and began to move off through the falling snow. Donal Cam followed. One by one, thirty-four others followed him. Even Thady Cooney, crying and terrified, followed because he could not imagine doing anything else.

They wended their way through a snowy wilderness that seemed more a hallucination than a reality. Joan's hand was lost in that of her husband. The two walked with their shoulders pressed together so that they moved as one.

Father Collins was most aware of the silence. He could not hear the crunch of their feet on the snow. Like magic, he thought. We are floating.

The O'Connor was aware that they were not floating, because his feet still hurt dreadfully. He marveled that their mysterious guide apparently was able to walk barefoot in the mountains in such weather. Hardy people, these northerners, he thought enviously. Almost as good as Kerry men.

If that one up there can do it, I can, he told himself.

But his pain was increasing. His legs had grown livid with ulcers. Once he thought the figure in white turned its head and glanced back toward him, as if aware of his condition.

"Your friend is very crippled," their guide said in a low voice which only Donal Cam heard. "We will find a horse down below and put him on it."

"Where will we find a horse in these mountains?"

"Be assured there will be one, when there must be," came the response.

They went on.

The snowy night enveloped them. In the darkness

each person could just make out the one in front of him. Donal Cam, in the vanguard, was the only one who could now see their guide, and trudged along blindly behind the figure, trying not to think.

Maurice O'Sullivan, directly behind him, continued to worry that it might be a trick of the Royalists. They were hopelessly vulnerable. They could be led to their deaths like sheep to the slaughter.

He wondered what Rory O'Sullivan would have done. For the first time, he regretted the mantle of leadership he had eagerly assumed. But he continued to follow Donal Cam.

Very late in the night their guide halted and turned to speak. "There is a little village up ahead, a place called Knockvicar. They will give you food, it will be paid for with this gold you have offered me, as you say it is all you have."

Their guide resumed walking and they followed, stumbling along stony trails. Afterward, none of them would be able to recall just what route they had taken. They would remember only the night, and the hush of the snow.

The trees gave way to reveal a tiny cluster of cabins in the lee of the hills. Their guide went up to one and rapped on the door with what Father Collins had perceived as a wand. The door soon opened. The figure spoke with whoever was inside, then turned and gestured to the others.

"You are very welcome here," they were told. "Go inside and warm yourselves by the fire. If there is not room for all of you within, the other villagers will make you welcome in their cabins."

Gratefully, the refugees stumbled inside. Food was brought to them and they ate, not really tasting, not really thinking. People spoke to them, commiserated with them, offered them blankets and warm clothing. The group spread itself among the few cabins, each of which soon had a fire blazing to thaw them and comfort them.

"We should not be divided like this," Maurice whispered urgently to Donal Cam.

"We are not staying, Maurice. We will go on as soon as we have recovered ourselves a little."

Maurice nodded dubiously.

Thomas Burke was raving with fever. One of the householders offered to give him a bed of straw and let him stay, but he roused himself enough to understand and refuse. "My place is with O'Sullivan Beare!" he proclaimed so loudly that no one repeated the suggestion.

Donal Cam ate sparingly to be sure there was enough food for the rest of his party. The village was small, its stores humble. He regretted depleting them further in the dead of winter, but the need of his refugees must be his first consideration. He went from one to the other as they ate and rested by the fire, casting an assessing eye at each and surreptitiously counting heads once more.

He paused by Father Collins. "Where is the other . . . where is your colleague?"

"Father Archer? He left us. Back there, somewhere. When our, ah, guide joined us. Father Archer turned a ghastly color and made some gestures in the air, then he just . . . went," the priest finished lamely. "I thought he would rejoin us, but I do not see him."

"Nor do I." Donal Cam left the cabin, went to the next and checked its occupants also. The O'Connor Kerry was sitting by the fire there, his destroyed feet thrust as close to it as possible while he chatted desultorily with Dermod O'Sullivan.

"Have either of you seen Father Archer?"

Dermod glanced up at his nephew. "I have not, nor am I looking for him. And neither should you be."

But he is on my conscience, Donal Cam thought.

He sought out the man who seemed to be senior in the village, the patriarch who had first opened his door to them. "Somewhere in this forest is a priest, a Jesuit, who was with our party. He seems to have gone astray. We will be leaving soon and cannot wait for him, but if he finds you, will you see to him?

"There is also a man called Rory O'Sullivan who has stayed behind. He may never come as far as this, but if you encounter him, I would be grateful for your kindness to him also."

"The gold we have been given is more than sufficient to purchase a vast amount of kindness to two poor men lost in the mountains," the villager assured Donal Cam with sincerity.

Donal Cam did not ask exactly how much of the gold given to his guide had been passed on to them. But from the expression on the faces of the villagers, he suspected it was most if not all of the treasure.

In the middle of a January night, wealth had been showered upon people who had probably never seen a gold Spanish coin in their lives.

Although he ached to sit by a fire and just close his eyes, Donal Cam looked for their guide to question him. But the stranger seemed to have disappeared. He was in none of the cabins and no one could say where he might be. Donal Cam expected to feel the old familiar prickling of danger at the back of his neck—but it did not come.

My senses are dulled, he thought. Too dulled. We had better get on to O'Rourke while there is any strength left in me.

He returned to the first cabin and issued the order to move out, then went into the second, which, like the others, was no more than one room made of timber and stone with clay plastered between the cracks, and an earthen floor. The man of the house was smoking a clay pipe; his wife sat shyly in the farthest corner of the room, clutching her apron anxiously in her two hands. Joan Ni Sweney was speaking gently to her, trying to befriend her, but the woman was patently uncomfortable in the presence of so many strangers.

Ah, she will be relieved when we go, Donal Cam thought. "Uncle? Sean? We must be on our way now."

Dermod eased himself to his feet with accompanying creaks and groans, but The O'Connor Kerry was not able to stand. His feet refused to bear his weight. Warming them so close to the fire had been a mistake. Donal Cam bent closer to look at them and saw great suppurating ulcers on the pitifully thin legs, and angry red streaks running up toward the knee.

The man of the house crouched beside him, making little sympathetic grunts and pointing to the legs with the stem of his pipe. "Very bad, that, very bad. Never seen worse. Leave him with us and we will care for him for you, though, and send him on when he is . . ."

The O'Connor bellowed, "I will not see my friends walk away without me!"

There was nothing for it but to carry him. Donal Cam organized the four strongest men and they hoisted the old chieftain onto their shoulders and bore him from the cabin. He gave directions at every step. "Mind my head, do not bump it on the lintel. Easy there. Be careful of the feet!"

They found the white-robed guide waiting for them outside.

"Where were you?" Donal Cam asked.

"Close by" was all the answer he got.

"You said there would be a horse when we needed it."

"There is, only a little distance farther. Bring your people and follow me." The guide moved off without looking back to see if they were following him.

People had streamed out of the cabins at Donal Cam's summons and formed a group in the trampled snow. They looked back longingly at the open doorways and the firelight. Maurice O'Sullivan muttered to Con O'Murrough, "This is all very strange. I do not like any part of this."

But there was no questioning the guide, who was gathering speed with every step. Donal Cam hurried after him and the others followed, into the night and whatever dawn awaited them.

Day Fifteen

January 14, 1603. *Loch Cé*, Lough Key, the Lake of the Geese

Daybreak found them treading their footsore way down from the snow-shrouded mountains, passing between two great lakes. On the ineffably serene surface of the first they saw, through falling snowflakes, a trio of swans.

One pair floated together in the dawn, their necks arched toward one another, their beaks almost touching.

The third kept a distance from them, a distance that gradually widened. The lone swan lifted its head and watched the pair drift away; its curved neck formed a question.

For Donal Cam, the sight was at once a benediction and a reminder of those left behind. He gazed at the lake and the swans for a long moment, his thoughts suspended in time. Then the sounds of those behind him roused him from his reverie and he went on, following their silent guide.

A horse had been found for The O'Connor Kerry, not

long after they left the village. The horse was a starving brute with a backbone like a ridge of mountains, but they had padded the bony spine with some of the blankets the villagers had given them and enabled the old man to ride without too much discomfort. The horse was a stray and all but blind; Peadar led him while Thady and another horse boy slapped his rump with their hands and bare branches to keep him moving.

With The O'Connor secure, Joan and Dermod had turned their efforts to helping Thomas Burke, who was in a bad way.

The big mercenary had never lost the ability to keep walking, but he was babbling like a child and totally unaware of his surroundings. He kept referring to Joan as if she were his mother.

"And so I am," she remarked to her husband. "The last of the women . . . I am mother to them all now, poor lads."

"Even a Connacht man?" Dermod teased her.

She answered seriously, "All of them, any of them. Be they from Connacht or Munster—or Leinster or Ulster, for that matter—I am mother to them all."

The snow swirled and billowed, encircling them within a lacy curtain. They peered out at the landscape through which they passed.

Morning.

And the last day surely. Donal Cam had promised they would reach O'Rourke and sleep in his castle this night. It seemed a dream too wild for realizing.

They were crossing a trackless wasteland between the two lakes, a route rarely used by anyone and therefore safe from Royalist interference. The morning was crystal clear. If any of them had been in a condition to appreciate beauty, they might have caught their breaths in wonder. Reeds were beaded with glittering ice. Shrubs were snow-spangled. Off to their right lay the second of the lakes, the one called Loch Cé, circled by mountain vistas, fringed with forest, bearing on its breast a scattering of wooded islands.

Their guide paused, looked back toward Donal Cam. The guide raised an arm and pointed. "Do you see that island? It is called Trinity, and the headless body of Sir Clifford Conyers is in the abbey there."

Donal Cam squinted, trying to make out the island that harbored the body of the former president of Connacht, victim of Young Brian of the Axes—now The O'Rourke.

Their guide extended an arm yet again. "And that way, if you travel without deviating, lies O'Rourke's castle. Go on with good heart and you shall be there by midday."

"Are you not going with us?" Donal Cam asked in surprise.

The other said softly, "I have done what I could. No one can do more than is allotted to them."

The figure in white turned away. Brushing past the refugees, it went back the way they had just come, along the neck of land between the two lakes. As Donal Cam stared after it, the snow swirled and billowed one last time, obscuring the image . . . then subsided. The trackway was empty.

The refugees were alone in the morning, just north of Loch Cé.

The thought crossed Father Collins's mind that perhaps they had been alone all night. Perhaps there had been no figure in white, but some sort of mass vision that had come to them all. If so, it had at least given them the impetus to come this far, almost within sight of their destination.

I wonder if we have seen a miracle? the priest asked himself, annoyed that he would never know the answer.

Of course, it could be something far less Christian. The mountains of Ireland are ancient and strange, and harbor relics of the Old Religion. And ghosts. Assuredly, ghosts.

Another mystery, when he had not yet resolved the one that had consumed him since the beginning of the long march.

He forced his aching leg muscles to catch up with Donal Cam. Falling into step beside him, he asked, "Do you know who our guide was?"

There was a pause before the other replied, "A kind individual who took pity on us poor Catholics."

"Is that all?"

"What else could there be?"

"Ah, indeed." A sensible answer, thought Father Collins, because Donal Cam is a sensible man. Not given to flights of fancy or extravagant imaginings.

So why . . . what . . .

They were heading for Leitrim. There was little time left. Father Collins would be staying with The O'Connor Kerry, and O'Sullivan Beare would doubtless go on to his own destiny, tangled though its threads had become. If curiosity was ever to be satisfied it must be done now.

Humbly, Father Collins began, "Curiosity is a terrible itch, a most unchristian passion. And I am sorely afflicted with it."

He glanced up and sideways at the haggard, aristocratic profile of the other man. Did he detect the faintest curve of a smile at the corner of the lips?

"Are you trying to tell me you want to ask a question?"

"I am. One I have no right to ask."

The smile deepened. "Surely anyone who has come all this way with me has the right to ask me anything."

"Ah. Ah." Father Collins tried to arrange his words

tactfully. But tact seemed to have been one of the early casualties of the long march; it required too much energy.

"Why did you give it up?" he was dismayed to hear himself blurt out. "You were safe enough. You could have lived out your life as the queen's O'Sullivan, with an English title and the retention of at least part of your estates, in the same way Thomond kept his. Why did you of all people throw that away to join the rebellion?"

Donal Cam turned to look him in the eye. "You are the first man who has had the courage to ask me."

"Am I?"

"People make their own assumptions about other people, and everyone has assumed I was inflamed with a glorious vision of Gael conquering Sasanach. A sense of destiny, a thirst for glory. There are many reasons for joining a rebellion, not the least of which is simply getting caught up in its momentum."

"Were any of those your reasons?"

"None," was the somber reply.

Donal Cam stared straight ahead at the midland landscape, but his mind's eye saw another landscape. A fishing village bathed in lambent light. Sea light, opalescent and unforgettable. In a faraway voice he murmured, "Bless me, Father, for I have sinned."

Startled, Father Collins protested, "But I am not your confessor . . ."

The faraway voice went on inexorably. "It has been more than a year since my last confession. A year. More. Since she . . ." The voice softened imperceptibly.

"Since she came running up to me with her hair flying," Donal Cam said. "Her hair was always wild. Always. Orla would never bind it like a proper married woman . . ." He paused, shook himself, threw off the mood. In a sharper voice he said, "She came running up to me crying; I had never seen her cry before. At first I could get no sense out of her.

"Then I began to understand. A party of Carew's soldiers had broken into her house. As captain of my guards, Rory had a fine house a little distance from the village. After he married Orla it was no longer appropriate that he live in rough quarters with the men-at-arms at Dunboy . . ."

His thoughts seemed to be wandering again. Father Collins recalled him by saying, "What had happened when the soldiers broke in?"

For a few moments he thought Donal Cam would not answer. The tall, dark man continued to stare into space, walking stiffly, as if his body were being propelled by some agency other than his mind. When he did speak each word came slowly, squeezed out of an inner darkness.

"They did not rape her. At first I thought they had, and I was angry, but I tried to calm her. Such things had become commonplace in Munster under Carew, but at least she was alive. To be brutally blunt, she was no virgin anyway. She had experienced unpleasantness, but it was over, I told her. She must try to put it out of her mind, I said. She would be making undue trouble for herself and Rory if she went to the English authorities and . . ."

"She interrupted me then and told me what had happened. She had been alone in the house except for her oldest boy, a lad of some seven years. Rory had taken the other two, the younger boy and the little girl, with him on some outing or other. Showing off small Sinead and the infant Hugh, no doubt. He doted on his family. We had that in common.

"I had similarly brought my son Donal out with me that day. Fortunately, he was not with me when Orla ran up to me, for he had gone with my attendants and Father Archer to inspect some hound puppies behind the cooper's house.

"I was alone when I heard Orla's story.

"When the soldiers broke in she thought they meant rape and pillage for amusement, for they had been drinking. She smelled it on them. She defied them, as she would. Her older boy was lying on the bed, for he had been ill, but he was not too ill to jump up and run to his mother's defense.

"She said he threw his little body in front of hers and held out his arms, shielding her from the soldiers. Five soldiers. One or two of them English, the others natives. *Irish.*" Donal Cam swallowed, hard.

"The soldiers laughed at first and tried to push the lad aside, but he would not be pushed. He would not give in, it was not in him.

"One of the soldiers reached past him and struck Orla on the head, knocking her down. She did not see what happened next. But she heard it.

"Another soldier had already taken out his sword. Then. He." Every word became an individual agony, wrenched from Donal Cam's guts. "He. Skewered. *Skewered.* The boy. Twisted the blade. In him.

"Skewered him like a pig. On his sword.

"And laughed."

Father Collins signed himself with the Cross, there being no other response to make.

"She showed me the blood on her hands and apron," Donal Cam said. "I was shocked, angry . . . I said something like, 'The nearest authorities must hear of this outrage. They have gone too far, killing my captain's son.'

"But Orla gave a great cry then and flung herself into my arms. 'Not Rory's son!' she cried. 'Yours!'"

Ah, thought Father Collins. Yes.

"I held her and we wept together, and said those things to each other that parents must say, which do not help, which change nothing. And as I held her in that sunlit marketplace, unaware of anyone or anything else, Father Archer came around a corner and saw us. I suppose there was no mistaking the tenderness between us in that moment. He was furious.

"But all my thoughts were of Orla, and the boy. My son! I swear to you I had not known for certain he was my son, though he was very like me in ways. But . . . I kept seeing it in my mind, you know. The sword entering his body. The deliberate cruelty. A child. A child!

"And it was happening to children throughout Munster, I knew that. Yet I had somehow thought to keep our own safe, to play politics with Carew and the deputies. I had congratulated myself on my cleverness at being able to conciliate them enough to protect my own people.

"Protect!" he spat the word. "In the heel of the hunt I had not even protected my own son!

"Taking Orla back to her house, I arranged for burial of the dead child. I asked Father Archer to give him the sacraments but he refused. Use their own priest, he said.

"I told him the dead boy was my son, and he must do it. I shall never forget the look he gave me then. 'You had never confessed this sin to me,' he said.

"That was all that mattered to him."

"The next evening, in the courtyard at Dunboy, I threw all my English goods into a great bonfire. My wife's English velvets and fine laces as well—she protested a bit, Honora. She loved her finery. But I was past listening to anyone's arguments.

"Rory O'Sullivan was at that bonfire. And Orla, standing as straight as an oak. They both heard me vow to drive the brutal blight from Munster. To make our land safe for the children again.

"She had not told him. I knew she had not told him, as I had not told anyone. Not because I was ashamed; what happened between us was natural and good. But private, you understand? She knew it and so did I. I was a man of great energy; when my wife was nursing our firstborn I had spent that energy on Orla as I had often done before my marriage. It was not a sin to me, merely a resumption of an old affection. We were easy together."

"You need not justify it to me," Father Collins said.

"Perhaps I am trying to justify it to myself. Had it not been my son who was killed so brutally, there is a chance I might never have joined the rebellion. I honestly do not know.

"Such a small thing, really," Donal Cam mused. "A lonely man with a wife recovering from childbed. A walk in the hills, an encounter with a friend . . . and here we are. Still walking among other hills. All but bereft of friends now.

"So that is the story of O'Sullivan's rebellion," he concluded. "Now you know. Not as nobly conceived as you imagined, was it?"

"It was nobly conceived," Father Collins contradicted, aware of the unconscious play on words, though Donal Cam, in his pain, obviously was not. "Surely every rebellion is born in a moment of agony such as yours, and springs from very human causes, not some ephemeral idealism. You are too hard on yourself surely."

"Thousands are dead who might not be dead if I had not led them to fight the English."

"They would have fought anyway, sooner or later. Carew will not rest until every pocket of resistance in Munster is destroyed. He would have gotten to you in his own time, and then all of your people might have died horribly, instead of at least having a chance to fight for their lives.

"And you have saved some, remember that." Father Collins turned and swept his arm in an embracing gesture, indicating the little band of refugees behind them. "You have saved these people."

Looking back at the group, Father Collins realized it was a pitifully small number to put into the scale on which the tormented Donal Cam was weighing his soul. But was not every life valuable?

He put a hand on O'Sullivan's arm. "Think of that young couple I married. They are not with us anymore, but I feel certain they will survive. Children will be born to them, and perhaps to some of those who follow us now. Unborn generations will owe their lives to you.

"You have done your best."

For a moment Donal Cam's face twisted so harshly he looked as if he were going to cry. I have gone too far this time surely, the priest told himself.

But O'Sullivan Beare recovered. Echoing another voice, he murmured, "No one can do more than is allotted to them."

They walked on.

After they had gone another mile, Donal Cam spoke for the last time on the subject. "The worst of it," he said abruptly, "is that Carew's soldiers were dressed in uniform. They tended to look alike. Until the day I die I shall never know for certain . . . if the hand that killed my son belonged to an English man, or an Irish one."

Step-by-step across frozen snow they crunched toward Leitrim. The Shannon was much narrower than it had been at Poll na gCapaill. They waded through its cold water at an ancient fording place. Beyond the holly bushes crowding the riverbanks like spectators at a fight they could see, in the near distance, the tall walls of O'Rourke's stronghold.

"At least for a time, we are home," Donal Cam announced. The final word caught in his throat.

The last weary steps were the easiest and the hardest.

A village stood near the castle, but Donal Cam made straight for the stronghold. Once its gates would have stood open all day, every day, offering Gaelic hospitality to any chance traveler. Now they were closed and barred, with a sentry posted. But the sentry offered no challenge to the ragged band. They were expected; he grinned and saluted.

Donal Cam stepped forward to pound his fist on the wooden gate, calling as loudly as he could, "I am O'Sullivan of Cork, and I bring you the army of Munster!"

From the depths of their exhaustion, the survivors summoned pride. By unspoken agreement they formed themselves into a rough approximation of a military column one more time. Father Collins and Joan Ni Sweney took their places with the other soldiers, and The O'Connor Kerry got down off his horse and walked, leaving tracks of blood. They trooped through the opened gates behind O'Sullivan Beare, with their heads held high. It was the best tribute they could give to the man who had brought them so far. A man who had believed, who had trusted, who had hoped for more than he got.

An extraordinary man.

"An extraordinary man!" cried Brian O'Rourke, hurrying forward to greet Donal Cam. "Here, let me look at you. By God, you are a disaster!"

"I am alive," Donal Cam replied.

"You are that, and we give thanks for it. We would have sent out scouts to look for you and lead you in but we did not know which direction you would come from, and we did not want to alert Lambert's scouts."

"You sent us no guide?"

"None. I just told you."

"Ah."

"Come into the hall, there is a fire and my wife waiting, and hot wine, and sack, and mead, even, for yourself and your companions. Warm beds, dry blankets. All you could wish."

"All I could wish," the gaunt man with the haunted eyes echoed.

They received a welcome that was too much for any of them to take in their condition. When the entire party had been made comfortable on benches in the great hall, Donal Cam recalled the noble courtesies and introduced them, one by one, to their host.

"I am anxious to meet him myself," Gerald Ryan confided under his breath to Hugh O'Flynn, as they awaited their turn. "He was Brian of the Axes, you know. We have the ax in common."

When Donal Cam came to his aunt, before he could say her name she gave him a meaningful scowl and drew him aside to hiss into his ear, "I am not supposed to be here. I was supposed to stay with your wife. O'Rourke's scribes will record this event, better I am not mentioned. Dermod, the old fool, is prickly about it."

"May I present our only surviving member of the gentle sex," Donal Cam then said to Brian O'Rourke, thoughtfully neglecting to mention the woman's name. But the mere fact of her existence was enough. Impressed, the lord of Breffni bowed low to Joan Ni Sweney.

When it came Father Collins's turn to be introduced, instead of calling him by his priestly title, Donal Cam simply said, "This is my friend."

The fire burned low in the great hall, but it would not go out. There were servants to keep watch. Donal Cam could rest at last.

Yet he lay awake, staring into the shadows.

He and Brian O'Rourke had talked late, long after the others were asleep. Sitting on either side of the hearth, they had discussed battles fought and battles yet to fight. At Donal Cam's insistence, O'Rourke had furnished his guest with a set of razors and shears to trim his beard, though he privately thought it a mad request from a man so obviously in need of more imperative aid. He had also furnished a fresh suit of clothing—Gaelic dress—and copious quantities of French brandy, which seemed to have no effect on O'Sullivan at all.

A most extraordinary man.

Donal Cam lay and waited for sleep to claim him. This was the time he feared most, when memories and apparitions had him at their mercy. Images he could keep at bay in the daylight could flood over him at night, drowning him . . .

In the far corner of the hall, O'Rourke's personal harper was still awake. At his lord's request he was playing very softly, his fingers stroking slow airs from the harp strings to soothe the refugees in their sleep.

Donal Cam turned onto one side and propped his head on his hand to listen to the music.

As he listened, the hall faded. He was transported to a different world, where women were as fair as swans and men had the faces of eagles. A place of exquisite craftsmanship and just judgments and and stylized battles between celebrated heroes. A world of leisurely pastoral rhythms, of abundance and freedom.

Donal Cam's eyes slowly closed. The last memory that came to him, before he fell asleep, was the smell of his wife's hair.

Afterword

O'Sullivan Beare stayed only briefly with Brian O'Rourke. As soon as he was somewhat rested he set off again. Driven by his obsession to join O'Neill and give new impetus to the rebellion, he put together an expeditionary force of some three hundred, joined Brian Maguire, and began fighting his way toward The O'Neill.

They successfully attacked a Royalist camp on the way, and O'Sullivan visited the garrisons on Lough Erne, taking savage vengeance on the queen's men there. But when he and Maguire reached the last reported stronghold of Hugh O'Neill, they learned they had come too late. Only a few days earlier, O'Neill, feeling all was lost, had formally submitted to the queen's Lord Deputy, ending his rebellion.

Cruelly, no one informed him that Queen Elizabeth of England had just died. O'Neill had outlived her.

He was given back his title as earl of Tyrone, which he held for a few more years before being driven into exile in Italy. Hugh O'Neill, on whom Ireland once pinned her hopes for freedom, died in Rome in 1616, a broken man.

After the great march from Cork to Leitrim, The O'Connor Kerry, together with one companion, set sail for Scotland. There he was welcomed as an honored guest by James the First, son of Mary, Queen of Scots—whom Elizabeth had beheaded. He would ultimately return to Ireland with honors and die a very old man.

Cornelius of clan O'Driscoll had succeeded in arranging passage from Ireland to Spain for Donal Cam's wife and infant son. There they were reunited with Donal Cam's eldest son, Donal, and Dermod's boy Philip, who was already receiving an education that would equip him one day to write the history of the great march, drawing on the memories of his father and uncle.

When Brian O'Rourke died of a fever, Donal Cam became the last prince of the Gael who was not either dead or forced into submission. His peers had bowed to the inevitable, accepting English titles and domination along with an English pardon.

But for O'Sullivan Beare there was to be no pardon. He alone would be perpetually outlawed; the man who refused to surrender. The man who could never go home.

Together with Dermod O'Sullivan, he set sail for Spain. There the king, in acknowledgment of his efforts on behalf of the Catholic faith, awarded him with a title, deeded estates to him, and granted him an income of three hundred gold pieces a month. When his son Donal was accidentally killed, the entire Spanish court mourned.

Dermod O'Sullivan and a number of other Irish nobles also received generous allowances from the king, permitting them to spend the rest of their lives in Spain in a golden exile.

For the next fifteen years, Donal Cam waited for some

word that the Irish were rising again. It never came. In 1618 he was killed, intervening in a duel—slain by the man he was trying to save.

The nobility of Spain marched in his funeral cortege.

Author's Note

Some readers may be surprised by the author's using the date of January 3, 1602, for the Battle of Kinsale. Kinsale is more commonly dated 24 December 1601 and is considered one of the decisive battles of Irish history.

The explanation is found in that unique research source, *The Annals of Ireland*, vol. 6, p. 2290. The *Annals* refer to the battle as having been fought "on the third day of the month of January." A footnote elucidates: "The Irish were defeated at Kinsale on the 24th of December 1601, *according to the old style then observed by the English, but on the 3rd of January 1602 according to the Irish and Spaniards.*"

In 1582, Pope Gregory XIII had ordained that ten days be dropped from the Julian calendar, thus creating the Gregorian calendar which is generally accepted today. As Catholic countries, both Ireland and Spain had already adopted this new calendar by the time of the Battle of Kinsale. England, however, would not adopt the Gregorian calendar until 1752, and was therefore still conforming to the "old style" of dating at the time of the battle.

In his definitive book on the subject, *Kinsale*, John J. Silke uses the 3 January date. So does *The Last Prince of Ire-*

land, which takes the Irish point of view and records dates as the Irish would have observed them at the time. A number of historians, however, do continue to use the old English date as it then obtained.

Such situations are indicative of the snares awaiting the historical novelist. Dates, places, and events in research material of acknowledged scholarship may contradict one another for a variety of reasons, and each contradiction must painstakingly be run to the ground if possible. On occasion an historical inaccuracy has originated with one source and been perpetuated, in all innocence, by a number of subsequent researchers and writers.

Mindful of this, the author confirmed the physical plausibility of the dates used in *The Last Prince of Ireland* by personally walking the route.

The author would like to express special gratitude to Donncha O'Dulaing, who followed in the footsteps of O'Sullivan Beare and recorded the history and folklore he discovered along the way for *Donncha's Historical Marches*, RTE Radio Series, Radio Telefis Eireann, Dublin, 1988. These recordings were of inestimable value in writing this book, but even more important was his great generosity in taking the time to retrace the walk with me to give me a deeper understanding of O'Sullivan's epic march.

Morgan Llywelyn
Dublin, Ireland

Bibliography

dc Blacam, Aodh. *O'Sullivan Bere*. The Capuchin Annual, Dublin. 1946–47.

Butler, William F. *Gleanings from Irish History*. London: Longmans, Green & Co., 1925.

Collins, M. E. *Ireland 1478–1610*. Dublin: The Education Company of Ireland Ltd., 1980.

D'Alton, E. A. *History of Ireland from the Earliest Times*. Dublin and Belfast: Gresham Publishing Co., Ltd., 1925.

Doherty J. E., and D. J. Hickey. *Chronology of Irish History Since 1500*. Dublin: Gill & Macmillan Ltd., 1989.

Dunleavy, Mairead. *Dress in Ireland*. London: B. T. Batsford Ltd., 1989.

Foster, Robert F. *Modern Ireland 1600–1972*. London: The Penguin Press, 1988.

Four Masters, The. *Annals of the Kingdom of Ireland*. Vol 6. Dublin: de Burca Rare Books, 1990.

Hayes-McCoy, Gerald A. *Irish Battles: A Military History of Ireland*. London: Longmans, 1969.

Healy, James N. *Castles of Cork*. Cork: The Mercier Press, 1988.

MacLysaght, Edward. *Irish Life in the Seventeeth Century*. Dublin: Irish Academic Press, 1979.

Moloney, Michael. *Irish Ethno-Botany*. Dublin: M.H. Gill & Son Ltd., 1919.

Moryson, Fynes. *An Itinerary*. 1617. Reprint. Glasgow: James Mac Lehose, 1907.

Norman, A.V.B., and Don Pottinger. *English Weapons and Warfare 449–1660*. Englewood Cliffs, N.J.: Prentice-Hall, Inc., 1979.

O'Brien, Barry. *Munster at War*. Cork: The Mercier Press, 1971.

O'Donnell, T.J. *Selections from the Zoilomastix of Philip O'Sullivan Beare*. Dublin: Stationery Office, 1960.

O'Faolain, Sean. *The Great O'Neill*. London: Longmans, 1942.

O hOgain, Daithi. *Myth, Legend, and Romance, An Encyclopedia of the Irish Folk Tradition*. London: Ryan Publishing Co., 1990.

O'Siodhachain, Donal. *The Great Retreat*. Cork: Clo Duanaire, 1987.

O'Sullivan, Don Philip. *Historical Catholicae Iberniae Compendium*. Translated under the title of *Ireland Under Elizabeth* by Mathew J. Byrne. Dublin: Sealy, Bryers & Walker, 1903.

Shaw-Smith, David. *Irish Traditional Crafts*. London: Thames & Hudson, 1986.

Silke, John J. *Kinsale*. Liverpool: Liverpool University Press, 1970.

Somerville-Large, Peter. *From Bantry Bay to Leitrim: A Journey in Search of O'Sullivan Beare*. London: Victor Gollancz Ltd., 1980.

After the Battle of Kinsale England came close to completing the conquest of Ireland. Centuries of oppression followed as the victors ravished the land and looted its resources. In spite of generations of subjugation and the horrors of the Great Famine, the Irish will to freedom was not destroyed. It surfaced again and again, culminating in the legendary Easter Rising of 1916. The Rising was put down and its leaders executed. But only five years later, in 1921.

Look out for the second volume

in Morgan Llywelyn's

1921

Coming in hardcover from Forge Books
in March 2001.

The headache was agonizing today. Sitting on the edge of the bed, Ned whispered "Please," to a god who did not seem to be listening.

A hand touched his shoulder. "Is it very bad?"

Ned looked up at Síle through slitted eyelids. Though it was past noon, her russet hair tumbled around the shoulders of her calico wrapper. In the privacy of their rooms she let it fall free because Ned liked it that way. She had so many small ways of pleasing him. Warming the sheets with her body before he got into bed; touching his shoulder for a moment when she passed behind his chair . . .

He forced a smile. "Not so bad."

"So you say. Why not lie back down?" Her voice caressed the sore places in his brain. "The washing is done and Precious is downstairs with Louise, so I can lie beside you for a while. You always say that eases your headaches." As she spoke she was unbuttoning her shirtwaist.

He sat watching her. Sat naked, watching her. In their bed Ned was always naked for Síle.

The warmth of her. The fragrance of her. A glimpse of

the soft down on the curve of her cheek, sweet as the down on a peach.

With a little moan he surrendered and let her press him back against the pillows.

She did not press her body against his but kept a small space between them; a space charged with desire. For the moment it was better than touching. In that tiny space the mingling of memory and anticipation became a passionate form of lovemaking all its own. Ned's senses rioted with heightened awareness and his headache receded, relegated to a distant pounding he could not separate from the pounding, rising tide of his blood.

When she shifted weight ever so slightly, his flesh knew exactly how it would feel if she were moving against him. Her soft, full breasts dragging across his bare chest. The tingling of his nipples as she teased them with her own. The sweet moist . . .

"Síle."

"Yes love."

"Touch me."

"I will."

"Now."

"Where? Here?"

She held her hand palm down over him, maintaining a hair's breadth of space between them. Yet the heat of her hand scorched him.

"Or here?"

She moved her hand lower. The heat followed.

She shifted weight again, bringing her hips fractionally closer to his. His erection leaped out to bridge the gulf between them but without seeming to move she avoided him. "Not yet. Not yet."

He closed his eyes. She entered into the darkness behind his eyelids and now they were touching, now her hands were moving sweetly down him, now her bare flesh was inviting his caresses, now her thighs were pressed against his thighs and then parting, parting sweetly, parting hungrily, and he was sliding into her, moist as he had known she would be, opening to him, sucking him into that secret, hidden mouth that was like a homecoming. The bliss became a knot at the base of his spine that moved out along all his nerves, gathering strength, and she with him, she with every movement, she inseparable from himself, one flesh one soul one great long shuddering explosion of joy that rocked the world and filled the universe with a silent shout and it was the two of them together, the two of them together always . . .

Then the slow, sweet shuddering, and the gentle drifting down, down, to find himself lying in Síle's arms and the pain gone. Magically gone.

He never let himself think about how she had acquired the skills of which he was the beneficiary. She was Síle. There was nothing else.

Ned stood up slowly, one section of himself at a time. "I have to get up. Henry's coming back today."

From the bed Síle said wistfully, "Everything's been so lovely with just the three of us up here under the eaves. Like having our own house almost."

"It's thanks to Henry that we have a roof over our heads at all," Ned reminded her.

When Ned and Henry worked together at the *Independent* they had shared a room, second-storey front, in Louise Kearney's lodging house for single men. There they dueled across a chessboard and became close friends. After the Easter Rising Henry had taken his cousin aside to explain, "Ned's been badly wounded, Louise. I have him well-hidden until the repercussions die down, but it's only a temporary arrangement. I want to bring him back here so we can keep an eye on him while he convalesces."

Louise Kearney was a sturdy middle-aged widow with a perpetual Celtic flush. Her jutting chin gave her the profile of a chest of drawers with the bottom drawer open. Yet a man had loved her once, and the warmth of that love would last her until the day she died. She had borne the late Mr. Kearney no children. "That was our Cross to bear," she said simply.

When Henry told her about Ned, her reply was, "You go fetch that poor lad home right now. Sure where else would he go?"

"Ah . . . there's a little more to it than that. You see, as soon as Ned's got his strength back he wants to get married. So I'm asking you to bend your rules about men only."

She was going to refuse; Henry could read it in her face. He spoke first. "Looking forward to marrying his sweetheart has been the only thing that's kept Ned alive."

Louise drew a deep breath. "Well . . . I suppose rules are made to be broken."

"So they are. I knew you would understand. And, ah, there is one other thing. Ned and his wife will be needing a bit of privacy, and I should like to have an office at home myself, come to that. So I've been thinking . . ."

Louise had listened with amazement to what Henry was thinking. "Go on out of that! It's impossible, I could never afford it."

"Nonsense. You're a businesswoman and this is a sound investment, it will increase the value of your property."

"I can't afford it," she had repeated less emphatically.

" 'There is no need like the lack of a friend,' " Henry quoted the old proverb. "Ned needs all his friends now, and that includes you surely." He sensed victory; it only remained to deliver the *coup de grâce*. "Besides, I'll pay for half the work myself."

"You're a most persuasive man, Henry Mooney."

"It's my stock in trade."

The next day a pair of workmen had arrived at Number Sixteen Middle Gardiner Street, where from disused maids' rooms and storerooms in the attic they had created two new apartments. One consisted of a large bedroom with a bookshelf-lined alcove that Henry called his study, whilst the other apartment had two bedrooms and a small sitting-room for Ned's family. Unlike the other lodgers, they took their meals with their landlady.

The arrangement seemed ideal, yet in spite of her gratitude Síle resented Henry's presence at the top of the house. The walls had been hastily erected and were thin. She tensed at the creak of his footstep on the floorboards, the rasp of his cough in the passageway, even his gentle chuckle when something amused him. Awareness of another man in their private space was like a splinter under Síle's fingernail. A painful reminder.

"I appreciate all that Henry's done for us," she assured Ned. "It's just that . . ."

"I know, I promised you a cottage on Howth." He paused; an Irish man did not discuss finances with his wife. Yet society's rules never applied to Síle. "For now all the money we have is what my brother sends me from the farm income," he said. "But Frank has our little sisters and our aunt to take care of, and the farm's not making much these days. If you and I didn't work around the house for Mrs. Kearney to help earn our keep, we'd be totally skint. No one else would employ me while my health's so uncertain."

"You were invited to teach at Saint Enda's," she pointed out.

"Ah, Síle, imagine what would happen when I had one of my dizzy spells and collapsed in front of the students. They would be frightened and I would be humiliated. No, teaching is out of the question. But when I sell my first novel we'll buy that cottage. You'll see."

Ned was getting dressed as he spoke. He was tall, dark, very thin, with intense green eyes fringed in heavy lashes. Síle thought he was beautiful. Their marriage was the fulfillment of the only dream she had ever allowed herself.

Ned's dreams were more ambitious. At the *Independent* he had been training to be a reporter, but he really wanted to be a novelist. Pádraic Pearse had told him he had a talent for creative writing and, to Ned, everything Pearse said was gospel.

Abruptly Síle threw back the sheets and stood up, gathering her abundant mane in both hands and twisting it atop her head. Proper married women put their hair up. She secured her willful locks with the tortoise-shell combs Ned had given her for Christmas, then busied herself dressing. She kept her back turned to her husband so he could not see the doubt in her eyes.

Sometimes Ned read aloud to her from the novel he was trying to write. The words sounded fine and grand, strung together so they danced on the tongue, but they did not relate to any life Síle knew. She could not believe in a future built upon fanciful adventures in faraway places. Castles in the air.

In her experience reality had a harder edge.

Mrs. Kearney met Ned at the foot of the stairs. "Is Síle coming down soon, Ned?" she asked as she dried her hands on her apron. "I need her in the scullery."

"She'll be here in a minute. She's tidying our rooms now."

Louise Kearney gestured with a nod. "Precious is inside, tidying the parlor."

Ned grinned. "Precious would tidy the world if we let her."

From the parlor doorway they observed a little girl enveloped in one of Louise's aprons. The garment went around her twice and was held in place by a wooden clothes peg. On the floor beside her was a basket containing a large tin of beeswax, a supply of rags, and a box of Keating's Powder, 'Guaranteed to Kill Moths Fleas and Bugs'.

Biting her lower lip in concentration, the child was polishing a table top. She swiped diligently, then squinted along the surface. When she found a tiny smear she polished the entire table again.

Henry Mooney called her Little Business.

After the third time she found salt in her sugar jar, Louise Kearney had suggested a better nickname might be Mischief.

Strangers sometimes felt sorry for the child because she had not inherited her parents' good looks. Although Ned and Síle were both tall, Precious was small for her seven years, and plain. Her hair had darkened from infant blonde to a nondescript brown. But there was a good reason why she had neither Ned's crisp black curls nor Síle's dramatically slanted eyes. The little girl was a waif from the Dublin tenements. She literally had fallen into Ned's arms during the Bachelor's Walk Massacre in 1914, when British soldiers fired on Dublin civilians.

Ned had rescued the terrified child and taken her to the Charitable Infirmary in Jervis Street. When the nuns asked her name, all she could tell them was, "My mama calls me Precious". In the days that followed no one claimed her. Dublin was teeming with tenement children; an abandoned one was not uncommon. Eventually Precious was consigned to an orphanage under the name of

'Ursula Jervis'. Thereafter Ned visited her as often as he could.

When the center of Dublin was under bombardment during Easter Week, Ned's fiancée Síle Duffy had gone to the orphanage to take Precious to safety. The matron had refused until Síle brandished a pistol in her face. The terrified woman had surrendered the little girl at once.

Precious had been theirs ever since. Theirs by right of love.

She called Henry 'Uncle Henry' and Mrs. Kearney 'Auntie Louise', and would not go to bed without kissing them both good night. At her recent First Communion Henry and Louise had sat with Ned and Síle. The family.

"Precious?" Ned called softly.

The child's sudden smile lit candles in her blue eyes. "Look Ned-Ned, I'm doing housework."

"So I see."

"I'm helping earn our sub-sis-tence." She ostentatiously returned to her dusting.

"You have another new word," Ned observed.

"Uncle Henry gave it to me."

Ned exchanged a knowing glance with Louise. Precious's vocabulary was a source of amusement. As soon as the child heard an unfamiliar word she seized upon it like a collector and allowed the adults in the house no peace until one of them told her its meaning.

"I didn't ask Precious to help with the housework," Louise said. "It was her own idea."

"I know."

"I would keep the three of you for nothing if I could afford to, Ned. It's small enough thanks for what you lads tried to do."

"You've done more than enough for us. You even let us get married in your parlor, when plenty of people in

Dublin wouldn't have allowed Síle through their front door."

"Whisht, go 'way out o' that!" Louise Kearney cast a furtive glance toward Precious, who seemed absorbed in her task. "You wouldn't want the child to be hearing such things about her mother."

"Síle *has* become her mother, hasn't she? And myself her father. Who's to know?"

"It's not that simple. Precious should be going to school, and when she does there'll be questions asked. They'll be wanting a copy of her birth certificate from the Custom House."

"We've decided not to send her to school, Louise. The national schools have windows but no light comes in. We're going to educate Precious at home."

"Can you?"

"Did I not have the best education in the world with Mr. Pearse at Saint Enda's? I can instruct her in Irish, Latin, Greek, history, literature, maths . . . and English grammar, of course. It's important that she speaks well. I don't want her labeled because of a Dublin tenement accent."

The front door opened; closed gently; stealthily. Louise motioned to Ned to stay where he was and went out into the hall. "God between us and all harm!" Ned heard her exclaim. "Henry Mooney, why are you sneaking into my house like an early autumn? Come into the parlor this minute."

Henry immediately went to one of the tall front windows and peered out from behind the curtains.

Precious tugged at his sleeve. "I've been ever so anxious for you to come home, Uncle Henry! I want to ask you—do men with beards put them under the bedclothes when they sleep, or leave them outside?"

"I don't know; I don't have a beard," said Henry distractedly, keeping his eyes on the street.

"It's not like you to ignore one of her questions," Ned observed. "What's wrong?"

"I think a British officer followed me from the G.P.O."

Ned made shooing motions at Precious. "Run along upstairs, pet. Go to Síle."

"But I haven't finished doing the . . ."

"Shift!"

She trotted obediently from the parlor and halfway up the stairs, then crept back down to sit on the bottom step, straining to overhear their conversation.

Ned joined Henry at the window. Together they scrutinized the street. Red brick boarding houses, their once-elegant Georgian facades smoke-grimed and shabby. A Jack Russell terrier lifting his leg against an ornate iron lamppost. A shawl-swathed woman with a shopping basket on her arm.

Louise Kearney went to the other window. "Just look at Dympna Dillon. Always late, that one. Pity her poor lodgers. I must remind her to do her shopping in the morning when everything's fresh. I don't see any soldiers, though. Perhaps you were imagining things, Henry."

"Or perhaps he recognized my name from my articles."

"If they were going to arrest you for sedition they would have done it while we were still under martial law."

"What makes you think we're not now?" Ned snapped. "When Maxwell was recalled it was supposed to be lifted, but I can't see much difference. They're still arresting people for singing rebel songs or insulting British soldiers. Do you realize that over two thousand were deported without any trial at all after the Rising? Including women? Many were innocent bystanders who just happened to be in the wrong place at the wrong time."

Henry said, "To be fair, at Christmas they did release the untried deportees. They only kept back the ones who'd been sentenced."

"They had no choice. So many angry Irishmen were turning British prisons into universities for revolutionaries."

Louise suggested, "If someone was following Henry he may really have been after you, Ned."

"If they're going to start harassing my friends, I'll make it easy to find me." He thrust his jaw forward stubbornly; the inherited Halloran cleft stood out in sharp relief.

"I despair of you, lad," said Henry. "One would think you want to go to prison."

"Better men than me have gone. Eamon de Valera, Michael Collins . . . even Madame."

Henry chuckled. "Countess Markievicz would be delighted to hear you classify her with 'the men'. I hear she's furious because she wasn't executed with Pearse and the others. Next thing you know, Madame will have the suffragettes demanding she be allowed equal rights to face the firing squad."

"Perhaps we could arrange to be shot together," Ned suggested. "Is there someone you know in the Castle who could organize that for us?" Gazing toward the ceiling he drawled, in an excellent imitation of an upper-class English accent, "How impressed dear Mater would be if I died beside a countess. She would welcome me into Heaven with the best tea service."

Henry laughed out loud, but Louise said angrily, "That isn't funny. I don't know how you can joke about such things. Tempting fate, that's what you are. I won't have you arrested and dragged out of this house, Ned Halloran."

He sobered at once. "Perhaps I should leave under my own power, then. I don't want to bring trouble down on you, not after you've been so good to us."

Louise Kearney looked horrified. "Take that sweet innocent child out of here to God-knows-what? I won't hear of it."